PENGUIN (P) CLASSICS

THE GOVERNMENT INSPECTOR
AND OTHER RUSSIAN PLAYS

DENÍS IVÁNOVICH FONVÍZIN graduated from the University of Moscow in 1762, the year of the accession of Catherine the Great. In 1782 he enjoyed great success with *The Infant*, a play genuinely original and genuinely Russian in which he expressed his own social views. Official disapproval forced Fonvízin to retire but did not silence him.

ÁLEXANDER GRIBOYÉDOV entered the University of Moscow in 1806 at the age of eleven and had taken degrees in Arts and in Law by 1812 when Napoleon invaded Russia. After the war he entered the Foreign Service and was posted to Tehran where he worked on his comedy, *Chatsky*, which was very popular in Russia even though it was banned by the Censor.

NIKOLÁY VASILÉVICH GÓGOL was born in 1809 in the country and went straight to St Petersburg on leaving school. He started writing at an early age; his first finished play was *The Government Inspector* (1835), which aroused such strong feelings that Gógol left for Rome, where he lived for twelve years, and where he wrote *Dead Souls*.

ALEXANDER OSTRÓVSKY was born in 1823. He read law at university but spent so much time at the Bolshóy Theatre that he left without a degree. His first full-length play was published in 1850. In 1859 *Thunder* appeared and startled audiences with its naturalism. The play has been popular ever since and was recently made into a film in the USSR.

JOSHUA COOPER was born in London in 1901. In 1915 he was awarded an open scholarship to Shrewsbury School, and in 1918 an open scholarship in Classics to Brasenose College, Oxford. He began to study Russian in 1921 at King's College, London, and took his B.A. with first-class honours in 1924. The following year he entered the Foreign Office where he remained until his retirement in 1961. He is the author of *Russian Companion*, a grammar and reader. Joshua Cooper died in 1981.

Four Russian Plays

Fonvízin: THE INFANT
Griboyédov: CHATSKY
Gógol: THE GOVERNMENT INSPECTOR
Ostróvsky: THUNDER

TRANSLATED FROM THE RUSSIAN
WITH AN INTRODUCTION AND NOTES
BY JOSHUA COOPER

PENGUIN BOOKS

PENGUIN BOOKS

Published by the Penguin Group
Penguin Books Ltd, 27 Wrights Lane, London W8 5TZ, England
Viking Penguin, a division of Penguin Books USA Inc.
375 Hudson Street, New York, New York 10014, USA
Penguin Books Australia Ltd, Ringwood, Victoria, Australia
Penguin Books Canada Ltd, 2801 John Street, Markham, Ontario, Canada L3R 1B4
Penguin Books (NZ) Ltd, 182–190 Wairau Road, Auckland 10, New Zealand

Penguin Books Ltd, Registered Offices: Harmondsworth, Middlesex, England

This translation first published as *Four Russian Plays* 1972
Reissued under this title 1990
1 3 5 7 9 10 8 6 4 2

Translation, introduction and notes copyright © Joshua Cooper, 1972
All rights reserved

Printed and bound in Great Britain by
Cox & Wyman Ltd, Reading
Set in Monotype Baskerville

All rights in these plays are reserved by the
proprietor. All applications for professional and
amateur performing rights should be addressed
to Curtis Brown Ltd, 1 Craven Hill,
London W2

for Pin

CONTENTS

TRANSLATOR'S PREFACE

THE translation of *The Infant* is based on the text of the first edition of *Nédorosl'* prepared with the approval of Fonvízin himself. Many later editions, published after the author's death, contain additional matter introduced by a nineteenth century editor who had access to the author's papers. Since Fonvízin appears to have deliberately discarded these passages when preparing the first edition (understandably, for they do nothing to improve the play) they have been omitted here.

The translations follow the usual English stage convention of beginning a new scene only where there is a change of location, or a time-break. Since Russian writers follow the continental practice of making a new scene every time a character comes on or goes off the stage, it has been necessary to write in a few stage directions for entrances and exits. Apart from these, and one or two places where it has been necessary to state in the English who is being addressed, when this is implied in the Russian, by the grammar, stage directions are as in the originals.

*

I should like to express my thanks to the Director of the School of Slavonic and East European Studies and to Mr C. Vaughan James of the University of Sussex for help in obtaining Russian editions of the plays, to Miss D. M. Messenger for typing the manuscript and to Mr James Cochrane and Mr Paul Foote for reading the manuscript and making valuable suggestions.

GREAT MISSENDEN
October 1971

INTRODUCTION

I. THE FOUNDATIONS OF THE RUSSIAN THEATRE

> I reckon that Russia has three tragedies – *The Infant,
> Chatsky* and *The Inspector* . . .
>> PRINCE V. F. ODÓYEVSKY (1803–69).

> (. . . built single handed) on the cornerstones laid by
> Fonvízin, Griboyédov and Gógol . . . (Only since Ostróv-
> sky) can we say with pride 'we have got our own National
> Theatre'.
>> IVAN A. GONCHARÓV (1812 91).

IT is a commonplace among critics and literary historians to
say that the three comedies translated in this volume under the
English titles *The Infant, Chatsky* and *The Government Inspector*
are of cardinal importance in the story of the emergence of
the Russian Theatre, a story that is consummated by the
life-work of Alexander Ostróvsky, who reached the height
of his fame with the production of *Thunder* which is the
fourth play here.

Odóyevsky however calls them 'three tragedies'; furthermore when Ostróvsky sat down to write *Thunder* he described
this play as a 'comedy' (like Chékhov's 'comedy' *The
Seagull* it ends with a suicide) and only as an afterthought
altered 'comedy' to 'drama'.

'How very Russian' some of us may say; and so it is,
only perhaps not in the way the expression 'very Russian' is
usually intended by English speakers. The first three plays
may certainly be said to be tragedies in the trivial sense that
all have unhappy endings. Fonvízin, in the last few seconds
of his play, contrives to enlist our compassion for the odious
Mrs Simple; Chatsky and Sophie, who might once have
marched together against the Philistines, go their separate
ways to loneliness and frustration; there is nothing at all

9

funny about Gógol's Final Tableau and audiences as a rule do not laugh at it. But there is or should be nothing 'sombre' about these plays; all three are sparkling, bubbling over, with the spirit of comedy.

Seriousness of purpose however has always been the keynote of the classic Russian Theatre, even in the most lighthearted of comedies, and this keynote is struck at once in the oldest play to have survived in the repertory – Fonvízin's *The Infant*. To understand and appreciate the work of the great Russian dramatists we need therefore to know something about the social problems of the times in which they lived.

The theatre in Russia is a transplant from Western Europe. Stage-plays were unknown in Muscovy till the late seventeenth century and did not strike roots there till well into the eighteenth. The medieval Russian church had no tradition of miracle plays or any form of religious drama, unless we count the one tremendous drama of the Liturgy, with its unconscious echoes of the long-forgotten theatre of the ancient Greeks. Anything to do with the Western Church was anathema to the clergy of Muscovy, but their Orthodox brethren in the Polish-dominated provinces of White Russia and the Ukraine, though also bitterly opposed to Roman Catholicism, were nevertheless receptive to cultural influences and from the end of the sixteenth century began to produce religious plays translated from medieval Latin or Polish originals.

Out of these beginnings there developed in the Ukraine a genuine native popular theatre, which was to have its influence, many years later, on the development of the young Gógol. When however these plays were carried into Muscovy on the great wave of culture and scholarship that came up with the influx of Ukrainian and White Russian clergy in the late seventeenth century, they remained no more than an academic exercise – 'Schoolplays' as they were called.

At about the same time the court of the Tsars had its first

experience of the secular theatre of the West. The Kremlin of those days was an unlikely kind of place for courtly entertainments such as were to be seen at St James' and Versailles. The Tsaritsa was always a native Russian, never (for religious reasons) a foreign princess, and sometimes even chosen in a kind of beauty competition. She never appeared in public unveiled, but spent her time in the *térem* or women's quarters among a host of pilgrims, nuns and other holy people. The political power of her family however was immense, for her relations automatically took over the chief offices of state. The Tsar, educated by the clergy and brought up in the seclusion of his mother's *térem*, had little relaxation from his official duties and the long ceremonies of the Church, other than all-male banquets where it was considered an act of disloyalty if a guest did not get drunk.

Tsar Alexius Mikhailovich, however, had begun to show interest in the outside world and in 1672 a play was performed in his presence. It was called 'The Comedy of Artaxerxes' and dealt with the Biblical story of Esther – a very suitable choice, for the setting was one readily recognizable to the audience. There was the beauty competition, the political intrigues in the *térem*, even the 'king's banquet of wine'. The 'comedy' had been written in verse in German by one Pastor Gregory, chaplain to the German community in Moscow, and translated into a kind of crude rhyming doggerel in a language that is an awkward mixture of Church Slavonic and native Russian; a copy was recently discovered at Lyons in France. Other plays by Pastor Gregory followed; there was one on Tamburlaine the Great, a character well remembered in Russia.

When Peter the Great, son of Tsar Alexius, came to the throne the flood-gates were opened for all kinds of Western influence. Ladies had to shed their veils and come out of the *térem*; their husbands were compelled to shave off their beards. A wooden theatre was set up on Red Square in

Moscow and Peter, predictably, made attendance compulsory; in spite of this however the enterprise did not prosper and it was not until 1756, thirty-one years after Peter's death, that the first permanent theatre was opened in St Petersburg, then growing up to be a beautiful city under the rule of the Empress Elizabeth Petróvna. Elizabeth was fond of the theatre and did much to encourage its development and soon there were theatres in Moscow and other towns, while wealthy gentlemen set up their own private companies of serf-actors and serf-ballets.

The repertory at first was largely foreign, either in the original French, German or Italian, or in translation, and many of the performers were foreign too. Even in original Russian plays there was wholesale copying of contemporary European models, and not in the best of taste – a Russian 'Hamlet' improved on Shakespeare to the extent of ending the play with a wedding march for King Hamlet and his Queen Ophelia!

But this second-rate, second-hand material served its purpose in providing a vehicle for the emergence of a first-rate native school of actors and actresses, quick to learn from the visiting companies from abroad. These actors had good audiences. There was by now a theatre-going public that if still a little naïve was always keen to 'identify' with the action on the stage and ready to stand up and shout applause at noble sentiments delivered in the stilted verse of Russia's first real playwright, Alexander Sumarókov (1718-77).

2. SERFDOM AND THE AGE OF CATHERINE II

> The age of grovelling and terror!
> That's what it was; disguised as zeal to serve the Tsar.
> CHATSKY.

What held Russian society together was the tradition of personal service. At its best it was manifested in selfless devotion, at its worst it could be perverted into toadyism and bullying. 'To serve his country and help his people' is according to Oldwise the function of a gentleman, and what makes the serf Mrs Jeremy break down and weep is not the brutality of her owners but the suggestion that she herself has done less for them than she might. 'When we don't know what more service we can give . . . when we'd gladly even . . . when we don't grudge our lives . . . and it's still not good enough!'

The Russian 'peculiar institution' of serfdom, that survived till 1861, was not a relic of feudal times. It did not receive sanction of law till the seventeenth century (though serfdom of a kind had existed to a limited extent before that) and it did not reach its full development till the reign of Catherine I I in the eighteenth century. But by the time that the peasantry of Russia were bound to the soil and made the personal property of the manorial gentry the point of view of the state was quite clear. A gentleman was obliged to serve the Tsar, and to enable him to do this he could claim service from his peasants. And in each case it was the superior who had an absolute right to determine what service was to be given, and he could vary the terms at his will. Peter the Great had stated what he required of a gentleman – full-time service from fifteen to sixty. Up to the age of fifteen a gentleman's son was a *nédorosl'* or a legal 'infant' and his parents were obliged to educate him, on pain of the Tsar's heavy displeasure. At sixteen, if his educational standard was adequate, he was to enter the army as a private soldier; if not, then he was to be sent to sea as an ordinary seaman. In consideration of this, he was given absolute power over his 'people'; his wealth was measured not in money or acres but by the number of 'souls' that he owned and his social status would depend on the rank that he had reached in the service hierarchy, according to the Tsar's famous Table of Fourteen Ranks, from

'Collegiate Registrar' in the Civil Service, equivalent to Ensign in the Army, up to Chancellor or Field Marshal. Since everybody, including gentry, had to enter the army as privates, commissioning from the ranks was the normal procedure and a career was open to all. If a commissioned officer or civil servant were not a gentleman by birth he would become one, and on reaching the eighth grade (Major in the Army) he would become a 'hereditary gentleman' which meant that his descendants would be gentry too. In this way many Russians of humble origin and many foreigners became founders of families of gentle-folk.

All this had to be paid for, and the Europeanization of government, the modernization of the Army and the improved standard of living of the educated gentry meant ever-increasing burdens on the serfs, who besides paying taxes to the State and providing recruits for the Army had to give their masters whatever they chose to ask in goods or in service; Mr Beast explains how he can always make up deficiencies by screwing a bit more from his own peasants.

Furthermore, as time went on the basis of Peter's system was gradually eroded. The obligation to enter as privates was evaded by a system of fictitious enrolment and promotion of 'infants', many gentlemen were provided with posts that enabled them to live comfortably at home and the term of their service was cut to twenty-five years. Then in 1762, on the accession of Tsar Peter III, grandson of Peter the Great, compulsory gentry-service was abolished altogether in the so-called 'Decree of Liberation of the Gentry'. In many cases this made little difference; the tradition of service was strong and fathers continued to use their parental authority to see that children were properly educated and went on to do their duty to the Tsar. But the fact remained that anyone could now resign whenever he liked and what had begun as a military caste of serving-gentlemen had become the only class in the country not liable to conscription. Justice and logic would seem to call for another decree emancipating the serfs, and the serfs were quick to see this.

But no such decree came, and the career of Peter III ended four months later in a Palace Revolution. He was succeeded by his widow, a German Princess without a drop of Russian blood and with no shadow of a claim to the throne which she held against the natural heir – her own son Paul – till a stroke took her, after thirty-four years. The reign of Catherine II ('The Great') is commonly reckoned a glorious period of Russian history, an age of brilliant cultural achievement and famous victories. For the common people however it was a black age. Catherine had arrived indoctrinated with the ideas of the eighteenth century enlightenment and ready to rule as a benevolent despot, but in fact she was riding on a tiger from the moment she accepted the supreme power at the hands of her husband's murderers. She knew that she could not hope to stay where she was without the support of the gentry; not only did she not reverse her husband's 'liberation decree' but she extended serfdom to areas where it had not existed before, such as the Ukraine, once the home of the Free Cossacks. The biggest serf-owner in the country was herself, and the peasants settled on Crown lands had always been relatively leniently treated; now she gave them away with both hands into private ownership.

Any sympathy she may have felt for the serfs was extinguished in the great peasant revolt of 1772, led by the cossack Pugachóv who claimed to be Peter III come back to put his wife in her place and set his people free. Thousands of country gentry and army officers were systematically exterminated by the rebels, and thousands more peasants were done to death by the returning forces of law and order. After that, the division of Russia into Two Nations was complete, and rivers of blood had flowed between them.

The rigid class system of Russian society was systematized and strengthened by Catherine's legislation, which lasted almost unchanged till the 1860s and in many respects right up to 1917. Each class managed its own internal affairs. The privileges of the gentry were consolidated and confirmed in a Charter of 1785; the gentlemen of each province had their own assembly, and elected a Marshal to lead them and make submissions on their behalf to the Central Authority as well as other officers to manage matters of common interest to the class, such as schools, orphanages and benevolent funds. Lawsuits between gentry were heard in the first instance by the District Judge, elected by the gentry themselves. The clergy formed another separate class, governed by their own hierarchy. There were two urban classes, the merchants, divided into three 'guilds' (nothing like West European guilds but simply a convenient stratification of merchants according to the amount of capital they possessed), and the 'townspeople' who included all those urban dwellers who were not serfs and had not the capital needed to belong to a 'guild' – artisans, shop assistants, etc. There was an elected Mayor (*Gorodskáya Golová*) with very limited powers; the real authority in the town was the Town Prefect (*Gorodníchi*) a civil servant who was at the same time Chief Magistrate and Chief Constable.

There were no rural magistrates and no justice for peasants other than what they might get from their owners, the gentry, who had the power to flog them, deport them to Siberia or draft them into the Army. A peasant-serf who had a grievance against a gentleman had practically no hope of redress. In extreme cases the Government might decree *sequestration* of a gentleman's property, on grounds of insanity, exceptional depravity, or gross extravagance, but such decrees were usually obtained by other members of the offender's family, never by serfs, who were actually forbidden, by a decree of Catherine's, to make any complaint against their owners. Only in rare cases (such as that of Dárya Saltykóva, convicted of torturing forty serfs to death) did the Government take sides against the gentry; Fonvízin's picture of Mr Trueman going round on a roving commission to stamp out cruelty is fiction.

The mistress of all Russia, Catherine II, was a well-educated and extremely intelligent woman – she corresponded with Voltaire, kept abreast of all the cultural developments of the Europe of her day, and herself wrote plays and satires and contributed to magazines. She also had great courage – at the worst crisis of the Pugachóv rebellion she was the one that kept her head. And she had a capacity for hard work and considerable charm. But she was entirely uninhibited by morality – she took a new lover about every two years – recklessly generous with the enormous wealth of her husband's family, and fair game for the most shameless flatterers. Naturally then her court, the central government of the Russian Empire, became a happy hunting ground for sneaks, pimps, careerists and general bootlickers. But these parasites never succeeded in driving away all the honest men, the men who were not afraid to speak their mind.

3. FONVÍZIN AND *The Infant (Nédorosl')*

You had better die now, Denís, or else not write again.
PRINCE POTEMKIN (ex-lover and chief minister of Catherine II) on the first night of *Nédorosl'*.

Denís Ivánovich Fonvízin was born about 1745 and graduated from the University of Moscow in 1762, the year of

Catherine's accession, entering the Civil Service in the Collegium of Foreign Affairs. The Fonvízins, like many other Russian gentry-families, were of foreign extraction, being descended from a German (or Swedish) prisoner captured in the Livonian campaigns of Ivan the Terrible; they had long become completely Russianized. In a personal memoir Denís tells us that his father was a man of the strictest principles who brought him up in the best tradition of the Russian serving-gentleman; he is no doubt the model for the father of Mr Oldwise as described in Act III of *The Infant*. Denís Fonvízin had taken a prominent part in University theatricals and on arrival in St Petersburg became friendly with the leading actor of the day, Iván Dmitrévsky, for whom he made a number of translations and adaptations of foreign plays. His first real success came (about 1760) when he was summoned to the Hermitage to read his comedy *The Brigadier* to the Empress. *The Brigadier*, a satire on the prevalent mania for aping all things French, is a great advance on his earlier work but is still derivative, being based on a Danish play called *Jean de France* by Baron Ludvig Holberg. After that he quickly came to the fore and in 1769 was made secretary to Vice-Chancellor Nikíta Pánin who was, in effect, Catherine's Foreign Minister.

In 1782 Fonvízin produced *The Infant*. This time he did not read it aloud at the Hermitage – there are lines here that one can hardly imagine anybody reading to Catherine – but had it performed at Kniper's Theatre in St Petersburg with Dmitrévsky as Mr Oldwise. The audience was wildly delighted – purses were thrown on to the stage. Here at last was something genuinely original and genuinely Russian. The dialogue is marvellously characterized, the totally unrefined vernacular of Mr Beast, the slightly top-dressed language of his sister, Oldwise with his downright directness and his antique affectation of 'thees' and 'thous',

Trueman with rather more pompous officialese. (Some expressions used by the Nurse are said to have been overheard by Fonvízin from two women fighting in the street.) The faults of construction are of course glaringly obvious; the plot is absurd, the construction is weak and the action is constantly being held up for one or other of the 'good characters' to deliver a lengthy lecture. But those of us who are inclined to smile, or yawn, or snort over Mr Oldwise should remember that in that age (and for that matter in every other age) Russians have never been averse from listening to a political debate at the Theatre. And we should realize, too, that Fonvízin was in deadly earnest, as will be seen from some of his other activities.

In the same year, 1782, his chief, Count Pánin, had a stroke, which left him paralysed but able to speak, and he sent for Fonvízin to take down his 'Political Testament' the nature of which can be judged from its title, which was as follows: 'A consideration of the total destruction of every form of state government in Russia, and of the parlous condition both of the Empire and of the Dynasty'. The testament contains a forthright denunciation of absolute power 'Subjects are enslaved to the Sovereign, and the Sovereign as a rule to an unworthy favourite. Greed and avarice complete the general depravity. Heads are occupied only with thoughts of the means of enrichment.'

This document was to be held by Fonvízin after Pánin's death, and delivered to the heir to the throne, the Grand Duke Paul, on his accession. It is reasonable to assume, given the circumstances, that Pánin did not dictate the 'testament' to Fonvízin, but that the latter drafted it and that it expresses views that the two men had held in common. What is here proposed is that the autocrat should exchange his absolute power for a Constitution with checks and balances (Fonvízin had visited Paris in 1778 and met Benjamin Franklin). There is no suggestion of democracy –

after Pugachóv the very idea of political power for the masses would have been enough to make any Russian gentleman shudder. Establish the rule of law, see that the gentry are properly educated and all will be well.

All this is strikingly similar to the doctrine expressed by Oldwise in *The Infant* and by Fonvízin himself in some of his other writings. His Ideal Gentleman need not devote his entire life to State service; he can also make important contributions to the commonwealth in trade and industry. The French notion that it is derogatory for a gentleman to engage in trade is (he says) mistaken; many years before he had translated a French treatise on this subject and had written an essay on the freedom of the French nobles, and the role of the Tiers-État. One sees already Starodúm, the businessman from Siberia.

Pánin died in the following year, and Catherine impounded and sealed all his papers, including the Testament, which was not released for publication from state archives until 1905 – the year of the first Russian revolution and the constitutional manifesto of Tsar Nicholas II.

Fonvízin was not employed again. In retirement he continued to press his views with remarkable boldness and to engage in a running debate with Catherine herself. There was a magazine called *Sobesédnik* ('The conversational companion for lovers of Russian speech') to which the Empress contributed a series called 'Bylí i nebylítsy' ('Truth and Fiction'). Fonvízin sent in a number of loaded questions 'for the author of "Truth and Fiction" ', which were published, with Catherine's replies, e.g.

Q. Why is it that marks of distinction, which ought to be recognition for genuine services to the State, seldom lead to any sincere respect for their recipients?
A. Because everybody admires and respects what is like himself, rather than the public and private virtues.

Q. Why do we see so many good men in retirement?
A. Presumably because they find it profitable to retire.

And so on; the repartee may not be up to the best Parliamentary level, but this comes very near to submitting that astonishing woman, the autocrat of All the Russias, to 'question time'.

He also contributed to the same magazine a 'dictionary of synonyms' showing how confusion of shades of meaning of near-synonymous Russian words could be avoided. Ostensibly this was intended for the compilers of the Academy Dictionary, then in preparation, but it contrived to convey messages of a quite different kind.

'*Injury and oppression. Injury* is damage to honour or to property, *oppression* is denial of rights. Where the *injured* are *oppressed*, the law is not operating.'

Another similar piece of philological parody was called 'An Universal Court Grammar'. Fonvízin planned to produce a journal himself, called 'The honest people's friend or Starodúm' in which 'Starodúm' ('Mr Oldwise') would provide answers to correpondents in need of advice. Many of the characters in *The Infant* reappear here; Sophia writes in distress to her Uncle – Milo has been unfaithful to her. A certain Durýkin ('Booby') a neighbour of the Simples, seeks advice about a tutor for his three sons. Should he perhaps get a Russian student – Germans do not seem to be reliable? He already has a tutor for his three daughters: 'Her name is Madam Ludo; she is of unknown nationality.'

But in the end Catherine's patience was exhausted and Fonvízin was silenced. It may well seem strange that she had stood him as long as she did – Púshkin thought that she was a little bit afraid of him.

Fonvízin's health declined after a seizure in 1785 and he died in 1791.

Catherine died in 1796. Her successor, the Tsar Paul, on whom such hopes had been fixed by Pánin and Fonvízin, turned out to be a madman.

4. GRIBOYÉDOV AND *Chatsky (Góre ot Umá)*

My characters are portraits? Yes! And if I haven't the talent of Molière I'm at least honester than he. Portraits and nothing else are the stuff of comedy and tragedy; they do however contain features in common with other people, some of them in common with all mankind in so far as each man resembles all his fellow-bipeds. I loathe caricature . . . I'll say one more thing about Molière: *Le Bourgeois Gentilhomme* and *Le Malade Imaginaire* are portraits, excellent ones; *L'Avare* is an anthropos that he has manufactured himself – and insufferable.

Talent rather than art? You couldn't pay me a better compliment!

GRIBOYÉDOV (Letter to P. A. Katénin).

Half the lines are bound to become proverbs.

PÚSHKIN.

In 1824 A. S. Griboyédov, a diplomat on leave in St Petersburg from service in Persia and the Caucasus, submitted to the Censor a comedy on which he had been working for a number of years. The Censor's reaction was to ban it; the utmost concession he would allow was publication of a few innocuous extracts in a theatrical magazine. Censorship was now a good deal tighter than it had been in Catherine's time, and the Tsar was surrounded by officials who had lived through the French Revolution and the wars of Napoleon, culminating in the invasion of Russia and retreat from Moscow, and were firmly convinced that change of any kind must be resisted. Tsar Alexander I had shed the 'liberalism' of his early days and become a man haunted by ghosts, seeking refuge in religious mysticism. Apart from a little well-intentioned but largely ineffective legislation by Alexander and by his father Paul, the state of the serfs was much as it had been forty years before.

Among the younger generation of gentry there was however a great ferment of thought. Russian armies had marched through Europe and occupied Paris and quite large numbers of army officers had had a chance to see what life was like in the West. They realized for the first time how backward and barbarous their country was, and some at least of them could see that serfdom was inherently beastly, not (as Fonvízin's generation had supposed) subject to abuses that could be corrected by the right kind of education. At the same time the great victory over Napoleon had given Russia a new sense of national greatness, a feeling even of a Messianic destiny ... There was a rampant growth of secret societies, some with frothy talk 'of Parliaments and juries, and Byron – serious things like that', some that really meant business.

It was the golden age of Russian poetry; Púshkin was twenty-five – already acclaimed as a national bard (most of his greatest work was yet to come) and the centre of a constellation of young poets; in the theatre however there had still been no new dramatist of comparable stature with Fonvízin. And all of this flowering of literature and political thought was confined to the gentry, or rather to a particular section of the gentry – mostly young army officers and young Civil Servants. The mass of the population were inarticulate, illiterate and quite unconcerned in the revolutionary projects of the secret societies.

At twenty-nine Griboyédov was slightly older than Púshkin and his associates. The Griboyédovs, like the Fonvízins, were an old-established family of Moscow gentry ultimately of foreign (Polish) extraction. The young

Alexander gave early promise of brilliance; he entered the University of Moscow at the age of eleven (decidedly early even for those days) and had taken degrees in Arts and in Law and was studying mathematics and science for a doctorate when Napoleon invaded Russia in 1812. He immediately threw up his university career (he was still only seventeen) and took a commission in the Hussars. After the war he came to St Petersburg and entered the Foreign Service, where in addition to his knowledge of classical and modern languages he learned Arabic and Persian. As an amateur pianist he was of near-professional standard, and he even composed a little music (a couple of waltzes by him have survived). Some people (including perhaps even Púshkin) seem to have thought it was slightly indecent for one man to have quite so many talents; Griboyédov was touchy about this and got really angry when his friend Thaddaeus Bulgárin put him into a novel under the name of Talántin. In St Petersburg he lived the life of a young man of fashion and spent much time in company with theatrical people, and had a hand, generally in collaboration with friends, in the production of a number of light theatrical entertainments, or 'vaudevilles' as they were called. As a result of his friendship (apparently quite innocent) with the great ballerina of the day, the Istómina who is mentioned by Púshkin in *Eugene Onegin*, he got mixed up in a tragic duelling affair and in the end was obliged to fight a duel himself, in which he received a slight wound on the little finger from an opponent who was deliberately trying to spoil his piano-playing. Perhaps in consequence of this very grave scandal, he was posted to Tehran in 1819, remaining on duty in Persia and in the Caucasus till 1823 when he came home on a long leave which was to last nearly two years. During the years abroad he had worked on his comedy *Chatsky*, a picture of the world he had left behind; at the beginning of his leave he stayed a while in Moscow to refresh his memory of the types he had portrayed and then took the finished work to St Petersburg.

The Censor could ban *Chatsky* but not suppress it. Night after night, Griboyédov was invited out to read his play, manuscript copies were made and circulated all over Russia; in the end it is said that there were 40,000 of them.

Shortly after his return to the Caucasus the Tsar Alexander I died and was succeeded by his brother Nicholas I. The secret societies, already working up for a coup, were stampeded into immediate action, resulting in the disastrous fiasco of the Decembrist mutiny, of 14 December 1825. In the inquiries that followed the collapse of the Decembrists, Griboyédov was arrested, taken to St Petersburg under escort and interrogated for several months. Eventually he was released and presented with a remarkable document which certified officially that he was not a member of a secret society. The whole truth will probably never be known, but it seems unlikely that he was really innocent.

He had only three more years to live. He returned to his post in the Caucasus, where he distinguished himself greatly in the Russo-Persian war that had just broken out, and in the peace negotiations afterwards, when Persia was forced to accept the extremely harsh terms of the Treaty of Turkmanchai. In reward for this he was chosen to carry the Treaty to the Tsar in St Petersburg, where he was received with gun salutes, decorated, and presented with a purse of gold.

He would have liked now to retire, and devote the rest of his life to literature, but the Tsar wanted him to go back to Tehran as Chargé d'Affaires, to supervise execution of the terms of the Treaty. He accepted this duty with a heavy heart; he knew he had many enemies in Persia and he took leave of his friends as one not expecting to see them again.

On his way through Tiflis he was married to Princess Nina Chavchavadze, sixteen-year old daughter of a Georgian Prince who was famous both as a general and as a national poet. She was, he wrote, like 'Murillo's shepherdess-Madonna on the right by the door as you go into the Hermitage'; their brief married life seems to have been wildly happy. She went with him into Persia as far as Tabriz, after which he went on to Tehran without her.

Soon after his arrival at the capital he ran into trouble. An Armenian eunuch (of all people, the comptroller of the Imperial Household) appeared at the Russian legation and asked for asylum. His master, the aged Fath Ali Shah, was indignant, but the eunuch had a clear right under the peace treaty to claim repatriation, for he had been born in the province of Erivan, which had just been ceded to Russia (it is now the Armenian Republic of the USSR), and had thereby become a subject of the Tsar. Griboyédov saw it as his duty to grant asylum to the eunuch, and to two Armenian girls who had escaped from the harem of the Shah's son-in-law; and also to start looking for other captives who might have a right to protection, and to make inquiries of a kind that were certain to infuriate Moslems – as he well knew.

On 30 January O.S. 1829 a crowd of fanatics broke into the Russian Legation at Tehran, killing Griboyédov and all but one of his staff. His mutilated body was recovered three days later, identifiable only by the old duelling scar on the little finger. He was just thirty-four years old.

In 1833 the Censorship relented to the extent of allowing public performance of a heavily cut text of *Chatsky* and the play was given for the first time in Moscow with a distinguished cast headed by Shchépkin as Fámusov and Mochálov as Chatsky. In 1861 all restrictions were removed and the full text published for the first time. It has remained in the repertory ever since, a virtuoso show-piece for generations of actors and more often quoted, consciously or un-consciously, than any other Russian play.

That it is still so little known in the English-speaking world is no doubt due to its being exceptionally hard to translate. Many have gone so far as to say that it is un-translatable, and indeed much of its unique flavour is bound to be lost.

The original is a national monument; the language is inimitable, even in Russian – it has been remarked that it has the supreme virtue of not being always too perfect! – and lines from the play are quoted, often unconsciously, every day. The combination of easy, colloquial diction with rhymed metrical verse results in what I. A. Goncharóv (author of *Oblómov*) has called an 'indissoluble fusion of prose and verse' which can hit its targets right in the centre again and again with a kind of neat inevitability.

The metre used in the present translation is broadly similar to that of the original, a mixture of iambic lines of any length from six feet down to one foot, but is unrhymed. Only those who can read Russian will know how much is lost by discarding the rhyme with its ever-changing, some-times complex, patterns and its unvarying alternation of monosyllabic and disyllabic endings. But for some reason the English theatre does not take kindly to rhymed verse, except for the pantomime, and it would be difficult to preserve the rhyme and at the same time keep faith with the sense; to reproduce the alternation of single and double rhymes in English would probably be impossible.

Such an irregular metrical system is however in danger of turning into prose, unless the ear can be given something to look forward to, as it has all the time in the rhymes of the Russian. To do something to meet this difficulty, the English version avoids *consecutive* lines containing less than five feet, though such lines are common enough in the original; a short line, when it comes, may therefore be regarded as a kind of 'suspension' to be 'resolved' by the immediately following full five foot line or six-foot alexandrine.

Russian verse, like English, is based on stress, but there are certain differences of practice. English allows an occasional trisyllabic foot in 'iambics' (especially with obscure vowels or with words such as *going* or *being* scanned as if monosyllables), a thing that classical Russian verse does not tolerate; here the translation has followed the English tradition. Griboyédov, like many Russian poets, observes a caesura both after the third foot of an alexandrine line and after the second foot of a five-foot line. The caesura is observed in the alexandrines of the translation (English tradition here varies – compare e.g. *The Faerie Queene* with *Childe-Harold*) and this has been marked with a little extra space in the middle of the line; it seems to help to give these lines (slightly exotic anyhow in English) a characteristic rhythmical contour and to keep them from looking and sounding like common 'blank verse' gone wrong. But it would be quite un-English to have a fixed caesura in five-foot lines and would make for monotony where, as here, the five-foot line is much the commonest measure; it happens to be rather rare in the Russian which is almost half alexandrines with four-foot lines the next commonest.

The original title of the play, *Góre ot Umá*, does seem to defy translation into English. The literal meaning is 'Grief from Mind' but there seems to be no way of conveying the sense of these three words in anything that looks like a possible title for an English play. 'Woe from Wit' and 'The misfortune of being intelligent' have been proposed in the past, but neither is satisfactory. The solution adopted here is to give the translation the new title of *Chatsky* with a sub-title *The misery of having a mind*, these last words being taken from the English version of the little epigram which Griboyédov prefixed to his play, the original of which also ends with the words *góre ot umá*.

5. GÓGOL AND *The Government Inspector (Revizór)*

> (Gógol's) characters were not realistic caricatures of the
> world without, but introspective caricatures of the fauna
> of his own mind. They were exteriorizations of his own
> 'ugliness' and 'vice'. *The Inspector* and *Dead Souls* were
> satires of self and of Russia and mankind only in so far as
> Russia and mankind reflected that self.
>
> D. S. MIRSKY.

> In *The Inspector* I had decided to collect into one heap
> everything that I then knew about that was bad in Russia,
> all the injustices that were being done at times and in
> places where there was greatest need for justice; and laugh
> at the whole lot in one go.
>
> GÓGOL.

> Well, what a play. Everybody caught it, most of all Me.
>
> TSAR NICHOLAS I.

Nikoláy Vasilévich Gógol was born in 1809. His family
were small gentry of Ukrainian cossack extraction, Russianized in that Russian, not Ukrainian, was spoken at home.
He was brought up in the country, where he would see the
Vertép or popular puppet-theatre (a descendant of the
religious drama and school-plays of the seventeenth century)
and would hear the blind minstrels' songs of the heroic days
of the Cossack Host and the Camp Below the Rapids. His
father too was the author of a number of plays based on
Ukrainian popular tales, which were performed at the Big
House near by. He went to school in the small town of
Nézhin, and took a leading part in school-theatricals; his
performance as Mrs Simple in a school production of *The
Infant* was long remembered.

On leaving school in 1829 he went not to University but
straight to St Petersburg, taking with him a sentimental
poem called 'Hanz Küchelgarten' that he thought would

bring him instant fame. It was received with derision and he bought up and burnt the whole edition. He entered the Civil Service but did not stay there long, as somebody got him a job as history teacher at a girls' school. He had small enough qualifications for this, but went on (incredibly) to be Professor of History at the University of St Petersburg, resigning the Chair after one very embarrassing session. During this period he started a historical drama on King Alfred of England, on the strength of having read Hallam's *View of the State of Europe in the Middle Ages* – in translation, for he knew no English. This he left unfinished.

But meanwhile he had found a better line. In 1831 he published a volume of tales of the Ukraine called *Evenings on the Farm near Dikánka* told in the mouth of an old beekeeper called Rudy Panko. This delighted everybody; other volumes followed with more tales of the Ukraine and, later, of St Petersburg; humorous, fantastic, sometimes tragic and heroic. These stories are shot through with a strong persistent eerie flavour, based partly on his reading of *The Tales of Hoffmann*, partly on Ukrainian legends of uncanny beings such as Viy, whose eyelids reach to the ground (Gwevyl, son of Gwestad in the Mabinogion, had a similar trick with his lip), but above all on something strange and sinister inside his own head.

It was however becoming plain that Gógol's real métier was after all the theatre. Like Dickens, he was a wonderful reader of his own works, and it has often been noticed how easy his stories are to dramatize. In 1832 he started a play called *The Suitors* which he put aside, finishing it ten years later and changing the title to *Marriage*. This hilariously funny comedy is the story of a girl who asks a professional matchmaker to find her a husband; in comes a procession of typical Gógol grotesques and a shy young Civil Servant who wins the girl, only to take fright at the last minute and jump out of the window. Psychologists see in this another reflection of the inner life of Gógol himself – he never married.

He started another play called *Vladímir Class III* about a decoration-hunting bureaucrat and abandoned it as being certain to be stopped by the censor. Then he asked Púshkin to give him a subject for a comedy, and Púshkin told him how once when he was travelling round collecting material for his *History of the Pugachov Mutiny* he was mistaken for an inspector.

The Censor would have banned *The Government Inspector* but for the Tsar having heard about it from the poet Zhukóvsky. Nicholas I commanded that the play be performed and went to see it himself on the first night at the Alexandra Theatre in St Petersburg (1835); his comment, quoted at the head of this section, was soon repeated everywhere. Even without this *The Government Inspector* was the talk of the town. Some saw in it no more than a good laugh, the progressives hailed it as a manifesto for social reform and the reactionaries raised a howl of protest. Bulgárin (once the friend of Griboyédov and now little better than a police nark) said it was a libel on Russia, and that flamboyant ruffian 'American' Tolstóy (Repetílov gives a thumbnail sketch of him in Act IV of *Chatsky*) demanded that Gógol be sent to Siberia to the chain-gang.

Gógol fled from the clamour and went to Rome, where he lived for most of the next twelve years. He was very disappointed with the production; Durr who took the part of Whippet played it as farce and many of the lines sounded all wrong when he heard them from the stage. The first Moscow performance, with the great Shchépkin as the Prefect, was rather better, but Gógol decided to rewrite the play, taking particular pains with the rhythm and the 'orchestration', as he called it, of the text. The second version, much superior to the first and used ever since, appeared in 1842.

In the same year he published the First Part of *Dead Souls* a novel (or as he called it a 'poem'). The triple pun in the title exemplifies the multiple levels of meaning in his work that make it so hard to pin down what Gógol really thought he was doing.

The story is of a gigantic swindle. Chíchikov travels round Russia buying up 'dead souls' (i.e. the title-deeds to serfs who had died since the last assessment and for whom the owner was obliged to go on paying poll-tax) with the intention of mortgaging them. But the serf-owners that Chíchikov meets on his travels are all themselves 'dead souls', killed by what to Gógol was the cardinal sin, the mixture of smug pettiness, indolence and complacency that is called in Russian *póshlost*. But there was a third meaning too; a journey among dead souls is a journey through Hell and Gógol saw in his work nothing less than Part I of a new *Divine Comedy*, with a new *Purgatorio* and *Paradiso* to follow.

The fact is that Gógol could see a lot more of the 'fauna of his own mind' than most men in that pre-Freudian age, and he was frightened. In 1847 he produced a piece called 'The Dénouement of *Revizór*', purporting to show that the whole thing was an allegory, and that the characters were citizens of what Bunyan called the City of Mansoul; the real Inspector was the true conscience of man which will awaken in his last hour, when it is too late for him to change.

Heaven knows how long it had taken him to think up this; it is hard to believe he had been at any rate conscious of any such idea when he wrote the play. Everybody was annoyed by it, and still more so when in the same year he published *Select Passages from a Correspondence with Friends*. To begin with, the title was dishonest; most of it was not correspondence at all but newly written. 'Select Passages' consists of a dreadful collection of sanctimonious platitudes purporting to justify all the evils of the Social Order in Russia including serfdom and flogging.

His progressive friends denounced him as a traitor to the cause, but that would not really do for Gógol. He had, it is true, always believed that theatre should be a serious thing; he had inveighed against the triviality of the 'vaudevilles' that were all the rage in his day and had talked of 'community comedy', abandonment of love interest and back to Aristophanes. But the truth is that he had never been really concerned in the reform of society, but rather in the regeneration of men . . .

Sincere believing Christians too were horrified and disgusted at what he had written, but the fact seems to be that he was going mad. In the following year (1848) he made a pilgrimage to Jerusalem, where he was disappointed to find he experienced no emotion at the Holy Places, and he came away more frightened than ever, believing himself to be damned. At last he went home to Russia and put himself under a spiritual director who told him that his writings had been sinful. He burned most of the manuscript of Part II of *Dead Souls*, which was to have been the story of Chíchikov's progress through purgatory; from what little is left, Part II seems to our taste greatly inferior to Part I, which remains as a first-rate picaresque novel.

He underwent an appallingly severe regime of fasting and died, one may say of starvation, in 1852.

He had been the first to bracket his work with that of Fonvízin and Griboyédov, who were he said the models for what he called 'community comedy'; and the general consensus of opinion is that *The Government Inspector* is not only the greatest of Odóyevsky's 'three tragedies', but the greatest play in the Russian language.

6. OSTRÓVSKY AND *Thunder (Grozá)*

A ray of light in the Kingdom of Darkness.

N. A. DOBROLYÚBOV.

It does us no harm to listen carefully to the Moscow *prosvírni*; they speak a marvellously pure and correct language.

PÚSHKIN.

Alexander Ostróvsky was 'mere Russian'. His father Nicholas was the son of an Archpriest from the province of Kostromá, his mother was the daughter of one of the 'Moscow prosvírni' (church baking-women who made the special loaves of bread used in the Holy Eucharist) commended by Púshkin for the purity of their Russian. Nikoláy Ostróvsky had entered the Civil Service and retired when he reached the eighth grade, which made him a hereditary gentleman, setting up in private practice as a lawyer. His son Alexander therefore carried a gentleman's passport, though his ancestors came from the clergy class. He was born in 1823, in the South Bank suburb of Moscow, a stronghold of the old traditional Muscovite way of life, hardly touched yet by Europeanization, where there were great sprawling houses, homes of wealthy merchants and their families, where things were kept up properly in the old style. The young Alexander Ostróvsky soon developed an ear for the speech of his father's clients, untouched by westernization or book-learning, but highly expressive and capable of rising into a kind of natural poetic diction. One is reminded of J. M. Synge listening through the floor of a loft to the kind of English spoken by Irish servants. At the same time he had the run of his father's excellent library and finished high school with good marks for Russian language and literature, going on to the university to read law. Here, he tells us, he and his fellow students spent much of their time at the Bolshóy Theatre, then used for drama; too much apparently, for he came away without a degree. His father got him a job at the 'Court of Conscience', a kind of arbitration tribunal to help people settle their differences without litigation, from where he went on to the Commercial Court, which was largely concerned with bankruptcy. All this gave him an extensive knowledge of the seamy side of life and the ways of minor officials. But his heart was in the theatre; about this time he began a lifelong friendship with the actor Probus Sadóvsky who was to create so many of his great parts.

In 1850 his first full-length play *The Bankrupt* or *We can settle this among ourselves* was published in the magazine *Moskvityánin*. The merchant community were indignant at a play which showed a Russian merchant committing a fraudulent bankruptcy and, worse still, getting away with it, and complaints reached the Tsar, who sent back a sharp minute saying that the play should never have been passed for publication and must not be performed. Ostróvsky was put under police surveillance and in the following year had to resign his civil service post. But critics had begun to take notice of him, as a playwright fit to be mentioned in the same breath with the 'immortal trio' – Fonvízin, Gribo-yédov and Gógol. In 1853 he had his first play performed. *Don't get into someone else's sledge* (in other words 'Stick to your own class') was the story of a merchant girl who falls in love with an untrustworthy gentleman, but in the end goes back to the merchant boy who really loves her. Nicholas I went to see this play, and approved it. The same year, 1853, saw the production of *Poverty is no Vice*, a simple story of the good poor boy that gets his love in the end, but marvel-lously adorned by the loving care with which Ostróvsky has recorded and reproduced every detail of the traditional life in a big merchant's house, especially the music – he uses twenty-three different folk-songs. After that he went on producing plays at the rate of over one a year until he died thirty-three years later.

In fact however Ostróvsky's talent was not of the same order as that of the 'immortal trio'. He is rather like a searchlight – he can pick out every detail in a small circle of light, surrounded by darkness, or he can suddenly shine down into some murky hole, revealing the strange creatures at the bottom of it.

One of the ways in which 'absolute power corrupts absolutely' is that it is self-propagating; an absolute ruler can only delegate power like his own – arbitrary and irresponsible, so that as soon as the door closes behind him each subordinate becomes himself another little autocrat, free to do what he thinks fit with nobody to say him nay. Ostróvsky invented a word for the type that says 'Here am I, you can't stop me, I don't care if it's right or wrong. I'm going to do it.' He called it a *samodúr*, a 'portmanteau' formed from the words for *autocrat* and *fool* – an 'autofool'; and since they have been (and still are) not uncommon characters in Russia, the word *samodúr* has become a permanent part of the Russian language. There are many types of autofool from the top downwards; there is for instance the pompous bureaucratic autofool, whom the Russians with the 'happy flexibility' of their language call a *pompadúr*. But Ostróvsky with his bright, narrow searchlight beam concentrates on the lowest level, the autofool in the family circle, and his plays often tell of the consequences, sometimes comic but more often tragic, of his activity, or rather of his or her activity – for many Russian autocrats, from the throne downwards, have been women and there seems to have been a strange substratum of matriarchal custom, at least in some districts, as we shall see later. In a country where the press is kept muzzled the autofools have things very much their own way – 'The tears that are shed, unseen and unheard, behind those bolted doors! ... All hidden, all kept dark'. Take one oppressed household, multiply it a thousand times for the rest of the town and then again for all the other towns in Russia and you get what the great radical critic N. A. Dobrolyúbov called 'The Kingdom of Darkness'; it is the subject of many Ostróvsky plays.

In 1855 Nicholas I died and his son Alexander II immediately started preparatory work for the abolition of serfdom, which took place in 1861. Among the research studies undertaken was a great economic and anthropological survey of the whole Volga basin. Ostróvsky immediately offered his services and was assigned to the section dealing with the upper Volga, the 800-mile stretch from the source to Nízhni Nóvgorod (Górki). This was the country where he had roots; his ancestors had come from Kostromá province, and he had by now inherited a property from his father at Shchelíkovo, near Kinéshma. Here was the typical landscape that recurs so often in his plays, the steep escarpment along the right bank of the great river, the little towns on top of the escarpment, each with its little promenade and view over 300 yards of water to the flat open country to the north.

What Ostróvsky learned in that journey down the Volga forms a basis for his play, *Thunder*, which appeared in 1859. In the town of Torzhók he found strange marriage customs, quite unlike the oriental *térem* seclusion that had prevailed once in Moscow. Young girls were allowed absolute freedom to go in and out of the house whenever they liked, and to walk the streets arm in arm with boys. But directly they were married (and marriage was commonly by elopement) they became virtually bond-slaves to their husband's mother and lived in strict seclusion till she died and they became matriarchs themselves. At Rzhev he heard a strange story of an underground passage with murals representing

37

the Last Judgement – the source of that curious and ominous structure, the 'Gallery' in Act IV of *Grozá*. Once again he used the folk-songs that he knew so well, and all the best of what he had collected of the natural poetic language of unlettered people is put into the mouth of his Catherine, the Catherine whom Dobrolyúbov in his great review of the play calls 'A ray of light in the Kingdom of Darkness.'

Naturalism was something of a novelty to Russian theatre audiences of the 1850s. Shchépkin, the great actor of the previous generation, is said to have walked out of the dress rehearsal of *Thunder*, protesting that he did not go to the theatre to smell sheepskins, and on the first night one puzzled merchant was heard to ask another 'How did they know about that?' But the play was an instant success, and has been popular ever since. In recent times it has been made into a film in the USSR, and has been used by the Czech composer Leoš Janáček as the basis of his opera *Katya Kabanova*.

In 1886 Ostróvsky died at his well-loved home at Shchelíkovo, six months after being appointed artistic director to the Imperial State Theatres. He left over fifty plays of every kind – drama, comedy, tragedy, historical plays, realistic plays, costume pieces, fairy tales (his 'Snow Maiden' was twice used as a libretto, by Tchaikovsky and by Rimsky-Korsakov) and translations (he was working on Shakespeare's *Antony and Cleopatra* when he died). This huge output is of uneven quality; nothing else that he wrote was ever quite so popular as *Thunder* but several other plays of his are still in the repertory. As a rule he was most successful with naturalistic plays taken from the world he knew so well, the world of merchants, townsmen and small government clerks. Towards the end of his life the public began to find that he was not giving them what they were used to expect from him and the word went round that his talents were failing. In fact however he was trying, and not altogether unsuccessfully, to adapt his work to the changed conditions of Russian society. The ascendancy of the gentry had ended with the abolition of serfdom, and both the grand gentleman and the old-time merchant were giving place to capitalist businessmen in European suits.

A 'Chekovian' situation, in fact, and some of his last plays show interesting anticipations of the work of Antón Chékhov, whose first full-length play *Ivánov* was written in the year that Ostróvsky died. In *Bespridánnitsa* (*A girl without a fortune*) which appeared in 1879 and which Ostróvsky himself thought was his best work, the heroine Larísa has been 'shot down' by a passing lady-killer, who reappears to pick her up at a luncheon party given by a rather uncouth young civil servant who has just got engaged to her. Russian authors are always sensitive to the meanings of proper names and it is perhaps no coincidence that Larísa means Seagull.

NOTE ON RUSSIAN NAMES

A WORD is needed to explain, perhaps to excuse, the treatment of personal names in these translations. Russian names often look strange to an English-speaking reader; they are hard to pronounce and hard to remember – hard too, sometimes, to tell apart. To make matters worse each character in a play or novel may be addressed at different times by totally different names or by variant forms of a name that imply (to a Russian) gradations in tone all the way from affectionate respect down to sheer contempt. Finally whether the names are real or absurdly improbable they frequently have meanings appropriate to the character that bears them. In an attempt to convey some of these nuances to the reader, many names have been more or less completely Anglicized.

As members of the Eastern or Orthodox Church, Russians have a very restricted choice of christian names. Every child must be baptized in the name of a saint taken from the Church Calendar, which is virtually a closed list, since for many centuries past the newly-added saints have been men and women who had themselves been baptized in one of the older names. These names are mostly Biblical or early Christian or, at latest, Byzantine; very few of them have anything particularly Russian about them. They are therefore part of the common heritage shared by both East and West, though some have gone out of fashion in the West today, where we have introduced a great many new names unknown to the conservative East. There is therefore nothing strange about Russian Christian names, except the forms in which they use them, and indeed they have a better reason to say that our names are strange to them.*

Christian names, therefore, have been Anglicized wherever possible, and in some cases rendered by their original Greco-Roman form. *Ósip* therefore becomes *Joseph* and *Savyól, Saul*; while *Avdót'ya* and *Khavrónya* become *Eudoxia* and *Febronia*. Similarly with diminutives; *Fómka*, e.g. becomes *Tom*, but since we have nothing in English to correspond with *Mitrofánushka* we have to use some added words to express the tone of fond complacency conveyed by this incessantly repeated form of the boy's name – 'Mitrofán, dear boy' or 'Our boy, Mitrofán'.

The patronymics, so much used by Russians, do not convey anything particular to an English ear other than 'strangeness' when in fact they are quite natural. Various expedients have been used to get rid of them from the translation; the aim being to find a form of address that would sound natural in English, in the given circumstances, and would convey the right kind of 'tone'. In *Chatsky*, e.g. an English lady's maid would not call her mistress 'Sophie, daughter of Paul' (Sóf'ya Pávlovna); she would say 'Miss Sophie'. Chatsky never once addresses Sophie by name (an interesting touch)† but when talking about her to her father he too calls her Sóf'ya Pávlovna. One might have expected him to use a plain Christian name (after all they were brought up together) but even if he hesitated at that, one

* 'Hence comes the holy virginal company
  Priscilla, Gertrude, Agnes and Cicely,
  With Lucy, Petronel and Thecla,
  Agatha, Barbara, Juliana.'

This list of girls' names is taken from a twelfth century Latin poem by Sigebert of Gembloux. All of them, except Gertrude, are names of virgin saints of the Early Church and therefore exist in some form as possible Russian Christian names; one is surprised to find how many 'Russian' names turn out to be *Latin*.

† She calls him plain Chatsky without Mr, which again would sound very odd in English – imagine Emma talking about 'Knightley'! But Russians are sparing in their use of titles and the tone implied by a plain surname is quite different from English.

would hardly expect an English Chatsky to be so stiff as to say 'Miss Sophie'. So the translation makes him compromise on 'Your daughter, Sophie', which seems to irritate the old man, for he mimics it in his reply. When however Fámusov himself addresses his daughter in this coldly formal way he is very angry with her, and the translation makes him call her Sophia instead of the usual Sophie. Again Repetílov in Act IV addresses Sophie's aunt as 'Anthusa, daughter of Nilus'; this is the sort of thing that makes English readers give up in despair, for there is nothing in the list of characters or anywhere else to suggest that this is her name and patronymic. An Englishman would use a title and surname, and call her Miss Khlyóstova.

Surnames have been differently treated in different plays. *The Infant* is typical eighteenth century and as in many contemporary English plays the surnames are conventional, more like 'character masks' than real names. It seems therefore in keeping with the period atmosphere to convert Prostakóv into Simple, Starodúm into Oldwise, etc. The Christian name 'Mitrofán' was also chosen for its meaning ('He that showeth forth the Mother' – Greek Metrophanes); the Prostakóvs have bestowed a rather grand Byzantine name on their precious son, one that is often assumed as a name-in-religion and therefore associated with bishops rather than with small boys.

Griboyédov's surnames are of various kinds. Tugo-úkhovsky ('Tight-ears') for the deaf Prince is of course quite artificial and in line with Fonvízin's practice, as are Molchálin ('Silence') for the secretary, Skalozúb ('Grinner') for the Colonel and Khlyóstova ('Whiplash') for a masterful old lady.* Others are thinly disguised names of contemporaries, 'Repetílov' is a conflation of French

* 'Miss Khlyóstova' is based on a well known character of the day named Nathalie Dmitrievna Ofrosímova, who also appears (though Tolstoy denied this) to have inspired the Akhrosímova of *War and Peace*. Ofrosím and Akhrosím are both Russian forms of Euphrosyne!

répéter and Shepetílov (an acquaintance of the author); other characters' names seem to have no obvious significance, or else the key is lost. Surnames in this play have been left unaltered.

Ostróvsky is a naturalist and uses genuine names, even taking the trouble to choose surnames that were current in the district in which the play is set. At the same time he contrives to give them symbolical meaning. In *Thunder* the play is opened by a self-educated working man who takes little part in the action but appears again and again, like a Greek Chorus, to comment on the story as it unfolds. He has a genuine love of nature, knows a little about Science and has read the poets of the eighteenth century. Unlike the others, he understands that the brutal and selfish society surrounding him is sick, but he has no remedy to offer other than a daydream of making a fortune and giving it away.

In giving the name 'Kulígin' to this man Ostróvsky was no doubt thinking of a famous self-taught craftsman called Kulíbin, who lived in the eighteenth century, but at the same time he makes the name symbolic of the future of the Russian people, for *kulíga* means 'a patch of forest ground cleared for cultivation'. Opposed to him are the denizens of the surrounding forest – Dikóy ('savage') and Mrs Kabanóva ('the wild sow'). Christian names, too, are symbolic in this play; Saul Dikóy has a moody violent temper, like his namesake King Saul, and Mrs Kabanóva is one of the 'Marthas' of this world – at least in her own estimation. So too with Barbara the 'wild' and Catherine the 'pure'; Tíkhon (Greek Tychon), like Mitrofán, is a rather unusual and monastic name, probably chosen because it sounds like the Russian word for 'quiet'.

The surnames in this play however are real Russian surnames, and the overtones of meaning that they carry could not be reproduced in English. They have therefore been retained in their original form.

Lastly, *The Government Inspector*, which stands apart from the main line of development. Gógol's names are neither conventional nor natural; they are queer. There seems no logical reason for calling one of the principal villains 'Strawberry' nor for calling the Police Chief 'Earwig', but Gógol has gone on to work this out down to the smallest details; a shopkeeper (Mr Pylebottom) who never appears and is only casually mentioned is given the name 'Pochechúyev', which means 'haemorrhoids'. This is all of a piece with that uncomfortable vein of nightmare fantasy that crops out all over Gógol's works, a presage perhaps of the insanity that ultimately overtook him; and if this non-sense is part of the essential Gógol it would seem worth-while to invent English equivalents for the surnames that he has given to his monsters (their Christian names are all good names out of the Calendar) and this has been done in the translation. But the names in their 'Englished' forms are still Gógol's names, and his too is the setting in time and space – a remote country town in the Russia of Tsar Nicholas I. Nothing is altered by calling the Prefect *Mr Huffam-Slydewynde* instead of Antón Antónovich Skvozník-Dmukhanóvsky, for neither of these is his real name. He is somebody that we all know. 'What are you laughing at?' he asks us. 'You are laughing at yourselves.'

THE INFANT

A Comedy in Five Acts by
Denís Ivánovich Fonvízin

CHARACTERS

SIMPLE, a country gentleman
  (Prostakóv)
MRS SIMPLE, his wife
  (Gospozhá Prostakóva)
MITROFÁN, their son, an infant (Nédorosl')[1]
MRS JEREMY, Mitrofán's nurse
  (Yeremáeevna)
SOPHIA, an orphan, living with Mr & Mrs Simple
  (Sófya)
OLDWISE, Sophia's uncle
  (Starodúm)
TRUEMAN, a member of the administration of the Lieutenancy
  (Právdin)
MILO, an army officer, in love with Sophia
  (Milón)
MR BEAST, brother of Mrs Simple
  (Gospodín Skotínin)
PRIESTLING, a seminary student
  (Kutéykin)
FIGGURES, a retired army sergeant
  (Tsýfrkin)
BOSCHMANN, a German tutor
  (Vral'man)
TRÍSHKA, a tailor
Mr Simple's servant
Mr Oldwise's valet

The action takes place at the SIMPLES'S *Manor.*[2]

ACT ONE

MRS SIMPLE, MITROFÁN, MRS JEREMY *are on stage.*

MRS SIMPLE [*looking over the caftan worn by* MITROFÁN]: The caftan is all spoilt. Jeremy, fetch that scoundrel Tríshka here.

[*Exit* MRS JEREMY.]

He's made it tight everywhere, the villain. Mitrofán dear boy! It must be choking you to death. Call your father here.

[*Exit* MITROFÁN; *enter* MRS JEREMY *and* TRÍSHKA.]

Come nearer, animal. Didn't I tell you to let that caftan out, you with that thieves' look on your ugly face? Firstly, the child is growing, and secondly, even without a tight caftan the child has a delicate constitution. What have you got to say for yourself, dolt?

TRÍSHKA: Why ma'am, I taught myself tailoring. I said to you at the time, may it please you ma'am, to send it to a tailor.

MRS SIMPLE: Do you really need to be a tailor to know how to sew a caftan properly? Just what an animal would think!

TRÍSHKA: But you see, ma'am, the tailor has been taught, and I haven't.

MRS SIMPLE: Still arguing. The tailor was taught by another tailor, and he was taught by a third tailor. Who was it taught the first tailor of all? Tell me that, animal.

TRÍSHKA: The first tailor of all . . . well, maybe his sewing was worse than mine.

[*Re-enter* MITROFÁN, *running.*]

MITROFÁN: I've called Papa. He says please he'll come directly.

MRS SIMPLE: Go and pull him out, then, if he won't come when he's called.

MITROFÁN: But here is Papa.

[*Enter* SIMPLE.]

MRS SIMPLE: What are you doing, pray, hiding from me? Do you see, Sir, the pass I've come to, and with your connivance? What sort of new clothes are these, for our son to wear at his Uncle's betrothal? And what sort of a caftan is this that Tríshka has gone and made for him?

SIMPLE [*stuttering nervously*]: A b ... b ... bit b ... baggy.

MRS SIMPLE: Baggy yourself, Mr Clever.

SIMPLE: But Mother, that's the way I thought you would see it.

MRS SIMPLE: Have you gone blind then?

SIMPLE: When I have your eyes, mine see nothing.

MRS SIMPLE: See what a wretch of a husband the Lord has sent me. Hasn't got enough sense to tell what's tight and what's loose.

SIMPLE: In that, Mother, I've always trusted you and always shall.

MRS SIMPLE: Then trust me in this too. I won't have the serfs pampered. Come, Sir, chastise him here and now.

[*Enter* MR BEAST.]

BEAST: Chastise who, and what for? On the day of my bethrothal? I beg you, Sister, on this festive occasion, to put it off till tomorrow, and tomorrow if it pleases you I'll gladly give a hand myself. I'd find 'em guilty, whatever the charge was, or my name ain't Tarasius Beast. You and I, Sister, are like-minded in that. What has made you angry?

MRS SIMPLE: Tell me now, Brother, how does this look to you? Come over here, Mitrofán, dear boy. Is this caftan baggy?

BEAST: No.

SIMPLE: I can see now, Mother, that it is too tight.

BEAST: I don't see that neither. Brother, it's quite a decently made caftan.

MRS SIMPLE [*to* TRÍSHKA]: Get out, animal. [*to* MRS JEREMY] Come, Jeremy, give the boy some breakfast. The tutors will be coming soon, I expect.

MRS JEREMY: Please, ma'am, he's already had five buns.

MRS SIMPLE: Wretch! Would you grudge him a sixth one! See how particular she is! Look at that, I ask you!

MRS JEREMY: 'Tis for his health, ma'am. I only said it for Master Mitrofán's own sake. He's been upset all night.

MRS SIMPLE: Holy Mother of God! What happened to you, Mitrofán, dear boy?

MITROFÁN: Well, Mamma, I was taken bad last night after supper.

BEAST: I think you did yourself pretty well at supper, young man.

MITROFÁN: Uncle, I hardly had any supper.

SIMPLE: Excuse me, my dear, I can remember you eating something.

MITROFÁN: What was it! About three slices of the salt beef, and some pies. I don't remember how many pies. Maybe five, maybe six.

MRS JEREMY: He kept on asking for drink in the night. He finished the whole jug of Kvas.

MITROFÁN: I still feel in a daze. I dreamed the most nonsensical dreams all night.

MRS SIMPLE: What sort of nonsense, Mitrofán, dear boy?

MITROFAN: Sometimes it was you, Mama, sometimes Papa.

MRS SIMPLE: What about us then?

MITROFÁN: Directly I got to sleep I seemed to see you, Mama, and you were beating Papa.

SIMPLE: Oh my grief! That dream's a true one.

MITROFÁN [*tenderly*]: And I was so sorry.

MRS SIMPLE [*annoyed*]: Who for, Mitrofán dear boy?

MITROFÁN: For you, Mama. You got so tired, hitting Papa.

MRS SIMPLE: Give me a hug dear. There's my little son, the only comfort I've got.

BEAST: Well, Mitrofán dear boy! I can see you are your mother's son, and not your father's.

SIMPLE: At least I love him as a parent should; he's a clever boy and a sensible boy, he's full of jokes and pranks; sometimes I'm quite beside myself with him, I'm so delighted I can hardly believe he is my son.

BEAST: But our little joker is looking rather glum at the moment.

MRS SIMPLE: Oughtn't I to send to town for the Doctor?

MITROFÁN: No, no, Mama. Better let me get well on my own. I'll run over now to the dovecote, or else maybe . . .

MRS SIMPLE: Or else maybe the Lord will be merciful. Run away and play, Mitrofán dear boy.

[*Exeunt* MITROFÁN *and* MRS JEREMY.]

BEAST: Why don't I see my bride? Where is she? The bethrothal is for this very evening; isn't it time to tell her that she is going to be married?

MRS SIMPLE: Time enough, Brother dear. Tell her that beforehand, and she may even think that we are coming to ask her leave. Of course she is only a connection by marriage, through my husband, but I do like to be obeyed, even by people who are not blood relations.

SIMPLE [*to* BEAST]: To tell you the truth, we have treated Sophia as a complete orphan. Her father died when she was a baby. Then, six months ago, her mother, who was a connection of mine by marriage, suffered a stroke. . . .

MRS SIMPLE [*making as if to cross her heart*]: Powers of the Holy Cross be with us.

SIMPLE: . . . which carried her into the next world. Her uncle, a Mr Oldwise, had gone to Siberia, and since there hasn't been a word of news about him for several years, we are presuming him to be deceased. Seeing that she was left alone, we took her into our manor, and we have been looking after her property as if it were our own.

MRS SIMPLE: What a lot of nonsense you are talking today, Mr Simple! Brother may be beginning to think that our motives for taking her in were not disinterested.

SIMPLE: Mother, how could he think that! Sure, it is not possible for us to pick up dear Sophia's estates and carry them here.

BEAST: Even if her chattels have been removed, I'm not one for the law. I don't like trouble, and I'm scared of it. However much my neighbours may have offended me, whatever damage they may have done to me, I haven't ever sued them. Anything that I may have lost, due to them, I screw out of my own peasants, and there's the end of the matter.

SIMPLE: You're right there, Brother. All the neighbours say that you are a past master at collecting your dues.

MRS SIMPLE: Do teach us, Brother dear, we're no good at it at all. Since we took everything that our peasants had, we haven't been able to screw any more out of them. It's dreadful.

BEAST: Sister, I'll teach you, if you please, I'll teach you; only marry me to little Sophie.

MRS SIMPLE: Do you really like the wench so much?

BEAST: No, it isn't the wench I like.

SIMPLE: Is it then having her manor near at hand?

BEAST: It isn't manors that I'm so dead set on, it's what's raised in the manors.

MRS SIMPLE: And what is that, Brother?

BEAST: Sister, I love pigs; and the pigs where we live are so big that there isn't one of them that wouldn't be a head taller than any of us, if you were to stand it on its hind legs.

[SOPHIA *comes in, holding a letter in her hand and looking merry.*]

MRS SIMPLE [*to* SOPHIA]: Why so merry, my dear? What are you so pleased about?

SOPHIA: I have just received some joyful news. My uncle, of whom we have for so long heard nothing, whom I love and esteem as my own father, has lately arrived in Moscow. Here is the letter that I have just had from him.

MRS SIMPLE [*frightened and angry*]: What! Your uncle Oldwise alive! And you, making out that he has risen from the dead! Here's a fine story!

SOPHIA: But he didn't ever die.

MRS SIMPLE: Didn't die! Whyever shouldn't he die? No, Madam, you have made up these stories of your uncle to frighten us into giving you your liberty. 'Uncle's a clever man,' says you. 'When he sees me in the hands of others he'll find a way to deliver me.' That's your joyful news, Madam, but I don't think you have much to be merry about: of course that uncle of yours hasn't risen from the dead.

BEAST: Sister, come now! Supposing he didn't die?

SIMPLE: God help us if he didn't!

MRS SIMPLE: Didn't die! Tell that to your grandmother! Don't you know that for several years I've been having his name remembered at the Prayer for the Repose of the Dead? Were my sinful prayers not answered? [*To* SOPHIA] Let me have that letter please. [*Almost snatches it from her.*] I bet it's some love-letter. And I can guess who from. That officer who was all for marrying you, and whom you yourself wanted to marry. There's a sly one for you, sending you letters without my leave! I'll get to the bottom of this! See what a pass we have come to. Writing letters to girls! Girls able to read!

SOPHIA: Read it yourself, Madam. You will see that nothing could be more innocent.

MRS SIMPLE: Read it yourself! No, Madam, that, thank God, is not how I was brought up. I can receive letters, but I always order someone else to read them. [*To her husband*] Read it.

SIMPLE: Tricky.

MRS SIMPLE: You were meant to be a pretty girl, my dear. One can see that from the way you were brought up. You try and read it, Brother.

BEAST: Sister, I've never done any reading in all my born days. God has saved me from that dull stuff.

SOPHIA: Permit me to read it.

MRS SIMPLE: Oh my dear I know you're first-rate at it, but Lord no! I wouldn't trust you so far. But look, I think that our boy Mitrofán's tutor is coming soon. I'll tell him to . . .

BEAST: Have you already started teaching the lad reading and writing?

MRS SIMPLE: Oh, but Brother dear! He's been having lessons for four years. No, nobody ought to say we haven't tried to educate our boy Mitrofán. We're paying out to three tutors. There's Mr Priestling, the clerk at St Mary's, he comes out to do reading and writing with him. For arithmetic, my dear, he has lessons from a retired sergeant called Figgures. Both these two come out from the town. Just two miles, you see, my dear, from here to the town. For French and all the arts he has lessons from Adam Boschmann, a German. He gets three hundred roubles a year, and boards with us. Our washerwomen do his linen. A horse, when he wants to go anywhere. A glass of something at mealtimes. A tallow candle to go to bed with, and has his wig seen to by our Tom, for nothing. Indeed I tell you we are pleased with him, Brother dear; he's no slave-driver to the child. Our boy Mitrofán is still an infant, and surely that, my dear, is the time to cosset him. Ten years or so from now, God help us, he'll be entering the Service, and he'll have a terrible lot to go through then. Some people are born lucky, Brother. Some of our family, the Simples, look you now, don't have to exert themselves in any way to go flying up the ladder of promotion. Why shouldn't our boy Mitrofán do as well? Ah! Here by good fortune comes our dear kind visitor.

[*Enter* TRUEMAN.]

Brother dear! May I introduce our guest, dear Mr Trueman and, Your Honour, may I introduce my brother to you?

TRUEMAN: I am pleased to have made your acquaintance.

BEAST: Good, Sir! And what is your surname, I didn't quite catch.

TRUEMAN: I'll repeat it for you. My name is Trueman.

BEAST: Where were you born, Sir? Where are your estates?

TRUEMAN: If you want to know, I was born in Moscow, and my property is in this Lieutenancy.

BEAST: And may I venture to ask, Sir – are there any pigs raised in your villages?

MRS SIMPLE: Now don't you start on pigs, Brother. We had better say something about our own trouble. [*To* TRUEMAN] Look, my dear Sir! God has commanded us to take charge of a girl. She, if you please, receives letters from her uncles. Her uncles write to her from the next world. Will you do us a kindness, my dear Sir, and be so good as to read this aloud to us all?

TRUEMAN: Pardon me, Madam. I never read letters without leave of the person to whom they are addressed.

SOPHIA: Please do so. I shall be most obliged to you.

TRUEMAN: If you so command. [*Reads.*] 'My dear niece! My affairs have compelled me to live for several years away from my nearest and dearest; and distance has deprived me of the gratification of receiving news of the family. I am now in Moscow, having spent several years in Siberia. I may serve as an example to show that a man may make his fortune by hard work and honesty. With these means, aided by favourable circumstances, I have acquired an estate worth ten thousand roubles a year. . . '

BEAST *and the two* SIMPLES: Ten thousand!

TRUEMAN [*reading*]: 'Of which, my dear niece, I am making thee my heiress . . . '

MRS SIMPLE: Made you his heiress! ⎫
SIMPLE: Sophia his heiress! ⎬ [*together*]
BEAST: He's made her his heiress! ⎭

MRS SIMPLE [*flinging her arms round* SOPHIA]: Sophie my dear, I congratulate you. Congratulations, my sweetheart! I am beside myself with joy. Now what you want is a husband. I . . . I couldn't wish for a better bride for our boy Mitrofán. There's an uncle for you! Good as a father to you! And I always did think that God would preserve him and that he would be still alive and well.

BEAST [*putting out his hand*]: Come Sister, let's clinch it at once.

MRS SIMPLE [*quietly to* BEAST]: Stay, brother, we must first inquire if she is willing to be married to you.

BEAST: What! Do that? You're not going to start asking her leave?

TRUEMAN: Will you permit me to finish reading the letter?

BEAST: But what for? You could go on reading for five years and not come to anything better than ten thousand a year.

MRS SIMPLE [*to* SOPHIA]: Now, Sophie, my love! Come with me to my bedroom. I really must have a talk to you.
[*Exit, taking* SOPHIA.]

BEAST: Bah! From what I see, it's unlikely there'll be any betrothal today.
[*Enter a* SERVANT.]

SERVANT [*breathless, to* SIMPLE]: Master, Master! The soldiers have come and they're staying in our village.

SIMPLE: What a calamity! They'll ruin us entirely.

TRUEMAN: Why are you alarmed?

57

SIMPLE: Ah my good kind Sir! We have seen this before. I durstn't show my face near them.

TRUEMAN: Do not be afraid. They are, of course, commanded by an Officer, who will not permit any sort of insolence. Come with me and meet him. I am sure that your anxieties are groundless.

[*Exeunt* TRUEMAN, SIMPLE *and* SERVANT.]

BEAST: They've all gone off and left me alone. I may as well take a turn round the farmyard.

ACT TWO

TRUEMAN *and* MILO *are on stage.*

MILO: How delighted I am, my dear friend, at this unexpected meeting with you! Tell me, how comes it . . .

TRUEMAN: As a friend, I will disclose to you the reason for my presence here. I have been appointed a member of the Administration of this Lieutenancy. I have instructions to travel round this district; and moreover by the promptings of my own heart I cannot fail to observe the presence of certain evil-minded and ignorant individuals, who make cruel and inhuman use of the absolute power that they hold over their people. You know the manner of thinking of our Governor-General. His eagerness to help suffering humanity! His zeal to execute the philanthropic designs of the Supreme Authority! In our region we have learnt by our own experience that where the Governor-General is the kind of man envisaged by the Statute,[3] the welfare of the population is safe and sure. I have been staying here for the past three days. I have found the squire to be inconceivably stupid, while his wife is a raging fury, whose hellish nature is creating unhappiness throughout their household. And what, my dear friend, are your plans? Tell me, will you be staying here long?

MILO: I am marching on from here in a few hours.

TRUEMAN: Why so soon? Stay and rest awhile.

MILO: I cannot. My orders are to bring the troops on without delay. . . . And besides that, I am burning with impatience to be in Moscow.

TRUEMAN: For what reason?

59

MILO: Dear friend! I will disclose to you the secret of my heart! I am in love, and it is my fortune to be loved. It is more than half a year since I was parted from one who is dearer to me than everything else in the world, and more grievous still, in all that time I had heard nothing of her. Often I had been bitterly tormented, attributing her silence to coldness, till suddenly I received news which has shocked me. Someone wrote to say that after her mother's death certain distant relatives carried her off to their estates. Who they are, and where they live, I do not know. It may be that she is in the hands of some mercenary people who are taking advantage of her orphanhood to confine her and ill-treat her. The very thought makes my blood boil.

TRUEMAN: I have seen inhuman conduct of that kind here in this very house. I console myself however with the hope of quickly putting a stop to the savagery of the wife and the stupidity of her husband. I have already made a full report to our Chief, and I have no doubt that measures will be taken to restrain them.

MILO: How fortunate you are, my friend, being in a position to alleviate the lot of the unfortunate. I am in an agonizing situation, and I do not know what I can do.

TRUEMAN: Permit me to ask her name.

MILO [in delight]: Oh! Here she is, herself.

[Enter SOPHIA.]

SOPHIA: Milo! Can it be you that I see!

TRUEMAN: What good fortune!

MILO: This is she who possesses my heart. Dearest Sophia, tell me, how do I come to find you here?

SOPHIA: How many sorrows have I endured, since the day of our parting! My unscrupulous relatives . . .

TRUEMAN: My friend! Do not question her on so painful a subject.... You shall learn from me of their brutalities...

MILO: Odious people!

SOPHIA: Today however, for the first time, the mistress of the house has changed her demeanour towards me. On hearing that my uncle was making me his heiress, she suddenly ceased her grumbling and scolding, and became fulsomely affectionate. From all her roundabout talk I can tell that she has destined me to be the bride of her son.

MILO [*impatiently*]: And did you not immediately apprise her of your utter contempt?

SOPHIA: No . . .

MILO: Did you not tell her that your heart was engaged, that . . .

SOPHIA: No . . .

MILO: Ah, now I see that I am lost. My rival's the lucky man! I won't deny him any good quality. He may be intelligent, educated, amiable, let him only match me in my love for you, let him . . .

SOPHIA [*smiling*]: Oh Lord! If you could see him you would be beside yourself with jealousy.

MILO [*indignant*]: I can imagine all his good qualities . . .

SOPHIA: You can't imagine them all. He isn't yet sixteen years old, and has already reached his highest pitch of perfection, and will go no further.

TRUEMAN: What, Madam, no further? He is working through his Primer;[4] after that one must suppose that they'll start him on the Psalms.

MILO: Well! Is that what my rival is like! Ah my dear Sophia! Why do you tease me with your jokes? You know how easily a passionate man can be hurt by the least suspicion. Tell me, then, what answer did you give her?

[*Here* BEAST *walks across the stage, deep in thought and nobody sees him.*]

SOPHIA: I said that my fate depended upon the wishes of my uncle, who has promised to come here himself. That was in his letter [*to* TRUEMAN], the end of which we were prevented from hearing by Mr Beast.

MILO: Beast!

BEAST: Here!

TRUEMAN: Mr Beast, you have stolen in on us. I had not expected that of you.

BEAST: I was walking past you. I heard my name called, and I answered back. That's what I always do; if anyone shouts out 'Beast' I shout back 'Here!' Come on, fellows; it's the truth I'm telling you! I served in the Guards and retired as a corporal. At roll-call in the guard-room, when they called out 'Tarasius Beast' I used to sing out 'Here!'

TRUEMAN: We weren't calling you now, and you can go on wherever you were going.

BEAST: I wasn't going anywhere. I'm wandering round and thinking. That's the way with me; once I get a thing into my head you couldn't knock it out again, not if you took a hammer and chisel to it. Listen, once a thing is in my head, there it stays. All my thoughts are of that – dreaming and waking, waking and dreaming I see it all the time.

TRUEMAN: What is on your mind then, now?

BEAST: Oh, my dear good fellow! Strange things have been happening to me. My sister fetched me over post-haste from my manor to hers, and if she sends me back just as quick from her manor to mine I shall be able to tell the whole world, with a clear conscience, that I came for nought and I've brought nothing back.

TRUEMAN: What a shame Mr Beast. Your sister is playing with you like a ball.

BEAST [furious]: Like a ball? God help me, I'll chuck her somewhere where the whole village won't find her in a week.

SOPHIA: Oh, you are angry!

MILO: What have they done to you?

BEAST: You're a sensible man, you can judge. My sister

fetched me over here to get married. Now she's the one that tries to get round me to put it off. 'What do you want with a wife, Brother?' says she. 'You'd better have a good pig, Brother', says she. No, sister, I'm going to manage my own little pigs and you shan't fool me.

TRUEMAN: It seems to me, Mr Beast, that your sister has got ideas about a wedding, but it isn't yours.

BEAST: There's a queer thing to say. I don't interfere with others. Let each man marry his own bride. I won't touch anybody else's and let them not touch mine. [*To* SOPHIA] Don't you be afraid, my sweetheart. Nobody's going to cut me out with you.

SOPHIA: What is the meaning of this? More surprises!

MILO [*exclaiming*]: Of all the confounded insolence!

BEAST [*to* SOPHIA]: What's frightened you?

TRUEMAN [*to* MILO]: How can you be angry with Mr Beast?

SOPHIA [*to* BEAST]: Can it be that I am fated to be your wife?

MILO: It is all that I can do to restrain myself.

BEAST: Fate's fate, sweetheart, there's no getting round fate. You've got no call to complain of your luck. Live with me, and you'll live in clover. Ten thousand a year of your own! That's a mighty big load of good luck; I haven't seen that amount of money in all my born days. Why, with that I'll buy up all the pigs in the whole wide world; and listen, I'll give 'em all something to shout about. Around here, they'll say, the pigs have the best of it.

TRUEMAN: But if only animals can be happy at your place, then what with them and what with you, your wife will be poorly lodged.

BEAST: Poorly lodged! Pooh, pooh! Aren't there enough parlours at my place? I'll give her a corner room all to herself, with a warm bench to lie on.[5] My good friend, never mind anything else, but if every one of my sows has a sty to herself, I'll find a little parlour for my wife.

MILO: What a beastly comparison!

TRUEMAN [*to* BEAST]: It's no good, Mr Beast, I tell you straight; your sister has got her marked down for her own son.

BEAST [*furious*]: What! An uncle cut out by his nephew? I'll knock hell out of him next time I see him. Let me be the son of a pig, if I'm not her husband, or Mitrofán a monster.

   [*Enter* MITROFÁN *and* MRS JEREMY.]

MRS JEREMY: There now, do a little bit of lessons.

MITROFÁN: One more word from you, you old harridan, and I'll say something you won't like. I'll complain again to Mamma and Her Ladyship will pull your hair for you, same as she did yesterday.

BEAST: Come over here, my young friend.

MRS JEREMY: Go on, go over to Uncle.

MITROFÁN: How do you do, Uncle, and please why are you so cross-looking?

BEAST: Mitrofán! Look me straight in the face.

MRS JEREMY: Look at him, dear.

MITROFÁN [*to* MRS JEREMY]: Why does Uncle behave so strangely? What is there to look at?

BEAST: Again I say, look me straight in the face.

MRS JEREMY: Now don't make Uncle cross. Look now, my dearie, see how wide he has opened his eyes. You open yours wide too.

   [BEAST *and* MITROFÁN *stare at one another, goggle-eyed.*]

MILO: Here's a fine set-to!

TRUEMAN: But how will it end?

BEAST: Mitrofán! You are now a hairsbreadth away from death. Tell me the whole truth; if I weren't afraid of the sin I wouldn't say one word more – I'd catch hold of you by the legs and sling you against a wall. But I won't take your life away without having found you guilty.

ACT TWO

MRS JEREMY [*trembling*]: Oh! He's going to make away with him! Whatever will become of me!

MITROFÁN: What's the matter with you Uncle? Have you gone crazy? I really don't know what you are going on at me about.

BEAST: Mind now, no prevarication, don't provoke me or I'll fetch you one blow that will knock the breath out of your body. No more meddling for you, then. On my own head be it. Guilty before God and the Tsar. Mind you don't say anything against yourself that ain't true, or you'll get a thrashing you don't deserve.

MRS JEREMY: God preserve us from false accusation.

BEAST: Do you want to get married?

MITROFÁN [*relaxing*]: Well, Uncle, for quite a while I've had a feeling that I'd like it.

BEAST [*flinging himself upon him*]: You cursed little swine you!

TRUEMAN [*restraining BEAST*]: Mr Beast! Keep your hands to yourself.

MITROFÁN: Nanny! Protect me.

MRS JEREMY [*getting in front of* MITROFÁN *with her fists up, in a fury*]: Let me die on this spot, but I won't give up the child. Come on, Sir, will you just please come on. I'll scratch out your eyeballs for you.

BEAST [*backs away, trembling and threatening*]: I'll do for you. [*Exit.*]

MRS JEREMY [*calling after him, trembling*]: I've got sharp claws too.

MITROFÁN [*calling after* BEAST]: Get along with you, Uncle, and be damned to you.

[*Enter* MR *and* MRS SIMPLE.]

MRS SIMPLE [*walking along, to her husband*]: There's no need for all that nonsense here. You go through life, Mr Simple, believing everything that those great ears of yours pick up.

SIMPLE: But he and Mr Trueman gave me the slip and vanished. What have I done that's wrong?

65

MRS SIMPLE [*to* MILO]: Ah, my dear Mr Officer, sir! I have been looking for you all over the village; I've run my husband off his legs, trying to bring our most humble thanks to you, my dear Sir, for your kind troops.

MILO: For what, Ma'am?

MRS SIMPLE: For what indeed my dear Sir! Such kind soldiers. All this time they haven't touched the least little thing. Please don't be annoyed my dear Sir, because this oaf of mine missed you. He never did have enough sense to look after a visitor. A natural-born dawdler, that's what he is, my dear.

MILO: I've nothing to complain of, Ma'am.

MRS SIMPLE: My dear Sir, he gets what in these parts we call the megrims. Sometimes he'll stand and stare, as if he was rooted to the spot, for a solid hour. What haven't I done to him, what hasn't he put up with from me? Nothing will shift him. And if the megrims does go off for a bit my dear the nonsense he talks! You'll pray God to have the megrims back again.

TRUEMAN: At least, Ma'am, you can't complain that he's ill-natured. He's quiet . . .

MRS SIMPLE: Quiet as a calf, my dear Sir, and that's how the whole household gets spoilt. He doesn't understand that you must be strict in the house, and that offenders must be properly punished. I manage everything myself, my dear. On the go from morning to night, my hands never still, scolding here and slapping there, that's how the house is managed, my dear.

TRUEMAN [*aside*]: It's going to be managed differently soon.

MITROFÁN: My Mama has had trouble with the serfs all morning.

MRS SIMPLE [*to* SOPHIA]: I was getting the house ready for your dear uncle. I'm dying to meet that distinguished old gentleman. I have heard so much about him. Even his enemies say no more than that he is a bit surly, but they say that he is an extremely clever man, and that if he does take a liking to anybody why, he really does like them.

TRUEMAN: And anybody he doesn't take a liking to is no good. [*To* SOPHIA] I have the honour to know your uncle; and this, together with what many people have told me about him, has given me a sincere respect for him. What is sometimes spoken of as surliness and roughness in him is no more than the effect of his straightforward nature. His tongue has never uttered the word 'yes' when his heart was thinking 'no'.

SOPHIA: And besides, he must have worked hard to make his fortune.

MRS SIMPLE: What a blessing for us that he did! All I want is for him to show fatherly kindness to our boy Mitrofán. Sophie, my sweet, will you please go and look at your uncle's room.

[*Exit* SOPHIA.]

MRS SIMPLE [*to her husband*]: Woolgathering again, my dear! Be so good as to accompany her, Mr Simple. You haven't lost the use of your legs.

SIMPLE [*going out*]: No, but they are sagging.

MRS SIMPLE [*to the visitors*]: My only care, my only joy is my boy Mitrofán. My days are passing away. I am preparing him for his career.

[*At this point* PRIESTLING *appears with the Primer, and* FIGGURES *with a slate and a slate-pencil. Both make signs to* MRS JEREMY *to ask whether to come in. She beckons them, but* MITROFÁN *waves them away.*]

MRS SIMPLE [*going on talking without seeing them*]: Please God there may be fortune written in his birth-lines.

TRUEMAN: Look round Ma'am. What's going on behind you?

MRS SIMPLE: Ah! These are Mitrofán's tutors, my dear Sir. Priestling . . .

MRS JEREMY: And Figgures.

MITROFÁN: May they drop dead, both of them, and Jeremy too.

PRIESTLING: Peace be unto the Lord of this house, peace and many years, with his children and his manservants and his maidservants.

FIGGURES: We wish Your Honour a hundred years of good health, then twenty more and another fifty; years past counting.

MILO: Hallo! You're one of us, a service man! Where do you come from, friend?

FIGGURES: I was in the Garrison troops, Your Honour! Now I've taken my discharge.

MILO: What are you doing for a living?

FIGGURES: Your Honour, I do what I can. I know a little bit of arithmetic, so I can get a living among the government clerks in the town, keeping accounts. The Lord hasn't revealed the art of it to all of them; those that don't understand it themselves hire me to check the books and add up the totals. That's what I live by; I don't like living in idleness. In my free time I teach boys. For two years and more this young gentleman and I have been battling with fractions, but they don't somehow come out right. Ah well, people aren't made all alike and that's the truth.

MRS SIMPLE: What? What's that nonsense you're talking, Figgures? I wasn't listening.

FIGGURES: I was reporting to His Honour. I was saying that ten years of hammering won't knock a thing into one man's head, while another will get it first time.

TRUEMAN [to PRIESTLING]: And you, Mr Priestling, are you not a scholar?

PRIESTLING: A scholar I am, my Lord! From the Diocesan Seminary here. I went even unto rhetoric, and by the grace of God I returned again. I laid a humble petition before the Consistory in which I wrote 'The Seminarist such and such, of the Sons of the Clergy, being in fear of profound learning, craves to be released therefrom.' Whereupon there quickly followed a gracious resolution with a note that said 'The Seminarist such and such is to be released from all study, for it is written – "Cast not your pearls before swine lest they trample them under their feet".'

MRS SIMPLE: And where is our Mr Boschmann?

MRS JEREMY: I went to speak to him, but it was all I could do to get away. A pillar of smoke, ma'am! He choked me, curse him, with his filthy tobacco. The wicked sinner.

PRIESTLING: Nonsense, Mrs Jeremy! Smoking tobacco is no sin.

TRUEMAN [*aside*]: Priestling has actually got some learning to show off!

PRIESTLING: It is permitted in many books. It is indeed printed in the Psalter 'And herb for the use of man'.

TRUEMAN: Well, and where else?

PRIESTLING: The same thing is printed in another Psalter. Our Archpriest has a little octavo one, and it is in that too.

TRUEMAN [*to* MRS SIMPLE]: I don't want to hinder your son's exercises. Your humble servant.

MILO: Nor I, Ma'am.

MRS SIMPLE: Where are you gentlemen going? . . .

TRUEMAN: I shall take him to my room. Friends who have not met for a long time have much to talk about.

MRS SIMPLE: Where do you wish to take your meal, with us or in your own room? It will be just the family at table, and dear Sophia.

MILO: With you, Ma'am, with you.

TRUEMAN: We shall both have that honour.

[*Exeunt* MILO *and* TRUEMAN.]

MRS SIMPLE: Come now, Mitrofán dear boy, just read over the old lesson in Russian.

MITROFÁN: Oh, I don't want that old lesson.

MRS SIMPLE: Live and learn, my love. That's the way.

MITROFÁN: Oh is it? If I were to give my mind to my lessons, you'd only bring a lot more uncles here.

MRS SIMPLE: What? What's that you're saying?

MITROFÁN: Yes! Any minute I might be knocked about by an uncle, and then have to do Primer after I'd got away from his fists. No thank you! I'd as soon make away with myself.

MRS SIMPLE [*terrified*]: What's that? What do you want to do? Be reasonable, darling.

MITROFÁN: You know that there's the river near here. I'll dive in and you'll never set eyes on me again.

MRS SIMPLE [*distraught*]: You've destroyed me, God help you. Destroyed me!

MRS JEREMY: It's all because his uncle frightened him. He all but grabbed hold of him by the hair. And no rhyme nor reason for it at all.

MRS SIMPLE [*furious*]: Go on . . .

MRS JEREMY: He kept on asking him 'Do you want to get married?'

MRS SIMPLE: Go on . . .

MRS JEREMY: And the child didn't deny it. 'For quite a while now Uncle,' says he, 'I've had a feeling I'd like it.' And then, my dear, he got into an awful rage, and he rushed at him . . .

MRS SIMPLE [*shaking*]: Go on . . . So you stood like a dummy, you wretch you! Didn't you stick your nails into that muzzle of his? Didn't you tear his face open, from the corners of his ugly mouth right back to the ears?

MRS JEREMY: I was going to! Oh, I was going to, only . . .

MRS SIMPLE: Only .. only what? . . . It wasn't your own child, wretch! You'd have let the boy be battered to death.

MRS JEREMY: Oh my Creator! Save me and have mercy

upon me! If your brother hadn't at that very moment gone out of the room, I'd have shown him something! I wouldn't have minded what happened to me. I'd have blunted these on him [*showing her fingernails*] and I wouldn't have spared these fangs either.

MRS SIMPLE: None of you wretches really care about us. It's all words.

MRS JEREMY [*bursting into tears*]: Me not care for you Ma'am! When we don't know what more service we can give . . . when we'd gladly even . . . when we don't grudge our lives . . . and it's still not good enough.

PRIESTLING: Do you wish us to go home?

FIGGURES: Where do we proceed to now, } [*together*]
Your Honour?

MRS SIMPLE: There you go, you old witch, howling away. Go on, give them their food with you, and bring them straight back here after dinner. [*To* MITROFÁN.] Come along with me, Mitrofán dear boy. I won't let you out of my sight now. I've got a little something to tell you about, and when you hear it you'll be glad you're alive. It isn't for ever, my love; you won't always have to go on with lessons. God be praised, you understand enough already to raise children of your own. [*To* MRS JEREMY.] I'll settle accounts with Brother, and it won't be done your way. Let good people see what the difference is between a child's nurse and its own Mother. [*Exit, with* MITRO-FÁN.]

PRIESTLING: Thy life, Mrs Jeremy, is like unto thick darkness. Let us now go to table, but first let us take a cup to drown our sorrows.

FIGGURES: And then another, and that's multiplication for you.

MRS JEREMY [*in tears*]: As I hope to be saved! I've been in service for forty years, and I've always had the same favours from them.

PRIESTLING: Is their bounty then great?

MRS JEREMY: Five roubles a year, and five face-slaps a day.
[PRIESTLING *and* FIGGURES *go off with her, each taking an arm.*]

FIGGURES: Let's work the sum out at table, and see how much your income is for a whole year.

ACT THREE

OLDWISE *and* TRUEMAN *are talking together.*

TRUEMAN: When we got up from table I went over to the window, and I saw your carriage. Immediately, and without a word to anybody, I ran out here to greet you with a hearty embrace. My sincere respect for you . . .

OLDWISE: Which, believe me, is something I find very precious.

TRUEMAN: Your friendship flatters me, the more so since you cannot be friendly with any save such as . . .

OLDWISE: Such as are like thee. I speak without regard to service rank. When rank comes in there's an end of sincerity.

TRUEMAN: Your manner of address . . .

OLDWISE: Many laugh at it. I know that. So be it. My father brought me up in the style of his day, and I have never found any need to re-educate myself. He served Peter the Great. In those days, one man was called 'thou', not 'you'. In those days, they did not know how to transmit to one another this infection that makes each man regard himself as several people, whereas nowadays many of them are not worth even one. My father at the court of Peter the Great . . .

TRUEMAN: But I have heard that he was in the Military Service . . .

OLDWISE: In that age the courtiers were warriors, not the warriors courtiers. My father gave me what was, for that age, the best possible education. At that time, facilities for study were few; they did not yet know how to cram another man's mind into an empty head.

73

TRUEMAN: The education of those days consisted indeed of a number of rules . . .

OLDWISE: Of one only. There was one thing that my father never ceased repeating to me 'Have a heart, have a soul, and you'll always be a man.' Everything else is fashion – fashion in minds, fashion in knowledge, as in buckles and buttons.

TRUEMAN: What you say is true. The real worth of a man is his soul . . .

OLDWISE: Without it, the most enlightened of scholars is but a poor creature. [*With feeling*] An ignorant man without a soul is a wild beast. The slightest impulse leads him into every kind of wickedness. He has no scales to weigh what he does against why he does it. It is from brutes of this kind that I have come to rescue . . .

TRUEMAN: Your niece. I know about that. She is here. Let us go.

OLDWISE: Stay. My heart is still boiling with indignation at the disgraceful behaviour of the master and mistress of this house. Let us wait here a few minutes. I have a rule – never to undertake anything on first impulse.

TRUEMAN: Few there be who can follow your rule.

OLDWISE: I have learnt it from my experience of life. Oh, had I been able to control myself earlier, I might have had the satisfaction of giving longer service to my country!

TRUEMAN: Nobody can be indifferent to the events in the life of a man of your qualities. I should be extremely obliged if you would tell me in what way . . .

OLDWISE: I never conceal it from anybody, so that others in a similar position may prove wiser than I was. When I entered the Military Service I became acquainted with a young Count, whose name I have no wish to recall. He was junior to me in the service, the son of a man in favour at Court, brought up in high society, with exceptional opportunities to learn things that did not then enter into our education. I made every effort to cultivate his acquaintance, so that by constant association with him I might make good the deficiencies in my education. Then suddenly, just when our mutual friendship had been firmly established, we heard that war had been declared. I was delighted, and rushed to embrace him. 'Dear Count! Here is a chance for us to distinguish ourselves. Let us at once go to the Army, and make ourselves worthy of the name of gentleman, with which we were born.' My friend the Count scowled furiously, and when he had embraced me 'Good-bye and good luck,' said he drily. 'For my part I am happy to say that my Papa will not wish to part with me'. There is nothing that I could compare to the scorn that I felt for him at that moment. I saw then that there is sometimes an immeasurably wide difference between honourable men and men in favour, that the meanest spirits are to be found in high society, and that the greatest enlightenment may go together with the greatest poltroonery.

TRUEMAN: True indeed.

OLDWISE: On leaving him I set out immediately to go where Duty called me. I had many opportunities to distinguish myself. My wounds are proof that I did not fail to take them. I had had a flattering reward for my service in the good opinion entertained of me by my superior officers and by my men, when suddenly I received the news that the Count, my former acquaintance, whom I had disdained to remember, had been promoted; while I, who at that time was lying gravely ill from wounds, I had been passed over. Stung to anger by such an injustice I immediately sent in my resignation.

TRUEMAN: What else would it have been proper to do?

OLDWISE: It would have been proper to come to my senses. I had failed to keep watch against the first impulses of my mortified ambition. I was so heated then that I did not stop to consider that the zeal of a properly ambitious man is directed towards action, not towards promotion; that promotion can not infrequently be had for the asking, but true respect has to be earned; that it is far more honourable to be passed over for no fault than to receive a reward that is not deserved.

TRUEMAN: But, is there no circumstance in which it is permissible to a gentleman to resign?

OLDWISE: One only; when he is inwardly satisfied that his service is bringing no direct advantage to his country. Ah, then you should go!

TRUEMAN: You bring home the very essence of a gentleman's duty.

OLDWISE: Having retired, I went to St Petersburg. There, blind chance led me to a part of the world, the thought of which had never entered my head.

TRUEMAN: Where was it?

OLDWISE: To the Court. I was taken to Court. Eh? What thinkest thou of that?

TRUEMAN: And what did you make of that part of the world?

OLDWISE: Curious. At first it seemed strange to me, that in that quarter hardly anybody travels on the straight highway, but all take crooked by-ways, in the hope of arriving sooner.

TRUEMAN: But though the road is crooked, is it not broad?

OLDWISE: Not broad enough for two that meet on it to pass by one another. One overthrows the other, and the one that stays on his feet never picks up the one that lies on the ground.

TRUEMAN: So there it's pride that . . .

OLDWISE: Not pride – call it rather selfishness. They have great love for themselves there; they care only for themselves, they are concerned only with the present moment. Thou wilt not believe it; I have seen many men there who have never in all their lives had occasion to give a thought either to their forebears or to their descendants.

TRUEMAN: But, those worthy men who serve the State at Court . . .

OLDWISE: Oh! Those are the ones who stay at the Court because they are useful to the Court; others stay there because the Court is useful to them. I was not numbered among the former, and did not wish to be numbered among the latter.

TRUEMAN: Of course you were not appreciated there?

OLDWISE: So much the better for me; I was able to get away without trouble. Otherwise, they would have got rid of me in one of two ways.

TRUEMAN: And what are they?

OLDWISE: My friend, there are two ways of getting rid of a man from Court. Either they quarrel with you, or they make you quarrel with them. I was not going to wait either for the one or the other. I concluded that it would be better to live my life in my own home, rather than in other men's anterooms.

TRUEMAN: So you came away from Court empty-handed. [*Opens his snuffbox.*]

OLDWISE [*taking snuff from* TRUEMAN]: Empty-handed? The price of a snuffbox is five hundred roubles. Two men went to a merchant. One paid the money and took home a snuffbox. The other went home without a snuffbox. And thinkest thou that the second man went home empty-handed? Thou art mistaken. He took home his five hundred roubles intact. I came away from Court without manors, without ribands, without promotion, but I took home inviolate what was my own – my soul, my honour, my principles.

TRUEMAN: Men with your principles ought not to be allowed to go away from Court; they ought to be summoned there.

OLDWISE: Summoned? But why?

TRUEMAN: For the same reason that the Doctor is summoned to a sick man.

OLDWISE: My friend! Thou art mistaken! It is no good sending for the Doctor for someone whose disease is incurable. The Doctor is no help then; he may even catch the infection himself.

[*Enter* SOPHIA.]

SOPHIA [*to* TRUEMAN]: I could not stand the noise of them any longer.

OLDWISE [*aside*]: Those are her mother's features. That's my Sophia.

SOPHIA [*looking at* OLDWISE]: Heavens! He called me by my name. If my heart doesn't deceive me ...

OLDWISE [*embracing her*]: It does not. Thou art my sister's daughter, the daughter of my heart!

SOPHIA [*flinging herself into his arms*]: Uncle! I am beside myself with joy!

OLDWISE: Dearest Sophia! I learnt in Moscow that thou wast being kept here against thy will. I have been in this world for sixty years. I have often had occasion to be angry, sometimes to be satisfied with myself. Nothing has ever roused my indignation so much as to see Innocence enmeshed in the snares of Guile; nothing has given me greater satisfaction than to be able to snatch its prey out of the hands of Vice.

TRUEMAN: How pleasant to witness this scene!

OLDWISE: Thou knowst that it is through thee alone that I am attached to life. Thou must provide the consolation of my old age. Thy happiness must be my care. It was I, when I retired, that laid the foundation for thy education, but I had no means of providing for thy fortune, save by parting from thy mother and from thee.

SOPHIA: Your absence was unspeakably painful to us.

OLDWISE [*to* TRUEMAN]: In order to ensure that she would

not want for the necessities of life, I decided to depart for a number of years to a land where money can be had without trading conscience in exchange for it, without stooping to servility, without robbing one's country, a land where money is sought from Earth herself, who is juster than human judges, knows no respect of persons, and pays fairly and generously for labour, and for that alone.

TRUEMAN: From what I have heard, you could have made incomparably more.

OLDWISE: But what for?

TRUEMAN: To be rich, as others are.

OLDWISE: Rich? But who is rich? Knowest thou that all Siberia is too small for the whims of one man? My friend! It is all a matter of imagination. Go by Nature, and thou shalt never be poor. Go by the opinion of men and thou shalt never be rich.

SOPHIA: How true it all is, what you are saying, Uncle!

OLDWISE: I have made enough for us not to be hindered, when it comes to thy marriage, by the poverty of a worthy bridegroom.

TRUEMAN: But when you marry her, it would not be amiss to provide for children as well . . .

OLDWISE: Children! Save up riches for the children? I wouldn't think of it. If they turn out intelligent they will manage without them; riches are no help to a son who is a fool. I have seen fine young men with coats of cloth-of-gold, and with heads made of lead. No, my friend! Cash in hand does not imply merit. A golden dunce is still a dunce.

TRUEMAN: For all that, we see that money often leads to promotion, that promotion commonly leads to honours, and that the holders of honours are accorded respect.

OLDWISE: Respect? The only kind of respect that ought to gratify a man is sincere respect, of which he is worthy, whose promotion is not gained through money, nor his honours through promotion.

TRUEMAN: Your conclusion is irrefutable.

OLDWISE: Halloa! What is that noise?

[*Enter* MRS SIMPLE *and* BEAST, *held apart from one another by* MILO.]

MRS SIMPLE: Let me go Sir, let me go! Let me get at his face, his filthy face!

MILO: Pardon me, Ma'am, but I will not let you go.

BEAST [*in a passion, straightening his wig*]: Be off with you, Sister! If it comes to a tussle, I'll twist you till your bones crack.

MILO [*to* MRS SIMPLE]: And you had forgotten that he was your Brother?

MRS SIMPLE: My blood's up, Sir. Let us fight it out.

MILO [*to* BEAST]: Is she not your sister?

BEAST: To tell the truth we are from the same litter. Hark how she squeals!

OLDWISE [*who has been unable to restrain his laughter, to* TRUEMAN]: I was afraid I was going to be angry. Now I have to laugh.

MRS SIMPLE: Who has to laugh and who is he laughing at? Who is this stranger?

OLDWISE: Pardon me, Ma'am, I have never seen anything more laughable in all my life.

BEAST [*holding his neck*]: He can laugh; you won't hear much of a laugh from me.

MILO: She didn't injure you, did she?

BEAST: I covered up in front with both hands, so she clawed into the back of my neck.

MILO: Did she hurt you . . . ?

BEAST: She pricked me a bit about the withers.

[*During the following speech by* MRS SIMPLE, SOPHIA *conveys to* MILO, *by glances, that he is in the presence of* OLDWISE. MILO *understands her.*]

MRS SIMPLE: Pricked you! . . . No, Brother, you have got this officer-gentleman to thank; but for him you wouldn't have held me off. I wouldn't spare even my own father, when I'm standing up for my son. [*To* OLDWISE] This is nothing to laugh at, Sir. Pardon me. I have a mother's heart. Whoever heard of a bitch that didn't protect her own puppies? You have been good enough to pay us a call here, but we don't know who you are nor who you've come to see.

OLDWISE [*pointing to* SOPHIA]: I came to see her. I'm her Uncle Oldwise.

MRS SIMPLE [*frightened and embarrassed*]: What! It's you, it's you my dear Sir! Our precious guest! Oh I'm an utter fool! And I ought to have received you like I would my own father, our one and only, nearest and dearest, the hope of us all. Forgive me, my dear sir. I'm a fool. I can't get over it. Where's my husband? Where's my son? Coming into an empty house like that! It's a judgement on us! We're all out of our minds. Girl! Girl! Pelagia! Girl!

BEAST [*aside*]: There you are! It's him! It's the uncle!

[*Enter* MRS JEREMY.]

MRS JEREMY: May it please you, Ma'am?

MRS SIMPLE: Bitch! Are you a girl? Haven't I got any servants in the house besides you, you ugly old thing! Where's Pelagia?

MRS JEREMY: Sick, ma'am. She's been in bed all the morning.

MRS SIMPLE: In bed, the wretch! In bed! Just like a lady!

MRS JEREMY: She's all to pieces with the fever, ma'am. She's raving all the time.

MRS SIMPLE: Raving, the wretch! Just like a lady! Go on then you, call my husband, my son. Tell them that by the grace of God we've got him here at last, our dear Sophia's Uncle. Go on! Run, stir yourself.

OLDWISE: Why all this ado, Ma'am? By the grace of God

I'm not your parent; by the grace of God I'm a stranger to you.

MRS SIMPLE: Oh my dear Sir! Your unexpected arrival has turned me out of my wits; only just let me embrace you properly – our benefactor! ...

[*During the following speech by* OLDWISE, SIMPLE *and* MITROFÁN *enter by the middle door and stand behind* OLDWISE. *The father is ready to embrace him as soon as his turn comes; and the son to kiss his hand.* MRS JEREMY *takes up a position to one side and stands with her arms folded, as if rooted to the spot; her eyes are fastened on* OLDWISE *with a submissive, slave-like expression.*]

OLDWISE [*reluctantly embracing* MRS SIMPLE]: This kindness, Ma'am, is quite superfluous! I could very easily do without it.

[*Extricating himself from her embrace, he turns to the other side, where* BEAST, *who is already standing there with outstretched arms, immediately grabs him.*]

Now who's got hold of me?

BEAST: It's me. I'm my sister's brother.

OLDWISE [*impatiently, seeing two more of them*]: Who are these then?

SIMPLE [*embracing him*]: I'm my wife's husband. ⎫

MITROFÁN [*catching hold of his hand*]: And I'm ⎬ [*together*] my Mamma's little boy. ⎭

MILO [*to* TRUEMAN]: I shan't introduce myself now.

TRUEMAN [*to* MILO]: I'll find an opportunity to introduce you later.

OLDWISE [*not letting* MITROFÁN *take his hand*]: This one is catching hold of my hand, to kiss it. They are evidently out to make a fool of him.

MRS SIMPLE: Go on, Mitrofán dear boy. Say 'Why should I not kiss your hand, Sir. You are my second father.'

MITROFÁN: Why shouldn't I kiss your hand, Uncle? You're my father ... [*To his Mother*] What sort of father was it?

MRS SIMPLE: Second.

MITROFÁN: Second? Second father, Uncle.

OLDWISE: Sir, I am neither thy father, nor thy uncle.

MRS SIMPLE: Why, my dear Sir, perhaps the child is fore-telling his own happiness; perhaps the Lord will find him worthy to be your nephew indeed.

BEAST: Really! And why not me be his nephew? Fie, Sister!

MRS SIMPLE: Now Brother, I'll have no shouting and screaming with you. [*To* OLDWISE] In all my life, dear Sir, I've never quarrelled with anybody. That's my nature. They may curse and swear at me, I'll never answer back one word. They can be as clever as they like; God will repay them for insulting a poor woman like me.

OLDWISE: So I observed, Madam, upon thy first appearance in the doorway.

TRUEMAN: For two days and more, I have witnessed the goodness of her nature.

OLDWISE: I haven't the time for that diversion. Sophia my dear, we are leaving for Moscow tomorrow morning, thou and I.

MRS SIMPLE: Oh but my dear Mr Oldwise! What has made you so cross?

SIMPLE: Why be unkind?

MRS SIMPLE: What! Part with Sophie? Our very dearest friend? I shall miss her so much I shan't be able to eat anything.

SIMPLE: That's done for me now, I'm finished.

OLDWISE: Oh, but if you love her so much, I'm bound to please you. I'm taking her to Moscow in order to provide for her happiness. A bridegroom has been proposed to me; a certain young man of great merit. I shall marry her to him.

MRS SIMPLE: Oh, he's destroyed me!

MILO: What's this I hear?

[SOPHIA *looks dismayed.*]

BEAST: Well I never!

[SIMPLE *throws up his hands.*]

MITROFÁN: Did you ever!

[MRS JEREMY *sadly shakes her head.*

TRUEMAN *looks surprised and pained.*]

}[all together]

OLDWISE [*observing the general consternation*]: What is the meaning of this? Sophia my dear, thou too lookest dismayed. Art thou then so distressed by my intention? I stand in place of thy father. Believe me, I know a father's rights. They extend no further than the protection of a daughter against unfortunate attachments; the choice of a worthy man is entirely dependent upon her heart. Set thy mind at rest my dear. Thy husband, if he is worthy of thee, will have a true friend in me, whoever he is. Marry whom thou wilt!

[*All begin to look cheerful.*]

SOPHIA: Uncle! Have no doubt about my obedience.

MILO [*aside*]: Admirable man!

MRS SIMPLE [*with a cheerful expression*]: There's a father! Hark at that! 'Marry whom thou wilt', if only the man is good enough for her. Yes, Mr Oldwise my dear, yes. Only, you mustn't overlook the eligible men here. If before your eyes you have a young person of gentle birth . . .

BEAST: Long past childhood . . .

MRS SIMPLE: With a bit of property, not much but . . .

BEAST: And a first-rate piggery.

MRS SIMPLE: Then in a holy hour, with angels' blessing . . .

BEAST: Then hey for a jolly feast, haste to the wedding.

}[together]

OLDWISE: Your advice is impartial. I can see that.

BEAST: You'll see more still when you get to know me better. Look here, this is a bear-garden. I'll come to you myself in an hour's time. Then we'll settle the business. Self-praise is no recommendation but I tell you there aren't many like me. [*Exit.*]

OLDWISE: That is highly probable.

MRS SIMPLE: You mustn't be surprised, my dear Sir, that my own brother . . .

OLDWISE: Your own brother?

MRS SIMPLE: Yes, Mr Oldwise, my dear. You see I'm a Beast on my father's side. My deceased father married my deceased mother. She was a Miss Quiverful. They had eighteen of us children; but by the Lord's will they all died except Brother and me. Three of them died of drinking milk out of a copper pan. Two fell off a belfry in Holy Week, and the others – why they just couldn't last out, Mr Oldwise, my dear.

OLDWISE: I see the kind of parents that you had.

MRS SIMPLE: Old-fashioned people, my good Sir! It wasn't like modern times. We weren't taught anything. Good folk used to come to Papa, and try to coax him into at least putting Brother to School. And was it any good? He just raged back at them, my poor dear father did, God rest his soul. Sometimes he used to shout out 'I'll curse the child that picks up anything from those damned heathen! If they want to learn anything then let their name not be Beast!'

TRUEMAN: But you are having your son taught something.

MRS SIMPLE: Times are different now, my dear! [*To* OLDWISE] We'd gladly give our last crust to have our son taught everything. Our boy Mitrofán sometimes doesn't get up from his book for a whole day on end. I've got a mother's heart. Sometimes you're sad, sad, till you think what a fine young man it will make of him. You see, my dear, he is going to be sixteen come

85

St-Nicholas-in-Winter. He's fit to marry anybody, but the tutors are still coming. They waste no time – there's two of them waiting outside now. [*Signs to* MRS JEREMY, *with a wink of the eye, to call them in.*] Besides that, we engaged a foreigner in Moscow, for five years, and got the contract registered at the Police Station so that nobody else could entice him away. He undertook to teach whatever we wanted, but as far as we're concerned – let him teach whatever he can. We've done our whole duty as parents; we've engaged a German and we pay him four months in advance. And I earnestly wish that you, my dear Mr Oldwise, might take a look at our boy Mitrofán, and examine him to see what he has learnt.

OLDWISE: I'm a poor judge of that, Ma'am.

MRS SIMPLE [*seeing* PRIESTLING *and* FIGGURES]: Here are the tutors! Our boy Mitrofán gets no rest, night or day. It's bad to be praising one's own child, but there'll be wonderful happiness for the girl that God sends to his wife.

TRUEMAN: That is all very well, but don't forget Ma'am that your guest has only just arrived from Moscow and that he needs to rest, much more than he does to hear the praises of your son.

OLDWISE: I'll admit that I would be glad of a rest, after the journey, and after all that I've seen and heard.

MRS SIMPLE: Oh, but my dear Sir! Everything is ready. I did the room for you myself.

OLDWISE: Thank you. [*To* SOPHIA] Sophia dear, show me the way.

MRS SIMPLE: And what about us! Do please let me and my son and my husband come with you Mr Oldwise my dear. We are all taking a vow to walk the whole way to Kiev, to pray for your health, if only our little business comes right.

OLDWISE [*to* TRUEMAN]: When do we meet again? I shall come back here when I have rested.

TRUEMAN: Then I shall have the honour to see you here.

OLDWISE: With all my heart.

> [*He sees* MILO *making a respectful bow to him, and civilly returns it.*]

MRS SIMPLE: Will you please come this way?

> [*All, except the* TUTORS, *go out.* TRUEMAN *and* MILO *to one side, the rest to the other side.*]

PRIESTLING: What a Pandemonium! It starts first thing in the morning; you can't get a word of sense out of anybody. Each day here dawns fair and then clouds over.

FIGGURES: That's life, for the likes of us. You can't get rid of a job by not doing it. It's hard on us if they don't feed us properly; like today, when we got short rations at dinner.

PRIESTLING: Had not My Lord granted me wisdom, to turn aside at the cross-roads on the way hither, and go in to our church baking woman,[6] verily I should be famished as a dog by the evening.

FIGGURES: Nice sort of officers, the gentry here!

PRIESTLING: Hast thou heard, Brother, how the servants here live? Though thou art an old soldier, though thou hast been in battles, fear and trembling would come over thee . . .

FIGGURES: What? Heard of it? I've seen it with my own eyes; you hear skirmishing here every three hours day and night. Oh ho! It makes me sad.

PRIESTLING [*sighing*]: Oh woe is me, poor sinner!

FIGGURES: Why do you sigh, Priestling?

PRIESTLING: Is not thy heart too oppressed within thee, Figgures?

FIGGURES: I can't help thinking . . . God sent me a pupil, the son of a lord. Three years I've been struggling with him and he can't count up to three.

PRIESTLING: Then we have the same affliction. For four years I have lived in torment. Sit with him for an hour, and he won't get one line beyond the last time's lesson: and even that, God forgive him, he mouths over syllable by syllable, or gabbles it without meaning.

FIGGURES: And whose fault is it? The minute he takes hold of the slate pencil, there's the German in the doorway. No more slate for him, and they're glad to shove me out.

PRIESTLING: Am I to blame? The minute I take hold of the pointer, there before my eyes is that heathen. One hand on the boy's head, and the other on my neck.

FIGGURES [*hotly*]: I'd give one of my ears to see that dirty sponger put through it properly, army fashion.

PRIESTLING: Chastise me even now, with rods; but first let me give that man of sin a good bang on the neck.

[*Enter* MRS SIMPLE *and* MITROFÁN.]

MRS SIMPLE: Just while he is resting, my love, do some lessons, so that he hears about how hard you work, Mitrofán dear boy.

MITROFÁN: Well and what then?

MRS SIMPLE: Then you'll be married.

MITROFÁN: Listen Mama, I'll do it to please you; I will do a lesson. Only let this be the last one, and let's have the betrothal today.

MRS SIMPLE: Please God, in His own good time . . .

MITROFÁN: It's my good time now. I don't want lessons, I want to get married. And you're the one that put me up to it so you may blame yourself. There now, I've sat down.

[FIGGURES *sharpens the slate pencil.*]

MRS SIMPLE: I'll sit here too for a while. I'll crochet a purse for you, my love. Something for you to put dear little Sophia's pennies into.

MITROFÁN: Come on, garrison rat, give me that slate. Tell me what to put down.

FIGGURES: Your Honour is always pleased to be needlessly abusive.

MRS SIMPLE [*working*]: Oh, good gracious me! The child mustn't even be allowed to be rude to Figgures. And now he's in a temper.

FIGGURES: Your Honour, why should I lose my temper? We have a Russian proverb 'The dog barks and the wind carries it away.'

MITROFÁN: Give me the sums we had last time, and buck up about it.

FIGGURES: It's always the same as last time for you, Your Honour, You'll always be kept on the same old sums.

MRS SIMPLE: That's no business of yours, Sergeant. I'm very glad that our boy Mitrofán doesn't want to stride ahead. With a mind like that he might take flight and go off! Heaven forbid!

FIGGURES: Problem. Suppose for instance that you and I were walking along the road together. And let's say that we took Mr Priestling with us too. Suppose for instance that the three of us . . .

MITROFÁN [*writing*]: Three.

FIGGURES: Found, in the road, three hundred roubles.

MITROFÁN [*writing*]: Three hundred.

FIGGURES: It was agreed to share it. Find out how much each of us got.

MITROFÁN [*calculating and muttering*]: Once three is three. Once nought is nought. Once nought is nought.

MRS SIMPLE: What's that? What's that about sharing?

MITROFÁN: It's the three hundred roubles we found, to be shared among three of us, you see.

MRS SIMPLE: My dearest love, the man is talking nonsense. If you find money, don't you share it with anybody. Keep it all for yourself, Mitrofán dear boy. Don't learn this stupid subject.

MITROFÁN: Listen, Figgures, give me another one.

FIGGURES: Put this down, Your Honour. You pay me ten roubles a year for tuition.

MITROFÁN: Ten.

FIGGURES: At present, it is true, you get nothing for it; but if you, young gentleman, were to learn something from me it wouldn't be amiss to add another ten.

MITROFÁN: Yes, yes. Ten.

FIGGURES: How much would that be for a year?

MITROFÁN [*calculating and muttering*]. Nought and nought is nought. One and one is . . . [*Pauses to think.*]

MRS SIMPLE: You needn't trouble yourself, my love. I'm not giving him a farthing more; there's no reason I should. That's the wrong subject. It's only a worry for you, and I can see it's all nonsense. If there's no money, why count it? If there is money, we can perfectly well count it without the Sergeant.

PRIESTLING: That's it, Figgures; time's up. Two problems solved. Nobody is going to check them, you know.

MITROFÁN: Never fear, man. My Mamma won't make any mistake about that. Come along now you, Priestling, let's have yesterday's lesson. [MITROFÁN *takes the pointer.*]

PRIESTLING [*opening the Primer*]: Let us begin with a blessing. Follow me attentively 'As for me, I am a worm.'

MITROFÁN: 'As for me, I am a worm.'

PRIESTLING: Worm signifieth an animal, a beast. It signifieth 'I am a beast.'

MITROFÁN: 'I am a beast.'

PRIESTLING [*in a classroom voice*]: 'And no man.'

MITROFÁN: [*in the same voice*]: 'And no man.'

PRIESTLING: 'A very scorn of men.'

MITROFÁN: 'A very scorn of men.'

PRIESTLING: 'And the out. . . .'[7]

[*Enter* BOSCHMANN.]

BOSCHMANN: Aie! Aie! Aie! Aie! Aie! Now do I see! Dey want to destroy de child. Have pity, dear Madam; think of your own womb, vot you carry him round in it for nine months – vot dey call de eighth wonder of de world! Send away those damned villains. Quickly shall dey turn dis head into a block of wood! He has de disposition for it, he has everything!

MRS SIMPLE: You are right there, Mr Boschmann. Mitrofán, dear boy, if study is so dangerous to your little head, then I think, my love, that you ought to give it up.

MITROFÁN: I've been thinking that too, for a long time.

PRIESTLING [*closing the Primer*]: Here endeth the lesson. Praise be to God.

BOSCHMANN: Dear Madam! Vot you vant? Liddle son like he is, mit health dat God give him; or liddle son wise how dey say like Aristotle, and den into de grave.

MRS SIMPLE: Oh but Mr Boschmann, how dreadful! Why only yesterday he was imprudent over his supper.

BOSCHMANN: Consider dear lady; if he cram too much de stomach – den is dere trouble. But dat head he got on him, you see, dat is much weaker than de stomach! Cram dat too much and God help him!

MRS SIMPLE: You are quite right, Mr Boschmann; but what would you do? Suppose now that the child goes to Petersburg without learning? They'll say he's a fool. There are so many clever folk about today; it's them that I fear.

BOSCHMANN: My dear Madam, vot is dere to fear? A clever man won't go near him, won't quarrel with him. Let him keep away from de clever folk and so will de Lord prosper him.

MRS SIMPLE: There, that's how you must live in Society, Mitrofán dear boy.

MITROFÁN: I don't care for those clever people, Mamma. People like ourselves are always best.

BOSCHMANN: Best of all dat he have his own company of friends.

MRS SIMPLE: Mr Boschmann! Who would you choose them from?

BOSCHMANN: Don't distress yourself dear lady. In society dere is millions and millions of peoples like your darling son. Why shouldn't he choose his own company?

MRS SIMPLE: Never mind about his being my son. He's a sharp boy, a quick boy.

BOSCHMANN: All de better den, dat dey don't go tiring him out mit lessons. Russian Grammar! Arithmetic! Oh my goodness me, how does he keep body and soul together! As if a Russian Shentleman couldn't make his way in de world no more, without Russian grammar.

PRIESTLING [aside]: Under thy tongue be mischief and vanity!

BOSCHMANN: As if before dey had arithmetic dey couldn't count all de fools in de world!

FIGGURES [aside]: I'll count your ribs for you when I get hold of you!

BOSCHMANN: What he wants is to know how to live in Society. I know Society by heart. Me, I'm de man about de town.

MRS SIMPLE: Of course you know all about Society, Mr Boschmann. I expect you have seen everything there is to see at Petersburg.

BOSCHMANN: Pretty well, dear Madam, pretty well. I always liked to look at de peoples. When de carriages mit de ladies and gentlemen met out at Katrinhof[8] on holidays I used to watch dem all de time. Not one minute did I get down off de box.

MRS SIMPLE: Off what box?

BOSCHMANN [aside]: Aie! Aie! Aie! Aie! What nonsense I talk! [Aloud] You know, dear Madam, dat it is always easier to see from on top. So I used to get up onto de carriage of somebody I know, and watch de high Society from de box.

MRS SIMPLE: Of course you can see better. A clever man knows where to climb up.

BOSCHMANN: Your darling son too will somehow get up into a place in Society, to watch de people and show himself off.

[MITROFÁN *stands and fidgets*]

A high-spirited boy! He's like de horse without de bridle; he won't stand still. Get along! *Fort!*[9]

[MITROFÁN *runs off.*]

MRS SIMPLE [*with a happy smile*]: He may be going to be married, but he's still a boy. All the same, I'd better go on after him; he wouldn't mean to, but in his playful way he might annoy the visitors.

BOSCHMANN: Go on, dear Madam! Dat one is a lively bird. You got to keep an eye on him!

MRS SIMPLE: Good-bye then, Mr Boschmann. [*Exit.*]

FIGGURES [*jeering*]: What an image of ugliness!

PRIESTLING [*jeering*]: A by-word among the nations!

BOSCHMANN: What for you ignorant fellows show your teeth at me?

FIGGURES [*slapping him on the shoulder*]: What are you scowling about, you flat-faced owl!

BOSCHMANN: Oy! Oy! Dat iron grip!

PRIESTLING: Thou triple abomination, thou great owl! Why blinkest thou thine eyes!

BOSCHMANN [*quietly*]: I'm done for. [*Aloud*] What for you make fun of me, boys? Eh?

FIGGURES: You don't earn your keep and you won't let anyone else do anything, and you stick your nose in everywhere.

PRIESTLING: Thy lips spake ever of pride, thou scorner.

BOSCHMANN [*moving away, alarmed*]: How dare you behave in dis ignorant way in de presence of a learned person? I'll call out de guard.

FIGGURES: Yes, and we'll salute you. I'll take this slate . . .

PRIESTLING: I'll take this Primer . . .

BOSCHMANN: I'll complain to de mistress about you.

[FIGGURES *brandishes the slate,* PRIESTLING *the Primer.*]

FIGGURES: I'll slice your foul face into five pieces!

PRIESTLING: I shall break the teeth of the sinner!

} [*together*]

[BOSCHMANN *runs away.*]

FIGGURES: Aha! Coward! You've shown us your heels!

PRIESTLING: The accursed one hath turned away.

BOSCHMANN [*in the doorway*]: Well, rascals, did you get me? Come on in here!

FIGGURES: Tucked away in there are you? We'd have given you a hammering.

BOSCHMANN: I'm not a bit frightened of you now, I'm not.

PRIESTLING: The unrighteous hath found a refuge. How many more of you heathen are there in there? Send 'em all out!

BOSCHMANN: You two couldn't take on one man! Hey boys, did you get me?

FIGGURES: I'll do you by the dozen, single-handed.

PRIESTLING: In the morning I shall smite all the sinners of the earth.

} [*All suddenly shouting*]

ACT FOUR

SOPHIA [*alone, looking at the time*]: Uncle is bound to come out soon. [*Sits down.*] I'll wait a while for him here. [*Takes out a small book and reads a little.*] That's true. How can the Heart not be content, when the Conscience is at rest! [*Again reads a little.*] It is impossible not to love the precepts of Virtue. They are the means to happiness. [*Reads a little, then looks up, sees* OLDWISE *and runs towards him.*]

OLDWISE: Ah! Here already, dear heart.

SOPHIA: I was waiting for you Uncle. I was just reading a little book.

OLDWISE: And what is that?

SOPHIA: It's French, by Fénelon,[10] on the education of girls.

OLDWISE: Fénelon? The author of Télémaque? Good. I don't know thy little book, but go on, read it, read it. The man that wrote Télémaque would never apply his pen to the corruption of morals. For your sakes, I'm afraid of the wise men of today. I have had occasion to read everything of theirs that has been translated into Russian. They are powerful eradicators of prejudice; that is true, but they also tear out virtue by the roots. Let's sit down.

    [*Both sit down.*]

It is my dearest wish to see thee as happy as it is possible to be in this world.

SOPHIA: Your instructions, Uncle, will be the foundation of all my welfare. Give me the rules that I must follow. Direct my heart; it is ready to obey you.

OLDWISE: Thy disposition pleases me. I'll gladly give

thee my advice. Listen to me with attention conformable to the seriousness with which I shall speak. Come nearer.

[SOPHIA *moves her chair nearer.*]

SOPHIA: Uncle! Every word of yours shall be engraved on my heart!

OLDWISE [*with solemn sincerity*]: Thou art now at the age when the Soul wants to delight in all its being, the Mind wants to know, and the Heart to feel. Thou art now entering into a world where the first step often decides the fate of a whole lifetime, where all too often the first encounter is with minds whose understanding has been corrupted, with hearts whose feelings are depraved. Oh my dear! Thou must know how to discriminate, to stay by the people whose friendship for thee will be a sure safe-guard for thy heart and mind.

SOPHIA: All my endeavours shall be directed to earning good opinions from decent people. But what can I do to prevent others from taking offence, when they see that I avoid them? Can I not find some way, Uncle, so that nobody in the world bears malice against me?

OLDWISE: Do not fret over the evil disposition of people that deserve no respect. Know that their malice is never directed against those whom they despise, but generally against those that have a right to despise them. It is not only wealth and rank that people envy; there are some too that envy virtue. They try with all their might to corrupt the innocent heart, so as to bring it down to their own level, and to beguile the inexperienced mind into a false notion of wherein its happiness lies.

SOPHIA: Uncle, I thought everybody was agreed wherein their happiness lay. Nobility, riches . . .

OLDWISE: Yes, my dear! I too agree in calling the noble and the rich happy. But first let us agree who is noble and who is rich. I have my own way of reckoning. I reckon degrees in nobility by the number of deeds that a great lord has done for his country, not by the number of deeds for which he has arrogantly claimed the credit. Not by the number of people that crowd into his anteroom, but by the number of people that have been contented by his conduct and his actions. My noble man is, of course, happy. So is my rich man. By my reckoning the rich man is not he that sets aside money in order to hide it away in a coffer, but he that sets aside what he has to spare, in order to help those that are in want for necessities.

SOPHIA: Is it possible, Uncle, that all hearts are not aware of truths such as these? Surely there can be nobody that does not ponder them? Where is the intelligence, of which they are so proud?

OLDWISE: My dear, what is there to be proud of in intelligence? Intelligence, if it be that and no more, is the merest trifle. Among the cleverest men we see bad husbands, bad fathers, bad citizens. It is Morality, which is immeasurably superior to any cleverness, that gives to intelligence its true value. Without it, the intelligent man is a monster. That can easily be understood by anyone who thinks carefully. There are many, many, different sorts of intelligence; it is easy to make excuses for an intelligent man, even if some mental quality is lacking in him. But if any quality of the Heart is wanting, an honest man can never be forgiven. He has to have them all; the merits of the Heart are indivisible. An honest man must be a perfectly honest man.

SOPHIA: Your explanations, Uncle, accord with my innermost feelings, that I had been unable to express. Now I have a lively sense of the merits of an honest man, and of his duty.

OLDWISE: Duty! Ah my dear! How they all keep that word on their tongues and how little they understand it! The hourly employment of that word has made us so familiar with it, that a man can now utter it without thinking or feeling anything. If people realized the gravity of that word, nobody could pronounce it without a sense of awe. Think what duty is. It is the holy vow that binds us to all those with whom we live and upon whom we depend. If they did their duty as well as they prate about it, men of every condition would achieve their aspirations and be perfectly happy. A gentleman, for example, would hold it in the highest degree dishonourable to do nothing, when there are so many things for him to do; he has his people to help, and his country to serve. There would then be none of those gentry, of whom we may say that their gentility is buried with their ancestors. A gentleman unworthy of being a gentleman – I know nothing on earth baser than that.

SOPHIA: Is it possible to descend so low?

OLDWISE: My dear! What I have said about a gentleman we may now extend to mankind as a whole. Everybody has his duties. Let us see how they are carried out, let us see for example what most husbands are like in Society today, and let us not forget the wives too. O my dearest heart! Now thou must give me all thy attention. Let us take as an example one of those many unhappy homes where the wife has no sincere affection for her husband, and he has no confidence in his wife; where both have gone their own ways, and turned aside from the path of virtue. Instead of a true and tender friend, the wife sees in her husband a brutal and debauched tyrant. On the other side, instead of the gentleness and candour that belong to a virtuous wife, the husband sees in his wife's soul only wayward, brazen impudence – and impudence in a woman is the hallmark of vicious conduct. They have become insupportable burdens to one another. Neither of them cares any more for their good name, for both have lost it. Can there be anything more dreadful than their condition? The home is abandoned. The servants see their own master a slave to his evil passions, and forget the obedience that they owe him. The property is frittered away; nobody will manage it, if the owner does not manage himself. The children, their unfortunate children, have father and mother alive, but are already orphans. Having no respect for his wife, their father hardly dares to embrace them, hardly dares to give way to the tenderest feelings of the human heart. The innocent babes are deprived, too, of a mother's affection. Unworthy to have children, she turns aside from their caresses, seeing in them either a cause of anxiety for herself, or a reproach for her misconduct. And what education can children expect, from a mother who has lost her virtue? How can she teach them morals, when she has none herself? What hell must there be in the souls of husband and wife when they turn their thoughts to the state of the children?

SOPHIA: Oh heavens! Why do such dreadful things happen?

OLDWISE: Because, my dear, in marriages today the heart is seldom consulted. Is the bridegroom noble? Is he rich? Is the bride good-looking? Is she rich? That is what matters; there is no question of morals. It never enters their heads that in the eyes of thoughtful people an honest man without high rank is a most noble person, that virtue can take the place of all else, but nothing can take the place of virtue. I'll confess to thee that my heart will not be at rest till I see thee married to the man who is worthy of thy heart, till your mutual love . . .

SOPHIA: But with a worthy husband, how can one not love him as a friend?

OLDWISE: Yes. Only, I think, do not have for your husband the love that is like friendship. Have for him the friendship that is like love. That will last much better. Then, after twenty years of marriage you will find in your hearts the old attachment to one another. A prudent husband! A virtuous wife. What could be more honourable than that? Thy husband, my dear, must be ruled by reason and thou by him, and all will go perfectly well with you both.

SOPHIA: All that you say touches my heart.

OLDWISE [*with the tenderest affection*]: And mine is delighted to see thy sensibility. Thy happiness depends upon thyself. God has given thee all the graces of thy sex, and I see in thee the heart of an honest man. My dearest dear, thou unitest in thyself the perfections of both sexes. I am happy to know that my affection is not deceiving me, that virtue ...

SOPHIA: It is thou that hast saturated my whole senses with it. [*Rushes to kiss his hand.*] Where is it?

OLDWISE [*himself kissing her hand*]: It is in thy soul. I thank God that I find a firm foundation for thy happiness in thee thyself. It will not depend upon rank or wealth. All of that may come to thee, but for thee there is a far greater happiness. It is to feel thyself worthy of all the blessings that thou mayest enjoy ...

SOPHIA: Uncle! My true happiness is that thou art with me. I know the value ...

[*Enter* MR OLDWISE'S VALET, *and hands him a letter.*]

OLDWISE: Where is this from?

VALET: From Moscow, by special messenger. [*Exit.*]

OLDWISE [*opening the letter, and looking at the signature*]: Count Honest. Ah! [*Begins to read but shows that his eyes cannot see clearly.*] Sophia my dear! My glasses are on the table, in the book.

SOPHIA: Directly, Uncle. [*Exit.*]

OLDWISE [*alone*]: Of course he's writing about the man on whose behalf he made the proposal to me in Moscow. I don't know Milo, but when his uncle, who is a true friend of mine, when the world at large regards him as an honest and worthy man ... if her heart is free ...

[*Re-enter* SOPHIA *and gives him the glasses.*]

SOPHIA: I've found them, Uncle.

OLDWISE [*reading*]: 'I have only just heard ... taking his detachment to Moscow. ... He's bound to go your way ... I shall be most pleased for him and you to meet one another ... do try to get to know his way of thinking.' [*Aside*] Of course I shall. I won't give her away without that. 'You will find ... Yours sincerely ...' Good. This letter has to do with thee. I was telling thee that a young man with admirable qualities had been proposed to me. ... My dearest heart, thou art troubled by what I am saying. I noticed that before, and I see it now. Thy confidence in me ...

SOPHIA: Can I have anything in my heart hidden from you? No, Uncle. I'll tell thee frankly ...

[*Enter* TRUEMAN *and* MILO.]

TRUEMAN: May I introduce my very good friend, Mr Milo.

OLDWISE [*aside*]: Milo!

MILO: I shall consider myself truly fortunate if I deserve to be well thought of by you, to be in your good graces ...

OLDWISE: Count Honest – is he a relative of yours?

MILO: He is my Uncle.

OLDWISE: I am very pleased to make the acquaintance of a man of your quality. Your Uncle has spoken of you to me. He does full justice to you. Particular merits ...

MILO: He is too kind to me. At my age, and in my position, I should be unforgivably conceited, if I were to think that a young man deserves all the good opinions that distinguished people hold about him.

TRUEMAN: I was sure in advance that if you could get to know my friend more intimately he would gain favour with you. He often used to visit your sister's house ...

[OLDWISE *glances at* SOPHIA.]

SOPHIA [*to* OLDWISE, *quietly and very shyly*]: And Mamma loved him as a son.

OLDWISE [*to* SOPHIA]: That pleases me very much. [*To* MILO] I hear you were in the Army. Your courage . . .

MILO: I was doing my duty. Neither my age, nor my rank, nor my situation has yet permitted me to show true courage, assuming that I have it in me.

OLDWISE: What! When you have been in battle, and exposed your life!

MILO: I exposed it as the others did. There, the quality of the heart, that the soldier was commanded to have by his leader, and the officer by his honour, was valour. I will frankly admit to you that I have not yet had any opportunity to show true courage, as I earnestly desire to do.

OLDWISE: I should be extremely curious to know wherein you consider true courage to lie?

MILO: If you will permit me to say what I think, I consider that true courage lies in the soul, and not in the heart. He that has courage in his soul will also without any doubt have a valiant heart. In our trade of war, the fighting man must have the valour; and the Army Commander, the courage. He considers in cold blood all degrees of danger, he takes the necessary measures, he prefers his glory to his life. But what is more than all, he will not be afraid to forget his personal glory in the interest of his country. His courage does not consist, therefore, in disregard of his own life, which is something he is always ready to hazard; he knows how to sacrifice that.

OLDWISE: Very just. So you consider true courage to be the quality of an Army Commander. Does it also belong to other walks of life?

MILO: It is a virtue; consequently there is no walk of life that cannot be distinguished by it. I think that the valour of the heart is shown in the hour of battle, but the courage of the soul in all the trials, all the situations of life. And what is the difference between the bravery of the soldier who together with others hazards his life in an assault, and the courage of the statesman who tells the truth to his Sovereign at the risk of making him angry? The judge who does justice to the helpless, without fear of revenge and of the threats of the powerful, is in my eyes a hero. How petty is the soul of the man who for some trifle sends out a challenge to a duel, compared with the man that stands up for someone who is absent, whose honour is being attacked by slanderers! That is how I understand courage . . .

OLDWISE: And that is how a man that has it in his soul ought to understand it! Embrace me, my dear! Pardon the simplicity of my heart. I am a friend of honest men. That sentiment was rooted in my upbringing. In thine I see and I respect virtue adorned by an enlightened intellect.

MILO: A noble soul . . . No . . . I can no longer hide my innermost feelings. No; the power of your virtue is drawing out all the secrets of my soul. If my heart is virtuous, if it deserves happiness, then it depends upon you to make it happy. For me, happiness means having your dear niece to be my wife. Our mutual affection . . .

OLDWISE [joyfully, to SOPHIA]: What? Could thy heart discover the man that I had intended for thee myself? Here he is – my bridegroom for thee . . .

SOPHIA: And with all my heart I love him.

OLDWISE: You are each worthy of the other. [Delightedly joining their hands together] From all my soul, I give you my consent.

MILO [embracing OLDWISE]: My happiness is beyond compare.

SOPHIA [kissing OLDWISE's hands]: Who can be happier than I! } [together]

TRUEMAN: I am sincerely delighted!
 [Enter BEAST.]

BEAST: And here I am.

OLDWISE: Why Sir, hast thou come to see me?

BEAST: It's about something I want for myself.

OLDWISE: And what dost thou want of me?

BEAST: Three words.

OLDWISE: What are they?

BEAST: Hug me tight, and say 'Sophie is thine'.

OLDWISE: But Sir, is not that an absurd thing to want?
Think well.

BEAST: I don't ever think and I was sure before I came
that if you didn't think neither, Sophie would be
mine.

OLDWISE: What? Dost thou want me to give my niece
away to somebody I don't know?

BEAST: If you don't know about me, I'll tell you. I am
Tarasius Beast, not the last in my family. The Beast
family is a great and ancient one. You won't find our
first ancestor in any book of heraldry.

TRUEMAN [laughing]: Will you have us believe, then, that
he was older than Adam?

BEAST: What do you think? Maybe a little older.

OLDWISE [laughing]: In other words, he was created on the
sixth day, the same as Adam, but a little earlier in the
day?[11]

BEAST: No, really? Then you think well of the antiquity of
my family?

OLDWISE: Oh, so well that I wonder how you in your
position can take a wife from any other family but the
Beasts?

BEAST: Think, though, how lucky Sophie will be, marrying
me. She's a simple gentlewoman . . .[12]

OLDWISE: What a man! If so, then thou are not the one to
marry her.

BEAST: It's what I've come to now. Let 'em talk, let 'em
say that a Beast has married some little gentlewoman.
It's all the same to me.

OLDWISE: It's not all the same to me that they should say that the gentlewoman has married a Beast.

MILO: Such inequality would create unhappiness for you both.

BEAST: Halloa! Is this a rival here? [*Quietly, to* OLDWISE] Trying to cut me out, is he?

OLDWISE [*quietly to* BEAST]: I think so.

BEAST [*same tone*]: But damn it, how?

OLDWISE [*same tone*]: It's difficult.

BEAST [*in a loud voice, pointing at* MILO]: Which of us is ridiculous? Ha, ha, ha, ha!

OLDWISE [*laughing*]: I can see which it is.

SOPHIA: Uncle! I love it when you are gay.

BEAST [*to* OLDWISE]: Halloa! So you're a gay one? Last time I saw you I thought you a bit stand-offish. You wouldn't say a word to me, and here you are now laughing with me.

OLDWISE: Such is man, my friend. Changing from hour to hour.

BEAST: So I see. But last time, you know, I was the same Beast and you were angry.

OLDWISE: I had a reason to be angry.

BEAST: And I know what it was. I'm like you about that. At home, if I go into the pigsties and find them in a mess, I get furious. And between you and me, when you came here and found my sister's house no better than a pigsty, you were furious.

OLDWISE: Thou art more fortunate than me. My concern is with people.

BEAST: And mine is with pigs.

[*Enter* MRS SIMPLE, SIMPLE, MITROFÁN *and* MRS JEREMY.]

MRS SIMPLE [*coming in*]: Have you got everything with you, Mitrofán dear boy?

MITROFÁN: Now don't you fuss yourself.

MRS SIMPLE: Mr Oldwise, my dear, we have come to trouble you now with a request on behalf of us all. [*To her husband and son*] Bow.

OLDWISE: And what is it, Ma'am?

MRS SIMPLE: In the first place, will everybody please sit down.

[*All sit down, except* MITROFÁN *and* MRS JEREMY.]

MRS SIMPLE: It is like this, Mr Oldwise my dear. The prayers of our parents were answered (what would have been the good of prayers from us sinners?) and the Lord granted to us our boy Mitrofán. We have done our best to make him as you see him today. My dear Mr Oldwise would you mind undertaking to examine him to see how he has been educated at home?

OLDWISE: Oh Ma'am! It has already come to my ears that this young gentleman has finished his education. I have heard who his tutors were. I can already tell what his reading and writing must be like, after studying with Mr Priestling, and his mathematics, after studying with Sergeant Figgures. [*To* TRUEMAN] I should be curious to hear about what the German has taught him.

MRS SIMPLE: All subjects, Mr Oldwise my dear.

SIMPLE: Everything, my dear Sir. } [*together*]

MITROFÁN: Anything you like.

TRUEMAN [*to* MITROFÁN]: Such as what? Give me an example.

MITROFÁN [*handing him a book*]: Here you are. Grammar.

TRUEMAN [*taking the book*]: This is a grammar. What is there in it that you know?

MITROFÁN: A lot. An adjective is attached to a noun.

TRUEMAN: What part of speech for example is 'door' – noun or adjective?

MITROFÁN: Door? Which door?

TRUEMAN: Which door? That one there.

MITROFÁN: That one? Adjective.

TRUEMAN: Why?

MITROFÁN: Because it's attached to its hinges. Down at the store-room there's a door that's been off its hinges for six weeks. That one's still a noun.

OLDWISE: Therefore you would say that the word 'fool' is an adjective, because it attaches to a stupid man.

MITROFÁN: Yes, indeed.

MRS SIMPLE: Well, what do you think, my dear?

SIMPLE: What do you think, Mr Trueman, Sir?

TRUEMAN: Couldn't be better. He is strong on grammar.

MILO: I expect he's quite as good on history too.

MRS SIMPLE: Why, he's always been fond of stories, my dear, ever since he was little.

BEAST: Mitrofán is like me. I could go on and on listening to my village headman, as long as he keeps on with his stories. He's one for telling them, the old devil. Where does he get them all from?

MRS SIMPLE: But he doesn't come up to our Mr Boschmann.

TRUEMAN: Have you gone a long way in history?

MITROFÁN: Gone a long way? What story is that? There's one in which you go flying over the nine-and-twenty lands and over the thirtieth kingdom.

TRUEMAN: Ah! Is that the sort of history that Boschmann teaches you?

OLDWISE. Boschmann? I think I know that name.

TRUEMAN: And have you the same sort of knowledge of geography?

MRS SIMPLE [*to her son*]: Do you hear what he says, my love? What subject is that?

MITROFÁN [*quietly, to his Mother*]: How should I know?

MRS SIMPLE [*quietly, to* MITROFÁN]: Don't be obstinate, darling. Now is the time to show yourself off.

MITROFÁN [*quietly, to his Mother*]: But I can't understand what they're asking about.

MRS SIMPLE [*to* TRUEMAN]: What did you say the subject was, Mr Trueman my dear?

TRUEMAN: Geography.

MRS SIMPLE [*to* MITROFÁN]: Do you hear? Georgie Ography.

MITROFÁN: But what is it, for goodness sake, that they're keeping on at me about!

MRS SIMPLE [*to* TRUEMAN]: There you see Mr Trueman my dear. If you'll be so kind as to tell him what the subject is, he'll say it for you.

TRUEMAN: Description of the earth.

MRS SIMPLE [*to* OLDWISE]: But to begin with, what good is that?

OLDWISE: To begin with, it would be useful if you happened to be travelling. You'd know then where you were going to.

MRS SIMPLE: Oh my dear Mr Oldwise, what are coachmen for? That's their job. That sort of thing isn't a gentlemanly subject. All a gentleman has to say is 'Drive me there', and they drive him to wherever he wants to go. Believe me, Mr Oldwise my dear, anything our boy Mitrofán doesn't know is sure to be rubbish.

OLDWISE: Sure to be, Ma'am. It is a great consolation for human ignorance to suppose that what we don't know is rubbish.

BEAST: And to prove to you that learning is rubbish, let's take my Uncle Oliver.[13] Nobody ever heard anything about books from him, and he didn't want to hear about them from other people neither. Yet what a headpiece he had on him!

TRUEMAN: What about it?

BEAST: Well, I'll tell you what happened once to him. He was riding a fast ambler and he was drunk and he rode into a stone gateway. He was a big tall chap, and the gateway was low and he forgot to duck, with the result that his forehead went smack against the lintel and down went Uncle with the back of his head on the tail-strap, and that lively horse carried him through the gate and up to the porch, lying on his back. I'd like to know if there's a learned forehead anywhere in the world that wouldn't have been shattered by a clout like that, but all my uncle asked about, after he had sobered up, God rest his soul, was whether the gate was all right.

MILO: You say yourself, Mr Beast, that you are no scholar, but I don't think that in a case like that your forehead would have proved any stronger than a scholar's.

OLDWISE [to MILO]: I wouldn't bet on that. I think that the Beasts are a hard-headed family.

MRS SIMPLE: But what enjoyment can one get out of learning, Mr Oldwise my dear? [To TRUEMAN] And look how hard you work, Sir. Why, just now, when I was on my way here, I saw them taking in some kind of packet for you.

TRUEMAN: A packet for me? And nobody tells me! [Rising] Please excuse me for deserting you. This may be some instructions for me from the Governor-General.

OLDWISE [rising as all the rest rise]: Go on then, my friend, but I shan't say good-bye to you.

TRUEMAN: We'll see each other again. Are you going tomorrow morning?

OLDWISE: Seven o'clock.

[Exit TRUEMAN.]

MILO: I'm moving off too with my detachment tomorrow, and we'll escort you. I'm going now to make the arrangements. [MILO leaves, with a farewell glance at SOPHIA.]

MRS SIMPLE [to OLDWISE]: Now my dear Mr Oldwise! Have you seen well enough what our boy Mitrofán is like?

BEAST: Well my dear good friend? Do you see what I'm like?

OLDWISE: I couldn't know you better than I do, either of you.

BEAST: Is Sophie going to marry me?

OLDWISE: She is not.

MRS SIMPLE: Is our boy Mitrofán going to be betrothed to her?

OLDWISE: He is not.

MRS SIMPLE: But what's to hinder it? ⎫
BEAST: What's up?   ⎬ [*together*]

OLDWISE [*taking them both aside*]: There's a secret that I can tell to you, and you alone. She is betrothed. [*Exit, signing to* SOPHIA *to follow him out.*]

MRS SIMPLE: Oh, villain!

BEAST: The man's daft.

MRS SIMPLE [*impatiently*]: When do they leave?

BEAST: Didn't you hear? Seven o'clock in the morning.

MRS SIMPLE: Seven o'clock.

BEAST: I'll be awake tomorrow directly it's light. He can be as clever as he likes, but you don't get away from a Beast in a hurry. [*Exit.*]

MRS SIMPLE [*dashing about on the stage and thinking furiously*]: Seven o'clock . . . We'll be up before that. . . . I'll get what I want, I'll have my own way. . . . All of you come over here!

[*All run up to her.*]

MRS SIMPLE [*to her husband*]: At six o'clock tomorrow you're to have the carriage brought round to the back porch. Do you hear? And don't you go and make a muddle of it.

SIMPLE: I hear you, Mother.

MRS SIMPLE [*to* MRS JEREMY]: And you stay outside Miss Sophia's door all night, and don't you dare go to sleep. Directly she wakes, run to me.

MRS JEREMY: I shan't close an eye, Ma'am.

MRS SIMPLE [*to* MITROFÁN]: And you, my love, you have got to be quite ready at six o'clock, and tell the men-servants they're not to go away from the house.

MITROFÁN: It shall all be done.

MRS SIMPLE: Go then all of you, and God bless you.
  [*All go out.*]
I know now what to do. Where there's anger, there's
mercy too. The old man will be angry for a while, but
he'll have to forgive us. And we shall take what is ours.

ACT FIVE

Early next morning. OLDWISE *and* TRUEMAN *are talking.*

TRUEMAN: That was the packet, the one that the lady of the house told me about yesterday, when you were with us.

OLDWISE: So now you have the means to put a stop to the inhuman behaviour of the squire's wicked wife?

TRUEMAN: My instructions are that on the first sign of violence, that might cause suffering among the people subject to her, I am to sequestrate the house and the manors.

OLDWISE: Thanks be to God that mankind is able to find protection! Believe me, where the Sovereign exercises reason, where he knows what makes for his true glory, there it is that mankind's rights must surely be regained. There it is that everyone is quick to perceive that each must seek his fortune and profit only within the law, and that oppression and enslavement of fellow men is against the law.[14]

TRUEMAN: I agree with you there; but how hard it is to get rid of the deep-rooted prejudices that base-minded people are able to turn to their advantage!

OLDWISE: Listen, my friend! A great sovereign is a wise sovereign. His task is to show the people their true good. The glory of his wisdom lies in directing people, since no great wisdom is required to direct dummies. The stupidest peasant in a village is usually chosen to mind the herd, because no great intelligence is needed to herd cattle. A Sovereign, worthy of the Throne, strives to uplift the souls of his subjects. We see this with our own eyes.

TRUEMAN: The satisfaction enjoyed by sovereigns who rule

over free individuals must be so great that I cannot understand what impulse could turn them aside . . .

OLDWISE: Ah! How great is the soul that a sovereign must needs have, to keep on the path of truth and never be diverted from it! To begin with there is a horde of greedy flatterers . . .

TRUEMAN: It is impossible to picture to oneself the character of a flatterer, without utter contempt.

OLDWISE: A flatterer is a creature who holds no good opinion of other men, nor indeed of himself. All that he strives for is first to blind a man's intellect and then to do with him whatever he wants to do. He is a thief in the night, who begins by putting out the light, and then sets about stealing.

TRUEMAN: The cause of people's misfortunes is of course their own depravity, but the means to make people good . . .

OLDWISE: Are in the hands of the Sovereign. As soon as everybody sees that nobody can take a place in Society without good morals, that rewards are to be earned for services rendered, not to be won by base time-serving, nor to be purchased for any money; that men are to be chosen for offices, rather than the offices to be snatched by the men – then everyone will see that it is to his advantage to be moral, and everyone will be good.

TRUEMAN: That is very just. A great sovereign gives . . .

OLDWISE: Grace and favour where he likes. Rank and office to them that deserve it.

TRUEMAN: In order that there may be no shortage of men of merit, special attention is now being given to education.

OLDWISE: That indeed must be the guarantee of the well-being of the State. We see all the unhappy consequences of bad education. Yes, and what is his Country to expect from the boy Mitrofán, for whom money is still being paid out by ignorant parents to ignorant tutors? How many gentlemen are there, who entrust the moral education of their little son to a so-called 'Uncle' – one of their own bond-slaves! Fifteen years later, and instead of one slave there are two – the old 'Uncle' and the young master.

TRUEMAN: But persons in high positions are giving enlightenment to their children ...

OLDWISE: All that is true; but whatever subject is being studied I should like it not to be forgotten that the principal aim of all human knowledge is good morals. Believe me, learning in the hands of a depraved man is a dreadful weapon for evil; it is only the virtuous soul that is uplifted by enlightenment. When educating the son of a gentleman of rank, for example, I should like to see his Governor every day unroll for him the Scroll of History at two places; one where great men have contributed to the good of their country, and the other where an unworthy magnate has used the power and trust confided to him for evil, and has been toppled from the height of magnificence into the abyss of scorn and contempt.

TRUEMAN: It is indeed necessary to have education appropriate to people of all conditions. Then one may be sure ... What is that noise?

OLDWISE: Whatever has happened?

[*Enter* MILO, SOPHIA, *and* MRS JEREMY. MRS JEREMY *is trying to clutch hold of* SOPHIA, MILO *is pushing her away and shouting at some* MENSERVANTS, *with a drawn sword in his hand.*]

MILO: Don't any of you dare come near me!

SOPHIA [*flinging herself on* OLDWISE]: Oh Uncle! Protect me.

OLDWISE: My dear! What is this? ⎫
TRUEMAN: What villainy! ⎪
SOPHIA: My heart is trembling. ⎬ [*together*]
MRS JEREMY: There goes my poor head! ⎭

114

MILO: The villains! I was passing by here and I saw a crowd of menservants who had seized her by the arms and in spite of her struggles and cries had got her out of the porch and were taking her to a carriage.

SOPHIA: This is my rescuer!

OLDWISE: My dear friend!

TRUEMAN [*to* MRS JEREMY]: Tell me at once, where were you going to take her, and how did you and that wicked woman . . .

MRS JEREMY: To be married, good Sir, to be married!

MRS SIMPLE [*off-stage*]: Rascals! Thieves! Scoundrels! I'll have you all beaten to death!

[*Enter* MRS SIMPLE, SIMPLE *and* MITROFÁN.]

MRS SIMPLE: What sort of mistress am I? In my own house? [*Pointing to* MILO] A stranger comes and threatens you, and my orders go for nothing.

SIMPLE: Is it my fault?

MITROFÁN: We'll teach those servants! ⎫ [*together*]

MRS SIMPLE: I don't want to go on living! ⎭

TRUEMAN: The offence, which I have myself witnessed, entitles you, as her Uncle, and you, as her betrothed . . .

MRS SIMPLE: Betrothed! ⎫

SIMPLE: Nice lot, we are! ⎬ [*together*]

MITROFÁN: To blazes with it all! ⎭

TRUEMAN: . . . to demand from Government that the outrage comitted by this woman be punished with the utmost rigour of the law. I shall immediately bring her before the Court, and charge her with breach of the Peace.

MRS SIMPLE [*falling on her knees*]: Oh my goodness! Forgive me!

TRUEMAN: The husband and the son must be regarded as accessories to the offence . . .

SIMPLE: I didn't mean to do it. ⎫ [*Together, falling on*

MITROFÁN: Forgive me, Uncle. ⎭ *their knees.*]

MRS SIMPLE: Bitch that I am! What have I done!
[*Enter* BEAST.]

BEAST: Well Sister, that was a nice business . . . Hey, what's this? The whole family on their knees!

MRS SIMPLE [*on her knees*]: Oh my goodness goodness me! You couldn't hurt a poor sinner! Not after she has repented. I have done wrong! Do not destroy me. [*To* SOPHIA] Dear kind lady, pardon me. Have mercy on me and [*pointing to her husband and son*] on these poor orphans.

BEAST: Sister! Are you in your right mind?

TRUEMAN: Silence, Beast!

MRS SIMPLE: God grant prosperity to you and to your dear betrothed too, what would you want with my head?

SOPHIA [*to* OLDWISE]: Uncle! I forget the injury done to me.

MRS SIMPLE [*raising her hands to* OLDWISE]: Mr Oldwise my dear! You pardon me too, pardon this sinner. I'm a human being you know, not an angel.

OLDWISE: I know, I know that human beings can't be angels. But still, they needn't be devils.

MILO: Her crime and her repentance are equally contemptible.

TRUEMAN [*to* OLDWISE]: The least complaint by you, one word to Government from you . . . and nothing can save her.

OLDWISE: I have no wish for anyone to be ruined. I pardon her.

[*All jump up from their knees.*]

MRS SIMPLE: He's pardoned me! Oh dear Mr Oldwise! . . . Now then! Now I'm going to teach those servants of ours, the blackguards! Now I'm going to have them all up, one by one. Now I'm going to go on till I find out who it was that let her slip out of their hands. No, you scoundrels! No, you thieves! This is a prank that I shan't ever forgive.

TRUEMAN: Why do you want to punish your own people?

MRS SIMPLE: Oh my dear Sir, what a question! Haven't I even got authority over my people?

TRUEMAN: Do you then consider that you have a right to strike them whenever you feel inclined?

BEAST: Do you mean to tell me that a gentleman hasn't got the right to clout a servant when he wants to?

TRUEMAN: When he wants to? But what a thing to want! A real Beast, you are. [*To* MRS SIMPLE] No, Madam, nobody is free to act the tyrant . . .

MRS SIMPLE: Not free! A gentleman not free to flog the servants when he wants to! What was the point, then, of giving us the Decree of the Freedom of the Gentry![15]

OLDWISE: A past-mistress at the interpretation of decrees!

MRS SIMPLE: You may be pleased to laugh, but I'm going to go through the whole lot of them and I'm going to . . . [*Breaks away to go.*]

TRUEMAN [*stopping her*]: Stay, Madam. [*Takes a paper from his pocket and addresses* SIMPLE *in a solemn voice.*] In the name of Government I order you to proceed forthwith to assemble your servants and your villagers for the proclamation to them of a Decree that in consequence of the inhuman conduct of your wife, which you have shown extreme weakness of character in permitting, I am commanded by Government to take your house and your manors into sequestration.

SIMPLE: Oh, what have we come to now!

MRS SIMPLE: What! More trouble! And what for, my dear Sir? Because I, mistress in my own house . . .

TRUEMAN: An inhuman mistress, whose immorality can no longer be tolerated in a well-ordered state. [*To* SIMPLE] Go on.

SIMPLE [*goes out slapping his hands*]: Who's responsible for this, Mother?

MRS SIMPLE [*distressed*]: Now I'm a wretched woman. Oh misery!

BEAST: Hey, I say! They can get me that way too. At that rate any Beast can find himself in sequestration. I'm getting out of here while the going is good.

MRS SIMPLE: Everything lost! Utterly ruined!

BEAST [*to* OLDWISE]: I was going to come and try to get some sense out of you. This betrothed of hers . . .

OLDWISE [*pointing to* MILO]: There he is.

BEAST: Oh well, in that case there isn't anything I can do here. Harness up the waggon and . . .

TRUEMAN: . . . go back to your pigsties. I advise you however to be careful. I have heard that you treat your pigs a great deal better than you do your servants.

BEAST [*slinking away*]: But my dear good Sir! How can I feel kindly towards servants? They are so clever, compared to me, but when I'm with the pigs I'm the cleverest of the lot. [*He leaves.*]

MRS SIMPLE [*to* TRUEMAN]: Don't ruin me, kind Sir; what good would that do you? Can't you somehow get the decree revoked? Are all decrees carried out?

TRUEMAN: I shall certainly not shrink from doing my duty.

MRS SIMPLE: Just let me have three days' respite. [*Aside*] I'll show them . . .

TRUEMAN: Not even three hours.

OLDWISE: No my friend! If she were up to her tricks for three hours she could do enough damage to last a lifetime!

MRS SIMPLE: But my dear Sir! How can you go into all the details yourself?

TRUEMAN: That is my business. Other people's property will be returned to the owners, and . . .

MRS SIMPLE: And what about the debts to be settled? The Tutors haven't been paid . . .

TRUEMAN: The tutors? [*To* MRS JEREMY] Are they here? Bring them in.

MRS JEREMY: I expect they'll have managed to get here. And what about the German, my master?

TRUEMAN: Fetch them all.

[*Exit* MRS JEREMY.]

TRUEMAN: You need not concern yourself with anything, madam, I shall satisfy all of them.

OLDWISE [*seeing* MRS SIMPLE *in distress*]: Madam! Thou wilt feel better for having lost the power to do harm to others.

MRS SIMPLE: Thanks for that mercy! What good am I, when I'm not free to use my own hands in my own house! [*Enter* MRS JEREMY, BOSCHMANN, PRIESTLING *and* FIGGURES.]

MRS JEREMY [*leading the* TUTORS *up to* TRUEMAN]: There you are, master, that's our whole gang.

BOSCHMANN [*to* TRUEMAN]: Your Lordship! Was you pleased to send for me?

PRIESTLING [*to* TRUEMAN]: I was called, and lo! I have come.

FIGGURES [*to* TRUEMAN]: What's the orders, Your Honour?

OLDWISE [*who has been looking hard at* BOSCHMANN *since he came in*]: Hallo! Is that thou, Boschmann?

BOSCHMANN [*Recognizing* OLDWISE]: Aie! Aie! Aie! Aie! Aie! It's you, it's my gracious master. [*Kisses* OLDWISE's *coat-tail.*] May it please you, my fader, are you keeping pretty well?

TRUEMAN: What! Do you know him?

OLDWISE: I do indeed. He was my coachman for three years.

[*All show astonishment.*]

TRUEMAN: A fine sort of tutor!

OLDWISE [*to* BOSCHMANN]: Art thou here as a tutor, Boschmann? I really thought thou wast a good man, who would stick to his trade.

BOSCHMANN: Vat can I do den, my dear Sir. I'm not de first nor de last. Three months I vander round Moscow mit no job, nobody is vanting coachman. Den it come dat I must either starve to death, or be tutor.

TRUEMAN [*to the* TUTORS]: As the Government-appointed sequestrator for this property, I discharge you.

FIGGURES: Couldn't wish for anything better.

PRIESTLING: It is your good pleasure to discharge me? First then let us settle accounts.

TRUEMAN: And what do you require?

PRIESTLING: Nay verily dear Sir, my account is not a little one. For half a year's tuition, for the boots that I have worn out in three years, for the lost time, when I used to come out all the way here for nothing.

MRS SIMPLE: There's no satisfying a greedy man like you, Priestling! What's all this about?

TRUEMAN: Madam, I must ask you not to interfere.

MRS SIMPLE: When you come to tell the truth, what did you teach our boy Mitrofán.

PRIESTLING: That's his business, not mine.

TRUEMAN [*to* PRIESTLING]: All right, all right. [*To* FIGGURES] Is there much owing to you?

FIGGURES: To me? Nothing.

MRS SIMPLE: He had ten roubles, Mr Trueman, for the one year, and he hasn't had a halfpenny yet for the other year.

FIGGURES: That's right. Those ten roubles cover wear and tear on boots for the two years. We're quits.

TRUEMAN: And what about tuition?

FIGGURES: Nothing.

TRUEMAN: Why nothing?

FIGGURES: I won't take anything. He never learnt anything.

OLDWISE: Nevertheless thou must be paid.

FIGGURES: There's nothing to pay me for. I served the Tsar for twenty years and more. I took money for service. I never took it for doing nothing, and I never shall.

OLDWISE: There's a real good man!

[OLDWISE *and* MILO *take money out of their purses.*]

TRUEMAN: Aren't you ashamed, Priestling?

PRIESTLING [*hanging his head*]: I am confounded and put to shame.

OLDWISE [*to* FIGGURES]: There, my friend, that's for thee, for kindness' sake.

FIGGURES: Thank you, my lord. I'm grateful. You're at liberty to make me a present. I'll never ask for what I haven't earned.

MILO [*giving him money*]: That's for you too, my friend!

FIGGURES: And thank you too.

[TRUEMAN *also gives him money*]

FIGGURES: But what is your Honour rewarding me for?

TRUEMAN: For not being like Priestling.

FIGGURES: Nay! I'm a soldier, Your Honour.

TRUEMAN [*to* FIGGURES]: Go, friend, and God be with you.

[*Exit* FIGGURES.]

TRUEMAN: As for you Priestling, will you call here tomorrow and try to work out your account with the lady herself?

PRIESTLING [*running away*]: With the lady herself? I renounce it all!

BOSCHMANN [*to* OLDWISE]: Don't forsake an old servant, Your Lordship. Take me back into your service.

OLDWISE: But Boschmann, I expect you have got out of the way of managing horses.

BOSCHMANN: Ah no my dear master! Living mit dese shentlemans and ladies I think I'm all de time mit de horses.

[*Enter* OLDWISE'S VALET.]

VALET [*to* OLDWISE]: Your carriage is ready.

BOSCHMANN: You tell me come along?

OLDWISE: Go on, get up on the box.

[*Exit* BOSCHMANN.]

OLDWISE [*holding the hands of* SOPHIA *and* MILO, *to* TRUE-MAN]: Now my friend, we are going. Wilt thou wish us . . .

TRUEMAN: All the happiness to which honest hearts have a right.

MRS SIMPLE [*rushing to embrace her son*]: I've one thing left to me, my own dear son Mitrofán.

MITROFÁN: Now Mother, you leave me be! Coming bothering me like that!

MRS SIMPLE: You too! You desert me too. Oh you ungrateful . . . [*Falls in a faint.*]

SOPHIA [*running up to her*]: Heavens! She's unconscious.

OLDWISE [*to* SOPHIA]: See to her, see to her.

[SOPHIA *and* MRS JEREMY *attend to* MRS SIMPLE.]

TRUEMAN [*to* MITROFÁN]: Good-for-nothing child! You of all people to be rude to your mother? It is her insane devotion to you, more than anything else, that has brought this misfortune upon her.

MITROFÁN: But she somehow seemed to . . .

TRUEMAN: Oaf!

OLDWISE [*to* MRS JEREMY]: How is she? How is she now?

MRS JEREMY [*looks closely at* MRS SIMPLE, *flings up her hands and claps them together*]: She's coming to, Master, she's coming to.

TRUEMAN [*to* MITROFÁN]: I know what to do with you, my young friend. You go and join the Service.

MITROFÁN [*with a wave of his hand*]: All right. I'll go where I'm told.

MRS SIMPLE [*coming to, in despair*]: I'm ruined entirely! My power has been taken from me! I can't show my face anywhere, for shame! I've lost my son!

OLDWISE [*pointing to* MRS SIMPLE]: There you have the deserved fruits of immorality!

CURTAIN

THE END OF THE COMEDY

Notes to *The Infant*

1. p. (48). In eighteenth-century Russia, a gentleman's son was called an 'Infant' (*nédorosl'*) until he was fifteen years old, when he became liable for military training. (See Introduction, Section 2.)
2. p. (48) No further indication of stage setting is given by the author; the time is round about 1782.
3. p. 59. By the Statute of 1775, which reorganized local administration, the Russian Empire was divided into fifty provinces, or 'governments', each of which was subdivided into districts. In some areas, a Governor-General (*Naméstnik*) was appointed with overall responsibility for a Lieutenancy, or group of about three provinces (*naméstnichestvo*).
4. p. 61. The Greek *Horologion*, like the Book of Hours and the Primer of the Western Church, was a shortened form of the monastic Divine Office, intended for use by the laity. The Russian version, like all other service-books, was printed in the medieval Church-Slavonic language. Although by now largely unintelligible to the Russian people, it was still used as a first reading-book for children.
5. p. 63. A *lezhánka*, or stove-bench, is a stone platform, big enough to lie on, jutting out from the side of a big stove and often independently heated.
6. p. 87. The woman who baked the bread used in Church at the celebration of the Holy Eucharist. (Compare Introduction, Section 6.)
7. p. 90. The Twenty-second Psalm.
8. p. 92. Ekaterinhof, outside St Petersburg.
9. p. 93. *Fort:* German for 'be off!'
10. p. 95. *De l'éducation des filles* was the first published work by François de Salignac de Lamothe-Fénelon (1651–1715), tutor to the sons of the Dauphin and later Archbishop of Cambray. His best-known book is *Les aventures de Télémaque*, a tale of the son of Ulysses, which also embodies his views on education. Sophia is exceptionally well-educated for an age when Russian ladies were still quite often illiterate; she can even read French, and it is significant that her uncle apparently cannot.
11. p. 104. In other words, he was a beast (Genesis I 24–27).
12. p. 104. Mr Beast claims descent from the Medieval Russian nobility. As such, he considers himself a cut above a 'simple gentlewoman', a daughter, that is, of one of the newer 'serving gentry' whose family honours had been granted for service to the Tsar.

13. p. 108 Mr Beast's uncle is called in the original Vavíla Falaléyich. The christian name Vavíla is the Russian form of the name of the Syrian martyr St Babylas (+ 250A.D.), whom few remember in England today; St Aldhelm wrote a life of him at Sherborne Abbey in the Seventh century! The name Oliver, used in the translation, was suggested by the patronymic; Falaléy is a Russianization of the Greek *thallos elaias* - an olive branch.

14. p. 112. Quite untrue, of course of eighteenth-century Russia, but Fonvízin seems to have regarded the legal institution of serfdom as susceptible of abuse, rather than inherently evil. (See Introduction Section 2.)

15. p. 117. The decree of Tsar Peter III of 1762, relieving the gentry-class of their obligations to serve the state and educate their children. (See Introduction, Section 2.)

CHATSKY

or

THE MISERY OF HAVING A MIND

A Comedy in Verse in Four Acts by

Alexander Sergeyevich Griboyédov

'Fate's a practical joker, giving out presents;
Each one gets what she thinks is a suitable kind:
For fools – the bliss of being mindless,
For the wise – the misery of having a mind.'

CHARACTERS

PAUL FÁMUSOV, director of a Government office

SOPHIE, his daughter

LIZA, Sophie's maid

ALEXIS MOLCHÁLIN, Fámusov's secretary, living at his house

ALEXANDER CHÁTSKY

COLONEL SERGE SKALOZÚB

NATHALIE and PLATO GÓRICH, a young married couple

PRINCE TUGO-ÚKHOVSKY, the PRINCESS his wife, and their six daughters

COUNTESS KHRYÚMINA the elder ('Grandmother Countess')

COUNTESS KHRYÚMINA the younger ('Granddaughter Countess')

ANTHONY ZAGORÉTSKY

MISS KHLYÓSTOVA, an old lady, Fámusov's sister-in-law

MR N.

MR D.

REPETÍLOV

PETER, Fámusov's manservant, and some other servants with speaking parts

Waiters at Fámusov's house. The Porter. Numerous guests of various types and (when they drive away) their footmen

The action takes place on a wintry day in the early 1820s, at FÁMUSOV'S *house in Moscow*

ACT ONE

The Drawing room; large grandfather clock; door right leading to
SOPHIE'S *bedroom, whence can be heard a piano with a flute,*
which presently stop; LIZA *is asleep in the middle of the room,*
dangling over an armchair. It is morning and day is just
breaking.

LIZA [*suddenly wakes up, gets up out of the chair, looks around her*]:
   It's getting light! Oh! Didn't the night go quick!
   I asked to go to bed, but 'No,
Our friend is coming, somebody must keep watch,
So you can stay awake   till you roll out of the chair.'
   I must have nodded off just now
And it's day! They'll have to be told!
      [*Knocks on* SOPHIE'S *door.*]
                                        Excuse me, please
   I say, Miss Sophie, this won't do!
You've gone and kept your party up all night!
Have you gone deaf? Mr Molchálin Sir
Miss Sophie, Miss . . . They're not a bit afraid!
      [*Comes away from the door.*]
Why, somebody who hasn't been invited
   Might come, and that's Papa!
Give me a post with a young lady in love!
      [*Goes back to the door.*]
   Come on Miss, break it up – it's morning!
SOPHIE [*off*]: What time is it?
LIZA: Everyone else is up.
SOPHIE [*from inside her room*]:
   What time is it?
LIZA: Past six . . . past seven . . . past eight

127

SOPHIE [*still from inside*]:
  It can't be.
LIZA [*coming away from the door*]:
                  Oh! Curse Cupid!
They hear all right, but just won't take it in;
Come on, we've got to get their shutters down!
There'll be a fuss, I know, but I'll put the clock on
    I'll make the music play.
    [*Climbs on a chair and moves the hand of the clock, which
    strikes the hour and plays a tune. Enter* FÁMUSOV.]
LIZA: Oh! It's the Master!
FÁMUSOV: Yes, it is the Master.
    [*Stops the clock music.*]
  So you're the joker, little hussy!
I couldn't think whatever was the matter,
I heard a flute, and then (I thought) a pianoforte.
  Couldn't be Sophie's; much too early . . .
LIZA: No Sir . . . You see . . . I accidentally . . .
FÁMUSOV: You accidentally! Your sort need to be watched!
    Of course it was on purpose . . .
  [*Squeezes and fondles her.*]
  Oh, you bad thing, you naughty little girl!
LIZA: Naughty boy, you!
Do you think it suits you to go on like that?
FÁMUSOV: So prim, and yet
There's nothing in this head but fooleries and nonsense.
LIZA: Nonsense yourself, Sir, let me go!
Remember now, you're an old gentleman.
FÁMUSOV: Hardly . . .
LIZA: What are we going to do, if someone comes?
FÁMUSOV: Who's going to come this way?
  Sophie's asleep – yes?
LIZA: Gone to bed just now.
FÁMUSOV: Now? What about last night?
LIZA·   She read all night.

FÁMUSOV: Whatever made her want to do a thing like that!

LIZA: She shut herself in there   all night and read aloud,
In French.

FÁMUSOV: Tell her, it's no use ruining her eyesight.
You can't get much good out of reading;
French books keep her awake   all night, and Russian ones
Send me right off.

LIZA: I'll tell her, Sir, as soon as she gets up.
And now please go, or I'm afraid you'll wake her.

FÁMUSOV: Wake her? And it was you who turned the
clock on
Blaring out symphonies for all the neighbours.

LIZA [*at the top of her voice*]:
Will you have done Sir!

FÁMUSOV [*stopping her mouth*]: Gracious, how you scream!
Are you going off your head?

LIZA: I'll tell you now, what I'm afraid of . . .

FÁMUSOV: Well?

LIZA: You ought to know by now Sir, you're no baby
How delicate is a young girl's morning sleep
You've only got to scrape a door, or whisper
They're sure to hear.

FÁMUSOV: You're sure to lie.

SOPHIE [*off*]: Hey, Liza!

FÁMUSOV [*hastily*]:   Sh!
[*He steals away from the room on tiptoe.*]

LIZA: He's gone! Oh! keep us clear of
gentry!
Look out for trouble every day with them,
And may we miss the worst of all
The Master's temper and the Master's love.
[*Enter from bedroom* SOPHIE *with a candle in her hand,
behind her* MOLCHÁLIN.]

SOPHIE: Liza, whatever happened to you?
That noise . . .

LIZA: Of course, it's hard for you to part
Shut up in there all night, and call that nothing?
SOPHIE: Oh, but it really has got light! [*Puts the candle out.*]
Here's light, and sadness ... don't the nights go quickly!
LIZA: Then you may pine away, it's hard enough
For other folk as well; your Father's been along –
    I nearly died!
I played him up – I don't know what I told him ...
What are you waiting for, Sir? Make your bow
    And go, with your heart in your mouth ...
Do you see the clock? Well, now look out of the window!
There have been people in the street for ages,
And stumping round indoors, sweeping and dusting.
SOPHIE: People don't watch the clock when they are happy.
LIZA: Don't then – it's up to you.
There's always me to take the consequences.
SOPHIE [*to* MOLCHÁLIN]:
Go on! ... Another endless boring day ...
LIZA: Oh come along, hands off!
    [*She parts them;* MOLCHÁLIN *collides in the doorway with*
    FÁMUSOV.]
FÁMUSOV: Hello, what's this? Molchálin, is it you, boy?
MOLCHÁLIN: Yes, Sir.
FÁMUSOV: What are you doing here? And at this hour?
    And Sophie too! ... Good morning, Sophie!
You *are* an early riser ... What's the matter?
And what brings you together at this odd time?
SOPHIE: He's just come in.
MOLCHÁLIN: I'm just back from a walk ...
FÁMUSOV: My friend, why don't you take your walks
In some sequestered spot – further afield?
And as for you, Miss, jumping out of bed
    To meet a man, a *young* man!
Is that the sort of thing a girl should do?

All night she goes on reading made-up stories
  And now we see what comes of books!
It's shops, shops, shops and everlasting Frenchmen.
That's where we get our fashions, authors, muses,
The ruination of our hearts and pockets!
Oh, when will the Good Lord deliver us
From all their hats and bonnets, pins and brooches,
  Their bookshops and their cake-shops!

SOPHIE: Please, dear Papa, my head is going round . . .
You gave me such a fright . . . It took my breath away!
You see . . . you dashed in here so suddenly –
  I'm all upset . . .

FÁMUSOV: Well, thank you kindly,
  So, I came dashing in on them too quickly
  I upset them! I frightened them!
Sophia! I'm put out, myself. I get no rest,
  Rushing about all day like a scalded cat
  And worrying over my Service duties:
  One buttonholes me, then another does
    They all want me!
  Hadn't I had enough of worry then,
  That I should be deceived?

SOPHIE [in tears]:   Papa! By whom?

FÁMUSOV: There! Now I'm going to get it!
They'll say that I'm unreasonable, and scold!
  Don't cry: I'm talking sense.
What about all the thought and care I gave
  To your upbringing – from the cradle!
Your Mother died, and I found Madame Rosier
  To be a second mother to you.
A treasure, that old woman was! So quiet,
So understanding, such high principles!
One thing was not entirely to her credit
When someone offered her five hundred more, she went.
  But never mind about Madame.

You don't want any other model now;
  Before your eyes you have – your Father!
You look at me, I hardly like to boast –
I've lived to see my hair grey – hale and hearty –
A widower, I'm free, I'm my own master;
And, I'm well known for my monastic way of life.
LIZA: If I may say so Sir . . .
FÁMUSOV: Be quiet!
Whatever can one do? This awful generation!
  They're all of them up to precocious tricks,
Daughters the worst of all. We parents are soft fools
  Gone crazy over foreign nations!
We find some penniless waifs, we take them in our houses,
Or pay them by the hour, as tutors for our daughters,
To teach 'em dancing, singing, sighs, tenderness, all that!
As if we'd bring 'em up to marry strolling players!
Now, Mr Visitor, what are you doing here?
You were a nobody. I took you in my household,
Got you a Grade Eight post, [1] made you my secretary,
Got you your transfer here; had it not been for me,
  You'd still be slaving out at Tver! [2]
SOPHIE: Why are you cross? I really can't imagine.
  Poor man, he happens to live in this house;
He made for one room and he landed in another.
FÁMUSOV: Where did he mean to land, I wonder?
But why together then? Can't be coincidence. . . .
SOPHIE: Coincidence is what it is however;
  When you and Liza were in here just now
  Your voice gave me a dreadful fright, and I
    Came rushing in . . .
FÁMUSOV: All right, then, I'm to blame for all the rumpus:
  I scared them with my voice at the wrong moment.
SOPHIE: It doesn't take a lot to scare a person
  After a nightmare; if I tell you about it,
    You'll understand.

FÁMUSOV: Why, what's all this?

SOPHIE: Shall I tell my dream?

FÁMUSOV: Go on
[*Sits down.*]

SOPHIE: Well, if I may . . . you see . . . at first there is
A flowery meadow, and I am looking for
    Some plant . . .
I don't remember now what sort it was.
Suddenly, someone very nice, the kind
  You meet, and feel you've always known,
Appears beside me . . . clever and attractive,
But shy . . . you know . . . someone who was born poor . . .

FÁMUSOV: My dear girl, let me off the rest of that!
  No poor man is a match for you.

SOPHIE: Then it all vanishes . . . the skies and meadow . . .
And we're in a dark room. Then, stranger still
  The floor bursts open, and you shoot out
As pale as death, your hair standing on end!
  Then there's a bang; the doors swing back,
And Things, not beasts, not people, come between us
And torture him who had sat there by me.
    He is, it seems,
My very dearest treasure of all treasures!
I try to get to him, you drag me back
    And all the while
The monsters moan, and roar, and laugh and whistle!
    And he calls after us!
Then I woke up . . . I heard somebody talking.
It was your voice. 'But why,' thought I, 'so early?'
  I ran in here and found you both.

FÁMUSOV: Yes, I can see, that was a horrid dream,
Everything in it, unless it be deceit:
Devils and love and flowers and terrors . . . Now, Sir,
What about you?

MOLCHÁLIN: I heard your voice . . .

FÁMUSOV: Now, that's amusing!
  My fascinating voice! So clear it rings
  And calls them all together, before the dawn!
  You rushed towards my voice . . . what for? . . . Come on!
MOLCHÁLIN: With papers, Sir.
FÁMUSOV: Well, that is the last straw!
  But, gracious me! What has come over you . . .
    This sudden zeal for paper-work?
      [*He gets up.*]
  Sophie, my dear, I'm going to let you rest;
  One sees queer things in sleep and queerer still awake –
  You went to look for plants, and found a friend instead . . .
    You'd better clear your head of rubbish!
  Where there are miracles, there's not much sense.
  Go back to bed, and go to sleep again.
[*To* MOLCHÁLIN]   Come on, let's see those papers.
MOLCHÁLIN: I thought I ought to show them to you, Sir,
  They can't go out as they stand . . . they're inconsistent
  In several ways, and lots of things aren't right.
FÁMUSOV: Sir, of one thing I live in mortal dread . . .
    Accumulating THAT STUFF!
  If I gave you your head, we'd be jammed up.
  But, whether anything is sense or nonsense
  I've got a rule in life – what's signed is signed
    It's off my back.
      [*Exit with* MOLCHÁLIN, *whom he lets through the door
      ahead of himself.*]
LIZA: Now wasn't that a lark! There's fun for you!
    But no, it's past a joke
  When eyes go dim and one is ready to faint;
  No harm in sin – till people start to talk.
SOPHIE: What do I care for talk? Let them think what
they like!
  Papa's the one to mind about;
  He's mean, never lets up, jumps to conclusions,

He's always been like that – now you can judge.

LIZA: Yes, Miss, I can. And not by hearsay.
Suppose he locks you up? It'll be all right
If I'm inside with you   but if I'm not, God help us,
Mr Molchálin and me,   we'll all be out in the street.

SOPHIE: You know, one's luck is so capricious!
Some people do worse things, and go scot-free.
But there we were, without a thought of sorrow,
Lost in the music . . . time went sailing by . . .
   You'd think that Fate was on our side,
Never a doubt, nothing to worry us . . .
And all the while, disaster round the corner!

LIZA: Well, there you are! You never bother, Miss,
To notice what you're told by silly me,
   Till suddenly – there's trouble!
Could anybody else   have given clearer warning?
I told you, nothing good would come of this love,
   World without end, Amen.
Your Dad's like all the Moscow gentlemen,
He wants a high-up son-in-law, with medals.
Now some, between ourselves,   have medals, but no money,
   And so, of course, he must be rich as well,
Able to live in style, and to give balls;
   There's Colonel Skalozúb, for instance,
Got pots of cash and aims   to be a general.

SOPHIE: What a nice man! Isn't it fun for me
To be told all about his lines and columns!
He hasn't made one sensible remark
   Since he was born!
I'd as soon drown myself as marry him.

LIZA: Yes, Miss, he talks a lot   and isn't very clever
   But, in or out of uniform,
Where will you find the sensibility
The gaiety, the wit, of Mr Chátsky?
   Of course, I don't want to upset you . . .

It's an old story, let's not rake it up . . .
But one remembers . . .
SOPHIE: What does one remember?
   He has the gift
Of making everybody else look silly,
  His chatter and his jokes amuse me.
And one's allowed to share   a joke with anybody.
LIZA: As if that's all! He was in floods of tears,
  Poor man, the day he said good-bye to you.
  'Why are you crying, Sir, Come, live and laugh!'
  And I remember what his answer was
  'It's not for nothing, Liza, that I'm crying.
  Who knows what I shall find, when I get back,
   Or what I may be giving up?'
  If he had known, poor thing, that three years later . . .
SOPHIE: Look here, don't you go taking liberties.
  I may have been extremely silly –
  I know, I blame myself, but who can say
  That I was fickle, or broke faith with him?
  Of course, I was brought up with Mr Chátsky
  We used to go about all day together
  And had a childhood friendship, till in the end
  He left us – seemingly our place had bored him –
   And didn't often come to see us.
  Then he came dashing back again, a lover,
   Very demanding, very touchy . . .
  He's eloquent, he's witty and he's clever,
  Exceptionally lucky in his friends –
  So he begins to think a lot of himself,
   And gets the urge to wander . . .
  Oh! If you are in love with somebody,
  Why all this cleverness and all this travel!
LIZA: Where is he off to now? What countries?
  They say, he went for a cure to take the waters.
   Most likely, his complaint was boredom.

136

SOPHIE: Sure, he'll be happy where he can laugh at people.
  The man I love is not like him.
 Mr Molchálin can forget himself
 And think of others, never gives offence,
  So modest always, and so bashful . . .
 Who else could stay all night with me like that?
 There we two sat, till the sky was light outdoors,
 What do you think we were doing?
LIZA: Goodness knows!
    Is it my place to say, Miss?
SOPHIE: He took my hand, and pressed it to his heart.
 And gave a sigh that came from his very soul.
 Never a risky word, and so the night passed by,
 Hands joined, and never once   did he take his eyes off
 me . . .
    You're laughing! Really now!
 What have I done, to start you off guffawing?
LIZA: Please Miss . . . I suddenly remembered
    About your Auntie . . .
 The time the young French boy ran away from her house.
 Poor dear! She couldn't hide her disappointment.
  So, she forgot to dye her hair
  And, after three days – she was grey! !
[*She goes on laughing.*]
SOPHIE [*offended*]:
Some day I'll be the one   they talk about like that.
LIZA: I'm sorry Miss. Honest to God,
 I only hoped perhaps my silly laughter
 Might cheer you up a little.
    [*Enter a Servant, followed by* CHÁTSKY.]
SERVANT: Mr Chátsky.   [*Exit.*]
CHÁTSKY: It's peep of day! You're up! And I am at your
feet.
    [*Fervently kisses her hand.*]
 Come on, a kiss! You weren't expecting me?

You're pleased to see me? No? Look in my face.
Surprised? No more than that? What a reception!
  As if it hadn't been a week,
As if it had been yesterday we met
And we had bored each other to extinction.
Love? Not a bit of it! Aren't you a fine one!
And I came blindly on, half in a daze,
Forty-five hours without a wink of sleep . . .
Nearly five hundred miles of tearing through the blizzards
I'm in a proper state, I've had so many spills.
  What a reward for my devotion!
SOPHIE: Oh, Mr Chátsky, I'm very pleased to see you.
CHÁTSKY: You are? That's good! But, even so,
  How does one act when one is *really* pleased?
  It seems to me that all I've done
  Is to get men and horses shrammed with cold,
    Just to amuse myself.
LIZA: Why, Sir, you should have been behind that door,
  I swear it, not five minutes ago.
Here in this room we were talking about you.
    Tell him yourself, Miss.
SOPHIE: Not only now, we always talked about you.
  You haven't any reason to reproach me;
  When anyone called, or looked in at that door,
    On his way through, or casually,
    Coming from foreign parts, or far away,
  I always asked (I even asked the sailors)
  Whether they'd met your post-chaise anywhere.
CHÁTSKY: Let's have it so, then.
Blessed is he that believes; he lives in a cosy world!
  O Lord! And am I here again,
In Moscow, at your house? And do I recognize you?
  Where are those days, the age of innocence,
    When, through long evenings, we two
  Appeared and disappeared, now here, now there,

Playing and romping round   among the chairs and tables ...
And your Papa sat – here,   with Madame, at piquet.
Wasn't it over there   we hid in the dark corner? ...
Remember how we jumped,   when doors or tables creaked?
SOPHIE: Nursery days!
CHÁTSKY: Yes, Miss, and now you're seventeen
  You've blossomed out, you're fascinating,
  Inimitable, and you know it too.
  That's why you're prim, why you won't look at people.
  Are you in love? I want an answer, please.
   Don't stop to think! Don't get so flustered!
SOPHIE: But it's enough to fluster anyone,
The way you stare at me   the way you fire off questions.
CHÁTSKY: Heavens! What else is there to wonder at,
  But you? And what has Moscow new to show me?
There was a ball last night,   tomorrow there'll be two –
Someone has got engaged,   and someone else has not –
  The same old talk, the same old album verses.
SOPHIE: Running down Moscow!
  That comes of seeing the world! Where is there better?
CHÁTSKY: Where there are none of us.
  Well – your Papa? Still at the English Club?
  The old-established, faithful, lifelong member?
     Your uncle? Still hopping round?
  Or has he hopped away to Kingdom Come?
  And ... what d'ye call him? ... Is he a Turk or a Greek? ...
  That dusky chap, long-legged like a stork. . .³
     I don't know what his name is.
  But, any place you go, he's always there
  At dinner-tables and in drawing rooms ...
     And then, the Boulevard Trio,
  Who have been keeping young for fifty years?
  They have relations by the million,
  And, with their sisters' help, they'll get in-laws
     All over Europe.

And what about Our Lovely One, Our Treasure?
Theatre and masquerade stamped on his forehead,
His house all painted like a greenwood scene . . .
  He's fat himself – unlike his artistes . . .
Do you remember the ball, when you and I
Got in behind a screen, in a secret room;
And found a man doing the nightingale –
The bird of summertime, singing in winter?
Then there's that man with the cough, who hates all books
    (A relative of yours)
They put him on the Education Panel[4]
    And he began to rant,
  Calling on one and all to swear an oath
That nobody should read, nor write, nor ever learn!
Is it my fate to see all them again?
  One soon gets tired of living with them,
Where is the man in whom no fault is found?
But, travel about a while, come back, and then –
'Even the smoke of home smells sweet and lovely'![5]
SOPHIE: You and my aunt should get together,
And make a catalogue of everyone we know!
CHÁTSKY: Your aunt? She's still unmarried? Still Minerva?
Ninety years' service as a Maid of Honour?[6]
Pugs and adopted daughters all over the house?
  Ah, that reminds me, education . . .
Still what it used to be in olden times –
Teachers recruited in battalions,
The greatest number at the cheapest rate?
Not that they need to be far gone in studies . . .
  For, we in Russia are commanded,
On pain of heavy fines, to cry up each man-jack
  As an historian and geographer!
Our tutor! Do you remember his cap and gown,
His index finger, all the signs of learning
How it all terrified our tender minds!

And how we came to believe, in early life
That without Germans we could not be saved!
And, Monsieur Guillaumet, the flippant Frenchman,
  Is he not married yet?
SOPHIE: Who to?
CHÁTSKY: Some dowager princess – Pulcheria for instance?
SOPHIE: The dancing-master! Come!
CHÁTSKY: Why not? He is a partner.
We are supposed to have high rank, and property.
  But Guillaumet . . . So, what's the present form
  At big assemblies and parochial fêtes;
  Still the confusion of tongues, with those of France
  And Nízhni-Nóvgorod prevailing?[7]
SOPHIE: A blend of tongues?
CHÁTSKY: Yes – always must have two.
LIZA: It'd want a clever man to make one more like
yours.
CHÁTSKY: At least it isn't pompous.
How strange! I take advantage of the moment,
  I'm all excited, meeting you,
And full of talk, but can't I sometimes be
  More fatuous even than Molchálin?
Where is he, by the way? Are his lips still sealed?
If he had seen a nice new song-book anywhere
He used to pester us 'Please could he have it copied?'
For all that, *he'll* get somewhere – nowadays
They like the dumb sort that don't answer back.
SOPHIE [*aside*]: It isn't human – it's a snake!
    [*Aloud, and in a forced voice*]
I'd like to ask you . . . has it ever happened
That laughing, or in grief, or by mistake,
You have said something kind about some person?
Not now, perhaps . . . maybe when you were little?
CHÁTSKY: When all was soft, and immature and tender?
Why go all that way back? What about you for kindness?

There was I, night and day,
The sleigh-bells tinkling in a desert of snow,
  Driving like mad to get to you . . .
How do I find you? All formality!
For half an hour I have endured your coolness;
  Doing the pious little saint!
And yet, I'm helplessly in love with you.
    [*A moment's silence.*]
Listen, is everything I say so cutting?
  And is it always meant to hurt?
If so, it's out of tune with what is in my heart.
  I see the funny side of some queer fellow,
    I laugh, and then forget about it;
But, order me into the fire, and I'll go, as I would to a
feast.

SOPHIE: That's all right if you burn – suppose you don't?
    [*Re-enter* FÁMUSOV.]

FÁMUSOV Another one!

SOPHIE: Papa! my dream come true!
    [*Exeunt* SOPHIE *and* LIZA.]

FÁMUSOV [*muttering after her*]:
Confounded dream!
    [*Speaks aloud, to* CHÁTSKY, *who is looking towards the door
    through which* SOPHIE *has gone out.*]
                    Well now, you've sprung one on us!
  Three years, and never write a line,
And then drop in, like a bolt out of the blue!
Hullo my dear, hullo my boy, hullo!
    [*They embrace.*]
  Let's have the story, I bet you've got a budget
  Of weighty news, come on and tell us! [*They sit down.*]

CHÁTSKY [*absent-mindedly*]
Your daughter Sophie, hasn't she got pretty!

FÁMUSOV: All you young men, you've nothing else to do
  But pass remarks about the girl's appearance.

142

She lets a word slip out,
And I suppose you're full of hopes, bewitched . . .

CHÁTSKY: Oh no! I haven't got   a lot of hopes to fool me.

FÁMUSOV: 'My dream come-true'
That is what our young lady whispered to me,
And so you thought . . .

CHÁTSKY: Me? Not a bit of it!

FÁMUSOV: Who did she dream about? What was the
dream?

CHÁTSKY: I'm not a dream-diviner.

FÁMUSOV: Don't you believe her –
All rubbish.

CHÁTSKY: What I believe is my own eyes.
I'll take my oath, never in all my days
Have I seen anything to equal her!

FÁMUSOV: He just goes on! But tell us properly
Where have you been, wandering all these years?
Where have you come from?

CHÁTSKY: I can't tell you now!
I meant to go all over the whole world,
And haven't seen the hundredth part of it!
    [Gets quickly up.]
Excuse me! I was in a terrible hurry
To see you, and I haven't yet been home.
    Good-bye! I'll be back in an hour,
And then I won't forget the smallest details
You'll have it first, and you can tell the others.
    [In the doorway]   So pretty!   [Exit.]

FÁMUSOV: [Alone]
Which of them is it then? 'Papa! my dream come true!'
    She said that to me, right out loud!
Well, I was wrong,   I'd gone completely off the track!
I'd had my doubts of late about Molchálin,
    But now . . .
Out of the frying-pan, into the fire!

That pauper, and this other fancy-friend,
Notoriously extravagant and wild . . .
What a commission Thou gavest me, O Lord,
Making me father of a grown-up daughter! [*Exit.*]

ACT TWO

FÁMUSOV: Peter, you're always one for something new
You've got your elbow torn, fetch me the almanack;
Now read, not like the Parish Clerk
But sensibly, with feeling, making pauses.
Wait now, turn to the page marked 'Memoranda':
Put down an invitation
From Parasceva – Tuesday of next week –
We're to have trout. The world is wonderfully made!
Philosophize, and you go dizzy . . .
Try to be careful, then – a dinner party:
Three hours of eating, three days' indigestion.
Put down same day – no, no!
Thursday it is I have the funeral.
Ah human race! You had forgotten
That each of you himself must creep into that box,
Where there's no standing, and no sitting up
But if you want to leave a name behind you,
Here's your example of a life well lived:
An Honourable Gentleman-in-waiting,
He wore the Chamberlain's key, he got it for his son. [8]
Wealthy, and married to a wealthy wife,
His children married off, grandchildren too.
He dies, and everyone remembers him with sorrow
'Kuzmá Petróvich – Rest his Soul!'
Ah what grand men they be, that live and die in Moscow!
Put down – Thursday again – one thing after another –
Or could be Friday, even Saturday,

I've got the christening   to go to, at the Widow's.
The Doctor's wife as was; she hasn't had the baby –
  But, counting up, I make it time she did.
     [*Enter* CHÁTSKY.]
  Ah, that you, Chátsky? Please come in
  And take a chair.
CHÁTSKY: You're busy?
FÁMUSOV [*to* PETER]:   You may go.
     [*Exit* PETER.]
  Yes, we were making notes of this and that,
     Things get so easily forgotten . . .
CHÁTSKY: You somehow don't seem to be very gay.
Tell me, is something wrong? I've come at a bad time?
Has something happened that   distressed your daughter
Sophie?
  You're looking, moving, like a worried man.
FÁMUSOV: Ah, my dear chap, you've solved the riddle!
  I am not gay, but when one gets to my age
  One can't squat down, kick out one's legs, and dance.
CHÁTSKY: Nobody wants you to do that;
I simply asked one thing   about your daughter Sophie;
     Is she perhaps not well?
FÁMUSOV: Tcha! God forgive me! Fifty thousand times
     He says the same old thing.
First, nobody on earth   can touch my daughter Sophie,
     And now, my daughter Sophie's ill!
        Tell me – you like her?
You've been all round the world – won't you be getting
married?
CHÁTSKY: Why do you ask?
FÁMUSOV: No harm,   if you were to ask me.
  You see, I am a kind of relative
At least, I've always been   supposed to be her father.
CHÁTSKY: What would you say, then, if I did come for her?
FÁMUSOV: Firstly I'd say – Don't play the fool,

And don't be slapdash, man, with property,
And, most important – go; do something, in the Service.
CHÁTSKY: I'd like the Service.
It's the servility that makes me sick.
FÁMUSOV: Ah! There you go! You're all so proud!
What did your fathers do? You should inquire,
And learn from the example of your elders;
People like me, or my lamented uncle.
My Uncle Maxim had no silver dinner-service,
He ate off gold! He kept a hundred servants!
Rode in a coach-and-six whenever he went out,
   Covered in medals!
Lived all his life at Court and what a court that was!
   Not like they have today;
He served Her Majesty the Empress Catherine!
When there were men of weight – two ton apiece –
Who didn't even nod when people bowed to them.
   Great lords in office – grander still;
They neither ate nor drank like other folk.
But Uncle! Where's your Prince or Count beside him?
His grave expression, and his haughty air!
Yet, when he'd got to show obsequiousness,
   He could bend over double too!
Once, on a levée day at Court, he tripped on something,
Fell backwards, nearly cracked his occiput –
   The old man gave a deathly groan . . .
There was vouchsafed to him the Smile of the All-Highest.
The Lady deigns to laugh – what does he do?
Gets up, straightens himself prepares to make his bow
   Tumbles again – this time on purpose;
Laughter grows louder still – he does it all a third time!
What do you think of that? I call it clever;
   He fell down sick, he rose up sound.
Who, after that, gets asked to whist most often?
Who comes to court, and hears a word of welcome?

My Uncle Maxim! Whom   does everyone respect?
  Joking apart – my Uncle Maxim!
  Who puts promotions through? Who gives out pensions?
  My Uncle Maxim! Yes, you modern men!
      Get along with you all!
CHÁTSKY: Indeed you might well sigh   and say the world's
gone silly,
  Looking at our age, and the age that's past.
It's well remembered still,   though hardly credible,
That honours went to him   that bowed his neck most often,
    And that it was in time of peace,
Not in the wars, that men   would put their heads in peril,
    And did not shrink
  From letting them go bump along the floor!
  Sneer at the needy – leave 'em in the dirt –
While weaving flatteries,   like lace around the mighty.
    The age of grovelling and terror!
That's what it was; disguised   as zeal to serve the Tsar.
    We won't disturb your Uncle's ashes;
I don't mean him – but who   would want to do it now,
  However keen he was to play the toady?
  Bravely to sacrifice his occiput
    Just to make people laugh!
  Only some little old contemporary
  Falling to bits inside his aged skin,
    Might perhaps say about those capers
  'Oh dear, why didn't that happen to me!'
  Of course, some people like that sort of thing;
  You find them everywhere, but nowadays
  They're curbed by shame, and fear of ridicule;
      And, understandably
They don't get very much   out of the Emperors.
FÁMUSOV: My God! He's joined the Carbonari![9]
CHÁTSKY: No, no! The world is not like that today.
FÁMUSOV: He's dangerous to know!

CHÁTSKY: People can breathe more freely,
There's no rush now to join   the regiment of buffoons.

FÁMUSOV: The things he says! And so pat with it all!

CHÁTSKY: To yawn at influential patrons' ceilings,
 To be seen and not heard, to kick one's heels, fetch chairs,
    To pick up handkerchiefs . . .

FÁMUSOV: He's on the verge of preaching liberty!

CHÁTSKY: People who travel, people who live in the
country . . .

FÁMUSOV: He doesn't recognize Authority!

CHÁTSKY: People who work for the job, not to please
others . . .

FÁMUSOV: I wouldn't ever have   those gentlemen allowed
 In gunshot range of Petersburg or Moscow.

CHÁTSKY: That's all; I'll let you have a rest.

FÁMUSOV: Exasperating! Unendurable!

CHÁTSKY: I've shewn no mercy to your generation;
    It's your turn now
 To throw some of it back at the modern age
    I won't cry if you do.

FÁMUSOV: I refuse to know you, Sir; I can't stand vice.

CHÁTSKY: I've finished speaking.

FÁMUSOV: Good, I've stopped my ears.

CHÁTSKY: What for? I shan't offend them.

FÁMUSOV [in a quick patter]:
 They go all round the world, they loaf about,
And then they come back here – so what can you expect!

CHÁTSKY: I'll say no more.

FÁMUSOV: Have mercy, I beseech you.

CHÁTSKY: I've no desire to go on arguing.

FÁMUSOV: Peace for one moment!
    [Enter Servant.]

SERVANT: Colonel Skalozúb.

FÁMUSOV [hearing and seeing nothing]:
 You'll be had up, as sure as eggs are eggs,

And put away.

CHÁTSKY: Somebody's come to call.

FÁMUSOV: Not listening! Had up!

CHÁTSKY: Your man's announcing someone.

FÁMUSOV: Not listening! Had up!   Had up!

CHÁTSKY: Turn round, you're wanted.

FÁMUSOV: [*turning round*]:

What? It's a mutiny? Now to see Hell break loose!

SERVANT: It's Colonel Skalozúb. Shall I show him up,
Sir?

FÁMUSOV [*getting up*]:   Asses! How often must I tell you?
Of course! Say 'Please come in'; say I'm at home!
Say I'm delighted. Off with you now and hurry.
      [*Exit* SERVANT]
Mind what you say, Sir, please, in front of this man;
  He is a most important person –
He has collected heaps of decorations,
Early promotion too, the lucky chap,
Any day now he'll be a general.
So please, no showing off in front of him;
  Chátsky, my boy, that's naughty of you!
He's always very good   about coming to see me –
  You know I'm pleased when anybody comes;
  But two and two makes five in Moscow.
In other words, they think   he'll marry little Sophie.
  Rubbish! Maybe there's nothing he'd like better,
But I don't see why I   should give away my daughter,
  Either this week or next – sure Sophie's young.
    But still – it's in the hands of God.
So please don't argue black   is white in front of him,
    And drop those cranky notions.
  But he's not here! What can have happened to him?
He must have gone for me   into the other room.
      [*He exits hurriedly.*]
CHÁTSKY [*alone*]:   What's all the fuss and all the hurry?

Sophie! Suppose she is getting engaged to someone,
 And that is why they treat me like a stranger?
  Then, why is she not here?
Who is this Skalozúb? Her father raves about him;
 Maybe he's not the only one who does . . .
  Ah, you may say farewell to love,
When you go on your travels for three years.

    [*Re-enter* FÁMUSOV *with* COLONEL SKALOZÚB.]

FÁMUSOV: Now, my dear Colonel, come this way.
 I do beseech you, Sir; it's warmer here.
 You're frozen with the cold – we'll get you warm
  Quick now, I'll open up the stove.

SKALOZÚB [*in a thick bass voice*]:
For goodness sake! You can't go clambering there yourself!
I am an officer and I'm a gentleman
  And I don't like it.

FÁMUSOV: Mustn't I do one thing to help my friends,
  My dear, dear Colonel?
 Put down your hat, Sir, and undo your sword.
 Spread yourself on the sofa, take it easy.

SKALOZÚB: Just as you say, if only you'll sit down.

    [*All three sit down –* CHÁTSKY *at a little distance*]

FÁMUSOV: Ah, my dear Sir, one thing, while I remember –
 May we regard ourselves as your relations?
Distant of course, no claim to share inheritance.
 Perhaps you didn't know, no more did I
Until the other day, your cousin kindly told me
 Where Anastásia Nikoláyevna
  Comes in on your side?

SKALOZÚB: Sorry, Sir, I don't know; I've never served
with her.

FÁMUSOV: Colonel! That isn't like you!
I feel quite overwhelmed when I discover kinship;
 I'd trace it to the bottom of the sea!

Very few people work   with me who aren't relations
  Most of them are my sister's children,
Or else my sister-in-law's;   there's only one exception –
Molchálin – that's because   he is so capable.
 But when it comes to putting up a name
 For a nice post, or some small decoration,
  One has to think of kith and kin!
 Your cousin told me – he's a friend of mine –
That he's had lots of help   from you, in his career.
SKALOZÚB: In the year '13 both of us got citations
In the 30th Chasseurs, and in the 45th.
FÁMUSOV: Happy the man who has a son like that!
Wasn't there something else   about a loop of ribbon
  With something pretty on the end?
SKALOZÚB: Stuck in the trenches on the Third of August;[10]
  He got a medal for it,
 And I was given a neck-decoration.
FÁMUSOV: Charming! And one can see   that he's the dashing type;
 Your cousin really is a splendid man!
SKALOZÚB: Oh, but he's all mixed up   with these new-fangled ways.
 Due for promotion, suddenly retired;
 Went to the country, started reading books.
FÁMUSOV: That's youth for you! They read – and then where are they?
  Now, you've done all the proper things.
Not in the Service long   and quite a senior Colonel.
SKALOZÚB: I had good luck with brother-officers;
You see, some senior men   were superannuated
  And others got killed off.
FÁMUSOV: Whom the Lord seeketh, him He raiseth up!
SKALOZÚB: One can have even better luck than mine;
 No need to look outside Fifteenth Division –
  Take now, our Brigadier.

FÁMUSOV: Goodness! What was there more you could have
had?

SKALOZÚB: I can't complain; I haven't been passed over
But still, it took two years to get a regiment.

FÁMUSOV: You were kept waiting for your colonelcy?
For something else, however, you'll come first –
The rest are nowhere.

SKALOZÚB: No Sir, there are some people in the Corps
Senior to me – I joined in eighteen-nine.
Yes, there are many channels for promotion –
I'm truly philosophical about it;
If only I could get to be a General.

FÁMUSOV: That's the right way to look at it; please God
You keep your health, and get made general.
But then, why put things off? Isn't it time
You broached the question of the General's lady?

SKALOZÚB: Marry? I don't mind if I do.

FÁMUSOV: Well? Someone's got a sister, niece, or daughter;
Moscow, you know, is never short of brides –
Short? Why, they get a fresh batch every year.
You must agree, my dear – go where you will
I don't suppose you'll find a capital like Moscow.

SKALOZÚB: Distances do pose problems of logistics.

FÁMUSOV: But, my dear Sir, we've got our taste, our
perfect style,
Our special rules for everything.
For instance, there's the immemorial custom
That sons inherit honours from their fathers;
A man may not be much himself – if he can muster
Two thousand souls on family estates,
He'll find a bride.
Someone else may be smart, stuffed with conceit;
Give him the name of being a clever chap
Nobody wants him in their family.
Whatever they may say about us,

This is the only place where gentle birth
    Still keeps its value.
And that's not all – take hospitality;
If anybody cares to come and see us,
   He's welcome – we keep open house.
It doesn't matter whether he's invited
(Specially when it comes to foreigners)
   Or whether he's an honest man.
It makes no odds to us   dinner is there for all.
   Take us from top to toe –
All Muscovites have got that special hall-mark.
Oblige me, please, by looking at our juniors;
   The boys, our sons and grandsons.
We grumble at them till – what do we find?
When they're fifteen, they start to teach their teachers!
And our old seniors? When the fire is in them,
   They speak their minds, lay down the law.
Look at their pedigrees! They don't care who you are!
  And, when they start about the government,
   It's just as well nobody's listening!
  Not that they want to see new ways brought in –
  No, no! Good gracious no! They storm along
   At this and that – sometimes at nothing –
  They argue and they rage, and then go home.
Such minds! You'd think they must   have all been Chancellors!
But, mark my words! Of course   the time's not ripe, but someday,
There'll be some work to do   that can't be done without them.
The ladies! Manage them?   Let's see you try to do it!
  They judge the world – nobody judges them!
And when a card table   explodes into a riot . . .
God give us patience; I   was married once myself.
   Put 'em to drill the troops on the parade-ground!

Send 'em and make 'em members of the Senate!
Irene Vlás'evna!   Glyceria Alexévna!
Tatiana Yúrevna!   Princess Pulcheria!
To see their daughters! That   would shatter anyone!
We had His Majesty   the King of Prussia here
  He was astounded by the Moscow girls;
    Not by their looks – by their deportment.
Indeed, could anyone   be better educated?
    For they can dress themselves
  In pretty velvets, taffetas and gauzes;
They never speak a word   without they pull a face;
  They'll sing you French Romances, and bring out
      All the top notes.
  They simply dote on military men,
    Because they are so patriotic.
    It's what I'm telling you; go where you will,
I don't suppose you'll find   a capital like Moscow.
SKALOZÚB: Well, I must say, I think the fire
Improved the look of Moscow quite a lot.
FÁMUSOV: Please don't remind us of it;
  The subject's still a very painful one!
    But since those days we've had
  Houses and streets and pavements – all brand new.
CHÁTSKY: New houses, but the same old prejudices;
Cheer up! Not years, nor fires   nor fashions can destroy
them.
FÁMUSOV [*To* CHÁTSKY]:
  Look here! You tie a knot in your handkerchief!
  I said keep quiet – it wasn't much to ask.
      [*To* SKALOZÚB]
  Sir, by your leave, I'd like to introduce . . .
Chátsky, a friend of mine,   old Andrew Chátsky's son.
  Not in the Service – doesn't see the point,
    But could be useful if he liked.
It's such a shame! The lad   has got a headpiece on him,

First rate at writing and translation.
A mind like his – one can't help feeling sorry.
CHÁTSKY: Have you got no one else   you must feel sorry
for?
It vexes me, even to hear you praise me!
FÁMUSOV: Not only me; all critics say the same.
CHÁTSKY: Critics – who are they? Men out of an antique age,
Relentlessly opposed,   therefore, to free existence!
   They dig up their ideas
From newspapers forgotten long ago –
'Ochákov stormed' 'Crim Tartary surrenders'[11]
   They're always ready, with a grumble,
   They're always harping on the same old string,
   Yet never realize that they themselves
   Are getting worse as they grow older.
Where are they, tell me now,   these fathers of our country,
   That we have got to take as an example?
   Are they the men, heavy with loot,
Whose friends and families   have saved them from the
Courts,
   Who build themselves enormous palaces,
   And fling their wealth about at feasts,
Where foreign hangers-on   would, if they could, revive
   The nastiest features of the Old Regime?
Does anyone live here   whose mouth they couldn't stop
   With dinners, balls and supper-parties?
   Or do you mean the man we used to visit
   When I was little, quite a baby?
I never did know why;   you must have had some reason
To take me when you went   to pay respects to him;
   That aged chieftain of the noble rips,
   Surrounded by the troop of servants,
   That took such care of him – time and again
   When he was fighting-drunk,
They saved his honour, even saved his life –

Till suddenly one day   he swapped them for three grey-
hounds![12]
  Is it the man who had the entertainments,
    The ballet troupe of serfs?
Many a waggon-load   of children he hauled in,
  Snatched from their mothers and their fathers.
Lost in his private dream   of little Loves, and Zephyrs
  Whose beauty was the wonder of the Town;
    Till he ran out of credit,
  And all the little Loves, and all the Zephyrs,
    Had to be sold in single lots!!![13]
  Those are the men who've lived to see grey hairs!
  The men we must respect – there's no one else!
  Those are our strict appraisers, and our critics!
    And now suppose that one of us,
That one young man is found   who doesn't tout for jobs,
  Who hasn't any use for rank and office,
    But thirsts for knowledge, set on study;
Or else, suppose the Lord   has raised in him a spirit
  Burning for beauty and creative art –
    They'll cry at once 'Fire, murder, thieves!'
  And he'll get called a dreamer! Dangerous!
  Uniform! Uniform's the only wear!
    In their young days,
  Gold lace and trimmings served to cover up
  Their feeble spirits and their want of wit;
So we must follow them   on that same road to fortune!
  Their wives and daughters too love uniform;
And, didn't I myself   once have a soft spot for it?
    And not so long ago, though now
  I have outgrown that sort of childishness . . .
  Yet, who would not have been swept off his feet
With all the rest of us   that time the Guards detachment
  Came to us from the Palace, on a visit?
    Hurrah! Hurrah!

The women cried and flung   their bonnets in the air!

FÁMUSOV [*to himself*]: He'll get me into trouble yet.

[*Aloud*]

Colonel, I'm going now   you'll find me in my study.

[*Exit* FÁMUSOV.]

SKALOZÚB: I rather liked the clever way you put it,

In your appreciation,

About the Moscow people's prejudice

In favour of their pets   – the Household Troops, the Guards!

They're dazzled by the gold and braid!

What's wrong with the First Army? Tell me that?

They're properly turned out, their waists are slim,

And I could even give   the names of officers

Who can talk French.

[*Enter* SOPHIE *followed by* LIZA. SOPHIE *runs over to the window.*]

SOPHIE: My God! He's fallen! He's killed!

[*She faints.*]

CHÁTSKY: Who is it?

SKALOZÚB: Who's been hurt?

CHÁTSKY: She's dead with fright.

SKALOZÚB: What's up? Who is it?

CHÁTSKY: What did he fall against?

SKALOZÚB: Don't tell me our old man has had a tumble?

LIZA [*busy over her mistress*]:

When a man's time has come   there's no avoiding Fate, Sir.

Mr Molchálin went to mount a horse.

He'd got his foot into the stirrup,

The horse reared and he fell – right on his head!

SKALOZÚB: Pulled on the reins! Well, he's a rotten horseman.

See where the damage is – his chest or side.

[*Exit* SKALOZÚB.]

CHÁTSKY: Tell me quick what to do to help her.

LIZA: There's water over in that room.
[CHÁTSKY *runs and fetches the water. What follows is all in
an undertone until* SOPHIE *comes round.*]

LIZA: Pour out a glass.

CHÁTSKY: Done that already.
Undo those laces, get them looser,
Rub vinegar upon her temples,
Sprinkle some water; there now, see
Her breathing's getting easier.
Something to fan her?

LIZA: Here's a fan.

CHÁTSKY: Look out of the window!
Molchálin's up, and on his feet already.
She gets herself upset for nothing.

LIZA: Yes, Sir, she's made like that, poor lady;
She can't stand by and watch, when people
Fall down head first.

CHÁTSKY: Sprinkle more water
That's it . . . go on . . . go on . . .

SOPHIE [*with a deep sigh*]:
Who's here with me? It's like a dream
[*Aloud and hurriedly.*]
Where is he? Tell me how he is!

CHÁTSKY: I don't care if he broke his neck;
He's very nearly been the death of you.

SOPHIE: Cold-blooded murderer! That's what you are!
I can't endure to see or hear you speak.

CHÁTSKY: You're telling me to worry about him?

SOPHIE: Run to him, go and see if you can help him.

CHÁTSKY: What? Leave you here alone and unattended?

SOPHIE: What does it matter about me?
Of course, you are amused by other people's troubles.
If your own father was killed, you wouldn't mind.
[*To* LIZA.]
Come, hurry up! Let's go!

159

LIZA [*taking her aside*]:   Steady now, Miss.
  Where are you off to? He's alive and well;
      Look out of the window!
      [SOPHIE *sticks her head out of the window.*]
CHÁTSKY: Distraught and fainting! Flustered, scared and angry!
  No one could get in such a state
Unless they were about to lose their only friend.
SOPHIE: They're coming in. He can't lift up his arm.
CHÁTSKY: I wouldn't mind if I was 'killed' like that as well . . .
LIZA: For company?
SOPHIE: No, leave it at the wish.
      [*Enter* SKALOZÚB *and* MOLCHÁLIN, *with his arm in a sling.*]
SKALOZÚB: Up and unhurt! His hand is slightly bruised;
  It's nothing but a false alarm.
MOLCHÁLIN: I must have frightened you; do please forgive me.
SKALOZÚB: Well, I was not to know why you were apprehensive.
  It made us jump, you rushing in like that,
    And fainting. All that fright for nothing.
SOPHIE [*not looking at anybody*]:
  I do see now, it wasn't serious
And yet, I'm shaking still.
CHÁTSKY [*to himself*]:   Not one word to Molchálin.
SOPHIE [*as before*]:   I will say this; I'm not a coward
  When I'm involved in accidents myself.
The carriage overturns – put it back on the road;
  I'm ready to go on again, full gallop.
  But the least thing involving other people
      Terrifies me –
  Even although it isn't serious
Or someone I don't know; that makes no difference.

CHÁTSKY [*to himself*]:   She wants him to excuse her
For having once felt sorry about someone!
SKALOZÚB: May I tell you a story?
There's someone here called Princess Lásova
  She is a widow, and she rides,
Though gentlemen don't often ride with her.
  The other day, she came a purler;
Her groom was half asleep or he'd have held her up . . .
Besides, she's got the name of being clumsy . . .
  So, now she's one rib short,
And looking for a husband – to support her.
SOPHIE: Now, Mr Chátsky
Lct's see you show yourself a real big-hearted man;
You're always so concerned   about your neighbour's
troubles.
CHÁTSKY: But that's exactly what I've just been doing!
  I took a lot of pains,
By dint of sprinkling you, and chafing you
To bring you back to life; who for, I do not know.
  [*Takes his hat and goes out.*]
SOPHIE: You'll come to us this evening?
SKALOZÚB: Is it early?
SOPHIE: Early-ish. Just a few friends of the family,
  A little dancing to the pianoforte;
We mustn't have a ball, as we're in mourning.
SKALOZÚB: I'll come, but I did promise your Papa,
  That I'd look in on him.
If you'll excuse me now.
SOPHIE: Good-bye.
SKALOZÚB [*shaking hands with* MOLCHÁLIN]:Your
                                              servant.
  [*Exit* SKALOZÚB.]
SOPHIE: Mr Molchálin!
I wonder that I'm still in my right mind!
You know how precious your life is to me,

Why play with it, in such a reckless way?
  Tell me, how is your arm?
Shall I give you the drops? Hadn't you better rest?
  Let's get the doctor, mustn't take it lightly.

MOLCHÁLIN: I used my handkerchief
  To tie it up. It hasn't hurt since then.

LIZA: I bet it's nothing serious;
He wouldn't want a sling only it looks becoming.
  I tell you though what will be serious –
  The talk! You can't escape it; Mr Chátsky
  Is going to have some fun, at your expense.
    The Colonel too, spinning his yarns,
  Will pile it on about the way you fainted.
  He's a great joker, aren't they all today?

SOPHIE: As if any of them mattered to me!
  I'll love if I want to, and I'll tell if I want to!
    Mr Molchálin!
  I did restrain myself, now didn't I?
  I never said one word when you came in,
  I didn't dare to breathe in front of them,
  Or ask you how you were, or look at you.

MOLCHÁLIN: Oh, no, Miss Sophie, you were much too
frank.

SOPHIE: How could I help giving myself away?
  I could have jumped out of that window to you.
  Who do I care for? Them? The whole wide world?
  They think it funny? Let them joke about it.
  If it annoys them, they can scold.

MOLCHÁLIN: I only hope this frankness won't have
harmed us.

SOPHIE: Surely they won't want you to fight a duel?

MOLCHÁLIN: Oh! Evil tongues are worse than any pistol.

LIZA: They're sitting now with your Papa.
  Why don't you go and slide in through that door;
    Show them a happy carefree face?

Tell any of us what we want to know,
  And see how quickly we'll believe you!
You only need to talk to Mr Chátsky;
  Go on a bit about old times,
And all the fun you used to have together.
  A pretty smile, and two kind words
Will make a man in love do anything.
MOLCHÁLIN: I won't presume to offer you advice.
    [*He kisses her hand.*]
SOPHIE: You want me to?
I'll swallow down my tears and go and be agreeable.
    Though I'm afraid
I may not have the strength to keep up the pretence.
  Oh, why did Mr Chátsky have to come!
    [*Exit* SOPHIE.]
MOLCHÁLIN: A cheery creature – that's what you are!
Lively!
    [*Tries to put his arms round her.*]
LIZA: Please let me go.
There's two of you already, without me.
MOLCHÁLIN: That dainty little face! I do love you!
LIZA: What about my young lady?
MOLCHÁLIN: She's for duty.
But you . . .
LIZA: For when you're bored. Please take your hands off.
MOLCHÁLIN: I've got three little pretty-pretty things.
  A dressing-case, awfully jolly,
With mirrors on the lid, inside and out,
And all done round with gilt and openwork.
A pin-cushion, with beads to decorate it.
And I've a toilet set – mother of pearl;
There's a sweet little needle-case and scissors,
And pearlies, all ground up to make pearl-white!
    Lip salve and ointment-creams,
Bottles of scent – jasmine and mignonette.

LIZA: I'll have you know, you can't catch me with presents.

You'd better tell me what it is that makes you

Shy with the mistress, saucy with the maid?

MOLCHÁLIN: I don't feel well today; I'll keep the sling on.

Come round at dinner-time   and stay a while with me

    I'll tell you the whole truth.

    [*Exit* MOLCHÁLIN *by a side-door. Re-enter* SOPHIE.]

SOPHIE: I went to find Papa, no one was there.

I don't feel well today.   I shan't go in to dinner.

  You'd better tell Mr Molchálin,

And say I'd like him to come round and see me.

    [*Exit* SOPHIE *into her room.*]

LIZA [*alone*]:   Well! People hereabouts!

  She's after him, he's after me, and I –

I am the only one   who's scared to death of love.

Could anybody though   not love Peter the footman!

ACT THREE

Scene One

Scene the same. Afternoon.

CHÁTSKY [*alone*]:   I'll wait for her and make her tell me,
Who is it, after all?   Molchálin? Skalozúb?
Molchálin always used to be so stupid!
   A miserable creature!
Surely he can't have suddenly got clever?
And what about the growling great bassoon,
   Half throttled in that collar,
The constellation of manoeuvres and mazurkas?
   Love's bound to be a game of blind man's buff.
   While I . . .
      [*Enter* SOPHIE.]
                    You here? I'm very glad.
   Just what I wanted.
SOPHIE [*to herself*]:   Just what I did not want.
CHÁTSKY: Of course, it wasn't me you came to look for?
SOPHIE: No, it was not.
CHÁTSKY: Maybe I'm not supposed to ask;
   If it's an awkward question, never mind –
   Who is it that you love?
SOPHIE: Why, goodness me!
   Everybody!
CHÁTSKY: Some more than the rest?
SOPHIE: Yes, lots . . .
   The family . . .
CHÁTSKY: All more than me?
SOPHIE: Some, yes.
CHÁTSKY   What do I want? It's all been settled!

165

I may go hang myself, she thinks it's funny.

SOPHIE: Do you want to know the truth? I'll put it in a
nutshell.

When you see anything the least bit odd in someone,
  You don't restrain your sense of humour.
  You're always ready with your witticisms,
  While you yourself . . .

CHÁTSKY: You mean, I'm funny too?

SOPHIE: Yes! That alarming eye! That cutting tone!
  You have a heap of eccentricities;
  Take a hard look at yourself – it'll do no harm.

CHÁTSKY: Odd am I? Well, who isn't odd?
  Some stupid fool like every other fool,
  Molchálin, for example.

SOPHIE: Your examples
  Aren't new to me; it's plain enough

That you are out to vent your spite on everyone
  So I won't hinder you; I'm going.

CHÁTSKY [holding her back]:
No, wait! [Aside] Just for this once I'm going to pretend.
[Aloud]   Let's stop this arguing.

I wasn't fair about Molchálin, please excuse me.
  Perhaps he isn't like he used to be
  Three years ago; all earthly things can change,
  Administrations, climates, customs, minds –
    There are important people,
  That used to have the name of being fools:
  One in the Army, one for his bad verses,
    And one I dare not name . . .

But everyone accepts that they've developed
Marvellous minds – particularly lately.
Granted, Molchálin has a lively wit,
A daring genius, but has he got
The sensibility, the fire, the passion,
That makes the whole world seem like dust and ashes

Except for you?
Accelerating every beat of the heart
    With love for you?
Every thought and deed inspired by you
    And pleasing you?
That is the way I feel; I can't express it
    It seethes, it surges, rages in me,
It's what I wouldn't wish   on my worst enemy;
    And he? He hangs his head and holds his tongue.
    Of course he's meek and gentle – that sort are . . .
    God knows what secrets lurk inside him!
God knows what kind of things   you have made up about
him –
    Things that have never crossed his mind!
You may be giving him   all sorts of qualities
(Your own in fact) because   you like the look of him.
    It's not his fault at all;
    You are a hundred times the more to blame!
No, no! Let's say he *is* intelligent,
    And getting more so all the time.
But – is he good enough   for you? That's all I ask.
If I'm to bear the loss   with equanimity,
    Tell me, as someone who grew up with you,
    Who is a friend and brother to you,
Prove to me that I can be sure of that!
        And then –
I shall be able to steer clear of madness
    Go right away, cool off, grow cold,
And think no more of love, but find some means
To lose myself in the world   amuse myself, forget.
SOPHIE [*to herself*]:
    There. And I never meant to make him crazy.
    [*Aloud*] What is the good of going on like that?
Mr Molchálin's arm might have been broken,
    I really was concerned about him.

You happened to be here; you never troubled
To understand that a girl can be kind to everyone,
    Without distinction.
  But maybe there's some truth behind your guesses;
  I do get heated, standing up for him.
  But why – I'm going to put it to you straight –
    Why don't you curb your tongue?
Why be so openly contemptuous of people?
  Why show no mercy, even to the humblest?
    One only has to mention him –
  Bang! There's a hail of caustic jokes from you.
  Jokes, jokes, nothing but jokes! How can you do it?
CHÁTSKY: Oh Lord! Surely I'm not the sort of man
  Who has no object in his life but laughter?
  I am amused when I meet funny people;
    More often though, I find them bores.
SOPHIE: That won't do now, you can keep that for others.
If you could get to know Mr Molchálin better,
    I hardly think you'd find him boring.
CHÁTSKY [*heatedly*]:
  How have you got to know the man so well!
SOPHIE: I didn't try to; God brought us together.
  Look, he's made friends with all of us who live here.
    He's served three years under Papa,
  Who often gets unreasonably angry,
    But he disarms him with his silence
  And, from the goodness of his heart, forgives him.
Another thing, he might go looking for amusement;
  Not he – he stays around with the old people.
    We rag about and laugh;
Whether he wants to or not, he sits with them all day,
    Plays cards . . .
CHÁTSKY: Plays cards all day?
  Says nothing when he gets a dressing down?
  [*Aside*]   She can't respect him.

SOPHIE: Of course, he hasn't got the kind of mind
  That's one man's genius and another man's ruin,
  That quickly makes a show, but soon disgusts,
    That damns the world outright
Just for the sake of getting talked about;
But, does a mind like that make for a happy home?
CHÁTSKY: Satire and morals? What does all this mean?
  [*Aside*] She doesn't care a halfpenny for him!
SOPHIE: In fact, his character is simply wonderful,
  He's modest, quiet, ready to give way,
  Never a shade of worry on his face
  He's got a conscience clear as clear can be,
  Doesn't tear strangers into little shreds ...
    There, that's why I love him.
CHÁTSKY [*aside*]: Playing the fool! It isn't him she loves.
    [*Aloud*]
I'll let that do for your description of Molchálin.
  But, Skalozúb! Now, there's a sight for you.
  He stands up for the Army like a rock;
    So straight and tall – that voice, that figure
  He's quite the hero.
SOPHIE: Not of my romance.
CHÁTSKY: Not yours? Then who can make you out!
    [*Enter* LIZA.]
LIZA [*in a whisper*]:
  Mr Molchálin's just behind me, Miss,
    He's on his way to see you.
SOPHIE: Excuse me, please, I must hurry away.
CHÁTSKY: Where to?
SOPHIE: The hairdresser.
CHÁTSKY: Bother the man.
SOPHIE: He'll get his curlers cold.
CHÁTSKY: Then let him.
SOPHIE: Can't; we're expecting people for a party.
CHÁTSKY: Bless you, that leaves me with the same old riddle!

But, won't you let me slip inside;
May I not come into your room a moment?
The walls, the air in there . . . it's all delightful!
The memories of what is gone for ever
Will warm me and revive me and refresh me.
I won't stay long, only two minutes . . .
And after that, I'll tell you what I'll do:
I am a member of the English Club
I'll go there, and devote whole days
To praying for Molchálin's mind
And for the soul of Skalozúb.

    [SOPHIE *shrugs her shoulders, goes into her room, followed
by* LIZA, *and bolts the door.*]

CHÁTSKY: Ah, Sophie! Who's her choice? Don't tell me
it's Molchálin!
Husband? Why not? He's weak on mind . . .
That all! When did that stop a man from raising children?
Obliging . . . unassuming . . . nice pink cheeks . . .

    [*Enter* MOLCHÁLIN]

There he is now, on tiptoe, keeping mum.
What magic has he used to creep into her heart!

    [*Addressing him*]

I say, Molchálin, you and I
Haven't had time to have a chat together.
Tell me, how's life? No troubles now? No griefs?

MOLCHÁLIN: Same as it always was, Sir.

CHÁTSKY: How was that?

MOLCHÁLIN: Day after day, today like yesterday.

CHÁTSKY: From desk to card table, card table back to
desk,
At the appointed hours of ebb and flow?

MOLCHÁLIN: Since I was moved to Archives,
My efforts and my energy have won me
    Three bonuses.

CHÁTSKY: Honours and social rank attract you?

MOLCHÁLIN: No, Sir,
  Each of us has his talent.
CHÁTSKY: What is yours?
MOLCHÁLIN: I've two, Sir,
  I'm economical and conscientious.
CHÁTSKY: Wonderful pair! Worth more than all of ours.
MOLCHÁLIN: You were passed over; did you blot your
copy?
CHÁTSKY: Promotion comes from human beings
  And human beings sometimes make mistakes.
MOLCHÁLIN: We were surprised!
CHÁTSKY: Whatever for?
MOLCHÁLIN: We felt so sorry for you.
CHÁTSKY: Needn't have.
MOLCHÁLIN: Tatiána Yúrevna told us a bit about it
  After she'd been to Petersburg.
She said you'd been well in with all the ministers,
  Then it went off.
CHÁTSKY: Why should she mind about it?
MOLCHÁLIN: Tatiána Yúrevna!
CHÁTSKY: But I don't know her.
MOLCHÁLIN: Tatiána Yúrevna!!
CHÁTSKY: I've never even met her.
  I've heard that she's a stupid woman.
MOLCHÁLIN: You can't mean who I mean; Tatiána
Yúrevna!!!
  A very well-known lady, and what's more
Senior officers and departmental chiefs
  Are all her friends and her relations.
Tatiána Yúrevna – at least you ought to call.
CHÁTSKY: Why ever should I call?
MOLCHÁLIN: One never knows.
Influence often comes from unexpected quarters.
CHÁTSKY: That isn't what I go to call on ladies for.
MOLCHÁLIN: So affable! So kind! So nice! So simple!

The balls she gives are truly sumptuous,
From Christmas time right up to Lent.
And garden parties at her summer villa.
I say, why don't you take a job with us in Moscow,
And get some bonuses and have a bit of fun?
CHÁTSKY: When I have work to do I keep away from fun,
And when I fool, I fool.
There's heaps of clever chaps who can combine the two,
But I'm not one of them.
MOLCHÁLIN: Sorry, but I can't see that it's a crime.
Look, Tom Fomích himself – you know him?
CHÁTSKY: Well?
MOLCHÁLIN: He's been a section head under three
ministers;
Now they've transferred him here.
CHÁTSKY: That beauty!
That superficial nincompoop!
MOLCHÁLIN: Now really,
Why, here his style is taken as a model!
Have you read anything of his?
CHÁTSKY: I don't read rubbish,
Particularly when it's model rubbish.
MOLCHÁLIN: Well, I've enjoyed it when I had to read him.
I'm not an author though.
CHÁTSKY: So one can see.
MOLCHÁLIN: I wouldn't venture to express my own
opinion.
CHÁTSKY: Why, what's the secret then?
MOLCHÁLIN: A man of my age
Should not presume to have opinions of his own.
CHÁTSKY: Good heavens, you and I aren't children!
Must other people's views always be sacrosanct?
MOLCHÁLIN: You see, one must depend on other people.
CHÁTSKY: Why must?
MOLCHÁLIN: One hasn't got the seniority.

CHÁTSKY: With sentiments like those, a soul like that?
Love him! The little rogue was laughing at me!

Scene Two

The same. Evening. All the doors (except the one leading into SOPHIE'S *bedroom) are opened wide, revealing a vista of a succession of brilliantly illuminated rooms. Servants are bustling about; one of them, the* HEAD SERVANT, *speaks.*

HEAD SERVANT: Come on now Tom and Phil, look lively there!
  Card tables, chalk, rubbers and candles!
  [*Knocks on* SOPHIE'S *door.*]
Quickly, Elizabeth, tell your young lady,
Here's Mrs Górich, and her husband with her.
And there's another carriage driving up.
  [*Exeunt in various directions, leaving* CHÁTSKY *alone. Enter* NATHALIE GÓRICH, *a young married lady.*]
NATHALIE: Surely I'm not mistaken! It's just like . . .
  Oh, Mr Chátsky, is it you?
CHÁTSKY: You look me up and down as if you weren't quite sure.
  Have three years changed me such a lot?
NATHALIE: I thought you were a long way off from Moscow;
Have you been here long?
CHÁTSKY: Just come.
NATHALIE: Are you staying?
CHÁTSKY: That depends.
  But wouldn't anybody be amazed
  Looking at you – you're plumper than you were,
    And you've got awfully pretty, too,
  Younger and fresher looking, fire and roses,
    Laughter and fun in all your features.

NATHALIE: I'm married.

CHÁTSKY: But you might   have told me that before!

NATHALIE: My husband – he's a dear – he's coming now –
  Would you like me to introduce him?

CHÁTSKY: Please.

NATHALIE: I've got a feeling that you're going to like him,
See him, and then you'll tell.

CHÁTSKY: I'm bound to – he's your husband.

NATHALIE: No, please, that's not the reason!
  You'll like him for himself, his mind, his ways,
    My one and only precious Plato!
  He's in retirement now, he was a soldier
  And everyone who ever knew him tells me
    That if he'd stayed on in the Army,
  He'd got the pluck, and the ability,
And he'd have ended up as Commandant of Moscow.
      [*Enter* PLATO GÓRICH.]
    This is my Plato.

CHÁTSKY: Bah!
  Old friend! Known him for ages! What a do!

PLATO: Hullo, Chátsky, old boy!

CHÁTSKY: Plato, dear chap, well done!
  Full marks to you for conduct.

PLATO: As you see,
  Old boy, I live in Moscow, and I'm married.

CHÁTSKY: The bustle of the Camp, friends, comrades, all
forgotten?
Quietly slacking?

PLATO: No, I have some occupation.
  I'm studying a flute duet,
A Minor.

CHÁTSKY: That's the one you had five years ago!
  Nothing like constant taste in married men.

PLATO: Old boy, if you get spliced, remember me!
  You'll whistle all day long the same old tune,

174

From boredom.

CHÁTSKY: What! Don't tell me you get bored!

NATHALIE: Several things my Plato likes to do
  He can't have now: parades, reviews,
  The riding-school . . . he does get bored some mornings.

CHÁTSKY: But, my dear chap! Who said you must do
nothing?
  Join up, you'll get a squadron. You're a Major?

NATHALIE: My Plato's health is very far from good.

CHÁTSKY: Bad health? Since when?

NATHALIE: He keeps on getting rheumatism and headaches.

CHÁTSKY: He wants more exercise.
  Try some warm country district – lots of riding –
  Country in summertime is paradise.

NATHALIE: My Plato likes to live in Town, in Moscow;
  Why should he waste his life, out in the wilds?

CHÁTSKY: In Town . . . In Moscow . . . You're a funny
          fellow!
  Remember how you used to live?

PLATO: Old boy,
  Things nowadays aren't what they were . . .

NATHALIE: My pet!
  The cold in here is simply terrible;
  Your coat's all open, and your waistcoat buttons.

PLATO: Old boy, I'm not the man I was . . .

NATHALIE: My dearest,
  Do what I ask you, quick, do up those buttons.

PLATO [coolly]: All right.

NATHALIE: And stand back further from that door,
  The draught is blowing on you from behind!

PLATO: Old boy, I'm not the man I was . . .

NATHALIE: My angel!
  For heaven's sake, get further from that door.

PLATO [raising his eyes to heaven]:
  Oh darling!

175

CHÁTSKY: Well, let God judge you;
So short a time, and not the man you were!
Wasn't it late last year   I knew you in the Army?
Up in the morning – boot and saddle –
And off you went, riding a lively stallion.
The autumn wind could blow   behind you or in front.

PLATO [*sighing*]: Old chap, it was a splendid life in those
days.

[*Enter* PRINCE *and* PRINCESS TUGO-ÚKHOVSKY *with
their six daughters.*]

NATHALIE [*In a thin, piping voice*]:
Prince Tugo-Úkhovsky!   Princess! Good gracious me!
Princess Zizí! Mimí!

[*Loud kissing; afterwards they sit round and look one another
up and down from head to foot.*]

FIRST YOUNG PRINCESS: Oh, what a pretty style!

SECOND YOUNG PRINCESS:
Look at the little pleats!

FIRST YOUNG PRINCESS: It's got a fringe all round.

NATHALIE: Ah, but you ought to see   my satin fascinator.

THIRD YOUNG PRINCESS:
Do look at this *écharpe*   a present from *mon cousin!*

FOURTH YOUNG PRINCESS:
Yes, and it's real Barège.

FIFTH YOUNG PRINCESS: How charming!

SIXTH YOUNG PRINCESS: Oh, how sweet!

THE PRINCESS [*their Mother*]:
Shh! Who was that man there   who bowed when we came
in?

NATHALIE: That's Mr Chátsky, he's a new arrival.

THE PRINCESS: Is he re-tired?

NATHALIE: He is; he's been abroad.
He's only just got back.

THE PRINCESS: Is he a ba-che-lor?

NATHALIE: No, he's not married.

THE PRINCESS: Prince! Prince! Here! Buck up!

THE PRINCE [*turning an ear-trumpet towards her*]:
Oh? Mm?

THE PRINCESS: Ask him for Thursday evening, quickly now!
  Nathalie Górich knows him – that man there!

THE PRINCE: Eh? Mm?

  [*Goes and hovers round* CHÁTSKY, *clearing his throat.*]

THE PRINCESS: There's children for you!
They want a ball, and so Papa must stump around.
  Partners are desperately hard to find . . .
  Is he a gentleman-in-waiting?

NATHALIE: No.

THE PRINCESS: Is he well off?

NATHALIE: Oh, no!

THE PRINCESS [*at the top of her voice*]: Prince! Prince! Come
back!!

  [*Enter the two Countesses* KHRYÚMINA, *grandmother and
  granddaughter.*]

GRANDDAUGHTER COUNTESS: Oh, *Grand'maman!* Why
does one come so early?
  We are the first!

  [*Disappears into a side room.*]

THE PRINCESS: That's all she thinks of us.
So she's the first, which means that we are nobodies!
  She'll make a sour old maid, God help her.

  [*Re-enter* GRANDDAUGHTER COUNTESS, *turning a
  double lorgnette on to* CHÁTSKY.]

GRANDDAUGHTER COUNTESS: M'sieu Chátsky! You in
Moscow! Still the same?

CHÁTSKY: How should I change?

GRANDDAUGHTER COUNTESS: Have you come back
unmarried?

CHÁTSKY: Who could I marry?

GRANDDAUGHTER COUNTESS: Who? And you in foreign
parts?

Oh, heaps of our men pick up wives abroad,
And bring us back in-laws, out of the hat-shops!
CHÁTSKY: The wretches! Must they stand reproached
By you, that take milliners for your models,
For daring to admire the original
>   More than the copy?
>   [*Enter a number of other guests, among them* ZAGORÉTSKY.
>   *Gentlemen appear, click their heels, go off to one side, drift
>   from room to room etc.* SOPHIE *comes out from her room; all
>   move towards her.*]

GRANDDAUGHTER COUNTESS:
Ah, there you are! Bonsoir!   Don't be too punctual;
We all like something to look forward to.
ZAGORÉTSKY [*to* SOPHIE]:
Have you a ticket for the show tomorrow?
SOPHIE: No.
ZAGORÉTSKY: May I be allowed to give you one?
Nobody else could have done this for you.
I've been here, there, and everywhere to get it.
>   Box office – all sold out.
Tried the Director – he's a chum of mine –
>   At dawn, at half-past five — no good!
People were turned away the night before.
>   I tried another and another . . .
Bothered the life out of 'em . . . till, at last
I snatched one by main force off somebody –
Elderly invalid – a friend of mine –
>   Well known not ever to go out;
Now he can spend his time in peace at home!
SOPHIE: Thank you for getting me the ticket
And thank you twice as much for all your trouble.
>   [*Still more guests appear. At the same time* ZAGORÉTSKY
>   *moves over to the gentlemen.*]
ZAGORÉTSKY: Good evening, Plato . . .

PLATO: Go away!

  Run to the women, lie to them and fool them.

  I'll tell true stories about you,

Far worse than any lie. [*To* CHÁTSKY] Old boy, I'll introduce

  This is – what's the polite name for them?

  A – how to put it kindly? – man of the world;

  A most notorious swindling knave,

  Anthony Zagorétsky is his name.

You watch your step with him, he sneaks, and he repeats things,

  And don't play cards with him – he'll skin you.

ZAGORÉTSKY: A character! He growls, without a trace of
                     malice!

CHÁTSKY: It would be ludicrous for you to take offence;

  Not being honest has its compensations.

People abuse you here, but somewhere else, they thank you.

PLATO: Brother, you've got that wrong, we all abuse him,

  Everywhere, and everyone receives him.

    [ZAGORÉTSKY *merges into the crowd. Enter* MISS
    KHYLÓSTOVA]

MISS KHLYÓSTOVA: No joke, you know, at sixty-five,

  To drag all over here to see my niece!

  It's torture! More than I can stand.

It took a solid hour to get here from Pokróvka;

  A dirty night, and dark as doomsday!

  To pass the time, I brought my black maid with me,

And a little dog; dear child see that they're fed some time.

  Send something down for them from supper.

      How do, Princess.

    [*Sits down.*]

Well, Sophie dear, what d'ye think of my maid,

  My negress! Woolly head and hunched up shoulders,

  And cross! Spits like a little cat!

Isn't she black! Enough to frighten you.
  Didn't the Lord create queer people?
A proper devil! In the maids' room now;
Shall I send for her?

SOPHIE: No, Aunt. Another time.

MISS KHLYÓSTOVA: Fancy! They walk them round, like
                      beasts at market,
So I've been told ... out there .. some place in Turkey ...
And who d'ye think it was that got her for me?
Anthony Zagorétsky!
    [ZAGORÉTSKY steps forward.]
A lying, gambling thief, that's what he is.
    [ZAGORÉTSKY vanishes.]
I really meant to close my doors to him,
  But he can get round anybody.
He bought two little black girls at a fair,
For me and for my cousin Parascéva.
  At least, that's what he says he did;
Probably won them in some dirty card-game.
But bless his heart! He gave me a nice present.

CHÁTSKY [with a loud laugh – to PLATO]:
  That sort of praise brings no blessings!
He's vanished; even he found that too much for him.

MISS KHLYÓSTOVA: Who is the humorist? What's his
position?

SOPHIE: That man? It's Mr Chátsky.

MISS KHLYÓSTOVA: What's the joke?
  What caught his fancy? What is there to laugh at?
    Mocking the aged is a sin.
I know! You often danced with him when you were little.
I used to pull his ear – I should have pulled it more.
    [Enter FÁMUSOV.]

FÁMUSOV [in a loud voice]:
  We're waiting for Prince Tugo-Úkhovsky,
    Here he is all the time!

And I've been hanging round the portrait gallery.
Now where's the Colonel? Colonel Skalozúb.
No? Can't be here. An easy man to see
Is Sérgius Sergéyich Skalozúb.

MISS KHLYÓSTOVA:
Mercy! He's deafened me! Louder than any trumpet!

[*Enter* SKALOZÚB, *followed later by* MOLCHÁLIN.]

FÁMUSOV: Colonel my dear, you're late!
And we were waiting, waiting, waiting for you.

[*Leads him up to* MISS KHLYÓSTOVA.]

My sister-in-law. She's heard a lot about you.

MISS KHLYÓSTOVA [*without getting up*]:
You came here once before . . . some regiment . . .
Was it the Grenadiers?

SKALOZÚB [*in a bass voice*]:
I think you meant to say The Grand Duke's Own
The Nova Zembla Fusiliers.

MISS KHLYÓSTOVA: I don't know how to tell t'other from
which
In regiments.

SKALOZÚB: But each has got distinctive marks
Piping and shoulder-straps and gorget-patches.

FÁMUSOV: Come, my dear Sir, I've got some fun for you.
Will you come with us, Prince? Our whist-school's quite
amusing.

[*Exit taking* SKALOZÚB *and* THE PRINCE *with him.*]

MISS KHLYÓSTOVA [*to* SOPHIE]:
Ooh! I was near as nothing caught that time!
Your father really must be crazy;
To introduce, without a 'by your leave'
The ten-foot warrior that he's so struck on.

MOLCHÁLIN [*handling her a card*]:
I've made your table up; there's Monsieur Kock
And Tom Fomích and me.

MISS KHLYÓSTOVA: Thank you my dear. [*Gets up.*]

181

MOLCHÁLIN: Isn't your doggie sweet! No bigger than a
          thimble;
  I stroked him down, his coat is just like silk.
MISS KHLYÓSTOVA: Thanks, honey.
     [*Exit followed by* MOLCHÁLIN *and many others.*]
CHÁTSKY [*to* SOPHIE]: There! He blew the clouds away.
     [*The remaining guests drift off while* CHÁTSKY *and*
     SOPHIE *talk together.*]
SOPHIE: Must you go on?
CHÁTSKY: Why not? Have I alarmed you?
  Seeing he pacified a very angry guest,
  I was going to praise him.
SOPHIE: Yes, with a sting in the tail.
CHÁTSKY: All right, I'll say what I was thinking.
  Old ladies are a fiery-tempered race;
    It does no harm to have on hand
  Some first-rate cavalier to dance attendance –
    Lightning conductor, you may call him.
  And who can do it better than Molchálin?
  Everything gets amicably settled;
    He's got the pug-dog ready petted,
  Slips her the little card at the right moment,
  While he lives, Zagorétsky will not die!
  Just now, you told me some of his good points;
  Aren't there lots more, that you forgot?
     [*Exit* CHÁTSKY.]
SOPHIE [*alone, to herself*]:   That man!
  He makes me furious, every time I meet him!
  He jeers, he loves humiliating people,
  He's jealous, he's conceited and ill-natured!
     [*Enter* MR N.]
MR N: [*Coming up to* SOPHIE]:
  You've something on your mind?
SOPHIE: Yes, Mr Chátsky.
MR N.: How do you find him, now that he's come back?

SOPHIE: He's not in his right mind.

MR N.: You don't mean off his head?

SOPHIE [*after a pause*]:
No, not exactly that . . .

MR N.: But there are symptoms?

SOPHIE [*with a hard look at him*]:
I think there are.

MR N.: Really? At his age!

SOPHIE: Well, there it is. [*Aside*] He's ready to believe it.
Now, Mr Chátsky!
You're fond of dressing people up as clowns,
Try how the costume fits on you.
[*Exit* SOPHIE.]

MR N.: He's off his head! . . . She thinks so, dear oh dear!
Where did she get it? Must be something in it.
[*Enter* MR D.]
You've heard?

MR D.: Heard what?

MR N.: Heard about Chátsky?

MR D.: What?

MR N.: He's off his head.

MR D.: What rubbish!

MR N.: I'm not the only one that's saying so.

MR D.: But you enjoy shouting it from the housetops?

MR N.: I'll go and ask – somebody's sure to know.
[*Exit* MR N.]

MR D.: Believe that chatterbox?
Picks up some trash, goes straight off and repeats it!
[*Enter* ZAGORÉTSKY.]

MR D.: Do you know about Chátsky?

ZAGORÉTSKY: Well?

MR D.: He's off his head!

ZAGORÉTSKY: Ah yes I did hear, I remember.
Of course I knew; it was a well-known case.
His wicked uncle got him certified,

They took him to the madhouse, chained him up.

MR D.: Good gracious! He was in this room just now.

ZAGORÉTSKY: Why then, they must have let him off the chain.

MR D.: Dear friend! When we have you   we need no newspapers.

　I must look into this – I'll go,
I'll ask around, but meanwhile 'Mum's the word'!

　　[*Exit* MR D.]

ZAGORÉTSKY: Which of them here is Chátsky? – Well-known name –
I used to know one of the Chátskys once.

　　[*Enter* GRANDDAUGHTER COUNTESS.]
You've heard about him?

GRANDDAUGHTER COUNTESS: Who do you mean?

ZAGORÉTSKY: Chátsky was in this room just now.

GRANDDAUGHTER COUNTESS:　　　　　　　　I know;
I talked to him.

ZAGORÉTSKY: Then I congratulate you.
The man's a lunatic!

GRANDDAUGHTER COUNTESS: What!

ZAGORÉTSKY:　　　　　　　　Yes, he's off his head!

GRANDDAUGHTER COUNTESS: Fancy! That's just what I was going to say!
I noticed it myself; I would have betted on it.

　　[*Enter* GRANDMOTHER COUNTESS.]
Ah, *Grand'maman*! The most amazing news!
　You haven't heard the trouble here?
Listen, a simply gorgeous thing has happened . . .

GRANDMOTHER COUNTESS:　　My dear, speak louder,[14]
My ears are blocked . . .

GRANDDAUGHTER COUNTESS: I haven't time,
I'm off to ask someone. [*Pointing to* ZAGORÉTSKY]
　　　　　　　　He'll tell you the whole story.

　　　[*Exit* GRANDDAUGHTER COUNTESS.]

GRANDMOTHER COUNTESS [*to* ZAGORÉTSKY]:
  Whatever is it? Is the house on fire?
ZAGORÉTSKY: No, no, it's Mr Chátsky – he's the trouble.
GRANDMOTHER COUNTESS: Did you say Mr Chátsky is
  in trouble?
  Is he in jail?
ZAGORÉTSKY: A bullet hit his head
  On operations, lodged, and turned his reason.
GRANDMOTHER COUNTESS:
  At the Freemasons' Lodge he turned a heathen?
ZAGORÉTSKY: Can't make her understand . . .
    [*Exit* ZAGORÉTSKY.]
GRANDMOTHER COUNTESS: Oh, Mr Zagorétsky!
Now he's run off; they're all   tearing around in terror.
    [*Enter* PRINCE TUGO-ÚKHOVSKY.]
    Prince! Prince! Oh, that poor Prince!
  Dragged round to balls when he can hardly breathe . . .
Prince! Have you heard?
THE PRINCE: Ah? Mm?
GRANDMOTHER COUNTESS: He doesn't hear a thing.
  Did you see the Police come here?
THE PRINCE: Eh? Mm?
GRANDMOTHER COUNTESS: Prince! Who took Mr
  Chátsky off to prison?
THE PRINCE: Ee? Mm?
GRANDMOTHER COUNTESS: He'll have to be a private
  soldier!
  Sidearms and knapsack now for him!
Nothing to laugh at! He's renounced the Faith!
THE PRINCE: Oo? Mm?
GRANDMOTHER COUNTESS: A heathen! Yes! A damned
Voltairean!
  Well, what? You're deaf, my Father; get your trumpet.
  Ah, deafness is a dreadful vice!
    [*Re-enter* MISS KHLYÓSTOVA, SOPHIE, MOLCHÁLIN,

PLATO *and* NATHALIE, GRANDDAUGHTER COUNT-
ESS, THE PRINCESS *with her daughters*, ZAGORÉTSKY,
SKALOZÚB, *followed by* FÁMUSOV *and many others*.]

MISS KHLYÓSTOVA: He's off his head! I ask you, honestly!
So sudden, and so quick! Have you heard, Sophie?

PLATO: Who started this?

NATHALIE: Oh, darling! Everyone.

PLATO: Why then, like it or not, one must believe it,
But still I'm doubtful.

[*Enter* FÁMUSOV.]

FÁMUSOV: What? Not about Chátsky?
Doubtful? I was the first! I found it out!
I'd wondered for some time why no one picked him up.
Try mentioning Authority to him;
He'll talk and talk and say the Lord knows what.
While anyone who bows, or shows profound respect,
Even in the presence of Their Majesties,
He calls a toady!

MISS KHLYÓSTOVA:
All of a piece with that, the way he keeps on laughing,
When I made some remark – he gave a great guffaw.

MOLCHÁLIN: He told me to give up my job in Moscow
Archives.

GRANDDAUGHTER COUNTESS: He kindly said that I was
like a milliner.

NATHALIE: He said my husband ought to live out in the
country.

ZAGORÉTSKY: All goes to show he's mad!

GRANDDAUGHTER COUNTESS: I saw it in his eye.

FÁMUSOV: He takes after poor Anne, his Mother.
She had eight separate attacks of madness.

MISS KHLYÓSTOVA:
Wonderful how such things can happen in the world!
So young, and suddenly goes crazy!
Probably drank too much for a man of his age.

THE PRINCESS: Sure to have done.

GRANDDAUGHTER COUNTESS: No doubt at all.

MISS KHLYÓSTOVA: Champagne! He used to swig it by
the tumbler.

GRANDDAUGHTER COUNTESS: Bottles! Whole mag-
nums!

ZAGORÉTSKY [*heatedly*]: Pardon me ma'am
He drank it by the hundred gallon cask.

FÁMUSOV: Come on! A lot of harm in that!
What if a man does take a drop too much?
Study – there is the plague, and learning – that's what
does it;
That's why we get so many more
Crazy folk, crazy actions, crazy notions.

MISS KHLYÓSTOVA: It's all enough to drive you off your
head;
The what's-its-names, the pensions, schools and lycées,
And Joseph Lancaster's Mutual Education.[15]

THE PRINCESS: No, it's that place in Petersburg,
The Pe – da – go – gic Institute, they call it.
The pupils there are trained in unbelief and schism.
Professors! One of our relations went there
When he passed out; he might as well
Have been a 'prentice in a chemist's shop!
He runs away from women, even me,
He's got no use for Service Rank . . .
Chemist and botanist! Prince Theodore, my nephew.

SKALOZÚB: I've got good news for you.
A rumour's going round about a plan
To teach these lycées, schools, gymnasiums,
Army-style, all by numbers – One! One-two!
And keep the books for best.

FÁMUSOV: No, my dear Colonel,
There's only one way left to crush this evil thing
Collect the books and burn the lot.

ZAGORÉTSKY [*diffidently*]: No, Sir, there's books and
books.

I'll tell you what I'd do if I were Censor;
I'd drop on fables! Oh! fables are deadly;
Nothing but jokes about the Lions and the Eagles.

People can call them what they like,
They may be animals but even so, they're Tsars.

MISS KHLYÓSTOVA: But my good Sirs, whether it's books
or drink,

What does it matter, now that he's gone mad?
I'm sorry about Mr Chátsky,
It's Christian-like, to feel compassion for him.
He was a clever man, and owned three hundred souls.

FÁMUSOV: Four hundred.

MISS KHLYÓSTOVA: Sir, it's three.

FÁMUSOV: Four hundred.

MISS KHLYÓSTOVA: No, three hundred.

FÁMUSOV: My almanack . . .

MISS KHLYÓSTOVA: Almanacks fiddlesticks!

FÁMUSOV: Four, four it is. Pooh, woman! How you argue!

MISS KHLYÓSTOVA: Wrong, it's three hundred. Do you
want to tell me

That I don't know what other people own?

FÁMUSOV: Look here, it's four.

MISS KHYLÓSTOVA: Three hundred, three, three, three!

[*Re-enter* CHÁTSKY.]

NATHALIE: Here he is!

GRANDDAUGHTER COUNTESS: Hush!

ALL: Hush! Hush!

[*They back away from him to the far side of the room.*]

MISS KHLYÓSTOVA: What if the fit is on him?
He'll have it out with us! He'll start a fight.

FÁMUSOV: O Lord, have mercy on us sinners!

[*Apprehensively.*]

Look, my dear fellow, you're not quite the thing.

After a drive like that you need some sleep,
  Let's feel your pulse, boy. You're not well.

CHÁTSKY: No, I can stand no more, after a million
torments . . .
  My chest is sore from friendly hugs,
  My feet from scraping, and my ears from screaming,
And most of all, my head from every sort of nonsense.
    [*Goes up to* SOPHIE.]
This place makes me feel all squeezed up inside and sad.
  I'm lost in the crowd, I don't know what I'm doing.
  No! I'm not pleased with Moscow.

MISS KHLYÓSTOVA: There you are!
    It's Moscow's fault!

FÁMUSOV: Keep clear of him!
    [*Makes signs to* SOPHIE.]
                          Hum! Sophie! She's not looking.

SOPHIE [*to* CHÁTSKY]: Tell me what's making you so
  cross?

CHÁTSKY: Nothing. Only a man I met in the next room,
  A little, puffed-out Frenchman from Bordeaux;
  He'd got quite an assembly gathered round him.
    He told them how with tears and terror
  He packed his bags to go to barbarous Russia;
And how he came, and found no end to all the kindness.
    Never a word of Russian;
  He never even saw a Russian face –
  He might have been in France, among his friends,
    In his own province!
  You see, he feels just like a little king
    At parties here – same ladies' dresses –
  Same ladies' conversation – he's delighted!
    But we are not delighted.
Yearning and sighs broke out all round, when he stopped
speaking
  'Ah France! There's no such country in the world!'

189

That was two young princesses, sisters,
Saying their piece, drummed into them from childhood;
There were no end of young princesses there!
  And I, standing afar,
Meekly but audibly put up my prayer,
That the Lord might cast out that unclean spirit
  Of vain, blind, servile imitation,
And drop His spark into the heart of someone
  Who by his words and his example
Would put a curb on us, and pull us back
  From this sick craving for abroad!
They'll call me 'bigot', 'old believer' – let them![16]
I hold our North one hundredfold the worse,
  Since we have traded all we had –
Our language, customs, ancient holiness –
  And taken on new ways;
Since we have laid aside our stately dress
  And put on clothes for clowns –
A tail behind, the front grotesquely cut away
Against all commonsense, regardless of the weather,
  And awkward when one moves!
Our faces marred – grey chins scraped ludicrously bare –
  Short coats, short hair, short wits!!
Oh, if we're born to borrow everything,
  Why don't we copy the Chinese
In their sage ignorance of foreigners!
When shall we rise against this alien tyrant, Fashion?
  Why! Our robust, sensible countrymen
  Might think we even talk like Germans?
'Can you draw parallels', somebody muttered,
'Between the European and native Russian?
  Isn't that rather odd?
Come, how would you translate *Madame* and *Mademoiselle*
Surely you wouldn't use the word *sudárynya*?'
Imagine then! They all began to laugh.

At my expense!
'*Sudárynya*! Ha! Ha! Ha! Ha! That's lovely!
Sudárynya! Ha! Ha! Ha! Ha! How frightful!'
But while in anger, cursing life,
I was preparing a reply to stun them,
They all went off and left me!
There you are; that's my case, and not a new one either –
In Moscow, Petersburg, all over Russia,
Anyone from the city of Bordeaux
Need only open his mouth – fortune is with him
He wins the sympathies of all the young princesses.
But, anyone in Petersburg or Moscow
Who doesn't like people got in from abroad,
Fal-lals and fancy language,
Who by ill-luck has got inside his head
Five or six reasonable notions
Let him once dare to tell them to the world,
Lo and behold! . . .
[*Looks around him; everyone is waltzing with the greatest
energy. The old people have drifted back to their card tables.*]

ACT FOUR

The grand entrance-hall of FÁMUSOV'S *house: main staircase descending from the floor above, joined by several branch staircases leading from an entresol. Below, on the right, the Porter's lodge and doors leading out to the porch; on the left at the same level,* MOLCHÁLIN'S *room.*
Night, dim illumination. Some FOOTMEN *are bustling round, others are asleep, waiting for their masters. Enter from above* GRANDMOTHER COUNTESS *and* GRANDDAUGHTER COUNTESS, *preceded by* FOOTMAN.

FOOTMAN: The Countess Khryúmin's carriage.
GRANDDAUGHTER COUNTESS [*while she is being wrapped up*]:
Fámusov's ball, that was! He got a lot of guests,
  Weird-looking beings out of the next world,
  No one to talk to, nobody to dance with.
GRANDMOTHER COUNTESS: Let's go, my dear!
  It's all too much for me, it really is.
    One of these nights,
  After the ball, I get into my grave.
    [*Both drive away. Enter from above* PLATO *and* NATHALIE
    GÓRICH, *with a* FOOTMAN *busily attending to them. The
    other* FOOTMAN *is standing by the porch and calling out.*]
FOOTMAN: Carriage for Major Górich.
NATHALIE: Angel mine,
  My precious Plato-poppet, why so sad?
    [*Kisses her husband on the forehead.*]
  Come on, say it was fun at Fámusov's.
PLATO: My dear Natásha, I   am half asleep at balls.
  I've not the faintest wish to go to one;
  I don't object, I go to fag for you,

Past midnight, and I'm still on duty,
And now and then, however glum I feel,
When I'm detailed to dance I up and dance, to please you.
NATHALIE: Now that's put on, and very badly done;
   You're in a frightful hurry to be thought old.
   [*Exit* NATHALIE *with* FOOTMAN.]
PLATO [*coolly*]: A ball's all right – what hurts is loss of freedom;
   Now, who compels us to get married?
Some men are born to it . . .
   [*Re-enter* FOOTMAN *from porch.*]
FOOTMAN: Beg pardon, Sir
Mistress is in the carriage, and is displeased.
PLATO [*with a sigh*]:   I'm coming, coming.
   [*He drives away.*]
   [*Enter from above* CHÁTSKY, *preceded by his* FOOTMAN.]
CHÁTSKY: Call them and tell them to buck up and bring it.
   [*Exit* CHÁTSKY'S FOOTMAN.]
   There now, so ends this day
And with it all the hopes that filled my heart,
Drifting away, like spectres on the mist . . .
   What, then, did I expect?
What did I think I'd find, when I got here?
The joy of meeting? Somebody who cares?
The happy cry? The arms around? All blank.
As on a road across a never-ending plain,
   While you sit idle in the carriage,
There's something you can see, always ahead of you,
Different-looking, blue and shimmering;
You drive one hour, two hours, all day, till suddenly
   Up comes the rest-house and the night-stop.
And then it's all the same whichever way you look;
   Flat, bare, dead, empty steppe. Utter frustration,
   The more you think about it . . .
   [*Re-enter* CHÁTSKY'S FOOTMAN.]
                              Is it ready?

CHÁTSKY'S FOOTMAN: No, Sir, you see they can't find
Coachman anywhere.

CHÁTSKY: Get out and look for him. We can't stay here
all night.

[*Exit* CHÁTSKY'S FOOTMAN.]

[*Enter* REPETÍLOV *from the porch, running; falls headlong
right in the entrance, then hurriedly picks himself up.*]

REPETÍLOV: Tcha! That was a mistake. – Good Lord!
Just let me rub my eyes ... where have you come from,
Stranger?

My dearest, closest friend! *Mon cher!*
You know how they keep on their nonsense about me;
I'm superstitious, I'm a bletherskite,
I go by omens and presentiments –
Now will they please explain!
I hurried to get here, as if I knew ... then crash!
Tripped on the doorstep, down I went full length!
Yes, you may laugh
At silly Repetílov and his rubbish ...
But I've a weakness, something draws me towards you,
A kind of love, or kind of passion ...
In all the world you'll never find another ...
Never upon my soul, so true a friend as me!
Even although I lose my wife and children,
And everyone abandons me,
Even although I die upon this very spot.
Yes, may God blast me ...

CHÁTSKY: Don't talk stuff.

REPETÍLOV: You don't like me; that's only natural;
I'm so-so when I'm with the others;
But when it comes to you, I go all timid,
Laughable, pitiable; a fool, an ignoramus.

CHÁTSKY: That's a strange kind of self-depreciation.

REPETÍLOV: Scold me! I too will curse the day that I
was born,

Every time I think   of all the time I've wasted.
I say, what is the time?
CHÁTSKY: It's time to go to bed.
  If you do turn up in the ball-room
  You'll only have to come straight out again.
REPETÍLOV: Brother, what good's a ball? We'll never break the yoke,
  Where we are shackled by convention
  From dusk to dawn – you've read that book about it?
CHÁTSKY: Have you been reading? Here's a problem for me,
  You – Repetílov?
REPETÍLOV: You may call me Vandal;
I well deserve the name –   the people I've admired
  Were worthless; I've spent all my life
  In a mad round of balls and dinner parties;
Unfaithful to my wife,   forgetful of my children;
    I've gambled and I've lost;
I've had my property   put into sequestration;
  I've kept a dancing-girl; not only one,
    Three at a time!
  I've been dead drunk; stayed up nine nights on end;
  Renounced the laws, my conscience and my faith!
CHÁTSKY: Listen! Talk nonsense, but know when to stop;
  You've said enough to make a man despair.
REPETÍLOV: Congratulate me; now that I know some people
  With really high intelligences,
  I don't go wandering around all night.
CHÁTSKY: What are you doing now?
REPETÍLOV: One odd night doesn't count.
But, ask me where I've been.
CHÁTSKY: That I can guess myself;
  Would it be at the Club?
REPETÍLOV: The English Club.

Here goes with my confession:
I've come here from an animated meeting –
Please keep this to yourself – I'm pledged to silence –
We've a society, we hold clandestine sessions,
On Thursdays. It's extremely secret.
CHÁTSKY: Oh Brother, you alarm me! At the Club?
REPETÍLOV: That's where it was.
CHÁTSKY: And that's the way to do it,
To have yourselves chucked out, you and your secrets.
REPETÍLOV: No need for you to get alarmed;
Even when we speak aloud no one will understand.
Often, when we get on to Parliaments and Juries,
And Byron – serious things like that –
Even I have to hold my tongue, and listen.
It's quite beyond me, man; I feel that I'm a fool.
Oh *Alexandre*! It's you that we've been missing;
Listen, dear chap, do one small thing to please me –
Come along with me now – we're half-way there;
I'll introduce you to some men
None of them in the least like me, *mon cher*.
Such men! The very cream of our enlightened youth!
CHÁTSKY: Bother the lot of you! What! Me go tearing off!
Why should I, in the middle of the night?
I'm going home, I want some sleep.
REPETÍLOV: Chuck it! Whoever goes to bed these days?
Come on, no havering, make up your mind!
We know our minds! We are that sort of people ...
The Fiery Dozen; that's who we are!
And when we shout, you'd think there were a hundred of
us.
CHÁTSKY: Why do you have to get in such a frenzy?
REPETÍLOV: We're animated, Brother, animated.
CHÁTSKY: You are? And is that all you do?
REPETÍLOV: I can't explain it here; I haven't time,
But it concerns the State,

You know, something that isn't yet quite ripe,
    Can't do it all at once!
Such men, *mon cher*, I won't be too long-winded.
I'll tell you – First, we have Prince Gregory!
Odd? He's unique! He makes us die with laughter!!
He's always with the English; has their ways –
Talks through his teeth – just like an Englishman,
    And wears his hair cropped, like a convict.
What? You don't know him? Oh, come on and meet him.
    Next there's Eudókimus Vorkúlov;
You've never heard him sing? He's marvellous!
My dear, you ought to hear   his special favourite
    '*Ah, non lasciarmi, no, no, no*'.[17]
        And then we have two brothers,
Leo and Boris, wonderful chaps they are!
One wouldn't know quite what to say about them . . .
But, if you like, I'll tell you who's a Genius!!!
Hippólytus Marcéllovich Udúshyev!!!
Have you read anything at all of his?
Do read him, Brother! He writes nothing now,
    People like that ought to be flogged,
And told with every stroke to write, write, write.
You can still find him in the magazines –
'A Glance', 'A Fragment' and a piece called 'Something'.
What's 'Something' all about? It's about everything,
    For he knows everything.
We've got him in reserve   against a rainy day.
But we've got one great mind like no one else in Russia
I needn't say his name – you'll know him from his
portrait;[18]
    He's a night robber, he fights duels,
They sentence him to exile in Kamchátka,
When he gets back again, he's an Aleut.
    He plays some pretty dirty tricks;
But then, a clever man   can't help being a rogue.

Yet, when he talks to us about High Honour,
  His eyes burn red, his face lights up;
It is as if some daemon had possessed him,
  He weeps, and we all sob.
There! Do such men exist anywhere else? I doubt it.
  Mind you of course, I'm nothing very special,
In company like that; it's terrible to think
  How backward and how slack I am!
But still, if I sit tight and strain my poor old mind
  It doesn't take an hour of labour,
Before, casual-like, out pops a pun.
  The others jump on my idea;
Six of them to cook up a little vaudeville,
  Another six to write the music for it
  The rest to clap when its performed.
  Man, you may laugh, but we enjoy ourselves!
  God didn't give me much ability,
He gave me a good heart – people are fond of me,
  And let me off when I talk nonsense . . .

FOOTMAN [*standing by the porch*]:
Carriage for Colonel SKALOZÚB.
REPETÍLOV: ·For who?
    [*Enter from above* SKALOZÚB. REPETÍLOV *goes towards
    him.*]
REPETÍLOV: Ah! Skalozúb my dear old fellow!
  Wait now, where are you off to? Do me a favour.
    [*Smothers him in hugs.*]
CHÁTSKY: Where can I go to get away from them?
    [*Goes into the Porter's Lodge.*]
REPETÍLOV [*to* SKALOZÚB]:
  We hadn't heard of you for ages.
They said your regiment had gone on active service.
  You know each other? [*Looks round for* CHÁTSKY.]
                        Skipped, the stubborn fellow!
Never mind, it was you I desperately wanted,

Come along now with me   we're taking no excuses.
  Prince Gregory has a big crowd tonight,
  You're going to meet something like forty people,
    And, man alive, such minds!
The talk goes on all night, it's never boring.
Firstly, they fill you up   with lashings of champagne,
  And secondly, you get instruction
In things that you and I,   of course, would never think of.
SKALOZÚB: Clear off, try someone else.   You can't fool me
        with learning.
  But if you like, I'll send a sergeant-major;
  He'll Voltaire you and your Prince Gregory!
    He'll fall you in threes,
  And if he hears one peep from you, he'll fix you.
REPETÍLOV: You've always got the Service on your mind!
    What about me, *mon cher*?
  I might have got a long way up the ladder,
  But no one ever had such wretched luck!
  I was a Civil Servant – there was the Baron,
Von Klotz, shooting to get   a ministerial post
    And there was I,
  Shooting to be the Baron's son-in-law.
I didn't stop to think;   I went for it bald-headed.
  I played to lose to him and to his wife
  God help me, what I let those two take off me!
    He had a house on the Fontánka;[19]
I built a house next door,   a huge affair, with pillars!
    That cost a pretty penny!
  Well, in the end I did marry his daughter,
And got no job at all   only a piddling dowry.
  What good's a German for a father-in-law?
  You see, he was afraid he'd be reproached
    For favouring his own relations.
  Damn him! Afraid! What help was that to me?
    Those clods of clerks he had,

Those pen-pushers, with itchy little palms
They've all gone to the top   they're all big men today.
Look in the Petersburg Directory!
Pah! Service and promotion! Decorations!
Vanity and vexation of the spirit!
It's marvellously put by A. Lokhmótyev.
'Radical remedies are indicated
  For total failure to digest.'

> [*Stops, on seeing that* ZAGORÉTSKY *has taken the place of*
> SKALOZÚB, *who meanwhile has driven away.*]

ZAGORÉTSKY: Do please go on; I'll be quite frank with you,
I'm just the same as you – an awful liberal!
  To think of all thát I have lost
By being straight, and bold to speak my mind! . . .
REPETÍLOV [*Frustrated*]: They all go off without a word;
One's hardly out of sight   before another's gone.
First Chátsky vanishes   and now it's Skalozúb.
ZAGORÉTSKY: What do you think of Chátsky?
REPETÍLOV: Clever chap.
We ran into each other here just now;
  We chattered about this and that
And had some serious talk on vaudeville.
Yes! Vaudeville's the thing; the rest's all rot.
  We have the same tastes . . . him and I.
ZAGORÉTSKY: You noticed that his mind   is seriously disturbed?
REPETÍLOV: What utter rubbish!
ZAGORÉTSKY: Everyone believes it.
REPETÍLOV: Twaddle.
ZAGORÉTSKY: Ask anybody.
REPETÍLOV: I say moonshine.
ZAGORÉTSKY: Well, look; here come Prince Tugo-Úkhovsky
The Princess and the young Princesses.

REPETÍLOV: Bosh!

[*Enter from above* PRINCE TUGO-ÚKHOVSKY, *the* PRINCESS *and the six young* PRINCESSES. *Bustle of* FOOTMEN.]

ZAGORÉTSKY: Your ladyships, please tell me what you think,

Is Chátsky mad or is he not?

FIRST YOUNG PRINCESS:

Whatever doubt is there of that?

SECOND YOUNG PRINCESS: The whole world knows it.

THIRD YOUNG PRINCESS: The Khvórovs, the Dryanskóys, Varlyánskys and Skachkóvs.

FOURTH YOUNG PRINCESS: Oh, that's stale news. Who hasn't heard it?

FIFTH YOUNG PRINCESS:

Who doubts it?

ZAGORÉTSKY: This man here doesn't believe it.

SIXTH YOUNG PRINCESS: You!

ALL TOGETHER: You, Monsieur Repetílov, you!

How can you go against all of the rest of us?

Why should you? Fie on you! It's ludicrous.

REPETÍLOV [*stopping his ears.*]: I beg your pardons.

I hadn't realized that this was common knowledge.

[*Enter from above* MISS KHLYÓSTOVA, *coming down the grand staircase on* MOLCHÁLIN'S *arm.*]

THE PRINCESS: Indeed it is; he isn't safe to speak to.

Should have been locked up long ago.

To hear him talk, you'd think his little finger

Knew more than all of us even the Prince, my husband!

I think he's just a Jacobin,

Your Mr Chátsky! Come on now, let's go;

Prince, you can take Zizí or Katie with you,

The rest will come with me, in the six-seater.

MISS KHLYÓSTOVA [*from the stairs*]:

Princess, the little cards account!

THE PRINCESS:
I'll owe it you, my dear.

ALL [*to one another*]:   Good-bye.
    [*The* PRINCE'*s family drives away; so also does*
    ZAGORÉTSKY.]

REPETÍLOV: Heavens above!
  Miss Khlyóstova! Dear, dear, poor Chátsky!
  There! That's our lofty mind, and all those labours!
  Why do we go on trying, here on earth?

MISS KHLYÓSTOVA: Yes, it's a judgement on him.
  Still, he'll get treatment, and maybe they'll cure him.
But you're a hopeless case my dear, we give you up.
  You condescended to be just in time!
  Molchálin, that's your cubby-hole, in there.
  Go on, God bless – I don't need seeing off.
    [*Exit* MOLCHÁLIN *into his room.*]
Good-bye to you my dear, high time you settled down.
    [*Miss* KHLYÓSTOVA *drives away.*]

REPETÍLOV: Where shall I make for now? It's getting on
towards morning.
    [*To his footman*]
  Come on, and get me back into my carriage
  And drive me off somewhere.
    [REPETÍLOV *drives away.*]
    [*The last lamp is extinguished;* CHÁTSKY *comes out from the
    Porter's lodge.*]

CHÁTSKY: Can I believe my ears? What's that? Not fun,
plain malice.
  How in the name of wonder was it done?
  What magic makes them all repeat in chorus
    That silly nonsense about me?
  For some of them you'd think this was a triumph;
    Others, though, do seem sympathetic . . .
Oh, but if one could get inside of people's skins,
  Which would be worst in them? Their tongues or hearts?

Who made this story up?
Some fools believed it, passed it on to others,
Then the old ladies . . . quick! Sound the alarm!
And there you have Public Opinion.
And that's my native land . . . No, I can see
It won't be long this time   before I've had enough.
Does Sophie know? Of course, they've told her.
I can't say it amuses her to hurt me,
   Not me, particularly.
It's all the same to her   whether it's true or not,
   Whether it's me or someone else;
 She doesn't really care for anybody.
But what about that faint? She was unconscious.
   Nerves over-cosseted, the vapours,
A trifle sets them off;   a trifle calms them down . . .
 I took it for a sign of deeper feelings –
 No, not a bit! She might have done as much,
When someone trod upon   a dog's tail, or a cat's.
      [SOPHIE *appears on the upstairs landing, with a candle.*]
SOPHIE: That you, Mr Molchálin? [*Hurriedly closes the door
      again.*]
CHÁTSKY: Her! Herself!
 My head's on fire, my blood's all seething.
She did appear, she's gone.   Could it have been a vision?
 Or am I really off my head?
 I'm quite prepared for strange occurrences;
But, there's no vision here;   a meeting's been arranged
 At a set time – why should I fool myself?
 She called Molchálin; that's his room, in there.
      [*Re-enter* CHÁTSKY'S FOOTMAN *at the porch.*]
CHÁTSKY'S FOOTMAN: Carriage . . .
CHÁTSKY [*pushing him back outside*]:
            Sh! I'll stay here   and I'll not close an eyelid
Till morning if need be.   If I must drain the cup,
 Better to do it here and now.

You can't get out of things by putting off.

That's the door opening. [*Hides behind a pillar.*]

    [*Enter from above* LIZA *with a candle.*]

LIZA: Oh dear, I do feel frightened!

The empty hall at night! I'm scared of bogeys.

  I'm scared of living people too.

God help my poor dear suffering young lady . . .

    That Mr Chátsky,

He follows her around, like something in her eye.

Fancy, she thought she saw him there downstairs!

    [*Looks around.*]

So likely that he'd want to hang about the hall.

Probably off the premises this long time;

He's put his love away until tomorrow,

    Gone home and gone to bed.

Come on, I've got to knock on Sweetheart's door.

      [*Knocks on* MOLCHÁLIN's *door.*]

  I say, Sir, will you please wake up?

My Lady's calling you, my Lady wants you.

    Quick, before someone sees us.

    [MOLCHÁLIN *comes out of his room, yawning and stretching.*
    At the same time, SOPHIE *appears above again, and begins to*
    creep stealthily downstairs; CHÁTSKY *remains in hiding*
    behind the pillar.]

LIZA: You must be made of stone, Sir, or of ice.

MOLCHÁLIN: Oh, Liza, are you speaking for yourself?

LIZA: I'm speaking, Sir, for my young lady.

MOLCHÁLIN: Who would have thought these cheeks and veins have never felt

  The blush of love go playing through them?

Do you always want to be the one that carries errands?

LIZA: When you go courting for a bride,

  You mustn't lounge about, you mustn't yawn;

A nice, attractive man won't eat his fill

Nor have his sleep out, till the wedding day.

MOLCHÁLIN: Wedding? Who with?

LIZA: My Lady.

MOLCHÁLIN: Oh, go on!
   I've got my future to consider.
It's just to pass the time; there'll be no wedding.

LIZA: Oh, Sir! What *are* you saying!
Who else do we intend   to have to be our husband?

MOLCHÁLIN: I wouldn't know. One thing gives me the shudders
   The very thought of it unnerves me;
Suppose one day we're caught   by Mr Fámusov?
   He'll send us flying with a curse . . .
Well, shall I open up my heart to you?
I don't see anything   attractive in Miss Sophie.
   God grant long life to her, and wealth;
She was in love with Mr Chátsky once,
   She'll drop me, just as she dropped him.
Oh, how I wish that I could feel for her
Half what I feel for you, my little angel!
   But no, however hard I practise,
I'm ready to be tender – till we meet.
Then I go cold.

SOPHIE [*aside*]: Oh, how contemptible!

CHÁTSKY [*behind the pillar*]:
   The cad!

LIZA: Aren't you ashamed?

MOLCHÁLIN: The last advice
   My father gave me on his death-bed,
Was – first and foremost, make yourself agreeable
   To one and all, without exception.
The master of the house   in which you have to live,
   The chief, with whom you will be serving,
His servant, who will clean your clothes for you,
Porters and messengers   in case they turn against you,
   The porter's dog, to make it friendly.

LIZA: Well, Sir, you have a lot   of people to take care of!

MOLCHÁLIN: That's why I undertake to play the lover,
   To oblige the daughter of a man . . .

LIZA: Who gives you food and drink   and now and then
promotes you?
   That's enough explanations; come on, do!

MOLCHÁLIN: Come on and share the love of our poor
Beauty . . .
Let's have one hug with you   with all my heart behind it.
   [LIZA *repulses him.*]
   Why couldn't she be you!
   [*He is about to go, but is prevented by* SOPHIE.]

SOPHIE [*almost in a whisper; the whole scene is in an undertone*]:
   Don't move from there, I've heard more than enough.
   You horror! Shame on me, shame on these walls.

MOLCHÁLIN: What? . . . It's Miss Sophie . . .

SOPHIE: Quiet, for Heaven's sake,
   Don't speak; I'm ready to do anything.
   [MOLCHÁLIN *throws himself on his knees.* SOPHIE *pushes
   him away.*]

MOLCHÁLIN: Remember! Don't be angry! Look towards
me! . . .

SOPHIE: Don't come and pester me,   I can remember
nothing
   I want no memories, I hate and loathe them.

MOLCHÁLIN [*crawling at her feet*]:
   Mercy . . .

SOPHIE: Don't be a worm, get up!
   I know your answer, I don't want to hear it,
   It'll be lies . . .

MOLCHÁLIN: One favour . . .

SOPHIE: No, No, No.

MOLCHÁLIN: It was a joke. I only meant to say . . .

SOPHIE: Stand back at once, I tell you.
   Or else I'll scream, and wake up the whole household,

Ruin myself, as well as you.

  [MOLCHÁLIN *gets up.*]

From now on, it's as if I hadn't ever known you.

  Don't you dare think I'm going to cry,

  Reproach you, or complain, for you're not worth it.

But, do not let the dawn find you still in this house.

  And may I never hear of you again.

MOLCHÁLIN: As you command.

SOPHIE: Or else, I'm going to be so angry

  I'll tell the whole truth to Papa.

  You know I don't care what becomes of me.

  Go on. No, stay. You may be glad

That when you were alone with me, in the still night,

  You showed the coy side of your nature

More even than you do by day, in company,

    When you are wide awake.

  There's not so much audacity in you,

    As crooked-mindedness.

  I'm only thankful to have found it out

At night, and not in front of disapproving people;

  As when I had that faint just now

With Mr Chátsky here . . .

CHÁTSKY [*Flinging himself between them*]:

               He's here, you little shammer!

LIZA and SOPHIE: Oh! Oh!

  [LIZA *drops the candle with fright;* MOLCHÁLIN *disappears into his own room.*]

CHÁTSKY: Go on and faint; it's quite in order now.

  You've got a better reason for it, this time.

  So, now at last the riddle's solved!

  That's who it was I was thrown over for!

  I don't know how I held my rage back!

  I watched, I saw, and I could not believe!

  While that dear friend, for whose sake you forgot

  Your old love and your womanly modesty,

Hides behind doors, afraid to face the music!
How can one guess what Fate is up to?
She wields her scourge on men of sensibility,
It's the Molchálins of this world are blest!

SOPHIE [*in floods of tears*]:
Don't, don't go on. I blame myself entirely.
Who would have thought he could be so deceitful?

LIZA: Noise! Running footsteps! Lord! It's the whole household coming.
There now, your father will be gratified.

[*Enter* FÁMUSOV *and a crowd of servants, with candles.*]

FÁMUSOV: This way! All follow me, and hurry, hurry!
Let's have more candles, get some lanterns!
Where are the bogeys? Bah! They're all familiar faces!
Sophia! You, my daughter, loose!
What are you doing here? Who with, you brazen hussy?
There's not a pick to choose between them,
Her and her mother, my lamented wife.
The minute she and I were parted
My better half would find a man somewhere!
Where is your fear of God? How did this man beguile you?
Why, you yourself said he was mad!
No! I've been overcome by blind stupidity.
There was a plot, and he was in it
As well as all the guests. Why have I been so punished! . . .

CHÁTSKY [*to* SOPHIE]:
Have I then you to thank for this invention too?

FÁMUSOV: No play-acting, my lad. I shan't be taken in,
Not even if you two start fighting one another.
[*To a* SERVANT] You, Philip, you're an utter dolt!
[*To the* PORTER]
This is the lazy loon I made my porter,
Deaf as a post and never knows a thing.
Have you been out? Where did you go to then?
Why was the hall door left unlocked?

Why weren't you looking? Why did you not hear?
You're for the Settlement the pair of you! Hard labour![20]
   You would have sold me for a sixpence.
    [*To* LIZA]:
All this comes of your pranks, you with the shifty eyes!
   The Moscow shops, smart clothes and fashions!
   That's where you learned to play the procuress!
   Wait now, and I'll set you to rights;
Back to your hovel, if you please – quick march!
   You go and mind the poultry!
    [*To* SOPHIE]:
And you my dear – I shan't neglect my daughter –
   Just you be patient two days more;
You can't stay here in Moscow, and meet people,
You must be got away from these wild boys.
Off to the country with you, to your Aunt,
   Out in the wilds, Sarátov province!
You will be sorry for yourself, down there;
Sit with a tambour-frame, yawn over holy books . . . .
    [*To* CHÁTSKY]:
   Now, Sir, I'm going to speak plainly;
You will please not again come near this house,
   Either the front way or the back.
After this final escapade of yours
You'll find all sorts of doors shut in your face!
   I'll do my best to see they are,
Raise the alarm, and make the whole town hum!
   I'll show you up before the nation,
I'll take you to the highest court in the land,
    To the Cabinet, to the Tsar.
CHÁTSKY [*after some moments of silence*]:
Excuse me if I don't come to my senses;
   I hear, but I can't understand,
As if there's something more they're going to explain,
   I'm puzzled what to think . . . waiting for something . . .
    [*Hotly*]   209

Blind! Who did I expect   was going to reward me
  For all my toil? I rushed! I flew!
I trembled at the thought   of happiness so near!
To whom did I, just now,   pour out those tender words
  So passionately and so humbly!
 And you! My God! *Who* was it that you chose!
 When I think *who* it was that you preferred!
Why did you lead me on   with hopes? Why not say straight
That you had taken the past   and made a joke of it?
That even the memory   had all gone cold on you,
Of how we used to feel,   the way our two hearts beat . . .
  Distance, distractions, change of scene –
None of them ever chilled   that memory in me.
I lived and breathed in it,   it filled me all day long!
 If you had said that my surprise appearance,
  The way I looked, the way I talked and acted,
    Were all revolting to you,
 I would have broken with you, then and there
Without wanting to know   who this dear friend might be
  Before I said good-bye for ever.
    [*Mockingly.*]
You'll make it up with him   when you've had time to think;
  For, why should you destroy yourself?
 There'll always be . . . someone you can protect,
  Wrap him up tight, send him on errands,
Husband-the-little-boy, husband-the-servant.
  One of my lady's pages –
Supreme ideal of all Moscow husbands . . .
Enough! I'm proud to say   that I have made the break.
Now Mr Father, you   so passionate for rank,
  May you doze on in blissful ignorance
  Don't be alarmed – I won't come courting –
There'll be another one, who's well behaved
A smooth, obsequious, oily operator.
 A man, in fine, whose qualities

Are worthy of his father-in-law-to-be.
    There now! I'm absolutely sane;
I've no more dreams, the scales   have fallen from my eyes.
Now it would do no harm   to take them all in turn –
    Daughter and father, and the brainless lover,
    And the whole world, and pour upon them
    All of my bitterness, all my frustration.
Who was I with? Where did Fate cast me up?
Tormentors, all of them;   cursing and persecuting,
    Treacherous lovers, unrelenting haters,
    And irrepressible tellers of tales.
    Unbalanced clever ones, sly simpletons,
        And sinister old ladies.
Decayed old men, brooding on made-up nonsense . . .
You all with one accord   declared that I was mad –
And you were right! A man   could go through fire unharmed
    If he could spend a single day with you,
    Breathe the same air as you, and keep his reason.
Out, out from Moscow! Now   no more I'll ride this way;
    I'm off, I'm running, I'm not looking back,
        I've gone to search the world,
    To find some niche, where outraged sense can shelter! –²¹
        My carriage! Get my carriage!
        [*He drives away.*]
FÁMUSOV [*to* SOPHIE]:
Well now, and can't you see   the man was off his head?
    I ask you, seriously,
He's mad! That awful stuff   he talked when he was here!
    Oily and smooth! Father-in-law!
    And Moscow too – so truculent about it!
    Then had you really meant to do me down?
        Isn't my case truly pathetic?
And – Oh my God! What is   the Princess going to say?

CURTAIN

Notes to *Chatsky*

1. p. 132. Grade eight post. See Introduction, Section 2.
2. p. 132. Tver. An ancient city on the upper Volga; now called Kalínin in honour of the first President of the USSR.
3. p. 139. Most, if not all of the characters described here by Chátsky are no doubt real people, whom a contemporary audience would have recognized, but not all can be positively identified today. This 'dusky chap' is a Bessarabian Greek called Metaxas, living in Moscow at the time.
4. p. 140. The Education Panel was a body attached to the Ministry of Church Affairs and National Education. It was concerned, among other things, with the censorship of school books.
5. p. 140. Quotation from a poem by Gabriel Derzhávin (1743–1816).
6. p. 140. Literally, 'Still a *Fräulein* of Catherine I?'; nobody alive in 1824 could possibly have been a *Fräulein* at the court of Catherine I, the widow of Peter the Great, who reigned from 1725 to 1727. Commentators do not seem to have noticed this line; it is simply a rather heavy-handed way of saying that the aunt is a very old maid, or very old-fashioned in her ways – in fact Miss Khlyóstova is a sprightly sixty-five. Or could it be an allusion to the Order of St Catherine, a decoration for Court Ladies, founded in 1714 in honour of the Empress?
7. p. 141. Nízhni-Nóvgorod. The great trading centre of the Volga, now called Górki, in honour of Maxim Gorki.
8. p. 145. A Court Chamberlain wore a coat, with a golden key embroidered on the back, symbolical of his right to enter the Imperial Apartment.
9. p. 148. The Carbonari was a revolutionary secret society, active in Italy and France at this period.
10. p. 152. An audience in 1825 would have remembered the Leipzig campaign well enough to know that the two regiments named by Skalozúb were never in action, and an armistice was in force on 3 August 1813
11. p. 156. Ochákov, on the Black Sea, was stormed, with fearful loss, by Russian troops under Potemkin in 1788. The Crimea was annexed in 1783.
12. p. 157. A true story of General Izmaílov, a notoriously bad serf-owner.

13. p. 157. Several men, among them the Izmaílov mentioned above, ruined themselves with these serf-theatres and serf-ballets.

14. p. 184. The Grandmother-Countess is a German, probably from the nobility of the Baltic Provinces of the Russian Empire (today the Estonian and Latvian republics of the USSR), many of whom married Russians. Some Russian editions of the play use phonetic spelling to represent her accent; this should not be exaggerated as unlike Boschmann in *The Infant* she speaks quite good Russian.

15. p. 187. Literally 'mutual instruction by maps (Landkarte)'. An untranslateable malapropism; what she means is the monitorial system of the English educationist Joseph Lancaster (1778–1838), much in favour among progressive people in Russia at that time.

16. p. 190. The 'Old Believers' were a religious sect who objected to changes in Church Ritual introduced in the XVII century, and to innovations in general.

17. p. 197. 'Ah, do not leave me, no, no no.' An aria from the opera 'Didone Abbandonata' by the Venetian Baldassare Galuppi, who was for many years resident composer for the St Petersburg Opera; he is best known to English speakers from a poem by Browning 'On a Toccata of Galuppi's'.

18. p. 197. This is an unmistakable portrait of Count Theodore Tolstóy, a kinsman of the great novelist, nicknamed 'American Tolstóy'. He was a notorious card-sharper and bully (said to have killed eleven men in duels). In 1803 he went on the first Russian voyage round the world, where he made himself such a nuisance on board that he was put ashore on one of the Aleutian Islands, from where he made his way to Kamchatka, and thence home overland. It is not clear that he was ever on the mainland of Alaska, then a Russian possession.

19. p. 199. One of the small rivers that intersect St Petersburg (Leningrad).

20. p. 209. Fámusov is exercising his right to deport his serfs to Siberia.

21. p. 211. Compare ALCESTE. . . . 'Et chercher sur la terre un endroit écarté Où d'estre homme d'honneur on ait la liberté'

(Molière, Le *Misanthrope*, Act V Scene 4)

THE GOVERNMENT INSPECTOR

A Comedy in Five Acts by

Nikoláy Vasilévich Gógol

'If your face is crooked, it's no good
blaming the mirror'. (*Popular Saying*)

CHARACTERS

MR ANTHONY HUFFAM-SLYDEWYNDE, Town Prefect[1]
  (*Antón Antónovich Skvoznik-Dmukhanóvsky*)
ANNE, his wife
  (*Anna Andréyevna*)
MARY, their daughter
  (*Márya Antónovna*)
MR LUKE WALLOP, Schools Superintendent
  (*Luká Lukích Khlópov*)
MRS ANASTASIA WALLOP, his wife
JUDGE AMOS SLAPPENCATCHIT, Judge of the District Court
  (*Ammós Fyódorovich Lyápkin-Tyápkin*)
MR ARTEMUS STRAWBERRY, Warden of Charitable Institutions
  (*Artémiy Filíppovich Zemlyaníka*)
MR JOHN PRY, postmaster
  (*Iván Kuz'mích Shpyókin*)
MR PETER DOBBIN
  (*Pyotr Ivánovich Dóbchinsky*)   } owners of property in the town
MR PETER BOBBIN
  (*Pyotr Ivánovich Bóbchinsky*)
MR JOHN WHIPPETT, a Government officer from St Petersburg
  (*Iván Aleksándrovich Khlestakóv*)
JOSEPH, his servant
  (*Ósip*)
DOCTOR CHRISTIAN FINISCHEM,[2] District Doctor
  (*Khristiyán Ivánovich Gíbner*)
MR THEODORE HUBBLY
  (*Fyódor Andréyevich Lyulyukóv*)   }
MR JOHN RATTUM   } Retired. Owners of property
  (*Iván Lázarevich Rastakóvsky*)   } and people of consequence in
MR STEPHEN CANISTER   } the town
  (*Stepán Ivánovich Koróbkin*)

CHARACTERS

CAPTAIN STEPHEN EARWIG, Police Superintendent
  (Stepán Ilyích Ukhovyórtov)

SERGEANT WHISTLER
  (Svistunóv)

SERGEANT BUTTONS
  (Púgovitsyn)   } Police Sergeants

SERGEANT HOLDMUZZLE
  (Derzhimórda)

MR ABDULLAH,[3] a shopkeeper
  (Abdúlin)

MRS FEBRONIA CLAPPERKIN, wife of a locksmith
  (Fevrónya Petróvna Poshlyópkina)

A SERGEANT'S WIFE

MIKE, Mr Huffam-Slydewynde's servant
  (Mishka)

Waiter at the Inn

Male and Female Guests, Merchants, Townspeople, Petitioners.

*The action takes place in a district town,
somewhere in Russia, in the 1830s.*

CHARACTERS AND COSTUMES

NOTES FOR THE LADIES AND GENTLEMEN
OF THE THEATRE

The Prefect has grown old in the service; in his own way he is a pretty shrewd man. Corrupt, but rather a dignified rogue; quite staid, even somewhat sententious; speaks neither too loudly nor too quietly, neither too much nor too little. Every word of his tells. His features are rough and coarse, as they are with any man who has come up on hard work from the lower ranks of the service. His transitions from fear to joy, from depression to exaltation, are rather rapid, as they are in a man whose sensibilities have been coarsened. Usually wears his uniform, with braided trimmings, cavalry boots and spurs. His hair is cut short and grizzled.

Anne, his wife, is a provincial coquette, not yet quite middle-aged, brought up half on novels and albums, half on the business of her pantry and sewing-room. Full of curiosity, and occasionally vain. Sometimes gets the upper hand of her husband, for the sole reason that he cannot find a way of answering her, but her power extends only over petty matters, and is expressed in scolding and jeering. Changes her dress four times in the course of the play.

Whippet is a young man, about twenty-three years old, lean and slim. Inclined to be a bit of a fool, and as the saying goes 'has no king inside his head', one of those people who get the name of being completely feather-brained at the offices where they work. Speaks and acts without thinking at all. Incapable of keeping his attention fixed on any notion. His speech is abrupt, and the words fly out of his mouth in a totally unexpected way. The more the performer exhibits candour and simplicity, the better he will succeed with the part. Fashionably dressed.

Joseph his servant, is the usual type of servant of a certain age. Speaks seriously, tends to look downwards, sententious and fond of lecturing his master. His voice, always quite level, takes on a severe, abrupt, quite rude tone when speaking to his master. He is more intelligent than his master, and therefore quicker on the uptake, but he does not like to talk much and goes about his knaveries in silence. His costume is a shabby grey or blue surtout.

Bobbin and *Dobbin* are both short and tubby and full of curiosity. They are extraordinarily alike; both have little round bellies, and the speech of both is rapid and much assisted by gesture and use of the hands. *Dobbin* is a little taller and more staid than *Bobbin*, but *Bobbin* is more relaxed and more lively than *Dobbin*.

Slappencatchit, the Judge, has read five or six books and is therefore something of a freethinker. Much given to conjecture, and therefore puts weight on every word he speaks. The performer of this part must always keep an important-looking expression on his face. Speaks in a deep drawling voice with a throaty wheeze, like an old clock that first makes a whirring noise and then strikes.

Strawberry, the Warden of Charitable Institutions, is a very stout, slow-moving and ungainly man, but for all that an adroit, insinuating knave. Very obliging, officious.

The Postmaster is ingenuous to the point of naïveté.

The other parts call for no special explanation. Their originals are to be seen almost everywhere.

Ladies and Gentlemen must pay special attention to the Final Tableau. The last word spoken must act upon all suddenly and simultaneously, like an electric shock. The whole group must change positions instantaneously. The sound of astonishment must burst out from all the women at once, as if from a single breast. Failure to attend to these notes can destroy the entire effect.

ACT ONE

A room in the PREFECT'S *house. On stage are the* PREFECT, *the*
WARDEN OF CHARITABLE INSTITUTIONS, *the* SCHOOLS
SUPERINTENDENT, *the* JUDGE, *the* CHIEF OF POLICE, *the*
DOCTOR *and two* POLICE SERGEANTS.

PREFECT: Gentlemen, I have invited you here in order to
communicate to you some most unpleasant news. We are
about to receive an Inspector.

SLAPPENCATCHIT: What? An Inspector?

STRAWBERRY: What? An Inspector?

PREFECT: An Inspector from St Petersburg, incognito,
and with secret instructions, too.

SLAPPENCATCHIT: Dear oh dear oh dear.

STRAWBERRY: Not a care in the world, and now look
what's happened!

WALLOP: Good Lord! And with secret instructions too!

PREFECT: I had a kind of presentiment. All last night I
dreamed about two extraordinary rats. I really never saw
such rats, black and unnaturally large! They came and
sniffed and went off. Look, I'll read you the letter that I
have had from Andrew Chipmouse – you know him, Mr
Strawberry. This is what he writes 'My dear old friend
and benefactor' [*mutters under his breath as he quickly scans
the paper*] '. . . and to let you know'. Ah, here it is 'By the
way, I hasten to let you know that an official has come
with instructions to inspect the whole province, and
especially our district [*holds up one finger with a meaningful
gesture*]. I have this from most reliable people, although
he makes himself out to be a private individual. As I
know that you like everybody else are sometimes a bit

221

naughty, being a sensible man who doesn't like to let slip anything that drops into his lap.' [*Pauses.*] Well, we all know each other here . . . 'I advise you to take precautions because he may arrive any time – if indeed he hasn't arrived already and isn't living somewhere incognito. . . . Yesterday I . . .' Oh, now it gets on to family matters. . . . 'Cousin Anne came to see us with her husband; Cousin John has got very fat and still plays the fiddle . . .' and so on and so on. There, that's the position.

SLAPPENCATCHIT: Yes, that's the position. Extraordinary, quite extraordinary. Must be some reason for it.

WALLOP: But Mr Slydewynde, why? What's it all about? Why should we have an Inspector?

PREFECT: Why? Well I suppose it's Fate. [*Sighs.*] Up to now, thank God, they have picked on other towns; this time it's our turn.

SLAPPENCATCHIT: Mr Slydewynde, I think there is some subtle motive here, rather of a political nature. Russia . . . yes, she is about to go to war, and the administration, you see, have quietly sent out an official, to find out if there's treason anywhere.

PREFECT: Oh, get along with you! And you an intelligent man! Treason in a district town! Is this on the frontier, or what? Why you could start from here and gallop for three years, and still not get to any foreign state.

SLAPPENCATCHIT: No, I tell you . . . I mean to say . . . you don't . . . They've got very subtle ideas at Headquarters; never mind about our being a long way off, they keep their eyes skinned.

PREFECT: They may or may not do that, but Gentlemen, I've given you advance warning. Look here, I have taken certain measures in my own department, and I advise you to do the same. Especially you, Mr Strawberry! There's no doubt that the very first thing a visiting official will want is to look at the charitable institutions

under your administration. So mind you see that everything is decent; better have clean nightcaps, better not
have the patients looking like blacksmiths, going round
half undressed, the way they usually do.

STRAWBERRY: Well, that's all right. I suppose we can
even manage the clean nightcaps.

PREFECT: Yes, and another thing. Have a notice in Latin
or some such language over each bed – Doctor, this is
your department now – name of illness, name of patient,
when taken ill, day of the week, day of the month . . . It
isn't nice to have your patients smoking such strong
tobacco, every time one comes in one gets a fit of the
sneezes. And there had better be fewer of them, or else it
will be immediately put down to bad management, or an
incompetent doctor.

STRAWBERRY: Oh, as regards treatment, we have our
own methods, the Doctor and I. The closer to Nature the
better; we don't use expensive drugs. Man is a simple
creature – if he dies, he dies; if he gets well, he gets well.
And talking to them would be difficult for Doctor
Finischern; he doesn't know a word of Russian.

[*The* DOCTOR *emits a sound that is a mixture of EE! and
EH!*]

PREFECT: You too, Judge, I'd like to advise you to pay
some attention to your Court-house. The watchmen have
been raising geese in that ante-room of yours, the place
where the litigants have to report, and the little goslings
keep getting under people's feet. Rearing domestic
animals is of course a laudable occupation, and why
shouldn't the watch do it? Only, you know, in a place
like that it isn't decent. . . . I had meant to mention this to
you before, only I somehow kept on forgetting.

SLAPPENCATCHIT: Then I'll tell them to take the whole
lot to the kitchen today. Would you like to come and
have dinner?

PREFECT: And besides, it isn't right for you to have all those untidy things hanging up to dry in the courtroom itself, and a hunting-crop right on top of the cupboard with the papers. I know you are fond of sport, but all the same it would be better to take it away for now, and then when the Inspector has gone on I suppose you can hang it up again. Also there's that Assessor of yours . . . of course he is a competent man, but he smells as if he had just come out of a distillery – that isn't nice either. I meant to speak to you about this some time ago; I can't remember what it was put it out of my head. There's something you can take for that, if it really is true what he says, that it's his natural smell. You might advise him to eat onions or garlic or something. This is where Doctor Finischem might be able to help with some of his medicines.

[*The* DOCTOR *emits the same sound.*]

SLAPPENCATCHIT: No, he can't get rid of it now; he says that his Nanny bumped him when he was a child and that ever since he has given off that slight odour of vodka.

PREFECT: Well, I just mentioned it. As regards your internal arrangements, and what Mr Chipmouse calls being a little naughty, I can't say anything. Yes, it's an extraordinary thing, but there's nobody who hasn't got some sin on his conscience. The Lord Himself has arranged it that way and it's no good the Voltaireans saying otherwise.

SLAPPENCATCHIT: But, Mr Slydewynde, what do you regard as being naughty? There's naughtiness and naughtiness. I tell everybody frankly that I do accept bribes, but what sort of bribes? Greyhound puppies. That makes all the difference.

PREFECT: Well, whether it's puppies or anything else, it's still bribes.

SLAPPENCATCHIT: Oh no, Mr Slydewynde. Suppose for

instance you get a man with a five hundred rouble fur
coat, or a shawl for the wife . . .

PREFECT: Well and what comes of your taking bribes of
greyhound puppies? The end of it is that you don't
believe in God; you never go to Church, while I am at
least firm in my faith and I'm in Church every Sunday.
Whereas you . . . Oh, I know you; if you start talking
about the Creation, it's enough to make one's hair stand
on end.

SLAPPENCATCHIT: Yes, you see that is the position that
I've come to, thinking it out in my own mind.

PREFECT: Yes, and having a lot of mind is sometimes
worse than having none at all. I only just mentioned the
District Court, though to tell you the truth I doubt if
anybody will look in there; it really is an enviable job,
under the special protection of Providence. Now Mr
Wallop, you, as Superintendent of Schools, have got to be
particularly careful about the teachers. Of course they
are learned men, and they have been educated at all sorts
of colleges, but they do have the most extraordinary
habits; and these, naturally, are things that can't be
separated from the teacher's vocation. One of them, for
instance, . . . you know, the one with the fat face . . . I
don't remember his name . . . he can't help it, but every
time he goes up to the daïs he makes a grimace like this
[*makes a grimace*] and then puts his hand up inside his
stock and starts to stroke his beard. It's all right, of course,
if he pulls a face like that at a pupil; it may even be a
necessary thing to do – I'm not in a position to pass judgement on that, but you can judge for yourself that if he
does that to a visitor it could be very bad; Mr Inspector,
or someone, might take it personally. And that might
be the deuce and all.

WALLOP: But what can I do with him, really? I have
already spoken to him about it several times. And look

what happened the other day; our Marshal[4] was just about to come into the class-room and I've never seen anything to equal the face he concocted. He meant well, but I got a reprimand for allowing the young people to get infected with subversive ideas.

PREFECT: I must say something too about the history teacher. He's a learned man – that's obvious – and he has got hold of lots and lots of facts, only when he's explaining them he becomes so heated that he forgets himself. I was listening to him once; well, it was all right as long as he was talking about the Assyrians and Babylonians, but I can't tell you what happened to him when he got on Alexander of Macedon. Honestly, I thought the place was on fire! He rushed down from the daïs and banged his chair on the floor, as hard as he could! Mind you, of course, Alexander of Macedon is a hero, but why smash chairs? It means loss to the Treasury.

WALLOP: Yes, he is fiery! I have spoken to him several times about it. 'As you please,' he says, 'but I'm going to give my life unsparingly to learning.'

PREFECT: Yes. Such is the inscrutable law of the Fates. Either a learned man drinks, or else he makes such awful faces that you can't have the holy icons in the same room with him.

WALLOP: God help anyone whose job has anything to do with education! You're afraid of everything, everybody interferes, everybody wants to show that he is an intelligent man too.

PREFECT: It would be all right if it wasn't for that confounded incognito. Suddenly he'll look in. 'Ah, there you are, my dears! And who,' he'll say, 'is the judge here?' 'Slappencatchit.' 'Then bring Slappencatchit to me! And who is the Warden of Charitable Institutions?' 'Strawberry.' 'Then bring Strawberry to me!' That's the horrid part of it.

[*Enter the* POSTMASTER.]

POSTMASTER: Will you explain to me, gentlemen, what is it, who is the officer who's coming?

PREFECT: Haven't you heard?

POSTMASTER: I heard from Peter Bobbin. He was with me in the post office just now.

PREFECT: Well then, what do you think about that?

POSTMASTER: What do I think? It'll be a war with the Turks.

SLAPPENCATCHIT: That's it! I thought the same myself.

PREFECT: Yes, and you're a pair of silly cuckoos!

POSTMASTER: That's right. A war with the Turks. It's the French up to their filthy tricks again.

PREFECT: War with the Turks? It's going to be trouble for us, nòt for the Turks. We know all about it; I've had a letter.

POSTMASTER: In that case, it won't be a war with the Turks.

PREFECT: Tell us then, Mr Pry, what do you make of it?

POSTMASTER: What do I make of it? What do you, Mr Slydewynde?

PREFECT: What do I make of it? I've nothing to fear, well nothing much . . . It's the merchant community and the townspeople that worry me. They say that I have made them smart, but honestly if I did take anything from anybody it was done without any ill feelings. Really I do wonder though [*takes him by the arm, and draws him aside*] I do wonder whether someone may have reported me. After all, why should we be the ones to get the Inspector? Listen, Mr Pry, can't you do something for the good of us all . . . every incoming and outgoing letter that comes to you at the Post Office – you know, just unseal it a little way to see whether there is anything in the way of a report, or whether it is just correspondence. If not, you can seal it up again; for that matter you could even deliver it as it is, unsealed.

POSTMASTER: I know, I know.... You can't teach me about that, I do it not so much by way of precaution, more out of curiosity; I just love to know the news of the world. It's very interesting reading, I can tell you. Sometimes you get a letter that's a joy to read – the way the various incidents are described ... so edifying ... better than the 'Moscow Gazette'.

PREFECT: Tell me now, you haven't in your reading picked up anything about an officer from St Petersburg?

POSTMASTER: No, nothing about one from St Petersburg, though there has been a lot of talk about officers from Kostromá and Sarátov. But it's a pity you don't read the letters – they've got lovely things in them. The other day now there was a subaltern writing to a friend and describing a ball ... very saucy ... very, very well done. 'My life, dear friend, is spent in the Seventh Heaven; lots of young ladies, the band playing, the colours flying ...' He describes it with great feeling, great feeling. I made a point of keeping that one by me. Would you like me to read it to you?

PREFECT: Come on, we haven't time for that now. Mr Pry, will you do me one kindness; if a complaint or report should happen to come in, have no compunction in holding it up.

POSTMASTER: I'll be delighted.

SLAPPENCATCHIT: You look out, you're going to catch it for this, one of these days.

POSTMASTER: Oh, dear me!

PREFECT: It's all right, it's all right. It would be different if you made any publicity about it, but this is a family thing, don't you know.

SLAPPENCATCHIT: Quite; it isn't a nice sort of thing to have started up. And I'll tell you what, Mr Slydewynde, I was just going to bring you a little present. A bitch puppy, and she's own sister to that dog that you know about. I expect you have heard that Mr Bonnet and Mr Flush are going to law; I'm on velvet – I get the hares on the land of both of them.

PREFECT: My dear man, I'm not awfully keen about your hares just now. I've got that confounded incognito stuck in my head. Waiting for a door to open, and then – pounce!

[*Enter, panting,* BOBBIN *and* DOBBIN]

BOBBIN: Extraordinary occurrence!

DOBBIN: Unexpected announcement!

ALL: What is it? What is it?

DOBBIN: Unforeseen development; we were going into the hotel . . .

BOBBIN [*interrupting*]: Peter and I were going into the hotel . . .

DOBBIN [*interrupting*]: Hey! Let me tell the story, Peter.

BOBBIN: No! You let me tell it . . . let me, let me . . . you haven't got the style for it . . .

DOBBIN: But you'll get into a muddle and you won't remember it all.

BOBBIN: I will remember it; I will, I will. Don't you interfere now, let me tell it, don't interfere. Gentlemen, kindly tell Peter not to interfere.

PREFECT: For goodness sake say what it is! My heart's in my mouth. Sit down, gentlemen! Get chairs! Here's a chair for you, Mr Dobbin.

[*All seat themselves round the two* PETERS.]

BOBBIN: Allow me, allow me; I'll tell it all in order. On having had the pleasure to leave your house after you, Sir, had received a worrying letter, yes Sir, I proceeded to run . . . Now, please don't interrupt, Peter! I know it all, Sir. All, all, all! Well, do you see Sir, I ran round to Mr Canister, and on not finding Mr Canister at home I looked in at Mr Rattum's house, and on not finding Mr Rattum, why I went to Mr Pry at the Post, in order to communicate the news that you had received, and on my way there I met Peter . . .

DOBBIN [*interrupting*]: By the stall where they sell pies.

BOBBIN: By the stall where they sell pies. Yes, and on meeting Peter I say to him 'Have you heard the news Mr Slydewynde has had in a letter from a reliable source?' And Peter has already heard about it from your housekeeper Eudoxia, who has been sent round, why I do not know, to Mr Philip Pylebottom.

DOBBIN [*interrupting*]: For a cask for French brandy.

BOBBIN [*pushing* DOBBIN's *hands away*]: For a cask for French brandy. So off we go, Peter and I, to Mr Pylebottom . . . Now look here, Peter, don't interrupt, please don't interrupt . . . Off we go to Mr Pylebottom, and on the way Peter says 'Let's look in,' he says 'at the Tavern. It's my stomach . . . I've had nothing to eat since morning, and I've got a wambly stomach . . .' Yes, Sir, it was Peter's stomach. 'And at the Tavern,' says he 'they've just had a delivery of fresh salmon, so we can have a snack.' No sooner are we in the hotel than all of a sudden a young man . . .

DOBBIN: Of prepossessing appearance and wearing plain clothes.

BOBBIN: Of prepossessing appearance and wearing plain clothes, walks into the room, just like this, with a judge-matical sort of a look on his face . . . his expression . . . his movements . . . lots and lots of everything up here. [*Sweeps his hand over his forehead in a circular gesture.*] I get a kind of presentiment and I say to Peter 'There's more in this, Sir, than meets the eye.' Yes. But Peter has already snapped his fingers to get the innkeeper to come over. Blazey, Sir, the innkeeper; his wife had a baby three weeks ago, such a bouncing boy, he'll keep an inn, just like his father. So when he has got Blazey over, Peter asks him, quietly like, 'Who is that young man?' says he.

'That,' says Blazey – now don't interrupt Peter, please don't interrupt! You're not going to tell the story, honestly now you're not. You've got a lisp; I know there's one tooth in your mouth that whistles . . . 'That', says he, 'is a young man, an official, travelling from St Petersburg, and his name,' says he, 'is John Whippett, Sir, and he is travelling,' says he, 'to Sarátov province, and his behaviour,' says he, 'is most peculiar. He's been living here for over a week, never goes out of the inn, has everything on account and won't pay a farthing.' And as he says that it comes to me in a flash. 'Hey!' I say to Peter . . .

DOBBIN: No Peter, it was I said Hey!

BOBBIN: You said it first and then I said it too. 'Hey!' we said, Peter and I. 'Now what is the point of his sticking here, when he is supposed to be going to Sarátov?' Yes, Sir! There you are, he is that official.

PREFECT: Who? What official?

BOBBIN: The official that your Honour got the notification about – the Inspector.

PREFECT [in terror]: What are you saying, good gracious, it isn't him.

DOBBIN: It's him! He doesn't pay any money, and he doesn't go out. Who would it be, if it isn't him? He's got an order for post-horses made out to Sarátov.

BOBBIN: It's him, it's him, I swear it's him. . . . He's so observant; looks at everything. He saw that Peter and I were eating salmon – more for Peter's sake on account of his stomach . . . yes, he actually eyed our plates. The terror of it struck right into me.

PREFECT: Lord have mercy on us sinners! Where is he staying there?

DOBBIN: Number Five, under the stairs.

BOBBIN: That's the same room where the officers had the fight, on their way through last year.

PREFECT: And has he been there for long?

DOBBIN: It's about two weeks now. He came on St Basil the Egyptian's day.

PREFECT: Oh my godfathers and godmothers! Take the holy icons out before I say something! In those two weeks there was the Sergeant's wife who was whipped! And the prisoners who didn't get their rations! The streets are a shambles! Filthy! Disgraceful! Shameful! [*Clutches his head.*]

STRAWBERRY: What will you do, Mr Slydewynde? Drive over to the hotel in full dress?

SLAPPENCATCHIT: No, no! Let the Mayor go ahead of you, and the Clergy, and the Merchant Community; you know, in that book 'The Acts of John the Mason'.[5]

PREFECT: No, no, leave this one to me. There have been some difficult situations in my life, but they passed, and I even got thanked in the end; maybe the Lord will bring me out of this one too. [*Turning to Bobbin*] A young man, you say?

BOBBIN: Yes, twenty-three or twenty-four and a bit.

PREFECT: So much the better; a young man is quicker to size up. The trouble is when you get an old devil; a young one has got it all on the surface. Will each of you gentlemen continue with his preparations in his own department; I shall go alone, unless I take Mr Dobbin. I shall go in my unofficial capacity; out for a walk, looking to see that travellers are not being inconvenienced. Hi! Whistler!

SERGEANT WHISTLER. Yes, Sir.

PREFECT: Go and get me the Chief at once. No, I want you here. Tell one of them out there that I want the Chief as quickly as possible, and come back here.

[*The* SERGEANT *scuttles out of the room.*]

STRAWBERRY: Come on, Judge, let's go. There might be really serious trouble.

SLAPPENCATCHIT: What have you got to be frightened

about? Get the clean nightcaps on to the patients and you're covered.

STRAWBERRY: Nightcaps! The patients were ordered gruel, and there's a smell of cabbages all down my corridors fit to make you hold your nose.

SLAPPENCATCHIT: I'm easy about this. After all, who is going to come into the District Court? And he'll get no joy out of the papers, even if he does look at anything. I've been on the bench now for fifteen years, and when I look at the Case reports – Oh! All I can do is to hold up my hands. Solomon himself couldn't understand what was right and what was wrong in them.

[*Exeunt* JUDGE, WARDEN OF CHARITABLE INSTITUTIONS, SCHOOLS INSPECTOR *and* POSTMASTER, *colliding with the returning* SERGEANT *in the doorway*.]

PREFECT: Well, have they got my droshky out there?

SERGEANT WHISTLER: Yes, Sir.

PREFECT: Go out into the street. . . . No, stay here! Go and get . . . Where are the others then? Don't tell me you are the only one! Surely I gave orders for Proctor to be here. Where is Proctor?

SERGEANT WHISTLER: Proctor is at the station, Sir, only he isn't in a serviceable condition.

PREFECT: In what way?

SERGEANT WHISTLER: Well Sir, he was carried in this morning dead to the world. He's already had two tubs of cold water poured over him and he still hasn't come round.

PREFECT: Oh Lord, oh Lord! Quick, get out into the street . . . No, run up to my room first — and listen! Bring down my sword and my new hat. Come, Mr Dobbin, let's go.

BOBBIN: Me too, me too! . . . Let me come too, Mr Slydewynde!

PREFECT: No, Mr Bobbin, no, you can't, you can't! It

would be awkward; anyway there isn't room for all of us in the droshky.

BOBBIN: All right, all right. I tell you what, I'll follow the droshky. I'll run along behind, run along behind. I only want to have a squint through the crack in the wall, and just pop my head round the door to see what he does . . .

PREFECT [*taking his sword, to the* SERGEANT]: Run at once and get the constables, and let each man take . . . Look how scratched this sword is! Confound that man Abdullah and his rotten shop – he can see that the Prefect has an old sword, and he hasn't sent up a new one. Oh, they're a sly lot! I shouldn't wonder if the scoundrels have got petitions ready to pull out from under their coats. Let each man take a street in his hand . . . damn, not a street . . . take a broom in his hand, and let 'em sweep the whole street leading up to the inn, and sweep it clean. . . . Do you hear! And look here, you! I know all about you; you go and chum up with them in there, and then you'll be slipping the silver teaspoons into your boot – Look here! I've got sharp ears! . . . What did you do to Blackman the draper? Eh? He gave you a yard and a half of cloth for a tunic, and you went off with the whole piece. Look here! You can't take things like that, not in your rank! Get going!

[*Enter the* POLICE CAPTAIN.]

PREFECT: Ah, Captain Earwig, will you tell me, for goodness sake, where did you vanish to? Is this a way to go on!

EARWIG: I was here just now, outside the gate.

PREFECT: Well then, listen, Captain Earwig! That officer from St Petersburg has arrived. What arrangements have you made?

EARWIG: Just what you told me. I have sent Sergeant Buttons with the constables to clean up the pavement.

PREFECT: And where is Holdmuzzle?

EARWIG: Holdmuzzle has gone out on the fire engine.

234

PREFECT: And Proctor's drunk?

EARWIG: Yes, he is.

PREFECT: How did you allow that to happen?

EARWIG: Heaven knows. A fight took place yesterday, outside the Town – he went there to restore order and returned drunk.

PREFECT: Listen now, this is what you are to do. Sergeant Buttons . . . he is tall, so let him stand on the bridge, in charge of Public Services. And quickly now, clear away that old fence, the one by the shoemaker's shop, and put some straw for a marker, something that'll look more like planning. The more demolitions you have, the more evidence there is of the activity of the Town Commandant. Oh Lord, and I forgot that about forty cartloads of every sort of muck had been dumped alongside that fence. What a nasty place this town is! You've only got to put up some sort of monument, or even a fence – up they come with the rubbish and where the Hell do they get it all from? [*Sighs.*] And if the visiting officer asks the men whether they are contented, they're to say 'contented with everything, Your Honour'. And if anyone isn't contented I'll give him something to be discontented about afterwards. Oh ho, ho, ho, ho! I'm a sinful man, a man of many sins. [*Picks up the hat-box instead of the hat.*] Grant me, O God, to get away with this one quickly, and I'll offer a candle such as no man has ever offered before. I'll have a hundredweight of wax off every one of those sly dogs of merchants. Oh Lord, oh Lord! Let's go, Mr Dobbin. [*Is about to put the cardboard box on his head instead of the hat.*]

EARWIG: Mr Slydewynde, that's the box, not the hat.

PREFECT [*throwing the box away*]: The box, so it is damn it, the box. And if anybody asks why the Chapel for the Charitable Institution, for which money was granted five years ago, hasn't been built, don't forget to say that the building was started, but it was burnt down. That's what

I have been putting in my report. Otherwise I expect somebody will be fool enough to forget himself and say it hasn't been started. And tell Holdmuzzle not to be too free with those fists of his; his idea of keeping order is black eyes all round – guilty or innocent. Come on Mr Dobbin let's go. [*He goes out and comes back.*] And don't let the soldiers out on to the streets improperly dressed. This rabble of a garrison just put their tunics on top of their shirts, with nothing below.

[*All go out.* ANNE *and* MARY *enter, running.*]

ANNE: Where are they? Wherever are they? Oh, heavens! [*Opens the door.*] Husband! Tony! Anthony! [*Speaking rapidly*] And this is all through you, all your fault. Going off rummaging: 'I want a pin, I want a scarf.' [*She runs to the window and calls*] Anthony, where are you going, where are you going? What? Has he come, the Inspector? Has he got a moustache? What sort of a moustache?

VOICE OF PREFECT: Presently, my dear, presently.

ANNE: Presently? I like that – presently! I don't want presently. . . . All I want is one word – what is he? A colonel? Eh? [*With scorn*] He's gone! I'll pay you out for this! All she says is 'Mummy, Mummy, wait till I pin up my scarf at the back; I'm just coming.' You and your 'just coming'. There you are now, we never found out anything! It's all that wretched vanity; she heard that the Postmaster was here and away with her to mince up and down in front of the looking-glass – first one side, then the other side. She thinks he's dangling after her, but all he does is to make a face when she looks the other way.

MARY: But Mummy what can we do? It'll be all the same in a couple of hours. We'll know all about it then.

ANNE: Couple of hours! Thank you very much! I'm obliged to you for your reply! I wonder you don't think to say that we'll know better still in a month. [*She leans out of the*

window.] Yoo hoo! Eudoxia! Eh! What's that, Eudoxia?
Did you hear? Has somebody arrived there? ... You
didn't hear? Stupid girl! He's waving good-bye? Even if
he is, you might have asked him something. You couldn't
find that out? Her head's full of nonsense; all she thinks
about is getting a husband. – What's that? They drove
away too quickly? You might have run after the droshky.
Go on, go on at once! Do you hear? Run! Ask where
they've gone to, and ask properly. Who is the visitor,
what is he like? Do you hear? Go and peep through a
hole and find out! Everything – what colour are his eyes?
Black or not? And come back this very minute, do you
hear? Hurry, hurry, hurry, hurry!

[*She goes on shouting till the curtain falls on the two of them
standing at the window.*]

ACT TWO

A small hotel room. Bed, table, trunk, empty bottle, boots, clothes-brush, etc. JOSEPH *is lying on his master's bed.*]

JOSEPH: Oh, to hell with it all, I'm hungry! And there's a rumbling in my belly that resembles the trumpeting of an entire regiment. We shan't get home at all, and then what will you have us do? It's over a month since we left Petersburg. Fiddled away his bit of money on the road, the dear boy, and now he's stuck here with his tail between his legs, and never a spark to be got from him. There was enough to pay for the post-horses, enough and to spare, but no – he must cut a dash, you see, in every town. [*Imitating him*] 'I say Joseph, go and look out a room for me, the best room, and order dinner, the best dinner they've got; I can't eat a bad dinner, I must have the best dinner.' I would be all right if there was anything to him, but sure what is he but a little slip of a grade 14 registrar?[6] He gets to know this fellow he meets on the road, and next thing it's the cards, and you see now what that has brought him to. Ah, I'm sick of this way of living; country life is better, it really is – there may not be so much *publicity*, but there's less anxiety. Get yourself a country wife, and you can spend all your days lying up above the stove and eating pies. But if you're going to be honest about it, then of course there's no denying that life in Petersburg is the best of all. If only there's the money, that's the genteel and *political* way of living – theatres, dogs to dance for you, everything you want. And all the delicate refinement of the conversation – it

238

nearly comes up to the gentry. Go into the Pike Market,
and the merchants call out 'Your Honour' to you!
Take the ferryboat, and you're sitting beside a government official. If you want company, go into a shop – there'll
be some army veteran in there, who'll tell you stories
about camp, and explain what every star in the sky
stands for. You can see it all spread out before you. An
old lady wanders in, she's an officer's wife; another time
a housemaid will give you such a look ... ooh! [*He
laughs and shakes his head.*] And the elegance, damn it,
of the etiquette! You never hear an impolite word,
everybody speaks civilly to you. When you're tired of
walking, you take a cab and sit in it like a lord. You
needn't pay if you don't want to; there's a side entrance
to every house and you can slip out the way the devil
himself wouldn't find you. There's one thing bad. You
get a grand feed one day and you're nearly destroyed
with hunger the next; like I am now, for instance. And
it's all his fault. What can you do with him? His Dad
sends him the bit of money, but will he hang on to it,
and make it last? Not he! He's off on the randan, riding
around in cabs – every day it's 'Go and get me a theatre
ticket,' till at the end of the week he sends me round to
the second-hand shops with his new frock-coat. Another
time he'll let everything go, down to the last shirt, till
there's nothing left on him but an old surtout and a
shabby overcoat .... Honest to God, it's the truth! And
that lovely English cloth! One frock-coat cost him a
hundred and fifty roubles, and he let it go in the market for
twenty; and as for trousers – no good talking about them,
they go for nothing. For why? Because he doesn't mind
his work. Gadding about on the Prospect, or playing
cards, when he ought to be in the office. Ah – ha! If the
old gentleman knew about that! He wouldn't stop to
think that you're a Government official, he'd lift your

shirt-tail and give you something that'd keep you scratching for four days. If you're in the service, do your duty. And you see what the innkeeper says now? 'I'll give you nothing to eat till you pay for the last lot', and suppose we don't pay? [*With a sigh*] Oh dear Lord, if it were only a drop of the cabbage soup! I think I could eat the whole world now. There's footsteps; that'll be him coming. [*Hurriedly scrambles off the bed.*]

    [*Enter* WHIPPETT.]

WHIPPETT: There, take that. [*Gives* JOSEPH *his cap and cane.*] Have you been lounging on the bed again?

JOSEPH: Why would I lounge on the bed? Haven't I ever seen a bed?

WHIPPETT: Nonsense, you have been on it. Look, it's all rumpled.

JOSEPH: What would I want with it? Don't I know what a bed is? I've got legs; I can stand. Why would I want your bed?

WHIPPETT [*walking round the room*]: Go and look if there's any tobacco in that pouch?

JOSEPH: What's the good of looking there for tobacco? You smoked up the last of it four days ago.

WHIPPETT [*walks about, pursing his lips into various shapes and at last speaks in a loud firm voice*]: Listen . . . I say Joseph!

JOSEPH: Yes, Sir?

WHIPPETT [*in a voice that is loud, but not so firm*]: You go there.

JOSEPH: Go where?

WHIPPETT [*in a voice that is not at all firm and not loud, very close to a request*]: Downstairs, to the dining-room . . . Tell them there . . . to give me some dinner.

JOSEPH: Ah no, I won't go.

WHIPPETT: Idiot, how dare you speak like that?

JOSEPH: Well you see, it makes no odds if I do go. The Guv'nor has said he isn't going to give you any more dinner.

WHIPPETT: How dare he not give me dinner! What nonsense!

JOSEPH: 'And, what's more,' says he, 'I'm going to the Prefect; your master hasn't paid for over a fortnight. You and your master,' says he, 'are rogues,' says he 'and your master's a scamp. Dirty bilkers,' says he, 'we've seen 'em before,' says he.

WHIPPETT: Brute! You enjoy repeating all that to me.

JOSEPH: 'Anybody can come here like that,' says he, 'make themselves at home and run up a bill, and then you can't get them out. I'm not going to shilly-shally,' says he, 'I'm going straight off with a complaint, so as to get them taken to the police-station and locked up.'

WHIPPETT: Now then, now then, that'll do, idiot. Go on, go on and speak to him. So beastly coarse.

JOSEPH: I'd better ask the Guv'nor to come and see you.

WHIPPETT: What do I want with the Guv'nor? You go and speak to him.

JOSEPH: But Sir, really.

WHIPPETT. Oh, go on, damn it, and get the Guv'nor.

[*Exit* JOSEPH.]

WHIPPETT [*alone*]: It's awful to be so hungry! I went for a bit of a walk, thinking my appetite might pass off, but it doesn't, damn it. Yes, and I'd have had the money to get home, if I hadn't blued it at Pénza. That infantry captain fairly rooked me: he's a deadly punter, marvellous how he does it, the clever devil. I sat in for a quarter of an hour, all told, and he scooped the lot. And I was still mad keen to have another go at him, only I never got the chance. What a filthy little hole this is! The greengrocers won't let you have anything on tick. Downright mean. [*Whistles, beginning with the air from 'Robert le Diable', going on with 'The Red Sarafan' and ending up with something nondescript.*] It's no go with any of them.

[*Re-enter* JOSEPH *and* WAITER.]

WAITER: The Guv'nor told me to ask what you wanted.

WHIPPETT: Hallo old fellow! How are you? Quite well?

WAITER: Quite well, God be praised.

WHIPPETT: Well and how are things with you in the hotel?
Everything going all right?

WAITER: Yes, praise be to God, pretty well all right.

WHIPPETT: Many travellers?

WAITER: Yes, a fair number.

WHIPPETT: Listen, my dear chap, they haven't yet brought
me my dinner, so will you please make them buck up and
bring it quickly – there's something I've got to do, you
see, after dinner.

WAITER: The Guv'nor said he wasn't going to let you have
any more. I think it's today that he was going to complain
to the Prefect.

WHIPPETT: Complain? What about? What do you think
we're going to do, my dear chap? You see, I must eat.
If I go on like this I may get quite thin. I'm very hungry;
I'm not joking.

WAITER: Yes, Sir. He said 'I won't give him any dinner
till he pays me for what he had before.' That was his
answer.

WHIPPETT: Then persuade him, you. Make him see reason.

WAITER: What am I to say to him, then?

WHIPPETT: You put it to him seriously, that I have got to
eat. Never mind about the money . . . He thinks that
because he's a peasant, and doesn't mind not eating for
a day, it's the same with other people. I like that!

WAITER: Maybe I will tell him.

[*Exeunt* JOSEPH *and* WAITER.]

WHIPPET [*alone*]: It's beastly, though, if they won't give us
anything to eat. I've never been so hungry before as I am
now. Couldn't I get something on my clothes? What
about selling the trousers? No, better to stay hungry for
a bit, and arrive home in a Petersburg suit. It's a shame

that Joachim's[7] wouldn't let me have the coach. Damn
it, it would have been fine to arrive home in a coach, and
go on in slap-up style, bowling up to the porch at some
neighbour's country place, with lamps, and with Joseph
in livery, up behind. I can imagine the commotion they'd
be in. 'Who is it? What is it?' And in comes the footman.
[*Stiffly erect, imitating the footman*] 'Mr John Whippett
from St Petersburg. Shall I say you are at home?'
Country bumpkins, they wouldn't understand what's
meant by 'Shall I say you are at home?' If some lout of a
squire comes to their house, he rolls in like a great bear,
straight into the drawing-room. You come up to some
pretty little daughter of the house 'Charmed, miss . . .'
[*Rubs his hand and scrapes his foot.*] Tcha! [*Spits.*] It makes
me feel quite sick, I'm so hungry.

[*Enter* JOSEPH.]

WHIPPETT: Well, what?

JOSEPH: They are bringing dinner.

WHIPPETT [*clapping his hands and bouncing softly on his
chair*]: They are! They are, they are!

WAITER [*entering with plates and a napkin*]: This is the last
time that the Guv'nor is doing it.

WHIPPETT: Oh, the Guv'nor, the Guv'nor . . . I don't give
a damn for your Guv'nor! What's that there?

WAITER: Soup and a roast.

WHIPPETT: What? Only two dishes?

WAITER: That's all, Sir.

WHIPPETT: What nonsense! I won't have this. You go
and tell him; what's this supposed to be? . . . It isn't
enough.

WAITER: The Guv'nor says it's more than plenty.

WHIPPETT: But why no sauce?

WAITER: There's no sauce.

WHIPPETT: Why ever not? I went past the kitchen and
saw for myself that there was a lot cooking. And I saw

two tubby little men in the dining-room this morning, eating salmon, and a lot else besides.

WAITER: Well, maybe that's something that's there, and isn't there.

WHIPPETT: How do you mean, isn't there?

WAITER: Well it just isn't.

WHIPPETT: But the salmon, the fish and the cutlets?

WAITER: They're for the quality, Sir.

WHIPPETT: Grr! You fool.

WAITER: Yes, Sir.

WHIPPETT: Dirty swine! . . . Why do they eat, and not me? Damn it, why can't I have some too? Aren't they travellers, the same as me?

WAITER: Indeed they are not!

WHIPPETT: What are they then?

WAITER: Ordinary sort of people! We know all about them – they pay cash.

WHIPPETT: I won't argue with a fool like you. [*Pours out some soup and eats.*] What sort of soup is this? You've just poured some water into a cup – it has no taste, only a nasty smell. I don't want this soup, give me something else.

WAITER: We'll take it away, Sir. The Guv'nor said that if you don't want it you needn't have it.

WHIPPETT [*guarding the food with his hand*]: Here, here, here . . . leave it you idiot! You're used to going on like that, with other people; I tell you, my friend, I'm not that sort of man! I advise you not to try it on with me . . . [*Eats.*] Lord! what soup! [*Goes on eating.*] I don't suppose there's another man in the world that ever ate soup like that! Some sort of feathers floating about in it, instead of butter. [*Carves a chicken.*] I say, I say, I say! What a chicken! Give me the roast. There's some soup left, Joseph, you have it. [*Carves the roast.*] What sort of roast is this? It isn't a roast.

WAITER: What is it, then?

WHIPPETT: The Deuce knows what it is, but it isn't a
roast. It's an axe that has been roasted, instead of beef.
[*Eats.*] Dirty swindlers, to serve stuff like that. It's enough
to give you a jaw-ache to eat one slice of it. [*Picks his
teeth with his fingers.*] Cads! Exactly like a piece of bark;
can't get it out anyway. Sort of stuff that makes your
teeth go black when you eat it. Swindlers! [*Wipes his
mouth with the napkin.*] Isn't there anything more?

WAITER: No.

WHIPPETT: Dirty cads! They might have let us have some
sort of sauce, or a pie. They're a rotten lot! All they can
do is to fleece travellers.

[*The* WAITER *collects the dishes and carries them out.*
JOSEPH *goes out with him.*]

WHIPPETT: Really I mightn't have eaten; all it has done is
to sharpen my appetite. If I had some small change I'd
send down to the market now, if only to buy a bun.

JOSEPH [*re-entering*]: The Prefect has come for something.
He's making inquiries and asking about you.

WHIPPETT [*terrified*]: Oh dear! It's that innkeeper gone
and got his complaint in, sly little beast. Suppose he
really does haul me off to jail? Well I suppose, if it's done
in a gentlemanly way . . . No, no! I won't! There are
officers and people strolling about in the town and of
course I had to put on a bit of side, and swap a couple of
winks with a shopman's daughter . . . No, I won't! . . .
What's he, after all? How dare he do it? What does he
think I am? A merchant or a townsman?[8] [*Plucks up
courage and straightens himself.*] Yes, I'll say it to him straight
'How dare you, how dare . . .'

[*The door-handle turns.* WHIPPETT *goes pale and shrivels
up. Enter the* PREFECT *with* DOBBIN. *The* PREFECT
*comes to a dead stop. Each gazes at the other in terror,
goggle-eyed, for several minutes.*]

PREFECT [*pulling himself together and coming to attention*]: How do you do, Sir!

WHIPPETT [*bowing*]: My respects . . .

PREFECT: I beg your pardon.

WHIPPETT: Granted.

PREFECT: As Commandant of this town, I am responsible for seeing that travellers and other gentlepeople are not in any way inconvenienced.

WHIPPETT [*stuttering a little at first, but speaking in a loud voice towards the end*]: But what could I do? . . . It's not my fault. . . . I will pay, really. . . . It will be sent to me from home. [BOBBIN *peeps round the door*.] It's more his fault; the beef he gives me is as hard as a brick, and the soup – goodness knows what sort of slops he shoved into it; I had to throw it out of the window. He's been starving me for whole days on end. The tea is queer – it stinks of fish, not like tea. Why should I . . . nice way to go on!

PREFECT [*timidly*]: Excuse me, it really isn't my fault. There is always good beef in my market. It is brought here by dealers from Kholmogóry, sober and well-behaved men. I don't know where he gets beef like that. But if anything is not as it should be . . . may I be allowed to suggest that you come along with me to other lodgings.

WHIPPETT: No, I won't! I know what 'other lodgings' means – it means jail. What right have you got to do it? How dare you? . . . I tell you . . . I am in Government service in St Petersburg . . . [*Plucks up courage*] I, I, I . . .

PREFECT [*aside*]: O Lord God! He *is* angry! He's found it all out; those confounded merchants have told him everything.

WHIPPETT [*putting a bold face on it*]: I tell you, you can bring the whole of your Force here – I won't come! I'm going straight to the Minister. [*Bangs his fist on the table.*] What do you mean by it? What do you mean by it?

PREFECT [*stiffly erect, and shaking all over*]: Mercy, don't ruin me! I've got a wife and small children . . . don't bring a man down to misery.

WHIPPETT: No, I won't come! What's all this? What's it got to do with me? Because you have got a wife and small children, I must go to jail! I like that!

[BOBBIN *peeps round the door, and withdraws in terror.*]

No, thank you very much, I won't come.

PREFECT [*trembling*]: It was due to inexperience, I swear it was, inexperience. Inadequacy of income . . . Judge, sir, for yourself; the Treasury salary doesn't cover tea and sugar, and if there has been any bribery it was very, very little – something for the table, or for a suit of clothes. As regards the Sergeant's widow, engaged in trade, that I am alleged to have whipped, it's a slander, I swear it – a slander. The people that made that up are evilly disposed towards me; the kind of people who would be ready to make an attempt on my life.

WHIPPETT: So what? They are nothing to do with me. [*Pauses to think.*] I don't know, however, why you are talking about evil people, or about some Sergeant's widow. A Sergeant's widow is quite another matter, but don't you dare to whip me. Keep that idea out of your mind. Look here! You see the sort of man I am . . . I will pay, I'll pay cash, but I haven't got it now. That's why I'm stuck here, because I haven't got a farthing.

PREFECT [*aside*]: Oh, very delicately put! So that's what he was getting at. Wrapping it up in all that fog and leaving it to you to puzzle it out, if you want to. You don't know which side to tackle him. But never mind that, come on, let's have a go. If something is going to happen, it will happen; let's have a go and chance it. [*Aloud*] Should you in fact be short of money, or of anything else, I am prepared to be of immediate service to you. It is my duty to assist travellers.

WHIPPETT: Do lend me some money, do! I'll settle the

innkeeper's bill at once. All I would want is a couple of hundred roubles, or even a bit less.

PREFECT [*holding out banknotes to him*]: Just two hundred roubles; you needn't even bother to count it.

WHIPPETT [*taking the money*]: Sir, I am most obliged. I'll send it to you at once from home . . . I'm suddenly all . . . I see you are a gentleman. That makes all the difference.

PREFECT [*aside*]: Well, thank the Lord, he's taken the money. I think it will go all right now. As a matter of fact I passed him four hundred, instead of two.

WHIPPETT: Hey, Joseph! Tell the waiter to come here.

[*Enter* JOSEPH.]

[*To the* PREFECT *and* DOBBIN] But why are you standing! Do please sit down. [*To* DOBBIN] Do, I beg you, sit down.

PREFECT: It's all right, we'll just stand.

WHIPPETT: Please be so kind as to sit down. I can see now the absolute frankness and warm-heartedness of your nature. Otherwise I would have begun to think that you were coming to . . . [*To* DOBBIN] Do sit down.

[*The* PREFECT *and* DOBBIN *sit down.* BOBBIN *peeps in at the door and listens.*]

PREFECT [*aside*]: We've got to be a bit bolder. He wants to be treated as incognito. All right, we'll trot out our own nonsense too, as if we hadn't got the least idea who he was. [*Aloud*] I was going on my duty rounds with one of the local landowners – Mr Peter Dobbin here, and we made a special call at the hotel, in order to ascertain whether the travellers were being properly looked after, because I am not one of those prefects who don't care about things. With me, on the other hand, with me it isn't only duty; there is also Christian loving-kindness to make me want to see that every mortal is accorded a good reception – and now, as a kind of reward, it has been my fortune to make a most pleasant acquaintance.

WHIPPETT: I'm very glad about it too. I must admit that if it hadn't been for you I might have been stuck here for a long time; I simply didn't know how I was going to pay.

PREFECT [*aside*]: Oh, what a story! Didn't know how he was going to pay! [*Aloud*] May I venture to ask, Sir, in which direction are you travelling, and what is your destination?

WHIPPETT: I am travelling to Sarátov Province, to my own village.

PREFECT [*aside, with an ironical expression on his face*]: What's that? To Sarátov Province! And he doesn't blush. Oho! You've got to keep wide awake with him. [*Aloud*] A fine thing for you to be doing, Sir. Well now, as regards travel; on the one hand, they say that there are annoyances due to delays over horses, and on the other hand, why there's diversion for the mind. I expect then that you travel mainly for your personal satisfaction.

WHIPPETT: No, my dad wants me to come. The old man is cross because I haven't had any recognition yet for my service in St Petersburg. He thinks that they pin a Vladímir medal on you as soon as you get there. I'd like to send him to knock around a bit in an office!

PREFECT [*aside*]: What about that for a yarn, I ask you! He's even worked in his old father! [*Aloud*] And will you be away for long, Sir?

WHIPPETT: I really don't know. You see, my Father is an obstinate old beggar with about as much sense as a block of wood. I shall put it straight to him; it's all very well, but I can't live away from St Petersburg. After all, why should I waste my life among a lot of peasants? One wants other things now; my soul is eager for enlightenment.

PREFECT [*aside*]: All beautifully tied up! He keeps on and on with it and never gets muddled. But you know, he's an insignificant-looking little man; you'd think you could

squash him with your finger-nail. Well just you wait,
you'll talk all right when I get you home. I'll make you
tell us a bit more of your story. [*Aloud*] A very just observation, Sir. What can one do in the wilds? Why, even
here, one stays awake all night, ungrudgingly doing one's
best for one's country, and there's still no knowing when
there will be any reward. [*Glancing round the room*] Isn't
this room a bit damp?

WHIPPETT: It's a foul room, and I've never seen anything
like the bed-bugs – they bite like dogs.

PREFECT: Really! An enlightened visitor like you, and
what has he got to put up with? Worthless bed-bugs, that
oughtn't ever to have been born into the world. Don't
you find the room dark as well?

WHIPPETT: Yes, quite dark. The landlord has got into the
way of not letting me have candles. Sometimes I want to
do something, to read a bit, or I get the fancy to write
something, and I can't – too dark, too dark.

PREFECT: May I venture to ask you . . . but no, I am not
worthy.

WHIPPETT: What is it?

PREFECT: No, no, I am unworthy, unworthy.

WHIPPETT: But whatever is it?

PREFECT: If I might be so bold . . . I've got a lovely room
for you in my house . . . it's bright and quiet . . . But no, I
feel myself that it would be too great an honour. . . .
Don't be angry – I assure you . . . It was naïve of me to
make the offer.

WHIPPETT: On the contrary, it was most kind of you. I
shall be delighted. It'll be much nicer for me to be in a
private house, instead of this dram-shop.

PREFECT: I shall be so pleased if you will! And my wife
will be overjoyed! That's the way it's been with me, ever
since I was a child – hospitality! Especially when the
guest is an enlightened man. Don't think that I said that

out of flattery. No, that's a vice I haven't got, I speak out from the fullness of my heart.

WHIPPETT: I am most grateful to you. I am like that too – I hate two-faced people. I do like your frankness and warm-heartedness, and I'll allow that I would ask for nothing more than that people should extend to me devotion and respect, respect and devotion.

[*Enter* WAITER *accompanied by* JOSEPH. BOBBIN *peeps in at the door.*]

WAITER: Did you want something, Sir?

WHIPPETT: Yes; give me the bill.

WAITER: But I've just given you the second bill.

WHIPPETT: I can't remember all your silly bills. Tell me, what does it come to?

WAITER: On the first day, Sir, you ordered dinner, and on the next day you only had a light meal of salmon, and since then you have gone over to putting it all down on the account.

WHIPPETT: Silly fool! Now he's starting to add it all up . . . What does it all come to?

PREFECT: Please don't trouble yourself about it; he can wait. [*To the* WAITER] Get out of here, it'll be sent to you.

WHIPPETT: That's right, it will be. [*Puts the money away.*]

[*Exit* WAITER. BOBBIN *peeps in at the door.*]

PREFECT: Would you like to come now and inspect some of the establishments in our town, such as the Charitable and other Institutions?

WHIPPETT: Why, what is there there?

PREFECT: Just for you to see how our affairs progress . . . our methods . . .

WHIPPETT: With great pleasure. I am ready.

[BOBBIN *sticks his head round the door.*]

PREFECT: Then, if such be your desire, we could go on from there to the District School, to look at the methods we employ for imparting knowledge.

WHIPPETT: Yes, please, yes please.

PREFECT: Then, if you would care to visit the lock-up and the town prisons, you could study our methods for dealing with delinquents.

WHIPPETT: But why go to the prisons? Wouldn't it be better for us to look at the charitable institutions?

PREFECT: As you wish. How would you like to . . . in your own carriage, or with me in the droshky?

WHIPPETT: I'd better go with you in the droshky.

PREFECT [*To* DOBBIN]: Well Mr Dobbin, there isn't room for you this time.

DOBBIN: That's all right. I don't mind.

PREFECT [*quietly to* DOBBIN]: Listen, will you run, and I mean run, as fast as you can, and take two notes, one to Strawberry at the Charitable Institution, and one to my wife . . . [*To* WHIPPETT] May I make so bold as to ask leave to write in your presence? Just a line to my wife, so that she may make ready to receive an honoured guest?

WHIPPETT: Oh, but why? . . . Anyhow here's the ink, only I don't know about paper . . . what about using this bill?

PREFECT: I'll write here. [*Writes, and at the same time speaks to himself.*] Now we'll see how it goes after a luncheon with some fat-bellied bottles! Yes, and we've got some of our local Madeira, not much to look at, but it would bowl an elephant over. If only I can find out what he is like, and how far you need to be careful with him. [*When he has finished writing he gives the note to* DOBBIN, *who makes for the door, but at that moment the door collapses and crashes on to the stage, together with* BOBBIN *who has been listening behind it. All exclaim.* BOBBIN *picks himself up.*]

WHIPPETT: I say, you haven't hurt yourself anywhere?

BOBBIN: It's all right, it's all right Sir. No trouble at all, only a small graze above my nose. I'll run round to Dr Finischem, he has those plasters; it'll go off then.

PREFECT [*to* WHIPPETT, *with a reproachful glance at* BOBBIN]: That's all right, Sir. I have the honour to invite you to be my guest; I'll tell your servant to carry your trunk over. [*To* JOSEPH] My good fellow, will you bring everything over to my house, the Prefect's house? Anybody will show you. Now Sir, I have the honour. [*Lets* WHIPPET *go ahead of him, but turns round and speaks reproachfully to* BOBBIN,] As for you! Couldn't you find somewhere else to fall over? Spread-eagled like an I don't know what!

    [*Exit, followed by* BOBBIN.]

ACT THREE

Same room as in Act One. ANNE *and* MARY *are standing in the same positions at the window.*

ANNE: There now, we have been waiting a whole hour, all thanks to you and your stupid titivating. She was perfectly well dressed, but no, she had to go and rummage again; I oughtn't to have taken any notice of her. So aggravating; and now of course there isn't a soul about; everybody might be dead.

MARY: Now really Mummy, we'll all know about it in a couple of minutes. Eudoxia is bound to come soon now. [*Looks out of the window and exclaims*] Oh, Mummy, Mummy! Somebody's coming, down there at the end of the street.

ANNE: Coming where? You're always fancying something. Why yes, there is somebody coming. Who is it then? Short ... frock-coat ... who is it? Eh? Oh, but this is aggravating! Whoever could it be?

MARY: It's Mr Dobbin, Mummy.

ANNE: Mr Dobbin indeed? You keep on suddenly imagining things like that! Certainly not Mr Dobbin [*waves her handkerchief*] Hi there you! Come here! Quickly!

MARY: It's Mr Dobbin Mummy, it really is.

ANNE: There now, you said that deliberately, simply for the sake of argument. I tell you it is not Mr Dobbin.

MARY: But Mummy, what do you mean? You can see it is Mr Dobbin.

ANNE: Why, so it is, it's Mr Dobbin. I can see now; what are you arguing about? [*Calling from the window*] Buck up, buck up! You're walking too slowly. Come on, where are they? Eh? Tell it me from there, never mind about that. What? Is he very strict? Eh? What about my husband? My husband? [*Steps back a little from the window, frustrated.*] Stupid man! Won't tell me anything till he gets into the room.

[*Enter* DOBBIN.]

ANNE: Will you tell me now please; come on – how can you do it to me? You were the one that I was relying on to be a decent man; they all suddenly dashed off and you went with them too wherever it was. And from that moment to this I haven't been able to get a word of sense out of anybody. Aren't you ashamed of yourself? I was your Johnnie's godmother, and your Lizzie's too, and now look at the way you treat me.

DOBBIN: So you were Godmother; and I declare to goodness that I'm all out of breath, running here to pay my respects to you. Best respects, Miss Mary.

MARY: How do you do, Mr Dobbin.

ANNE: Well then! Come on and tell me, what happened there, how did it go?

DOBBIN: Mr Slydewynde has sent a note to you.

ANNE: But who is he? Is he a general?

DOBBIN: No, not a general, but not far short of one. Such education, ma'am, and such grand ways.

ANNE: Ah! Then it is the man that my husband had the letter about.

DOBBIN: Absolutely. And I was the first to discover him, Peter and I were.

ANNE: Will you tell me now what happened, and how it went?

DOBBIN: Yes, thank God all's well. At first he was all for being a bit stiff with Mr Slydewynde. Yes ma'am; he was angry and said that everything in the hotel was nasty, and that he wouldn't come along with him, and that he wasn't going to go to prison on his account. Afterwards though, when he realized the innocence of Mr Slyde-wynde, and had had some more intimate conversation with him, he quickly changed his ideas, and thank God it all went off all right. They have gone now to look at the charitable institutions. . . . At first, though, I don't mind telling you, Mr Slydewynde was beginning to think that there might have been some secret report on him; I was a bit scared myself.

ANNE: What had you got to be afraid of? You're not in the service, are you?

DOBBIN: Well you know, one does get a feeling of fright when a Great Chief is speaking.

ANNE: Come now . . . but that's all rubbish. Tell me, what is he like? Is he young, or old?

DOBBIN: Young, a young man, about three-and-twenty. But he talks just like an old man. 'I shall go there, please,' says he, 'and there.' [*Waves his hand.*] And that's that. Everything fine. 'I like', says he, 'to write a bit, and to read a bit, but I'm hindered', says he, 'because the room is rather dark.'

ANNE: But what does he look like? Is he dark or fair?

DOBBIN: No, more of an auburn, and his eyes dart like the eyes of a wild beast; it really is quite upsetting.

ANNE: What is he writing to me here in this note? [*Reads.*] 'I hasten to let you know, my love, that I was in a most grievous situation. But, resting my hopes upon God's loving-kindness, extra for two pickled cucumbers and one half-portion of caviare, one rouble twenty-five kopecks...' [*Stops.*] I don't understand it at all, what's all this about pickled cucumbers and caviare?

DOBBIN: Oh, Mr Slydewynde wrote on a piece of scrap paper to save time; there was some kind of bill written on it.

ANNE: Ah yes, that's it. [*Goes on reading*] 'But resting my hopes upon God's loving-kindness I think that it is all going to end well. Quickly get a room ready for an important guest, the one with the yellow wallpaper. You needn't trouble to do extra for dinner because we are going to have refreshments with Artemus Strawberry at the Charitable Institution, but order some more wine. Tell Abdullah at the shop to send up his very best, or I'll have the whole of his cellar searched. With a kiss for your hand, my love, I remain yours Anthony Huffam-Slydewynde.' Oh good gracious! Come along now, we've got to hurry. Hi, who's there? Mike!

DOBBIN [*runs and shouts at the door*]: Mike! Mike! Mike!

    [*Enter* MIKE.]

ANNE: Listen; run to Abdullah's ... wait now, I'll give you a little note. [*Sits at the table and writes a little note, speaking as she does so.*] You give this note to Isidore the coachman, and tell him to run with it to Abdullah's and bring back the wine. And go at once yourself, and get that room made nice for a visitor. Put in a bed and a washstand and so on.

DOBBIN: Well, I'll run along quickly now, Mrs Slydewynde, and see how he is getting on with the inspection.

ANNE: Go on, go on! I won't keep you.

    [*Exit* DOBBIN.]

Now Mary dear, you and I have got to attend to our toilet. He's a city swell; heaven forbid that he should find anything to laugh at. I think that the most suitable thing for you would be to put on your blue dress with the little frills.

MARY: Oh Mummy, not the blue! I simply hate it; there's Mrs Slappencatchit going about in blue, and so is the Strawberry girl, she wears blue. No, I had better put on my flowery dress.

ANNE: The flowery dress! ... Really, you say that only for the sake of contradicting. It would be much better for you, because I am going to put on my pale yellow; I'm very fond of pale yellow.

MARY: Oh Mummy! Pale yellow doesn't suit you.

ANNE: Pale yellow not suit me?

MARY: It doesn't, honestly and truly it doesn't; you want to have quite dark eyes for it.

ANNE: I like that! Do you mean to say my eyes aren't dark? They're as dark as can be. What nonsense she talks! Of course they're dark; when I try the cards I always go by the Queen of Clubs.

MARY: Oh Mummy, you're more the Queen of Hearts.

ANNE: Rubbish, absolute rubbish! I've never been the Queen of Hearts. [*She goes out hurriedly accompanied by* MARY, *talking as she does so.*] What a thing to imagine, all of a sudden! Queen of Hearts! Whatever next!

[*After they have gone,* MIKE *throws out sweepings at the open door. Enter by another door* JOSEPH, *with the trunk on his head.*]

JOSEPH: Which way now?

MIKE: This way Uncle, this way.

JOSEPH: Wait now, let me rest first. Ah, but it's a hard life. Any load'll weigh heavy if your belly is empty.

MIKE: Tell me now, Uncle, will the General be here soon?

JOSEPH: What General?

MIKE: Why, your master.

JOSEPH: Is it the master? What sort of a general is he?

MIKE: He is a general, isn't he?

JOSEPH: He is, only he's a contrariwise general.

MIKE: What's that? More or less than a real general?

JOSEPH: More.

MIKE: There you are! That's what's started up all the commotion here.

JOSEPH: Listen my lad; I can see you're a smart boy. Will you get me something to eat now, in there.

MIKE: But there's nothing ready yet for you Uncle. You wouldn't wish to eat anything that's plain. But when your master sits down to table, they'll put out some of the same collation for you.

JOSEPH: Well, what have you got to eat that's plain?

MIKE: Cabbage soup, porridge and pies.

JOSEPH: Give me that then, soup, porridge and pies! It's all right, we'll eat anything. Come along, let's carry the trunk. Is that another way out, over there?

MIKE: It is.

[*They carry the trunk between them into a side room.* POLICE SERGEANTS *open both halves of the double door. Enter* WHIPPETT, *followed by the* PREFECT, *then the* WARDEN OF CHARITABLE INSTITUTIONS, *the* SCHOOLS SUPER-INTENDENT, DOBBIN *and* BOBBIN *(with a plaster on his nose). The* PREFECT *points out to the* POLICE SERGEANTS *the piece of paper on the floor. They run to pick it up, colliding in their haste.*]

WHIPPETT: Nice institutions. I like the way you show everything in the town to travellers. Nobody showed me anything in the other towns.

PREFECT: I would venture to observe that in the other places the Town Commandants and their staff are – put it this way – more concerned with their own advantage. But here we may say that we have no thought in our minds, save that of earning a good opinion from Head-quarters, by orderliness and vigilance.

WHIPPETT: The luncheon was very good. I have positively overeaten. Do you have it like that every day?

PREFECT: It was special for such a pleasant visitor.

WHIPPETT: I like a bit of something to eat. Isn't that what we live for – to pluck the flowers of pleasure? What was that fish called?

STRAWBERRY [*running up*]: Pickled cod, Sir.

WHIPPETT: Very tasty. Where was it we had luncheon? Hospital, wasn't it?

STRAWBERRY: Quite correct, Sir; at the Charitable Institution.

WHIPPETT: I remember, I remember. There were beds there. But had the patients recovered? There didn't seem to be very many of them.

STRAWBERRY: There aren't more than ten of them left. The rest have all recovered. We have got it arranged that way now, it's our method. You may find this hard to believe, but since I took charge they've all been recovering like flies. A patient is hardly admitted to the Infirmary before he recovers, and not so much through drugs as through conscientiousness and method.

PREFECT: May I venture to put it to you how perplexing are the responsibilities of a Town Commandant! So many things of every kind waiting to be done, solely in connection with cleaning, repairs and alterations . . . in a word, enough to baffle the cleverest of men. Yet, thanks be to God it is all going ahead in a satisfactory manner. Some Prefects, of course, would consult their own interests; but believe me, even when one lies down to sleep one thinks all the time 'O Lord, my God, how can I so order things that Headquarters may see my zeal and may be pleased'. They can of course reward me, or not as they think fit; at least my heart will be at rest. When everything in the town is orderly, the streets swept, the prisoners properly secured and the drunkards few in number . . . what more could I wish? No, no, I want no honours. Of course one is attracted by them, but set beside virtue all else is dust and ashes.

STRAWBERRY [aside]: How he does pile it on, the old rascal! It's a gift from God, that's what it is.

WHIPPETT: That is true, I confess that there are times when I too like to give rein to my musings, sometimes in prose, at other times by throwing off some little verses.

BOBBIN [to DOBBIN]: How right it is, Peter, how right it all is! The observations he makes . . . clearly he's a well-educated man.

WHIPPETT: Tell me, please, do you have any amusements here? Clubs, for instance, where one can get a game of cards.

PREFECT [*aside*]: Ho! Ho! We know what you are getting at, my dear. [*Aloud*] God forbid! We have never heard of such clubs here. I've never touched a card in my life; I don't even know how those card-games are played. I have never been able to remain indifferent to the sight of playing cards. If I happen to see a King of Diamonds, or anything else of that kind, such utter loathing comes over me that I feel I want to spit. As a matter of fact I did once build a house of cards, to amuse my children, but after that I dreamt of the accursed things all night. Let's not think about them. How can people waste such valuable time on them?

WALLOP [*aside*]: Cad! He won a hundred roubles off me yesterday.

PREFECT. Better that I should devote that time to the interests of the Empire.

WHIPPETT: Well never mind then, only . . . It all depends on the way one looks at a thing. If for instance you stand pat when you ought to double three times . . . well then of course . . . No, say what you like, a game of cards can be very tempting.

[*Enter* ANNE *and* MARY.]

PREFECT: May I venture to introduce my family; my wife and daughter?

WHIPPETT [*bowing*]: Charmed, ma'am, to have the special treat of meeting you.

ANNE: It is even nicer for us, to meet such a personage.

WHIPPETT [*with a flourish*]: Gracious no, ma'am, quite the contrary, it is nicer still for me.

ANNE: Really now, Sir! You say that out of politeness. Do please sit down.

WHIPPETT: Even to stand beside you is bliss, but if you

insist, I will sit down. How happy I am, now at last to be sitting beside you.

ANNE: Goodness, I wouldn't dare take that as intended for me . . . After the Capital, it must have been very unpleasant for you to be *en voyage*.

WHIPPETT: Extraordinarily unpleasant. When one has been accustomed to living, *comprenez-vous*, in Society, and one suddenly finds oneself on the road, filthy inns, the murk of ignorance . . . but for this good fortune [*looking towards* ANNE *and striking an attitude*] which I'm bound to say has compensated me for all that.

ANNE: It really must have been most unpleasant for you.

WHIPPETT: Yes, ma'am, but at the moment it is extremely pleasant . . .

ANNE: Really, Sir! You do me too much honour. I don't deserve it.

WHIPPETT: Not deserve it! Why not? Madam you do deserve it.

ANNE: I live in the country.

WHIPPETT: Yes, but the country too has its little hillocks and its rills . . . Though of course it's not to be compared with Petersburg. Ah, Petersburg! What a life indeed. Perhaps you think that I do nothing but copying work; on the contrary, the section head is on friendly terms with me. Slaps me on the shoulder and says 'Come along and have dinner old boy.' I only look in at the Office for a couple of minutes, just to say 'Do it this way, do it that way.' The clerical officer is already there, little rat of a man, off he goes on the letters, scratch, scratch, scratch with his pen. They were even going to make me an Assessor, grade eight, but I thought 'What's the point?' And the office-keeper comes flying down the stairs after me with a brush. 'Mr Whippett,' says he, 'will you permit me to give your shoes a shine?' [*To the* PREFECT] Gentlemen, why are you standing? Do please sit down.

PREFECT: My rank ... I can go on standing.⎫
STRAWBERRY: We'll stand.   ⎬ [together]
                                           ⎭

WALLOP: Please don't put yourself out!

WHIPPETT: Let's forget about rank, please sit down.

[*The* PREFECT *and all sit down.*]

I dislike ceremony, in fact I always try to slip in un-noticed. But concealment is quite impossible, quite impossible! No sooner do I go anywhere than they say 'There,' they say, 'there goes Mr Whippett'! Once I was taken for the Commander-in-Chief; the guard turned out and presented arms. Afterwards, an officer that I know very well said to me 'My dear old boy, we really did take you for the Commander-in-Chief.'

ANNE: Fancy that!

WHIPPETT. I know some pretty actresses. You see, I've done vaudeville sketches too ... I often meet literary men. I'm on friendly terms with Púshkin. I often used to say to him, 'What ho, Púshkin laddie.' 'Well, laddie,' he used to answer, 'everything's more or less ...' He's a great character.

ANNE: So you write as well. It must be nice to be an author! I suppose you put things in the magazines, too.

WHIPPETT: Yes, I do sometimes put things in the magazines. But there are a lot of my works: 'The Marriage of Figaro', 'Robert the Devil', 'Norma'. I can't even remember the titles. And it all came about by chance; I didn't want to write, but the theatre management said 'Please, my dear fellow, write something.' 'All right, my dear fellow,' thought I. 'Maybe I will.' And I wrote it all then and there, in a single evening. Everyone was amazed. I have an extraordinary facility of thought. Everything that was put out under the name of 'Baron Brambéus',[9] 'The Frigate of Hope'[10] and the 'Moscow Telegraph'[11] – I wrote all that.

ANNE: Fancy, then you were 'Brambéus'?

WHIPPETT: Rather, and I correct all their articles for them. Smírdin[12] gives me forty thousand for that.

ANNE: Then I expect 'Yúri Miloslávsky' is your work too?[13]

WHIPPETT: Yes, that's my work.

ANNE: I guessed it at once.

MARY: Oh, Mummy, it says on the book that it is by Mr Zagóskin.

ANNE: There now, I knew you would argue, even here!

WHIPPETT: Oh yes, that is true; it is indeed by Zagóskin, but there is another 'Yúri Miloslávsky' and that one is mine.

ANNE: Well then, I expect yours was the one I read. So well written!

WHIPPETT: I tell you, I live for literature. My house is the first house in Petersburg. It is quite well known – 'The John Whippett House'. [*Addressing the whole company*] Ladies and Gentlemen, will you do me a kindness; if you are in Petersburg, please, please come and see me. You know that I give balls, too.

ANNE: I can imagine how magnificent and how tasteful they are, those balls!

WHIPPETT: Don't mention it. On the table, for instance, there's a water-melon, a seven hundred rouble water-melon. Soup in a casserole, direct by steamboat from Paris; open the lid – an aroma, the like of which cannot be found in nature. I go to balls every night. We have got up a whist-school at our place; the Foreign Minister, the French Ambassador, the British and German Ambassadors, and me. It's awful, though, you can just destroy yourself playing cards. You run upstairs to your room on the fourth floor, and just say to the cook 'There's my overcoat, Maura'. What am I talking about? I'm forgetting that I live on the first floor. At my place the staircase alone cost ... It's amusing to look into my ante-room before I am awake; counts and princes jostling and buzzing there like bumble-bees. All you can hear is buzz, buzz, buzz . . . Once in a while the Minister himself . . .

[*The* PREFECT *and the others get up shyly from their chairs.*] They actually put 'Your Excellency' on my envelopes. On one occasion I even managed the Department. It was a queer situation; the Director had gone away, and nobody knew where he had gone to. Well, naturally, they began to discuss ways and means – who was to fill the post? There were a lot of Generals who were keen to do it, and they were taken on – but when they got down to it, oh no – they found that it wasn't so simple. At first sight it seems easy, but when you come to look at it, it's the very devil! In the end, they saw that there was nothing for it but to come to me. And the next minute there were couriers in the streets. Couriers and couriers and couriers! Imagine it, nothing but couriers – thirty-five thousand of them! 'What is the situation?' I ask. 'Mr Whippett, will you come and manage the Department?' I'll admit that I was a bit taken aback, as I had come out in my dressing-gown; I wanted to refuse, but I thought, 'This will go to His Majesty, yes and it will be entered on my Service record-sheet too.' 'Very well Gentlemen, I accept the post. I accept it,' I say, 'So be it', I say, 'I accept it. Only none of that with me! I tell you, I'm wide awake!' And that's just how it was; it used to be like an earthquake every time I walked through the Office; they all trembled and shook like leaves . . .

[*The* PREFECT *and the others shake with terror.* WHIPPETT *gets more and more heated.*]
Oh, I don't care to fool about. I put the fear of God into them all. Even the Council of the Empire is afraid of me. Yes, indeed! That's the sort of man I am, I don't mind who it is . . . I say to them all 'I know myself, I do'. I am everywhere, everywhere, I go to the Palace every day.

Tomorrow as ever is, I'm going to be promoted to Field-Marsh . . .

[*He slithers and nearly flops on the floor, but is respectfully supported by the officials.*]

PREFECT [*coming towards him, shaking all over, and speaking with an effort*]: B – b – but . . . Your . . . Your . . . Your . . .

WHIPPETT [*in a quick, jerky voice*]: What's up?

PREFECT: B – b – but . . . Your . . . Your . . . Your . . .

WHIPPETT [*in the same voice*]: Can't make it out at all. All rot.

PREFECT: Your . . . your . . . ness, Excellency, d–don't you wish to take a rest? . . . Here's a room, and everything you need.

WHIPPETT: Take a rest – rot. All right, I'm ready for a rest. Gentlemen, your luncheon was good . . . I am satisfied, I am satisfied. [*Declaiming*] Pickled Cod! Pickled Cod!

[*He goes into a side room followed by the* PREFECT.]

BOBBIN [*to* DOBBIN]: There's a man for you, Peter. That's what you can call a man! Never in all my born days have I been in the presence of such an important person; I nearly died of fright. What do you think, Peter? What rank do you make him out to be?

DOBBIN: I think he's not far short of a general.

BOBBIN: I tell you what I think. I think a general wouldn't be fit to black his boots! If he is a general, then he must be the Generalissimo himself. Did you hear the way he came down on the Council of the Empire? Let's go quickly, and tell Judge Slappencatchit and Mr Canister. Good-bye, Mrs Slydewynde.

DOBBIN: Good-bye, Godmother.

[*Exeunt* DOBBIN *and* BOBBIN.]

STRAWBERRY [*to* WALLOP]: Terrifying, simply terrifying. Yet one doesn't know why. We hadn't even got our uniforms on. He'll sleep it off, and then what? Away goes the adverse report to Petersburg. [*Goes out, pensive,*

together with the SCHOOLS SUPERINTENDENT, *saying*]
Good-bye, ma'am.

ANNE: Oh what a nice man!

MARY: Oh what a darling!

ANNE: But such refined behaviour! You can see at once
that he is a City Swell. His manners and all that . . . .
Oh how nice! I'm awfully fond of young people like that!
I'm crazy about them! And besides, he liked me very
much; I noticed that he kept on glancing at me.

MARY: Oh Mummy, it was me he was glancing at!

ANNE: Oh, get along with you do, you and your nonsense!
It's quite out of place here.

MARY: But he was, Mummy, really.

ANNE: Now, now, for pity's sake don't start arguing! I won't
have it, so stop it! Why should he look at you? What call
had he to look at you?

MARY: Really, Mummy, he was looking at me all the time.
When he started to talk about literature, he shot a glance
in my direction, and again when he was telling us about
how he played whist with the Ambassadors – he looked
at me then too.

ANNE: Well he may have done it just once, but only once,
if he did it at all. 'Well,' says he to himself, 'let's have a
look at her now.'

[*Enter the* PREFECT, *on tip-toe.*]

PREFECT: Shh! Shh!

ANNE: What is it?

PREFECT: I wish I hadn't got him drunk. Suppose, now,
that even the half of what he said was true. [*Pauses to
think.*] And why shouldn't it be true? When a man has
had a drop to drink he gives everything away. What's in
the heart, the same is on the tongue. Of course he did put
in a few lies; but you know, if you don't do that you can't
talk at all. Plays cards with Ministers, and goes to the
Palace . . . Yes, indeed, and the more you think about it

... You never know, damn it, what is going on in his head. It's just like as if you were standing on top of a belfry, or as if you were going to be hanged.

ANNE: I never felt the very least shyness with him. What I saw in him was simply an educated man, fashionable and extremely well-bred. I didn't need to concern myself about his ranks.

PREFECT: Oh you women! That's done it; that one word was enough. So far as you are concerned, it's all fiddle-faddle! Suddenly without any rhyme or reason they go and blurt out the word. You'll get a whipping, and that's all you'll get, but your husband will go where he'll never be heard of again. My dear, you were as free and easy with him as if he were somebody like Peter Dobbin.

ANNE: I shouldn't let that worry you. We know a thing or two. [*She glances towards her daughter.*]

PREFECT [*alone*]: Talking to you! ... It's a rum business; it really is! I'm still half dizzy with fright. [*Opens the door and speaks outside*] Mike, call Sergeant Whistler and Sergeant Holdmuzzle; they're somewhere not far away outdoors. [*After a short silence*] The whole world has gone queer; people might at least look distinguished, instead of which you get a thin, scrawny little man – how are you to know who he is? As long as a man's in the forces it does at least show, but when he gets into a twopenny-halfpenny frock-coat – why he looks like a fly with its wings clipped. Sure, he held out a long while at the hotel this morning, cooking up all those allegories and conundrums, till you'd think life isn't long enough to get to the bottom of it all. And in the end, you see, he gave way. Yes, and he said a lot more than he need have. One can see he's a young man.

[*Enter* JOSEPH. *All run to meet him, beckoning to him.*]

ANNE: Come here, my dear!

PREFECT: Shh! Well? Is he asleep?

JOSEPH: Not yet, he's stretching himself a bit.

ANNE: Listen, what's your name?

JOSEPH: Joseph, Ma'am.

PREFECT [*to his wife and daughter*]: That'll do, that's enough from you. Now then, my friend, have you been well fed?

JOSEPH: I have, thank you very kindly, Sir. Well fed.

ANNE: Come on now and tell me; I believe an awful lot of counts and princes come to see your master.

JOSEPH [*aside*]: What'll I say? If they've fed me well now, then they'll feed me even better afterwards. [*Aloud*] Yes, we do get counts.

MARY: Joseph, honey, isn't your master a nice-looking man!

ANNE: And tell me please, Joseph, how does he . . . ?

PREFECT: And will you please stop it! You're only hindering me with all your silly talk. Now, my friend . . .

ANNE: What sort of rank is it that your master has?

JOSEPH: The usual sort of rank.

PREFECT: Oh my God! You and your silly questions! You don't let me get a word in edgeways about business. Now, my friend, what's your master like? . . . Strict? Is he fond of using the rough side of his tongue? Or isn't he?

JOSEPH: Yes, he likes things to be tidy. You've got to have everything just so with him.

PREFECT: I rather like your face. You must be a good man, my friend. Well now . . .

ANNE: Listen, Joseph, when your master is up in Town does he wear uniform or . . . ?

PREFECT: That's enough clack from you, I tell you! This is a serious matter: it involves a man's life . . . [*To* JOSEPH] Well now, my friend. I rather like you, I do. You know, there's no harm in having the odd cup of tea on the road – it's chilly now. There you are, there's a couple of roubles for tea.

JOSEPH [*taking the money*]: Thank you very kindly, Sir, and

may God grant you the best of good health! You have
given help to a poor man.

PREFECT: Good, good. Pleased to do it. Now then, my
friend . . .

ANNE: Listen, Joseph, what colour eyes does your master
like best?

MARY: Joseph, honey, what a sweet little nose your master
has!

PREFECT: Steady on now and let me speak! . . . [*To*
JOSEPH] Now then my friend, I want you to tell me
please. What is it that your master notices most, I mean
to say, what pleases him most when he is on the road?

JOSEPH: What does he like? . . . That depends. What he
likes best of all is a good reception. Good hospitality.

PREFECT: Hospitality?

JOSEPH: Yes, hospitality. Take me now. I'm a bond-servant,
but he even sees to it I get well looked after. Honest to
God. Suppose now we had been making a call at some
place. 'Tell me, Joseph, did they do you well?' 'They
did not, your lordship.' 'Ah, Joseph,' says he, 'that's a bad
host. Will you remind me,' says he, 'when I get back.'
'Ah' thinks I to myself [*waves his hand*], 'bless him! I'm
a simple man.'

PREFECT: Good, good. You're talking sense. I've just given
you something for tea, and here's some more to get cakes
to go with it.

JOSEPH: Why is your lordship so good to me? I'll have to
drink your health.

ANNE: Come over here, Joseph, and you'll get something
from me too.

MARY: Joseph, darling, give your master a kiss.

[*A faint cough is heard from* WHIPPETT *in the next room.*]

PREFECT: Shh! [*Stands on tip-toe – the whole scene is in an
undertone.*] Heaven preserve you from making a noise. Get
along now, that's enough from you.

ANNE: Come on, Mary dear! There was something I noticed about our guest that I can't tell you till we're by ourselves.

PREFECT: Oh, they'll talk away in there. If anyone were to listen to them I expect the next thing would be that he'd want to stop his ears. [*Turning to* JOSEPH] Well, my friend . . .

[*Enter* SERGEANTS HOLDMUZZLE *and* WHISTLER.]

PREFECT: Sh-Shh! Clumsy bears, stamping in your great boots! Rolling in here like somebody dumping a half-ton load out of a cart. Where the devil have you been off to?

HOLDMUZZLE: Proceeding in accordance with instructions . . .

PREFECT: Shh! [*Shuts his mouth.*] Hark at him, croaking like a crow. [*Imitates him.*] 'Proceeding in accordance with instructions.' Booms like a voice out of a barrel. [*To* JOSEPH] Now, my friend, will you go in there and get ready whatever's needed for your master. Ask for anything that's in the house.

[*Exit* JOSEPH.]

And you stand in the porch and don't budge. And don't let any outsiders into the house, especially merchants! And if you do let one of them in . . . The minute you see somebody coming with a petition, or even without a petition if he looks like the sort of man who might be going to present a petition about me, take hold of him by the scruff of the neck and shove! Like that! Properly! [*Illustrates with his foot.*] Do you hear? Shh! Shh!

[*He tiptoes out after the* SERGEANTS.]

ACT FOUR

The same room in the PREFECT's *House. Enter cautiously, almost on tiptoe,* SLAPPENCATCHIT, STRAWBERRY, *the* POSTMASTER, WALLOP, DOBBIN *and* BOBBIN, *in full dress uniform. Conversation is in an undertone throughout.*

SLAPPENCATCHIT [*forming them all up in a semi-circle*]: Quickly now gentlemen: for Heaven's sake, form a ring and let's have a bit more order. Bless the man! He goes to the Palace and he tells the Council of the Empire what he thinks of them! Get into military formation; I must have military formation! Dobbin, will you run round to this side, and will you, Bobbin, stand just there?

[DOBBIN *and* BOBBIN *run round on tiptoe.*]

STRAWBERRY: It's up to you, Judge, but we have got to get on and do something.

SLAPPENCATCHIT: What's it to be then?

STRAWBERRY: Well, you know what.

SLAPPENCATCHIT: Slip him some . . .

STRAWBERRY: Well yes, slip him some.

SLAPPENCATCHIT: Deucedly risky! Suppose he cuts up rough? He's a big man in the Government. Hadn't we better make out that it's donations for some monument, from the gentlemen of the district?

POSTMASTER: Or else you might say 'Look, here's some money that has come through the post, and we don't know who it belongs to.'

STRAWBERRY: Look out he doesn't send you through the post to some place that's rather a long way off. Listen; this isn't the way things are done in a well-ordered state. Why is there a whole squadron of us? We've got to go in

272

ACT FOUR

and present ourselves to him one at a time. You know ...
strictly private and confidential. Do it properly so that
nobody else can overhear. That's how things are done in
a well-ordered society. Come on, Judge. You go in first.

SLAPPENCATCHIT: It had better be you. It was at your
institution that the distinguished guest was entertained.

STRAWBERRY: Wallop, as bearer of enlightenment to the
young, would be better still.

WALLOP: I can't, Gentlemen, I can't! To tell you the truth,
it's the way I have been brought up. If anybody one rank
above mine speaks to me, I'm lost, I'm tongue-tied, no
heart in me at all. No, gentlemen, let me off, do let me off.

STRAWBERRY: There you are, Judge, nobody can do it
but you. You and your flights of the purest Cicero.

SLAPPENCATCHIT: What's that? What's that? Cicero!
What's all this made-up story? Just because once in a
while a man lets himself go, talking about a leash of grey-
hounds at his place, or about his bloodhound bitch ...

ALL [*Pressing round him*]: No, it isn't only when you are
talking about the hounds, it's the same when you get on
to the Tower of Babel ... No, Judge! Don't leave us, be
our father! No, Judge!

SLAPPENCATCHIT: Gentlemen! Will you let me be!

[*At this point, a sound of footsteps and throat-clearing is
heard from* WHIPPETT's *room. All stampede for the door,
crowding together and struggling to get out, in the course of
which some of them get crushed. Smothered exclamations.*]

VOICE OF BOBBIN: Hi! Peter, Peter, you're treading on my
toe!

VOICE OF STRAWBERRY: Leave me, gentlemen, leave me
to make my peace with God! You've squashed me flat.
[*Several more cries of Hi! Hi! At last they all squeeze out
and the room is left empty. Enter* WHIPPETT, *sleepy-
eyed.*]

WHIPPETT: I must have had a good old snore. Where did

they get those mattresses, and those feather-beds? I'm positively sweating. They must have slipped me something at lunch-time yesterday; my head is still ringing. From what I see, a good time could be had here. I do like it when people are kind, and I must say I prefer being entertained out of goodness of heart, and not with some ulterior motive. The Prefect's little daughter isn't half bad, and the mother too has possibilities . . . No, I don't know, but this really is the sort of life I like.

[*Enter* SLAPPENCATCHIT.]

SLAPPENCATCHIT [*stops and speaks to himself*]: O Lord, O Lord! Get me out of this safely; my knees are giving way. [*Stands stiffly and lays his hand on his sword and says aloud*] I have the honour to present myself: Judge of the District Court, Assessor grade eight, Slappencatchit.

WHIPPETT: Please sit down. So you're the Judge here?

SLAPPENCATCHIT: At the desire of the Gentlemen of the District, I was elected for a three-year term in the year '16, and I have been in post ever since.

WHIPPETT: So then, do you do well out of being a Judge?

SLAPPENCATCHIT: After three three-year terms I was recommended, with Departmental approval, for the Vladímir medal, class four. [*Aside*] I've got that money in my fist, and it's making it red-hot.

WHIPPETT: Oh, I like the Vladímir. Third class St Anne doesn't come up to that.

SLAPPENCATCHIT [*thrusting his clenched fist slightly forward*]: Good God! I don't know what I'm sitting on. It feels like hot coals underneath.

WHIPPETT: What's that you've got in your hand?

SLAPPENCATCHIT [*panicking, and dropping the notes on the floor*]: Nothing, Sir.

WHIPPETT: What do you mean, nothing? I can see, isn't that money fallen down there?

SLAPPENCATCHIT [*his whole body shaking*]: Oh no, Sir.

[*Aside*] Lord! Here am I as good as in the dock, with the cart at the door to take me off.

WHIPPETT [*picking it up*]: Yes, it's money.

SLAPPENCATCHIT [*aside*]: It's all up now; I'm done for, done for!

WHIPPETT: I'll tell you what! You lend it to me.

SLAPPENCATCHIT [*hastily*]: Why Sir, why Sir . . . with the greatest pleasure. [*Aside*] Boldly now, boldly! Holy Mother of God, bear me out of this!

WHIPPETT: I ran short on the road . . . you know . . . this and that . . . But I'll send it straight to you from home.

SLAPPENCATCHIT: Oh for goodness sake, really! Besides, it's such an honour . . . Of course with my poor strength, with my zeal, and my concern for Headquarters, I try to be of service. [*Rising from his chair, and standing stiffly to attention*] I won't venture to trouble you further with my presence. Would you perhaps have some instructions for me?

WHIPPETT: What sort of instructions?

SLAPPENCATCHIT: I thought you might be going to issue some instructions to the local District Court.

WHIPPETT: Whatever for? Why, I don't want it for anything at the moment.

SLAPPENCATCHIT [*bowing himself out, aside*]: Well, the Town's ours!

WHIPPETT [*after he has gone*]: Nice man, the Judge!

[*Enter the* POSTMASTER.]

POSTMASTER [*Standing stiffly with his hand on his sword*]: I have the honour to present myself. Postmaster, Counsellor grade seven, Pry.

WHIPPETT: Ah, pleased to meet you. I'm very fond of pleasant company. Sit down. So you have always lived here?

POSTMASTER: Quite correct, Sir.

WHIPPETT: I rather like this little town. Not many people

here, of course but – well, you know this isn't the Capital.
That's right, isn't it? You know this isn't the Capital.

POSTMASTER: Perfectly true.

WHIPPETT: You know, it's only in the Capital that you get
the *Bon Ton* and no country bumpkins. Isn't that so?
What do you think?

POSTMASTER: Quite correct Sir. [*Aside*] Well anyway he
isn't a bit grand; he asks one about everything.

WHIPPETT: Besides, don't you know ... you will allow
that one can live happily even in a small town, don't you
know.

POSTMASTER: Quite correct, Sir.

WHIPPETT: What does one want? I'll tell you what I
think; all that one wants is to be respected and sincerely
loved. Isn't that true?

POSTMASTER: A perfectly just observation.

WHIPPETT: I must tell you that I'm glad that you agree
with me. Of course, they'll say that I'm a strange person,
but there it is, that's my nature. [*Looking into his eyes, and
talking to himself*] Come on, let's ask the Postmaster for a
loan. [*Aloud*] An extraordinary thing happened to me; I
ran right out of money on the road. I suppose you couldn't
lend me three hundred roubles?

POSTMASTER: But why not! I should be extremely happy
to do so. Here you are, my dear Sir. Only too glad to be
of service to you.

WHIPPETT: I'm most grateful. I must say I simply hate
having to do without things, when I'm travelling. And
why should one? That's right, isn't it?

POSTMASTER: Quite correct, Sir. [*Rises and stands stiffly
with hand upon his sword.*] I won't venture to trouble you
further with my presence ... Would you perhaps have
some remarks as regards the postal administration?

WHIPPETT: No, nothing.

[*The* POSTMASTER *bows himself out.*]

WHIPPETT [*puffing at a cigar*]: I think that the Postmaster is a very nice man too. Obliging, to say the least of it. That's the sort of people I like.

[*Enter* WALLOP, *almost pushed through the door. Behind him is heard in an almost audible voice* 'Don't be so shy!']

WALLOP [*standing stiffly, though shaking a little, with his hand on his sword*]: I have the honour to present myself. Schools Superintendent. Counsellor grade nine, Wallop.

WHIPPETT: Ah, pleased to meet you! Sit down, sit down. Won't you have a cigar? [*Offers a cigar to him.*]

WALLOP [*to himself, irresolute*]: Oh dear! I never thought of that one. Do I accept it or not?

WHIPPETT: Go on, go on; it's quite a decent little cigar. Of course, not like you get in Petersburg. I used to smoke cigars there, my dear Sir, costing twenty-five roubles a hundred; you feel simply gorgeous after one of them. Here you are, light up. [*Hands him a candle.*]

[WALLOP *tries to light the cigar, but shakes all over.*]

WHIPPETT: Not that end!

WALLOP [*drops the cigar in fright, spits, gesticulates, and says to himself*]: Oh, confound it all! That cursed shyness; it's done for me!

WHIPPETT: I can see you're not keen on cigars. I must admit that they are a weakness of mine. It's the same too with the female sex; I can't ever remain indifferent to them. How about you? Which do you like best? Brunettes or blondes?

[WALLOP *is completely at a loss what to say.*]

WHIPPETT: No, tell me frankly – brunettes or blondes?

WALLOP: I wouldn't dare to know.

WHIPPETT: No, no! No more excuses. I must insist on knowing your taste.

WALLOP: I venture to submit . . . [*Aside*] I don't know what I'm saying.

WHIPPETT: Aha! You don't want to tell me. I expect some little brunette has got her hooks into you. Hasn't she? Own up!

[WALLOP *is silent.*]

WHIPPETT: Aha! You blushed! See that! See that! Why don't you tell me then?

WALLOP: Your hon . . . your ex . . . your serene . . . I feel so shy. [*Aside*] It's let me down! My confounded tongue has let me down.

WHIPPETT: Shy, are you? There is indeed something in my eyes, that makes people shy. At least, I know that no woman can ever resist them. That's right, isn't it?

WALLOP: Quite correct, Sir.

WHIPPETT: Look, a most extraordinary thing happened to me; I ran right out of money on the road. You couldn't lend me three hundred roubles?

WALLOP [*to himself, slapping his pockets*]: Here's a do now, if I haven't got it! Yes I have, I've got it! [*Takes out the notes and hands them over, trembling.*]

WHIPPETT: I'm most grateful.

WALLOP [*standing stiffly, with his hand on his sword*]: I won't venture to trouble you further with my presence.

WHIPPETT: Good-bye.

WALLOP [*flies out, almost running, and saying, aside*]: Well thank God! Maybe he won't look at the classes.

[*Enter* STRAWBERRY.]

STRAWBERRY [*standing stiffly with his hand on his sword*]: I have the honour to present myself, Warden of Charitable Institutions. Counsellor grade seven, Strawberry.

WHIPPETT: How do you do? Please take a chair.

STRAWBERRY: I had the honour to accompany you, and to receive you personally at the Charitable Institutions entrusted to my care.

WHIPPETT: Ah yes! I remember. You gave us a very good lunch.

STRAWBERRY: One's glad to do what one can for one's country.

WHIPPETT: I admit it's a weakness of mine, but I do like good cooking. Tell me please. I thought you weren't quite so tall yesterday evening. Isn't that so?

STRAWBERRY: Quite possible. [*Silence.*] I may say that I carry out my duties with ungrudging zeal. [*Moves his chair closer and speaks in an undertone*] Look, the Postmaster here does absolutely nothing; all his work is in a complete muddle, the deliveries are being held up. You, Sir, might see your way to make a special investigation. The Judge too, who was here just now before I came in, spends all his time coursing hares. He keeps hounds on the Court premises, and quite frankly his behaviour – of course it is for the sake of the country that I am obliged to speak in this way, although he is related to me and a friend of mine – his behaviour is most reprehensible. There is a landowner here, a Mr Dobbin – you have met him, Sir – and as soon as this Mr Dobbin goes out of the house, there he is sitting with his wife. I'm prepared to take an oath on it . . . You've only got to look at the children; not one of them is like Mr Dobbin, but all of them, even the little girl, are living images of the Judge.

WHIPPETT: Fancy that now! I'd never have thought it.

STRAWBERRY: Then there's the local Schools Superintendent . . . I don't know how Headquarters could have entrusted such a post to him; he's worse than a Jacobin, and he indoctrinates the young people with principles which are so pernicious that I can hardly bring myself to speak about them. You might perhaps prefer to ask me to put it all down on paper?

WHIPPETT: Fine, you can put it on paper. I'd be delighted. Just what I like, you know; something amusing to read when I'm bored . . . What is your surname? I keep on forgetting.

STRAWBERRY: Strawberry.

WHIPPETT: Ah yes, Strawberry. Well now, tell me please, have you any children?

STRAWBERRY: Why, yes, Sir. Five; two of them already grown up.

WHIPPETT: I say! Grown up, are they? And what are their, what are their er . . .

STRAWBERRY: What you are kind enough to say is that you would like to know their names.

WHIPPETT: Yes, what are their names?

STRAWBERRY: Nicholas, John, Elizabeth, Mary and Perpetua.

WHIPPETT: That's nice.

STRAWBERRY: Not venturing further to trouble you with my presence, taking up time alloted to your sacred duties . . . [*Bows and makes to go.*]

WHIPPETT [*accompanying him*]: No, that's all right; it's all very amusing, what you told me. Some other time again, please. I liked that very much. [*Turns round, opens the door and calls after him*] Hi you, what's your name? I keep on forgetting your first name.

STRAWBERRY: Artemus, Sir.

WHIPPETT: Will you do me a kindness, Artemus? An extraordinary thing happened to me; I ran right out of money on the road. I suppose you haven't got any money you could lend me – four hundred roubles?

STRAWBERRY: Yes, I have.

WHIPPETT: I say, isn't that handy! I'm most grateful to you.

[*Exit* STRAWBERRY. *Enter* BOBBIN *and* DOBBIN.]

BOBBIN: I have the honour to present myself. A local resident, Peter Bobbin, son of John Bobbin.

DOBBIN: Peter Dobbin, son of John Dobbin, landowner.

WHIPPETT: Ah yes, I've seen you before. Didn't you fall over? And how's your nose?

BOBBIN: Quite all right; please don't worry about it, it has dried up, quite dried up now.

WHIPPETT: Dried up, that's good. I'm glad . . . [*Suddenly, in a jerky voice*] Haven't you got the money?

BOBBIN: Money? What money?

WHIPPETT [*loudly and rapidly*]: To lend me a thousand roubles.

BOBBIN: Honest to goodness I haven't got that sort of money. You haven't got it, have you, Peter?

DOBBIN: I haven't got it on me, Sir. You see, Sir, my money is on deposit at the Social Protection Office.[14]

WHIPPETT: Then if you haven't got a thousand, make it a hundred.

BOBBIN [*fumbling in his pockets*]: You haven't got a hundred roubles, have you, Peter? All I've got is forty in notes.

DOBBIN [*looking in his wallet*]: Just twenty-five roubles.

BOBBIN: Go on, now Peter, have a better look! I know you've got a hole in your right-hand pocket, so I dare say some of it has fallen down into the hole.

DOBBIN: No, really; there's nothing in the hole.

WHIPPETT: All right then. You see, I just . . . good, let it be sixty-five roubles. That's all right. [*Takes the money.*]

DOBBIN: I venture to make a request to you, concerning a certain very delicate circumstance.

WHIPPETT: And what is it?

DOBBIN: It's a matter of a very delicate nature Sir. It's my eldest son; you see, Sir, I got him before I was married.

WHIPPETT: You did?

DOBBIN: That's only in a manner of speaking, because I got him in precisely the same way as if I had been married, and I settled everything afterwards, with bonds of legal matrimony, Sir. So, you'll please understand that what I want for him now is to be quite . . . I mean to say, my legitimate son, Sir, and to have the same name as me, Dobbin, Sir.

WHIPPETT: Fine, let him have it! That can be done.

DOBBIN: I wouldn't have troubled you only it's a shame on account of his ability. He's such a lad ... shows great promise; recites several poems by heart, and anywhere he can get hold of a penknife he starts straight off and makes little droshkies. Clever as a conjurer, Sir. Peter here knows.

BOBBIN: Yes, he has great ability.

WHIPPETT: Fine, fine! I'll see what I can do about it, I'll speak ... I hope ... all that shall be done, yes, yes ... [*Turning to* BOBBIN] You haven't got anything to speak to me about?

BOBBIN: Yes, I have. I have a very modest request.

WHIPPETT: What is it? What is it about?

BOBBIN: I most respectfully request that when you get to Petersburg you should say to all the various great chiefs there – the senators and the admirals – 'Look, your Serene Highness (or your Excellency). In such and such a town there lives Peter Bobbin'. Just say that – there lives Peter Bobbin.

WHIPPETT: Very well.

BOBBIN: And if you should have occasion to see the Emperor, then say it to the Emperor too 'Look', you would say, 'your Imperial Majesty. In such and such a town there lives Peter Bobbin.'

WHIPPETT: Very well.

DOBBIN: Excuse me for having burdened you in this way with my presence.

BOBBIN: Excuse me for having burdened you in this way with my presence.

WHIPPETT: Not at all, not at all! I'm delighted.

[*He shows them out.*]

WHIPPETT [*alone*]: Lot of civil servants here. I think, though, that they are taking me for some big man in the Government. I suppose I must have spun them a bit of a yarn yesterday. Silly idiots! Let's write to Johnny Raggett in Petersburg, and tell him the whole story; he does little pieces for the newspapers – let him have a crack at them. Hey, Joseph. Get me paper and ink!

[JOSEPH *puts his head round the door saying* 'Coming directly'.]

Yes indeed; you have to look out for yourself if Johnny Raggett gets hold of you. He wouldn't spare his own father, if there were a good story, and he likes the cash too. But you know, they are kind people, these civil servants; it's a point in their favour that they lent me money. I'd better have a look and see how much I've got. Here's the three hundred from the Judge; here's the three hundred from the Postmaster, six hundred, seven hundred, eight hundred – what a filthy dirty note . . . eight hundred, nine hundred . . . Oho! It's gone over the thousand. Now then, Captain, now then! Just you run into me now, and we'll see who's who!

[*Enter* JOSEPH *with paper and ink.*]

WHIPPETT: Do you see now, idiot, the way I'm received, and entertained?

JOSEPH: I do, and thank God for it. Only you know what, Master John.

WHIPPETT: Well, what?

JOSEPH: Get away out of this. I tell you, it's time to go.

WHIPPETT: [*writing*]: What rot! Why?

JOSEPH: Well it is. Don't you mind any of them. You've had two good days of fun – that's enough now! Why would you want to go on having any truck with them? To blazes with them! It's a tricky sort of a time, there's somebody else might turn up. Really, Master John. And there are some grand horses here; they'd get us clear away.

WHIPPETT [*writing*]: No, I want to stay on here a bit longer. Make it tomorrow.

JOSEPH: Why tomorrow? Let's go, Master John, we must, really! Of course it's a great honour for you; but still, you know, it is better to get quickly away, for the fact is that they have mistaken you for somebody else . . . and your Dad will be cross with you for going on dawdling like this. You could get away in grand style, indeed you could! And they'd give you elegant horses here.

WHIPPETT [*writing*]: All right then. Only take this letter first; you might as well take the order for the post-horses at the same time. And mind you get good horses on it! Tell the drivers that I'll be giving a rouble apiece for them to drive like Imperial Couriers, and sing songs . . . [*Goes on writing.*] I can imagine Raggett dying with laughter . . .

JOSEPH: I'll get the servant here to take it, Sir. I'd better get on with the packing myself, so as not to lose more time than we need.

WHIPPETT [*writing*]: All right, only get me the candle.

JOSEPH [*goes out and speaks off-stage*]: Hey my lad, listen to me! You're to take a letter to the Post, and you're to tell the Postmaster that he is to accept it without payment. And tell him that they are to bring round the best three-horse team for the gentleman at once – the courier's team. And tell him that the gentleman doesn't pay for post-horses; tell him he says to charge it to Treasury account. And buck up about it; the gentleman says he's going to be very cross if you don't. Wait now, the letter isn't ready yet.

WHIPPETT [*going on writing*]: I wish I knew where he is living now – Post Office Street or Peasepudding Street? He's another one who's fond of changing his lodgings without paying up. I'll chance it and write to Post Office Street.

[*He folds the letter and addresses it.* JOSEPH *hands him the candle and he seals the letter. At the same time the voice of* HOLDMUZZLE *is heard.*]

VOICE OF HOLDMUZZLE: Where are you off to, Whiskers? You've been told; nobody is allowed past here.

WHIPPETT [*handing the letter to* JOSEPH]: There you are. Take that.

VOICES OF MERCHANTS: Let us in Governor. You can't not let us in, we've come on business.

VOICE OF HOLDMUZZLE: Get out, get out! He won't see you. He's asleep.

[*The noise grows louder.*]

WHIPPETT: What's that there, Joseph? See what the noise is about.

JOSEPH [*looking out of the window*]: It's some merchants who want to come in, and the Police Sergeant won't let them. They're waving papers; it must be you they want to see.

WHIPPETT [*going up to the window*]: What is it, my good fellows?

VOICES OF MERCHANTS: We appeal to Your Grace. Will your Lordship give an order for a petition to be taken in?

WHIPPETT: Let them in, let them in! They can come. Tell them they can come, Joseph.

[*Exit* JOSEPH.]

WHIPPETT [*takes petitions in through the window, opens one of them and reads*]: 'To the Right Honourable, the most noble Lord High Financier, from the merchant Abdullah . . .' What the devil is this? There's no such title!

[*Enter* MERCHANTS *with a hamper of wine and sugarloaves.*]

WHIPPETT: What is it, my good fellows?

MERCHANTS: We make humble petition to Your Grace.

WHIPPETT: Well, and what do you want?

MERCHANTS: Your Lordship? Do not destroy us! We have done nothing to deserve the shameful treatment we are receiving.

WHIPPETT: From whom?

MERCHANTS: From the Prefect here, it's all his doing. Never before, Your Grace, has there been such a Prefect.

The outrages that he commits are quite indescribable. His billeting has been the ruin of us – we may as well go and hang ourselves. His behaviour is most improper. He'll seize you by the beard and say, 'Ah you old heathen.' On my oath! And it isn't as if we had been in any way disrespectful to him, for we always do the proper thing; a dress-length for his lady-wife and another for his young daughter – we don't mind about that. But no, you see, that's not enough for him – no Sir! He'll come into the shop, and take whatever's there, anything. He sees a piece of cloth, and he says 'Hullo my dear, that's a nice bit of cloth, take it round to my place.' So you take it round and there'll be the best part of three dozen yards in the piece.

WHIPPETT: Is it possible! Oh, what a scoundrel!

MERCHANTS: Indeed I tell you, nobody can remember such a Prefect. You have to hide away everything in the shop, when you see him coming. And it isn't as if there were any niceness about him; he takes any rubbish. Prunes, that have been seven years in the barrel, stuff that my shop-boy wouldn't eat, and he sticks his hand in and grabs a fistful. St Anthony's day is always his name-day, and you go on bringing things to him till you'd think he wanted for nothing; but no, you're going to have to give it all over again. He tells you that St Humphrey's day is his name-day too. What can you do? You bring it on St Humphrey's day as well.

WHIPPETT: But he's simply a robber!

MERCHANTS: Ay! Ay! And if you try to answer back he'll land a whole regiment on to you, to be billeted in your house, and if you say anything he'll order your shop to be closed. 'I won't give you corporal punishment,' says he, 'or have you tortured, because that,' says he, 'is forbidden by the law. But you, my good friend, can come to me now, and you shall have salt herrings to eat.'

WHIPPETT: Oh, what a scoundrel! But he can go to Siberia for that.

MERCHANTS: It's all right wherever your Grace has him put, so long as he is well away from here. You are our Father; don't disdain our hospitality. Here's a bit of sugar and a little hamper of wine to greet you with.

WHIPPETT: No, you mustn't think of such a thing. I never accept any kind of bribe. But suppose now that you were to offer me a loan – say three hundred roubles – why then it would be quite another matter; I can accept a loan.

MERCHANTS: Oh please! Our Father! [*Bringing out the money*] But what's three hundred! Wouldn't it be better to take five? It can only help.

WHIPPETT: All right, thank you. If it's a loan I've nothing to say; I'll accept it.

MERCHANTS [*presenting the money on a silver salver*]: And will you please take the salver as well?

WHIPPETT: Well, I can take the salver too.

MERCHANTS [*bowing*]: And won't you, just this once, take a little bit of sugar?

WHIPPETT: Oh no, I never accept any kind of . . .

JOSEPH: My Lord! Why not accept it? Take it! It's all useful on the road. Will you give me here the sugarloaves and the bag! Let's have it all; it'll all come in handy. What's that? String? Give me the string too – string is another thing that's useful on the road; a waggon may break down, or something, and you can tie it up.

MERCHANTS: So then, will your Serene Highness do us this kindness? Because we don't know what is going to become of us, if you don't help us over our petition; we might as well go and hang ourselves.

WHIPPETT: Surely, surely! I'll do my best.

[*The* MERCHANTS *go out. A woman's voice is heard.*]

WOMAN'S VOICE: No, don't you dare not let me in. I'll

complain about you to the gentleman himself. Don't you push me like that! You're hurting me.

WHIPPETT: Who is there? [*Goes up to the window.*] What's the matter, mother?

VOICES OF TWO WOMEN: Welcome to you, kind Sir! Will Your Lordship give an order that we are to be heard?

WHIPPETT [*through the window*]: Let her in.

[*Enter* LOCKSMITH'S WIFE *and* SERGEANT'S WIFE.]

LOCKSMITH'S WIFE [*bowing at his feet*]: Your Honour's welcome . . .

SERGEANT'S WIFE: Your Honour's welcome . . .

WHIPPETT: What women are you?

SERGEANT'S WIFE: Mrs John, the Sergeant's wife.

LOCKSMITH'S WIFE: I'm a locksmith's wife, kind Sir! I'm Mrs Febronia Clapperkin. I'm a townswoman and I live here.

WHIPPETT: Steady now, one at a time. What do you want?

LOCKSMITH'S WIFE: Your Honour's welcome, and I make humble petition to you against the Prefect! God send all manner of evil on him! May his children never prosper in anything, nor his uncles, nor his aunts!

WHIPPETT: But why?

LOCKSMITH'S WIFE: My husband! He made them shave his forelock off[15] and he sent him for a soldier! And it wasn't our turn, the dirty swindler! Besides, it's against the law – he's a married man.

WHIPPETT: But how could he do that?

LOCKSMITH'S WIFE: He did it, the swindler, he did it – God smite him in this world and in the next! Let everything that is nasty come upon him, and upon his aunt if he has an aunt, and if his father's alive then may he too die like a dog, the old rascal, or else choke to everlasting. Dirty swindler! He was supposed to take the tailor's son, and a drunken little sot he was, but the parents gave him a fat present so he picked on Mrs

Pantaloon the shopkeeper's son. Then when Mrs Pantaloon went sneaking round with three pieces of linen for
his lady, he came to me. 'What do you want with a
husband?' says he. 'Sure he's no good to you.' And I'm
the one who knows whether he is or he isn't; it's my
business, dirty swindler. 'He's a thief,' says he. 'He may
not have stolen yet, but never mind that,' says he, 'he
will steal, and in any case he'll be taken for a recruit next
year.' And what's to become of me without a husband?
Dirty swindler! I'm a poor weak creature, you nasty mean
thing you! May none of your kindred ever come to see
the light of day! And may your mother-in-law, if you
have a mother-in-law . . .

WHIPPETT: All right, all right. Now what about you?
[*Shows the old woman out.*]

LOCKSMITH'S WIFE [*going out*]: Don't forget me kind Sir,
be gracious to me!

SERGEANT'S WIFE: I've come about the Prefect, mister.

WHIPPETT: Well, what is it then? Tell me in a few
words.

SERGEANT'S WIFE: He whipped me, mister.

WHIPPETT: What!

SERGEANT'S WIFE: It was a mistake, kind Sir! Some of us
women got fighting in the market, and the police didn't
get there in time, and they grabbed hold of me. So I was
reported – I couldn't sit down for two days.

WHIPPETT: Then what do you want done now?

SERGFANT'S WIFE: Well of course there isn't anything that
can be done. But you can order him to pay a fine for the
mistake. If I can get a windfall I may as well have it, and
the money would come in very handy, just now.

WHIPPETT: All right, all right. Go on, go on; I'll see to it.
[*Hands, holding petitions, are thrust in through the window.*]

WHIPPETT: Who is it there now? [*Goes over to the window.*]
No, I won't, I won't! I don't want it, I don't want it.

[*Stepping back*] Oh hell, I'm fed up with them. Don't let them in, Joseph.

JOSEPH [*shouting out of the window*]: Be off with you, be off! Time's up; come tomorrow.

[*The door opens and a figure appears in a frieze greatcoat with an unshaven chin, a swollen lip and a bandaged cheek. Behind it is seen a vista of several others.*]

JOSEPH: Get out, get out! Where do you think you're going?

[*He gives the first man a push in the stomach and shoots out after him into the anteroom, slamming the door behind him. Enter* MARY.]

MARY: Oh!

WHIPPETT: Why so frightened, Lady?

MARY: No, I wasn't frightened.

WHIPPETT [*with a flourish*]: Good gracious! Lady, I'm delighted to think that you took me for the sort of man who ... May I make so bold as to ask you where you intended going?

MARY: I really wasn't going anywhere.

WHIPPETT: Then, why weren't you going anywhere?

MARY: I thought perhaps Mummy was in here.

WHIPPETT: But I'd like to know why you weren't going anywhere.

MARY: I disturbed you. You were doing important business.

WHIPPETT [*with a flourish*]: But your eyes are better than the important business. You can't possibly disturb me, not by any manner of means; on the contrary, you can bring me happiness.

MARY: You're talking like City people.

WHIPPETT: For such a lovely person as you. Dare I aspire to the great happiness of offering you a chair? But no! You ought to have not a chair, but a throne.

MARY: I really don't know ... I ought to be going. [*Sits down.*]

WHIPPETT: What a beautiful handkerchief you have!

MARY: You're a mocker; all you do is to laugh at provincial people.

WHIPPETT: How I wish, Lady, that I were your handkerchief, so that I might clasp your lily-white neck.

MARY: I haven't the least idea what you are talking about. Some handkerchief . . . What extraordinary weather it is today!

WHIPPETT: But your lips, Lady, are fairer than any weather.

MARY: You're still talking in that way . . . I'd like to ask you . . . hadn't you better write some piece of poetry for me in my album, as a souvenir? I'm sure you know a lot.

WHIPPETT: For you, Lady, it shall be whatever you wish. Command me – what poem will you have?

MARY: Oh, any sort of thing. Something good and new.

WHIPPETT: Well, what's poetry? I know lots of it.

MARY: Tell me then what you are going to write for me.

WHIPPETT: What's the point of reciting it? I know it anyway.

MARY: I'm very fond of poetry . . .

WHIPPETT: I know a lot of poems of all kinds. Suppose now I did this one for you?
'O Man, that in thy vain repining
Dost murmur at the Lord thy God' . . .[16]
Oh well, I know others too. . . . I can't recollect them just now. . . . But that's all by the way; what I'd better do instead is to offer you my love, which from the moment I saw you [*moving his chair up towards her*] . . .

MARY: Love! I don't understand love . . . I've never even known what love is . . . [*Moves her chair away.*]

WHIPPETT [*moving his chair up*]: Why do you move your chair away? We'd be more comfortable sitting close to one another.

MARY [*moving away*]: But why close? We're all right far apart.

WHIPPETT [*moving up*]: But why go farther away? We're all right close.

MARY [*moving away*]: But what's the point of this?

WHIPPETT: You see, you only think that it's close; imagine to yourself that we're far apart. How happy would I be, Lady, if I could take you in my arms and press you to me.

MARY [*looking out of the window*]: What was that? I thought something flew up; was it a magpie or some other bird?

WHIPPETT [*kissing her on the shoulder and looking out of the window*]: It's a magpie.

MARY [*standing up, indignant*]: No, that's really too much . . . the impertinence . . .

WHIPPETT [*holding her back*]: Forgive me, Lady. I did it out of love, just out of love.

MARY: You take me for the kind of provincial girl who . . . [*Struggles to get away.*]

WHIPPETT [*continuing to hold her back*]: It was love, it really was love. I only did it for a joke, Miss Mary, don't be angry! I'm ready to go on my knees to ask your pardon. [*Falls on his knees*] Forgive me, do forgive me. See I'm on my knees.
   [*Enter* ANNE.]

ANNE [*seeing* WHIPPETT *on his knees*]: Goodness gracious me!

WHIPPETT [*getting up*]: Oh damn!

ANNE [*to her daughter*]: What is the meaning of this, Miss? What are you doing, behaving in this way?

MARY: Mummy I . . .

ANNE: Go on, leave the room. Do you hear? Go on, go on! And don't dare to show your face again.
   [*Exit* MARY *in tears.*]
I beg your pardon. I must confess that I was taken aback . . .

WHIPPETT [*aside*]: She's another tasty morsel, not half bad. [*Throws himself on his knees.*] Lady, you see, I am on fire with love.

ANNE: What are you doing, kneeling! Oh get up, do; the floor here is dreadfully dirty.

WHIPPETT: No, I'll kneel. I absolutely must! I want to know what is fated for me – Life or Death?

ANNE: Excuse me, but I still don't quite understand what these words mean. Unless I am mistaken, you are making a declaration with regard to my daughter.

WHIPPETT: No, I am in love with you. My life hangs on a hair. If you do not set the crown upon my constant love, then I am unworthy to exist upon the earth. With a flame in my bosom I ask for your hand.

ANNE: But permit me to remark – In a way. . . I am married.

WHIPPETT: That doesn't matter! Nothing makes any difference to love, and as Karamzín says 'It is the law condemneth'.[17] Let us go far beyond the waves . . . your hand, I ask for your hand.

[MARY *suddenly runs in*.]

MARY: Mummy, Daddy says will you . . . [*Sees* WHIPPETT *on his knees and shrieks*] Goodness gracious me!

ANNE: Now what are you doing? What's all this? What do you want? Here's a flighty sort of a way to go on. Suddenly dashing in like a scalded cat. Come on, what was it that you found so surprising? Whatever were you thinking of? Really she's like a child of three. Nobody would imagine that she was eighteen. Nobody, nobody, nobody! I don't know! When are you going to have some more sense? When are you going to start acting like a properly brought-up girl? When are you going to know what is meant by rules of conduct and dignified behaviour?

MARY [*tearful*]: Mummy I truly didn't know . . .

ANNE: You've always got some flighty nonsense in your head; you take your cue from Judge Slappencatchit's daughters. What do you want to go by them for? You shouldn't go by them. There are other examples for you.

Right here now you have your Mother. That's the kind of example you ought to be following.

WHIPPETT [*seizing the daughter by the hand*]: Mrs Slydewynde, don't stand in the way of our happiness! Give your blessing to our constant love.

ANNE [*bewildered*]: So she is the one that you . . . ?

WHIPPETT: Decide. Life or Death?

ANNE: Now do you see, you stupid girl. Now do you see? Here's our visitor gone down on his knees for a rubbishy little chit like you, and you suddenly come dashing into the room like a mad thing. Really and truly now I ought to simply refuse. You don't deserve such good fortune.

MARY: I won't do it again Mummy, I truly won't do it again.

[*Enter the* PREFECT, *panting.*]

PREFECT: Your Excellency! Don't ruin me, don't ruin me!

WHIPPETT: What's the matter with you?

PREFECT: Those merchants that have been complaining to Your Excellency! I assure you on my honour that not half of what they said was true. They cheat people themselves; they give short measure. The Sergeant's wife lied to you, making out that I whipped her; she's talking nonsense, I swear it's nonsense. She whipped herself.

WHIPPETT: Confound the Sergeant's wife, she's nothing to do with it.

PREFECT: Don't believe them, don't believe them! They are awful liars . . . why not even a little child would believe them. They're well known all over the town as liars. And as for swindles – I take the liberty of informing you that there haven't ever been swindlers like these in all the world before.

ANNE: Do you know about the honour that Mr Whippett is bestowing upon us? He is asking for our daughter's hand.

PREFECT: Get along with you . . . you've gone crazy,

Mother. I do beseech Your Excellency not to be annoyed. She's a little bit silly; her Mother was that way too.

WHIPPETT: But I really am asking for her hand. I'm in love.

PREFECT: Your Excellency, I can't believe it.

ANNE: Not when the gentleman is telling you?

WHIPPETT: I am not speaking to you in jest. I am capable of becoming mentally unhinged, through love.

PREFECT: I dare not believe it; I am unworthy of such an honour.

WHIPPETT: If you don't consent to give me Miss Mary's hand, damme I don't know what I won't do!

PREFECT: I cannot believe it. Your Excellency is pleased to jest!

ANNE: Oh you great gawk! With the gentleman explaining it to you and all!

PREFECT: I cannot believe it.

WHIPPETT: Do give your consent, do! I'm a desperate man, I'm prepared to go to any length; when I shoot myself they'll have you up before the court.

PREFECT: No, no! So help me God, I'm not guilty! Neither in thought nor deed! Please don't be angry! Please act in whatever way Your Lordship thinks fit! I really now ... my head ... I don't know what's happening. I've made a fool of myself now, the biggest fool that ever was.

ANNE: Go on, bless them!

[WHIPPETT *comes forward with* MARY.]

PREFECT: God bless you, and I'm not guilty.

[WHIPPETT *and* MARY *kiss. The* PREFECT *looks on.*]

PREFECT: Well I'll be damned! Look at that! [*Rubs his eyes.*] They're kissing! Oh by Jiminy they are kissing. Well and truly engaged! [*Shouting and jumping for joy.*] Yo ho Anthony! Yo ho Anthony! Yo ho the Prefect! Look what's gone and happened now!

[*Enter* JOSEPH.]

JOSEPH: The horses are ready.

WHIPPETT: All right then . . . just a moment.

PREFECT: Why Sir, are you going away?

WHIPPETT: Yes, I'm going.

PREFECT: But when – I mean to say . . . it was you yourself, Sir, that passed the remark; something about a wedding, I think.

WHIPPETT: But it's . . . only for one minute . . . for one day, to my uncle – rich old gentleman – back tomorrow.

PREFECT: I wouldn't presume to do anything to detain you. We'll be looking forward to your safe return.

WHIPPETT: Oh yes, rather. I'll be straight back again. Good-bye my love . . . no, I simply can't express it. Good-bye, darling. [*Kisses her hand.*]

PREFECT: Isn't there anything you want for the road? Excuse me, Sir, but I think you were short of cash.

WHIPPETT: Oh no! What would I want it for? [*After a moment's thought*] Ah well, perhaps.

PREFECT: How much would you like?

WHIPPETT: Look here, you gave me two hundred last time, that's to say not two hundred but four hundred – I don't want to take advantage of your mistake – shall we say the same again now, making it just up to the eight hundred?

PREFECT: Right you are! [*Takes the money from his wallet.*] Nice new notes, too, as it happens.

WHIPPETT: Ah yes! [*Takes the notes and examines them.*] That's fine. You know the saying, don't you – new notes, new luck.

PREFECT: That's right, Sir.

WHIPPETT: Good-bye, Mr Huffam-Slydewynde! I am most obliged for your hospitality. I say it in all sincerity – I haven't had such a good reception anywhere. Good-bye, Mrs Huffam-Slydewynde! Good-bye Miss Mary, my darling.

[*All go outside. Voices are heard off-stage.*]

VOICE OF WHIPPETT: Good-bye, Miss Mary, angel of my heart.

VOICE OF PREFECT: But what's this? Are you really travelling like that, in a post-vehicle?

VOICE OF WHIPPETT: Yes, I'm used to it. A sprung carriage makes my head ache.

VOICE OF DRIVER: Whoa . . .

VOICE OF PREFECT: Well, at least let's put something for you to sit on, even if it's only a rug. Wouldn't you wish me to tell them to get you a rug?

VOICE OF WHIPPETT: No, what for? It doesn't matter. Ah well, perhaps they might put a rug.

VOICE OF PREFECT: Hi there, Eudoxia! Go to the store room and get out the best rug – the one with a blue background, the Persian rug. Be quick!

VOICE OF DRIVER: Whoa . . .

VOICE OF PREFECT: When do you wish us to expect you?

VOICE OF WHIPPETT: Tomorrow or the next day.

VOICE OF JOSEPH: Ah, is that the rug? Let's have it here, put it like this. Now let's have a bit of hay in on this side.

VOICE OF DRIVER: Whoa . . .

VOICE OF JOSEPH: Now this side! In here! A bit more! Good. That'll be fine! [*Slaps the rug with his hand.*] Will you take your seat now, Your Honour!

VOICE OF WHIPPETT: Good-bye, Mr Huffam-Slyde-wynde!

VOICE OF PREFECT: Good-bye, Your Excellency!

VOICES OF WOMEN: Good-bye, Mr Whippett.

VOICE OF WHIPPETT: Good-bye, Mummy!

VOICE OF DRIVER: Fly away, my beauties!

[*A bell tinkles. The curtain is lowered.*]

ACT FIVE

Scene. The same room in the Prefect's house. The PREFECT,
ANNE *and* MARY.

PREFECT: Well, Mrs Slydewynde? Eh? Did you imagine
anything like this? A big catch, the baggage! Come be
honest and admit it, did you ever even dream of it – just
a prefect's wife, and all of a sudden . . . ooh! you little
baggage! . . . to find yourself related to that sort of a
devil!

ANNE: Of course I did; I've known it for a long time. You
think it marvellous because you're a common man; you
haven't ever seen decent people.

PREFECT: Mother, I am a decent person. But really now,
Mrs Slydewynde, what do you think? What sort of birds
have you and I become now, eh, Mrs Slydewynde? High
flyers, damn it! But wait a bit. I'm going to tickle up all
these people who are so keen on handing in petitions and
laying informations and I'm going to do it right now.
Hallo, who's that there?

[*Enter* POLICE SERGEANT.]

Oh, it's you, John. Just tell 'em to come here, lad, those
merchants. I'll teach 'em, the scamps! Complain about
me, would you? Look here you race of god-damned Jews!
Just a moment, my dears! I've given it to you hot before,
but this time I'm going to give it to you hot and strong.
Take all their names, anyone who came and humbly
prayed for help against me, and look here, most important of all, get the names of those writer-fellows, the
writer-fellows who got up the petitions for them. Publish
it abroad, let 'em know! 'Look', you can say, 'look what

298

an honour the Lord has sent down upon the Prefect —
he's giving his daughter in marriage, and not to any
ordinary sort of a person, but to a man such as there
never was before in the world, one who can do everything,
everything, everything.' Publish it abroad, let 'em all
know. Shout it to all the people, ring the bells backwards,
damn it! Talk about a triumph!

[*Exit* POLICE SERGEANT.]

What about that, Mrs Slydewynde, eh! And what about
us now? Where are we going to live? Here or Petersburg?

ANNE: Naturally, in St Petersburg. How can we stay here?

PREFECT: Well, in Petersburg then, in Petersburg; but it
could be all right here too. I tell you what I think though
— it's to hell with the Prefecture now, eh, Mrs Slydewynde?

ANNE: Naturally, what's a prefecture?

PREFECT: But, you know ... What do you think, Mrs
Slydewynde? I can land myself a big position now, because he hobnobs with all the Ministers, and goes in and
out of the Palace, so it follows that he can put through
promotions till in time one will even get up to be a
general. What do you think, Mrs Slydewynde; can I get
up to be a general?

ANNE: I should think so! Of course you can.

PREFECT: Damn it though, it would be fine to be a general.
They put the riband of the Order over your shoulder
when you get a knighthood. Which order's better to have,
Mrs Slydewynde, the one with the red riband or the one
with the sky-blue?[18]

ANNE: Well of course the sky-blue's better.

PREFECT: Eh? So that's what she wants! The red's all
right too. Shall I tell you why I want to be a general?
Because suppose now you're travelling somewhere ...
there's couriers and aides-de-camp galloping ahead of
you all over the place. 'Horses!' And then they won't let

anybody have them at the post-stages, they've all got to wait. All those grade nine counsellors and captains and prefects, and you don't give a damn. And when you're having dinner with the Governor at some place – steady, Prefect! Ha – ha – ha! [*Goes off into peals of helpless laughter.*] And that's what's the attraction, you baggage you!

ANNE: You always like anything coarse. You ought to bear in mind that you're going to have to make a complete change in your life, and that your acquaintances aren't going to be like that sporting judge that you go hunting hares with, or Mr Strawberry. Quite the contrary; your acquaintances will be people with the most refined manners – counts and all sorts of society people . . . only to tell you the truth, there's one thing I'm afraid of about you – you sometimes come out with a little word of a kind that is never heard in good company.

PREFECT: What of it? Why, a word's no harm.

ANNE: It was all right as long as you were a prefect. But life there is altogether different.

PREFECT: Yes; there's two sorts of little fish they have there. Whitebait and smelts. You fairly dribble when you put them in your mouth.

ANNE: That's all he would think about – little fish! I want nothing less than for our home to be the first house in the capital, and I want to have such a perfume in my room that you don't have to go in – you just have to close your eyes like this. [*Screws up her eyes and sniffs.*] Mm, how lovely!

[*Enter* MERCHANTS.]

PREFECT: Ah! Hullo, my bold lads!

MERCHANTS [*bowing*]: Our best respects to you, good Sir!

PREFECT: Well, my dears, how are you doing? How's trade? What's this? The tea-kettle mongers and the cloth-stretchers complaining? The arch-diddlers, the master-

fiddlers and the run-of-the-mill rogues complaining?
Well, did you get much? 'Have him put into jail' – that's
what they thought. And do you know, seven devils and
one witch on the teeth of you, that . . .

ANNE: Oh, my goodness Tony, your language!

PREFECT [*irritated*]: Never mind about the language now!
Do you know, that that very same officer that you've been
complaining to is now going to marry my daughter?
Well? Eh? What have you got to say now? I'll give it you
now . . . ooh! . . . you swindle the country . . . Yes, you,
you take a Government contract and do the Treasury
down to the tune of a hundred thousand by supplying
rotten cloth, then you bring out a handsome present of
thirty yards of stuff and expect to be given a bit more in
return for that! And if they'd known, they'd have done
something to you . . . His belly sticks out in front – that's
a merchant, mustn't touch him. 'We're no less good than
the gentry,' says he. But a gentleman . . . aah you there
with the ugly face! – a gentleman studies to be a scholar;
they may beat him at school, but it's for his good, so that
he may know something useful. And what do you do?
Start off on learning dirty tricks, and your boss beats you
because you don't know how to swindle. Still a little boy
who can't say his 'Our Father', but you're already giving
short measure; and as soon as that belly of yours pushes
out, and you cram your pockets, you'll have begun to put
on airs. Ooh, aren't you a wonder! Swill down sixteen
pots of tea a day – is that anything to put on airs about?
We don't give a damn for you and your fine airs!

MERCHANTS [*bowing*]; Mr Slydewynde, we've done wrong!

PREFECT: Complain! And who helped you with your
fiddle when you built the bridge, and put down twenty
thousand for timber when there wasn't a hundred
roubles worth of it there? I did, you with the beard like a
billy-goat! Have you forgotten that? You're another one

I could have shown up and got sent to Siberia! What have you got to say? Eh?

ONE OF THE MERCHANTS: Mr Slydewynde, we've done wrong before God! It was the Evil One that led us astray. And we repent and promise never to complain any more. Anything you like by way of satisfaction, only don't be angry with us!

PREFECT: Don't be angry! Look at you now, grovelling at my feet. For why? Because I'm on the up and up. And if things had gone the least bit your way, you twister, you'd have stamped me right down into the mud and chucked a tree trunk in on top of me.

MERCHANTS [*bowing at his feet*]: Don't ruin us, Mr Slyde-wynde!

PREFECT: Don't ruin you! It's 'don't ruin us' now, but what was it before? I'd like to . . . [*waves his hand*]. Well, God forgive you, let's say no more! I don't bear malice, only look out now and mind yourselves! I'm not marry-ing my daughter to any ordinary gentleman; when it comes to congratulations let's have . . . you understand? You can't get out of this one with a back-fillet of pickled sturgeon, or a sugarloaf. Go along now and good-bye!

[*Exeunt* MERCHANTS. *Enter* SLAPPENCATCHIT *and* STRAWBERRY.]

SLAPPENCATCHIT [*still in the doorway*]: Mr Slydewynde, am I to believe the rumours about some extraordinary good fortune having come your way?

STRAWBERRY: I have the honour to congratulate you on your extraordinary good fortune. I was absolutely de-lighted when I heard. [*Kisses* ANNE's *hand.*] Mrs Slyde-wynde! [*Kisses* MARY's *hand.*] Miss Mary!

[*Enter* MR RATTUM.]

MR RATTUM [*coming in*]: Mr Slydewynde I congratulate you, and may God grant long life to you and to the newly

engaged couple, and may He give you numerous descendants, grandchildren and great-grandchildren.
[*Kisses* ANNE's *hand.*] Mrs Slydewynde! [*Kisses* MARY's
hand.] Miss Mary!

[*Enter* MR *and* MRS CANISTER *and* MR HUBBLY.]

MR CANISTER: I have the honour to congratulate Mr
Slydewynde! Mrs Slydewynde! [*Kisses* ANNE's *hand.*]
Miss Mary! [*Kisses* MARY's *hand.*]

MRS CANISTER: My heartiest congratulations, Mrs
Slydewynde on your new happiness.

MR HUBBLY: I have the honour to congratulate you, Mrs
Slydewynde. [*Kisses her hand and then turns towards the
audience and clucks his tongue with an impudent air.*] Miss Mary!
I have the honour to congratulate you. [*Kisses her hand
and turns towards the audience with the same impudent gesture.*]

[*Enter many Guests in surtouts and frock-coats. They come up
and kiss* ANNE's *hand saying* 'Mrs Slydewynde!', *then*
MARY's *saying* 'Miss Mary!']

[*Enter* BOBBIN *and* DOBBIN, *jostling one another.*]

BOBBIN: I have the honour to congratulate . . .

DOBBIN: Mr Slydewynde! I have the honour to congratulate you . . .

BOBBIN: On a happy event!

DOBBIN: Mrs Slydewynde!

BOBBIN: Mrs Slydewynde!

[*Both bend over her hand at the same moment and their fore-
heads collide.*]

DOBBIN: Miss Mary! [*Kisses her hand.*] I have the honour to
congratulate you. You will be in great, great happiness
and go about in a gold dress and partake of various kinds
of delicate soups; you will pass your time in the most
entertaining way.

BOBBIN [*interrupting*]: Miss Mary! I have the honour to
congratulate you! God send you every kind of wealth,
pieces of gold and a little son ma'am – so big, look just so

big ma'am [*illustrating with his hand*] so he'll be able to sit on the palm of your hand, yes ma'am! And all the time the little boy will cry 'Wah! Wah! Wah!'.

[*Several more guests come up and kiss the ladies' hands. Enter* MR *and* MRS WALLOP.]

WALLOP: I have the honour . . .

MRS WALLOP [*running forward*]: Mrs Slydewynde I congratulate you! [*They kiss.*] And I really was so overjoyed. They say to me 'Mrs Slydewynde has a marriage arranged for her daughter.' 'Oh Heavens!' I think to myself and I'm so overjoyed that I say to my husband 'Listen, Lukey-boy, here's wonderful happiness for Mrs Slydewynde'. 'Well,' I think to myself, 'the Lord be praised', and I say to him, 'I'm so delighted that I'm burning with impatience to go and say it to Mrs Slydewynde herself.' And 'Oh Heavens!' I think to myself, 'A good marriage for her daughter was the very thing that Mrs Slydewynde was waiting for, and look what fate has brought to her! The very thing that she wanted has come off.' I really was so overjoyed that I couldn't speak. I cry and cry, I positively sob. So then Mr Wallop says to me, 'What are you sobbing about Anastasia?' 'Lukey-boy,' I say, 'I don't know, but the tears are pouring out like a river.'

PREFECT: Ladies and Gentlemen, will you pray be seated.

[*The guests sit down. Enter* EARWIG *and* POLICE SERGEANTS.]

EARWIG: I have the honour to congratulate your honour, Sir, and to wish you many years of prosperity!

PREFECT: Thank you, thank you. Please sit down, gentlemen.

[*The guests settle down.*]

SLAPPENCATCHIT: Will you tell me now, Mr Slydewynde, how did all this begin? I mean, how did the case go, step by step?

PREFECT: The case went in an extraordinary way; he actually made a proposal in person.

ANNE: In a very respectful and most refined manner. He said it all extraordinarily nicely. 'Mrs Slydewynde,' he says, 'it is out of pure respect for your merits that I . . .' And such a good-looking well-educated man, and so aristocratic in his behaviour! 'Believe me, Mrs Slyde-wynde, life to me isn't worth a farthing; I'm saying this simply out of respect for your rare good qualities.'

MARY: Oh Mummy! It was me he said that to.

ANNE: Be quiet, you don't know anything so mind your own business! 'Mrs Slydewynde, I am amazed . . .' He kept on pouring out that sort of flattering language . . . and just as I was going to say 'We cannot possibly dare to hope for so great an honour' he suddenly dropped down on his knees and in the most aristocratic way 'Mrs Slydewynde,' he said, 'don't make me the most unhappy of men! Consent to requite my feelings or I shall end my life in death.'

MARY: Really, Mummy, he said that about me.

ANNE: Yes, of course . . . it was about you that he said it, I'm not denying that.

PREFECT: He was positively terrifying, he said he was going to shoot himself. 'I'll shoot myself, I'll shoot my-self,' says he.

MANY GUESTS: Fancy that!

SLAPPENCATCHIT: What a do!

WALLOP: There now, that really must have been fated.

STRAWBERRY: Fate be blowed, my dear Sir! It's his services to the State that have led to this not fate. [Aside] The luck drops into his mouth all the time, the old swine!

SLAPPENCATCHIT: Mr Slydewynde, maybe I will sell you that hound dog you were after.

PREFECT: No, I'm not interested in hound dogs now.

SLAPPENCATCHIT: All right, if you don't want him we can settle for one of the other hounds.

MRS CANISTER: Mrs Slydewynde, I am so pleased about your good fortune! You can't imagine.

MR CANISTER: And where, may I ask, is the distinguished visitor now? I heard that he had gone away for some reason.

PREFECT: Yes, he has gone for one day, on most important business.

ANNE: To his uncle, to ask for a blessing.

PREFECT: To ask for a blessing, but tomorrow as ever is . . .
[*He sneezes, the congratulations merge into a continuous buzz.*] I am most grateful! But tomorrow as ever is he comes back. [*He sneezes.*]
[*Buzz of congratulations. Some voices stand out more loudly.*]

VOICE OF EARWIG: Our very best respects to your Honour, Sir.

VOICE OF BOBBIN: A hundred years and a sackful of golden money.

VOICE OF DOBBIN: God preserve your life for years and years and years!

VOICE OF STRAWBERRY: Confound you!

VOICE OF MRS CANISTER: Devil take you!

PREFECT: Thank you very much and the same to you.

ANNE: We are planning now to live in St Petersburg. The air here . . . I really must say . . . altogether too rustic . . . Most unpleasant, I must say . . . my husband now . . . he will receive the rank of general there.

PREFECT: Yes, gentlemen, I must say, God damn it I would like to be a general.

WALLOP: Please God you get it.

RATTUM: Humanly impossible, but to God all things are possible.

SLAPPENCATCHIT: Great ships need deep waters.

STRAWBERRY: As an honour, in recognition of your services.

SLAPPENCATCHIT [*aside*]: Nice thing, if he really does get made a general! A general's rank would suit him about as well as a saddle on a cow! No, old man, come on, that's still a far cry. There are bigger nobs than you, and they still aren't generals.

STRAWBERRY [*aside*]: Here I say, damn it all, he's out to be a general now. Perhaps he will be, you never can tell. He's got the bounce, and if the devil doesn't get him, he'll do. [*Turning to the Prefect*] Don't forget us then, Mr Slydewynde.

SLAPPENCATCHIT: And if anything should arise; something needed in business for instance, you won't fail to stick up for us?

MR CANISTER: I'm taking my boy up to St Petersburg next year, to serve his country, so will you be kind enough to use your influence for him and to stand *in loco parentis* for a fatherless child?

PREFECT: For my part I'm ready, I'm ready to try.

ANNE: Now, Tony, you're always ready to make promises. In the first place, you won't have the time to think about that. And how can you burden yourself with all these promises? What's the point of it?

PREFECT: But why my love? Sometimes one can.

ANNE: One can, of course; but surely you aren't going to go on using your influence for every Tom, Dick and Harry?

MR CANISTER: Did you hear the way she speaks about us?

A FEMALE GUEST: Yes, she's always been like that. I know her – show her the food and she'll have her feet in the trough . . .

[*The* POSTMASTER *rushes in panting, with an opened letter in his hand.*]

POSTMASTER: An amazing thing, Ladies and Gentlemen!

The officer that we took to be the Inspector, was not an inspector.

ALL: What! Not an inspector?

POSTMASTER: Definitely not an inspector – I've found that out from a letter.

PREFECT: You've what? You've what? From what letter?

POSTMASTER: Why, from his own letter. A letter was brought to me for the Post. I glanced at the address and when I saw 'Post Office Street' I went all numb. 'That's it,' I thought, 'he must have found irregularities in the Postal Department, and he is advising Head Office.' So I took and opened it.

PREFECT: But how . . .

POSTMASTER: *I* don't know, some supernatural force impelled me. I was just going to call a courier, so as to send it by special messenger, but I was overcome by such curiosity as I had never felt before. 'I can't, I can't!' I heard a voice telling me I couldn't do it, but something drew me on and drew me on. In one ear I heard 'Hi there! Don't you open that or you'll get your neck wrung like a chicken,' and a sort of demon was whispering into the other ear, 'Open it, open it, open it.' And as I pressed down on the wax my veins were on fire, but when I opened it they were frozen – honest to God! Frozen! My hands shook, and everything went dim.

PREFECT: But how dare you open the letter of a plenipotentiary personage!

POSTMASTER: The thing is that he isn't a plenipotentiary and he isn't a personage!

PREFECT: What do you suppose he is, then?

POSTMASTER: Neither the one nor the other. The Deuce knows what he is.

PREFECT [*blazing up*]: What do you mean – neither the one nor the other? How dare you call him 'neither the one nor the other' and 'the Deuce knows what'! I put you under arrest. . . .

POSTMASTER: Who, you?

PREFECT: Yes, me.

POSTMASTER: You can't touch me!

PREFECT: Do you know that he is going to marry my daughter, and that I am going to be a great man and that I can send you packing all the way to Siberia?

POSTMASTER: Siberia? Oh Mr Slydewynde, Siberia's a long way off. Look, I'd better read it to you. Ladies and gentlemen, will you permit me to read the letter?

ALL: Go on, read it!

POSTMASTER: 'I hasten to tell you, Raggett my dear, what wonderful things have been happening to me. On the way here I got completely cleaned out by an infantry captain, so much so that the innkeeper was on the verge of having me jailed; and then, what with my clothes and my Petersburg face the whole town suddenly took me for a governor-general. So, now I'm staying with the Prefect, living on the fat of the land and making desperado advances to his wife and daughter, the only thing being that I can't make up my mind which of them to begin with – I think I'll start with the mother, because she looks ready to do anything for you right away. Do you remember how we used to fiddle our dinners, you and I, when we were hard up? And that time when the pastry-cook nearly grabbed me by the collar for having eaten his pies and charged them to the King of England's account? It's quite the opposite now. Everybody lends me as much as I want. They're an awfully queer lot. You'd die laughing. I know you write little bits for the papers; put them into your literary work. First, there's the Prefect – he's got about as much sense as an old grey gelding.

PREFECT: It can't be that! That's not there!

POSTMASTER [showing the letter]: Read it yourself!

PREFECT [*reading*]: 'As an old grey gelding'. It can't be that! You wrote that yourself!

POSTMASTER: How do you suppose I could have written it?

STRAWBERRY: Go on, read it!

WALLOP: Go on, read it.

POSTMASTER [*continuing to read*]: . . . the Prefect – he's got about as much sense as an old grey gelding.

PREFECT: Damn it! Must you repeat it again. As if we didn't already know it was there?

POSTMASTER [*continuing to read*]: . . . hm . . . hm . . . hm . . . hm . . . 'grey gelding. The Postmaster, too, is a good man.' [*Stops reading.*] I say, he's used an indecent expression about me too.

PREFECT: Never mind, go on, read it!

POSTMASTER: But what's the point?

PREFECT: Go on damn it, if you're going to read it, read it! Read it all!

STRAWBERRY: Allow me, I'll read it. [*Puts on spectacles and reads*] 'The postmaster is the spit image of Micah, the office-keeper. So I expect he's a cad too, and drinks like a fish.'

POSTMASTER [*to the audience*]: All I can say is that he's a dirty little boy, who ought to be whipped!

STRAWBERRY [*continuing to read*]: 'The Warden of Charitable Instit . . . er . . . er . . . er . . .' [*He stutters.*]

MR CANISTER: What are you stopping for?

STRAWBERRY: The writing isn't clear . . . anyway you can see he's no good.

MR CANISTER: Give it to me. I think my eyes are a bit better. [*Takes hold of the letter.*]

STRAWBERRY [*not letting go of the letter*]: No, you can leave that bit out, it gets more legible further on.

MR CANISTER: Let me have it, I know now what it says.

STRAWBERRY: If anyone reads it, I'll read it myself. It really does get quite legible further on.

POSTMASTER: No, go on, read it all; why, everything was read out before.

ALL: Let him have it, Mr Strawberry, let him have the letter! [*To* MR CANISTER] Go on, read it.

STRAWBERRY: Just a moment. [*Gives him the letter.*] Look, allow me . . . [*Covers it with one finger.*] Look, read on from there.

[*All come up towards him.*]

POSTMASTER: Go on, read it! Rot, read it all!

MR CANISTER [*reading*]: 'The Warden of Charitable Institutions, a Mr Strawberry, is exactly like a pig in a skull-cap!'

STRAWBERRY [*to the audience*]: It isn't even witty! A pig in a skull-cap! Where was there ever a pig in a skull-cap!

MR CANISTER [*continuing to read*]: 'The superintendent of schools absolutely stinks of onions.'

WALLOP [*to the audience*]: Honestly, I never put an onion into my mouth.

SLAPPENCATCHIT [*aside*]: Thank goodness, at any rate there's nothing about me.

MR CANISTER [*reading*]: 'Judge . . .'

SLAPPENCATCHIT: Dear, oh dear. [*Aloud*] Ladies and Gentlemen, I think this letter is too long. What the devil's the use of reading out all this rubbish?

WALLOP: No!

POSTMASTER: No, go on, read it!

STRAWBERRY: No, go on and read it!

MR CANISTER: 'Judge Slappencatchit is the last word in *mauvais ton*' . . . [*Stops.*] Those words must be French.

SLAPPENCATCHIT: What the blazes do they mean? It's all very well if it's only a swindler, but it could be something even worse than that.

MR CANISTER: 'But after all, they are good-hearted, hospitable people. Good-bye, Raggett my dear. I want to follow your example and go in for literature myself.

This is a dull sort of life, old boy; after all one does want nourishment for the soul. I can see that one really must somehow concern oneself with higher things. Write to me at the village of Rollingholme, Sarátov Province. [*Turns the letter over and reads the address.*] John B. Raggett Esq., third floor on the right after turning into the courtyard, 97 Post Office Street, St Petersburg.'

A LADY: What an un-called for reprimand!

PREFECT: He's carved me up, that's what he's done, carved me up! I'm down, I'm down, I'm down and out! I can't see a thing. All I can see is a sort of pigs' snouts instead of faces ... Get him back, get him back! [*Waves his arm.*]

POSTMASTER: What's the good of saying 'Get him back?' I made a point of telling the Overseer to give him the best three-horse team; I was damned fool enough to give him forward orders too.

MRS CANISTER: Well really now, what unexampled confusion!

SLAPPENCATCHIT: But ladies and gentlemen, damn it all, he borrowed three hundred roubles from me.

STRAWBERRY: Three hundred roubles from me too.

POSTMASTER [*sighing*]: Oh! And three hundred roubles from me!

BOBBIN: He borrowed sixty-four roubles from Peter and me, Sir. In depreciated notes, Sir. Yes, Sir.

SLAPPENCATCHIT [*spreading out his hands in bewilderment*]: But, ladies and gentlemen, how did this happen? How in fact did we come to make such a mistake?

PREFECT [*slapping his forehead*]: How did I come to, you mean, how did I, the old fool? Silly old tup, you've out-lived your wits. Thirty years I've been in the service; never a merchant, never a contractor that I couldn't get the better of; swindlers upon swindlers and I fooled them, cheats and tricksters out to rob the whole world and I got

them on the hook. I've fooled three Governors. . . .
Governors indeed! [*Waves his arm.*] No need even to
mention Governors.

ANNE: But, Tony, this isn't possible; he's engaged to our
Mary!

PREFECT [*in a rage*]: Engaged! Snooks to you and snooks
to the engagement! Double snooks! The engagement was
to pull the wool over my eyes! . . . [*Beside himself.*] Come
and see, let all the world come and see, all Christendom,
all of you see how the Prefect has been diddled. Diddled,
the poor old beggar, diddled! [*Shaking a fist at himself.*]
Ah you! You with the fat nose! A snivelling little squirt
like that and you took him for an important person! There
he goes now, jingling his bells all along the road! He'll
spread the story all over the world. And as if you weren't
enough of a laughing-stock already, one of these pen-
pushing ink-slingers is going to come along and put you
in a comedy. That's what's so shameful. He'll show no
regard for rank or position, and everybody will grin and
clap their hands. What are you laughing at? You're
laughing at yourselves! [*Stamps on the floor with rage.*] I'd
like to fix all those ink-slingers! Ooh you pen-pushers,
god-damned liberals, spawn of the Devil! I'd like to tie
you all up in a bundle, and grind you all down to powder
and let the Devil have you for stuffing. Stuffing for the
lining of his cap! [*Lashes out with his fist and bangs the floor
with his heel. After some moments of silence.*] I still can't get
over it. Look it's true that if the Lord wants to punish
a man he begins by taking away his reason. Come on,
what was there about that little flippertigibbet that looked
like an inspector? There wasn't anything! Not so much as
a likeness in the half of his little finger – and suddenly
they all started 'Inspector, Inspector'. Come on, who
was the first to give out that he was the inspector? Answer
me that!

313

STRAWBERRY [*spreading out his hands*]: How did it happen? Now that's something that for the life of me I can't explain. The Devil led us astray, a kind of fog came down over us.

SLAPPENCATCHIT: Who gave it out? That's who gave it out! Those beauties! [*Points to* DOBBIN *and* BOBBIN.]

BOBBIN: Honestly now it wasn't me! I never thought ...

DOBBIN: I did nothing. Absolutely nothing.

STRAWBERRY: Of course it was you!

WALLOP: It stands to reason. They came running in from the tavern like lunatics 'He's arrived, he's arrived, and he isn't paying any money ...' You found the big man.

PREFECT: Of course it was you. You're the gossip-mongers of the town, you god-damned liars!

STRAWBERRY: To hell with you and your stories and your inspectors!

PREFECT: Nosing around the town and upsetting everybody! That's all you do, you blasted blatherskites! Jabbering magpies, spreading the gossip.

SLAPPENCATCHIT: Dirty damned oafs!

WALLOP: Imbeciles!

STRAWBERRY: Pot-bellied little runts!

[*All crowd around them.*]

BOBBIN: Honest to God, it wasn't me. It was Peter.

DOBBIN: Ah no, Peter; why you were the first to er ...

BOBBIN: No, I tell you! The first was you.

The Last Scene

[*Enter a Gendarme.*]
GENDARME: An officer from St Petersburg, who has been
commanded by His Majesty to proceed here, requires
your presence forthwith. He is staying at the hotel.
[*The words uttered strike them all like a thunderbolt. A sound
expressive of astonishment breaks, with one accord, from the
mouths of the ladies; the whole group makes a sudden shift of
positions, and then stops petrified.*]

Dumb Tableau

[*In the centre, the* PREFECT, *standing like a pillar with arms
outspread and head thrown back. On his right, his wife and
daughter, their whole bodies strained towards him; behind
them the* POSTMASTER, *transformed into a note of interroga-
tion, facing the audience; behind him* WALLOP *in a state of
utterly innocent helplessness; behind him at the extreme edge
of the stage, three ladies leaning against one another and looking
straight towards the* PREFECT *and his family with most
satirical expressions on their faces. To the left of the* PREFECT:
STRAWBERRY *with his head slightly on one side as if he
were listening for something; behind him the* JUDGE, *arms
stuck out, squatting down almost to the ground, and moving his
lips as if he were about to whistle, or to say ' There you are,
Grannie, we're sold again!'*[19] *Behind him,* MR CANISTER,
*facing the audience with a wink and a sarcastic leer aimed at
the Prefect; behind him at the extreme edge of the stage*
DOBBIN *and* BOBBIN *with arms outflung towards one*

another, goggling at each other open-mouthed. The other Guests simply stand motionless.
This position is held by the petrified group for almost a minute and a half. The Curtain is lowered.]

Notes to *The Government Inspector*

1. p. 216. Town Prefect. See Introduction, Section 2.
2. p. 216. Gógol's name for the Doctor is Gibner, a normal Russian spelling for the German name Huebner. But spelt like that it is reminiscent of the Russian gíbnut' = to perish.
3. p. 217. A Tartar, probably a Moslem; he complains that the Prefect calls him a heathen. Many shopkeepers at this period were Tartars, or of Tartar extraction.
4. p. 226. The Marshal of the Gentry. See Introduction, Section 2.
5. p. 232. A Russian translation of a piece of English eighteenth-century Masonic literature. The Judge is living up to his character of a daring freethinker, for this book, and everything else to do with Freemasonry, was banned at the time in Russia.
6. p. 238. The lowest grade in Peter The Great's Table of Ranks. See Introduction, Section 2.
7. p. .243 A well known St Petersburg carriage-dealer.
8. p. 245. Townsman. See Introduction, Section 2.
9. p. 263. Nom-de-plume of J. J. Senkówski, a popular journalist.
10. p. 263. Novel by A. A. Bestúzhev, sentenced to five years in Siberia for his part in the Decembrist mutiny (see Introduction, Section 4); served very gallantly afterwards as a private soldier in the Caucasus.
11. p. 263. A journal, edited by N. Polevóy. Suppressed in 1834.
12. p. 264. Name of a publisher.
13. p. 264. Historical novel by M. N. Zagóskin.
14. p. 281. A government organization, responsible for finance of hospitals, orphanages etc. Also acted as a kind of savings bank, paying interest on deposits.
15. p. 288. Done to recruits, to prevent them from deserting.
16. p. 291. Opening lines of the 'Ode, taken from the 38th to the 41st chapters of the Book of Job' By M. V. Lomonósov (1711–1765). An exceedingly well-known schoolroom repetition piece.
17. p. 293. 'It is the Law condemneth
        The object of my love . . .'
    (Song from 'The Isle of Bornholm' a sentimental romance by N. M. Karamzín.)
18. p. 299. Sky-blue for the Order of St Andrew The First-Called (the

premier Russian order); red for St Alexander Névsky (the second highest order).

19. p. 315. Literally 'There's St George's day for you, Grannie.' A proverbial expression for disappointment; before the introduction of serfdom peasants had the right to move from one manor to another on St George's day (26 November).

THUNDER

A Drama in Five Acts by

Alexander Nikoláyevich Ostróvsky

CHARACTERS*

SAUL PROKÓFIEVICH DIKÓY, *a merchant, a person of consequence in the town*

BORÍS GRIGÓRIEVICH DIKÓY, *his nephew, a decently educated young man*

MARTHA IGNÁTIEVA KABANÓVA* ('The Wild Sow')*, *a wealthy merchant's widow*

TÍKHON IVÁNYCH KABANÓV, *her son*

CATHERINE, *Tikhon's wife*

BARBARA, *Tikhon's sister*

KULÍGIN, *a townsman,*[1] *a self-taught clockmaker, who is searching for Perpetual Motion*

JOHNNY KUDRYÁSH, *a young man, Mr Dikóy's clerk*

SHÁPKIN, *a townsman*

FEKLÚSHA, *a pilgrim*

GLÁSHA, *a maid at Mrs Kabanóva's house*

LADY with TWO FOOTMEN, *an old lady of 70. Half mad*

TOWNSPEOPLE *of both sexes*

The action takes place in the town of KALÍNOVO *on the Volga, one summer in the late 1850s. Between Acts Three and Four there is an interval of ten days.*

* All the characters, except BORÍS, are dressed Russian-fashion.

ACT ONE

*A public park on the high bank of the Volga; across the Volga, a
view of the countryside. On the stage, two benches and some bushes.*
KULÍGIN *is sitting on the bench and looking across the river.*
KUDRYÁSH *and* SHÁPKIN *are walking about.*

KULÍGIN [*sings*]: 'A lofty oak on a gentle hill
       All in a spreading vale . . .' [*He stops singing.*]²
Marvellous, really and truly you have to say it's marvel-
lous! Here am I, Kudryásh my dear fellow, and I've been
looking across the Volga every day for fifty years and I
still can't have enough of it.
KUDRYÁSH: Enough of what?
KULÍGIN: The view! The extraordinary view! The beauty
of it! It's a joy to the heart.
KUDRYÁSH: I don't know . . .
KULÍGIN: Glorious! And you don't know! You must have
got used to looking at it, or else you don't understand
about the beauty that is poured out in Nature.
KUDRYÁSH: Ah now, what's the good of talking to you!
You're our odd man out, you and your chemistry.
KULÍGIN: Mechanics. I'm a self-taught mechanic.
KUDRYÁSH: All the same thing.
    [*Silence.*]
KULÍGIN [*pointing to one side*]: Will you look now, Kudryásh,
who is it over there waving his arms like that?
KUDRYÁSH: That? That's Dikóy, giving his nephew a
dressing-down.
KULÍGIN: What a place to choose!
KUDRYÁSH: Any place will do for him. He's got Mr Borís
where he wants him and he can trample on him.

321

SHÁPKIN: You'd go a long way to find anyone with a flow
of language like our Mr Saul Dikóy. He'll tear a man to
bits for nothing at all.

KUDRYÁSH: The fellow can screech all right.

SHÁPKIN. Another one who's good at it is the wild sow of
the woods – old Mother Kabanóva.

KUDRYÁSH: Ah, but at least she makes out that she does it
in the name of godliness, but that man goes on as if he
had broken free from a chain.

SHÁPKIN: He's on the warpath now, and there's no holding
him.

KUDRYÁSH: There aren't enough lads like me around, or
we'd teach him to stop his capers.

SHÁPKIN: What would you do?

KUDRYÁSH: Put the fear of God into him.

SHÁPKIN: How would you do that?

KUDRYÁSH: Why, four or five of us would have a private
talk to him in some side alley, and then he'd go all soft as
silk. And he wouldn't utter a squeak to anybody about
the lesson we'd given him, only he'd watch out in the
future.

SHÁPKIN: No wonder he wanted to send you for a soldier.

KUDRYÁSH: He wanted to, but he didn't do it, so it comes
to the same thing as if he hadn't wanted. He won't send
me; he can tell with that nose of his that I wouldn't sell
my life cheaply. The thing is that you're frightened of
him, but I know how to talk to him.

SHÁPKIN: Oh yes?

KUDRYÁSH: What do you mean, oh yes? I'm reckoned to
be a rough customer, what does he keep me for? Must
be because he needs me. In other words, I'm not afraid
of him and maybe he is afraid of me.

SHÁPKIN: Are you making out that he doesn't swear at you?

KUDRYÁSH: Of course he does! He can't breathe without
that. But I don't let him get away with it. If he says one

word – I say ten; he spits and goes off. No, I'm not going
to grovel to him.

KULÍGIN: What, follow his example! It would be better,
now, to put up with him.

KUDRYÁSH: Look here, if you're so clever you go and
teach him manners and then you can show us. It's a pity
that those daughters of his are all young girls, there isn't
one of them grown up.

SHÁPKIN: Suppose there was one, then?

KUDRYÁSH: I'd play up to him. I'm pretty hot on the girls.
    [DIKÓY and BORÍS approach. KULÍGIN takes off his hat.]

SHÁPKIN [to KUDRYÁSH]: Let's keep clear, he might pick
on us, too.
    [They move further away.]

DIKÓY: Did you come here to loaf about, or what? Sponger!
Damn you and blast you!

BORÍS: It's a holiday; what is there to do at home?

DIKÓY: You'd find something to do, if you wanted to. I've
told you once, I've told you twice 'keep out of my way'.
Can't do a thing with you! Isn't there enough room for
you? Wherever I go, there you are! Tcha! Curse you!
Look at you standing there like a dummy. Are we talking
to you, or are we not?

BORÍS: I can hear, but what more is there for me to do?

DIKÓY [looking at BORÍS]: Go to blazes! I don't want to
talk to a Jesuit like you. [He turns to go.] Foisting yourself on us like that! [He spits and goes off.]

KULÍGIN: Whatever have you got to do with him, Sir? We
just can't understand. Do you want to live with him and
put up with his insults?

BORÍS: Indeed I don't Mr Kulígin, it's slavery.

KULÍGIN: But why Sir, may I ask, why this slavery? Will
you tell us Sir, if we may ask.

BORÍS: Why shouldn't I tell you? You knew my grandmother, Mrs Amfisa Dikóy?

KULÍGIN: Yes, of course I knew her!

KUDRYÁSH: Of course we did.

BORÍS: My grandmother, you see, she turned against my papa, because he married a high-born lady. That's why Papa and Mama went to live in Moscow. Mama told me she couldn't stand to live for three days with the family; she found it all so savage.

KULÍGIN: Savage is the word for it! What else could you call it? It takes a lot of getting used to, Sir.

BORÍS: My parents had us educated in Moscow; well educated, they grudged us nothing. They sent me to the Commercial Academy and my sister to a boarding-school, till at the time of the Cholera all of a sudden they both died and there we were, orphans, my sister and I. Then we heard that my grandmother was dead too, and that she had left a will saying that Uncle was to pay over our portions whatever was due to us when we came of age, but with a condition attached.

KULÍGIN: What was that, Sir?

BORÍS: That we should be respectful to him.

KULÍGIN: Sir, that means you won't ever see your inheritance.

BORÍS: Yes, and that's not all, Mr Kulígin. He starts by jeering at us, then he swears at us, using any language he fancies, and he always ends up by saying that he's going to give us nothing, or if he does it will be some small amount. And what's more, he'll say that we don't deserve even that and that he's giving it to us out of charity.

KUDRYÁSH: That's the way with our merchants. Besides, even if you had been respectful to him, who's going to stop him saying that you hadn't?

BORÍS: That's it. Why, even now he sometimes starts saying 'I've got children of my own; why should I give away money to other people's? By doing that, I'm injuring my own family.'

KULÍGIN: Then you're in a bad way, Sir.

BORÍS: If I was alone, it wouldn't matter. I'd chuck everything, and go. As it is, though, I'm unhappy about my
sister. He wanted to have her sent here too, but my
mother's relations wouldn't let her go; they wrote and
said she was ill. What sort of life would she have here? It
frightens me to think of it.

KUDRYÁSH: Stands to reason. They wouldn't know how
to behave, would they?

KULÍGIN: But how do you live with him, Sir? On what
footing?

BORÍS: No footing at all. 'You can live with me', he says,
'and you can do what you're told, and your wages will
be what I say.' In other words, at the year's end he'll
make it come to whatever he likes.

KUDRYÁSH: That's just his way. None of us ever dares to
utter a squeak about wages, or he'd damn the daylights
out of us. 'How do you know what's in my mind?' says
he. 'Don't tell me you can read my thoughts! Perhaps,
now, I'm going to be in the sort of mood when I'll give
you five thousand.' You try talking to him! Only he hasn't
ever once been in that sort of mood, not in all his life.

KULÍGIN: What can you do, Sir? You must try somehow
to please him.

BORÍS: The thing is, Mr Kulígin, that it simply can't be
done. Even his own family can't even please him, so how
can I?

KUDRYÁSH: Who's going to please him, when his whole
life is founded on cursing and swearing? Most of all in
money matters; no account ever gets settled without a
row. Some people would gladly give up what was due to
them, if he'd only shut up. And there'll be trouble if
anyone crosses him in the morning! He'll go on picking
quarrels with everybody all day.

BORÍS: Every morning my aunt implores us all, with tears

'Don't make him cross, my dears! Darlings, don't make him cross!'

KUDRYÁSH: As if you could help it! He gets to the market, and that's the end. He goes round swearing at all the peasants. Even if a man asks under cost price he still won't get off without a row. That starts him up for the whole day.

SHÁPKIN: In one word – a fighter!

KUDRYÁSH: And what a fighter, too.

BORÍS: The trouble comes when somebody he daren't swear at is rude to him; then let the family look out!

KUDRYÁSH: Oh, my word! What a laugh we had! That time the hussar cursed him up and down on the Volga ferry-boat! That worked miracles!

BORÍS: And what about the family? They all hid in lofts and store-rooms for a fortnight after that.

KULÍGIN: What's that? Isn't it the people coming out from Vespers?

[*Several people pass across the back of the stage.*]

KUDRYÁSH: Come on, Shápkin, let's have some fun! Why stand about here?

[*They bow and go out.*]

BORÍS: Ah, Mr Kulígin, it's terribly hard for me here, not being used to it. They all look at me so savagely, as if I wasn't wanted here, as if I was in their way. I do understand that it's all Russian, all our own kith and kin, but still I can't get used to it anyhow.

KULÍGIN: And you won't ever get used to it, Sir.

BORÍS: Why not?

KULÍGIN: The ways of our town are cruel, Sir, cruel! You'll see nothing but roughness, Sir, and stark poverty, among the townsmen. And we won't ever break out of it, Sir. Because honest labour won't ever earn us more than the day's daily bread. And if anyone has got some money he tries to get some poor man under his thumb, Sir, work-

ing for him for nothing so that he gets even more. Do you
know what your Uncle Saul said to the Prefect? Some poor
peasants came and complained to the Prefect, because
he wouldn't give any of them the right amount. So the
Prefect went and talked to him about it 'Look here,
Dikóy,' says he, 'you settle with the peasants properly!
They are coming to me with complaints every day.'
Your uncle clapped the Prefect on the shoulder 'Your
honour!' says he. 'Is it worthwhile for you and me to
talk about such trifles! I have a lot of people through
my hands in a year and if I knock off a farthing from
each of them that will come to thousands a year for me,
and it's to my advantage to do just that.' There you are,
Sir! And, Sir, how do they go on among themselves? Un-
dermining one another's businesses, and not so much for
profit as out of jealousy. They're all at enmity one with
another; into those grand mansions of theirs they entice
drunken clerks. The sort of clerk, Sir, that has no human
look about him, all semblance of humanity is lost and
gone. And for a pittance, Sir, these men will take pieces of
paper stamped with the regulation stamp, and draw up
wicked plaints against their neighbours. And that, Sir,
leads to suits in the courts, and misery that hath no end.
They go on and on with their suits here, and then away
with them to the Provincial Court, where the lawyers
have been expecting them and clap their hands with
delight. The tale is quickly told, but the deed is not
quickly done. They get led on and on, the case is dragged
out and dragged out, and still they are glad to have it so;
it's just what they want. 'I'm spending a bit of money,
but it's costing him a pretty penny too!' I was going to
put it all into poetry.

BORÍS: Can you do poetry?

KULÍGIN: In the old-fashioned style, Sir. I've read quite a
lot of Lomonósov and Derzhávin[3]. . . . Lomonósov was

a sage, who inquired of Nature. And what's more, do you know that he was one of us, a common man?

BORÍS: You ought to write it down. It would be interesting.

KULÍGIN: How could I, Sir! They'd eat me, they'd swallow me down alive. I'm catching it already, Sir, for talking too much; but I can't help it, I like to go round and talk to people! There now, and I wanted to tell you some more, Sir, about family life, but it'll have to be some other time. And that's something to hear about, too.

[*Enter* FEKLÚSHA *and another woman.*]

FEKLÚSHA: The fair beauty of it, my dearie, the fair beauty! The wondrous loveliness! What can I say, 'tis in the Promised Land that ye live! And the merchant community are a godly people, adorned with manifold virtues! With bounty and manifold charities! I have been filled, my dear, filled to the neck! They have not forsaken us, and may bounties be multiplied ever more upon them, and especially upon the house of Kabanóv. [*They go out.*]

BORÍS: Kabanóv?

KULÍGIN: A holy fraud, Sir. Gives to all the beggars, and makes life a misery for everyone at home.

[*Silence.*]

If only I could discover Perpetuity of Motion!

BORÍS: What would you do?

KULÍGIN: Why Sir, you know the English would give a million for it; I'd use all the money for the support of the townsmen's community.[4] Work must be found for them; the hands are there, and no work for them.

BORÍS: Do you hope to discover Perpetual Motion?

KULÍGIN: I'm bound to, Sir! All I want now is to get hold of a bit of money for the models. Good day to you, Sir! [*He leaves.*]

BORÍS [*alone*]: It's a shame to disillusion him! What a nice man! He's got his dreams, and he's happy. But it looks as if I'm going to have my young days blighted in this hole.

Here am I now, going about all beaten down and yet I'm filling my head with foolishness! What business have I to do it? Me going in for sentimentality! Cowed and crushed, and fool enough to go and fall in love. And who with? A woman that I shan't ever so much as speak to. [*Silence.*] And yet, no matter what I do, I can't get her out of my head. Here she is! Walking with her husband, and that's her mother-in-law with them as well! I'm a fool, aren't I? Better watch from round the corner, and then go home.

[*Exit* BORÍS. *Enter* MRS KABANÓVA, TÍKHON, CATHERINE *and* BARBARA *from the opposite side.*]

MRS KABANÓVA: If you want to be obedient to Mother, you'll do what I've been telling you when you get there.

TÍKHON: Mama! How could I disobey you?

MRS KABANÓVA: People haven't got much respect for their elders today.

BARBARA [*To herself*]: Not be respectful to you, I like that!

TÍKHON: Mama! I don't think I've gone one step outside of your wishes.

MRS KABANÓVA: I'd believe you, my dear, if I hadn't seen with my own eyes and heard with my own ears the kind of respect that children have for their parents today! They might remember the pain that mothers undergo for their children.

TÍKHON: Mama! I . . .

MRS KABANÓVA: And if a mother ever should say anything to offend your pride, I think you young people might put up with it. What do you think, then?

TÍKHON: But, Mama! when haven't I put up with you?

MRS KABANÓVA: Mother's old, Mother's stupid; well then, you clever young people shouldn't be too hard on us fools.

TÍKHON [*aside, with a sigh*]: Oh, Lord! [*To his mother*] But, Mama! would we dare to think such a thing?

MRS KABANÓVA: You know, it's love that makes parents strict with you, love that makes them scold you. All that they think of is to teach you what's right. And that's not popular, nowadays. So off go the children, spreading it about that Mother is a grumbler, that Mother won't leave them alone, that she's bothering the life out of them. And pray God she doesn't say something that displeases her daughter-in-law, for then round goes the word that her mother-in-law has been making her life a misery.

TÍKHON: Mama! Does anyone talk about you?

MRS KABANÓVA: I haven't heard it my dear, I haven't heard it; I wouldn't tell you a lie. But if I had heard it, my dear, I wouldn't be speaking to you like this. [*Sighs*] Ah, the grievous sin! It doesn't take long to fall into sin. Something is said that comes too close to your heart, and you sin; you become angry. Ah well, my dear, you say what you like about me. You can't prevent someone speaking; if they're afraid to say something to your face they say it behind your back . . .

TÍKHON: May my tongue dry up . . .

MRS KABANÓVA: Stop, stop, don't bring God into it! That's a sin. I've known for a long while now that your wife is dearer to you than your Mother. I haven't seen the old love from you, since you got married.

TÍKHON: Mama! What makes you think that?

MRS KABANÓVA: Why, my dear, everything. A Mother may not see a thing with her eyes, but she has second sight in her heart, she can feel through the heart. But whether it's your wife, or what, that's taking you away from me, that I don't know.

TÍKHON: No, Mama, for goodness' sake, what are you saying!

CATHERINE: Mama, you're just the same to me as my own mother; yes, and Tíkhon loves you too.

MRS KABANÓVA: I think you might have kept quiet, since

your opinion wasn't asked. Don't interfere, young woman, and I shan't offend you; you needn't worry! You know he's my son as well – and don't you forget it! What are you doing, with all this parade of affection? Do you want us to see that you love your husband, or what? We know that, we know that; it's something you show off in front of everybody.

BARBARA [*to herself*]: What a place to choose for a lecture.

CATHERINE: It isn't fair to talk like that about me, Mama. Whether people are there or whether they aren't I'm always the same; I don't show off.

MRS KABANÓVA: I hadn't meant to speak about you at all; the subject came up quite by chance.

CATHERINE: Even if it did, why should you say hurtful things about me?

MRS KABANÓVA: Hoity-toity! Now she's offended.

CATHERINE: Does anybody like being treated unfairly?

MRS KABANÓVA: I know, I know that what I say doesn't suit your tastes, but what can I do? I'm not a stranger to you, my heart is sore for you. I've seen for a long time that what you want is freedom. All right then, you can wait for it. You'll live in freedom when I'm gone. Then you may do what you like, and there won't be any older people over you. And then perhaps you'll remember me.

TÍKHON: Mama, we pray for you night and day; and, Mama, we ask God to grant you health, prosperity and success in your affairs.

MRS KABANÓVA: Now that will do, please stop. Maybe you did love me when you were a bachelor. What do you want with me? You've got a young wife.

TÍKHON: But, please Mother, the one doesn't hinder the other. The wife is one thing, and the respect I have for the parent is another.

MRS KABANÓVA: Would you give up your wife for your Mother? Nothing will ever make me believe that.

TÍKHON: But, Mother, why should I have to give anyone up? I love you both.

MRS KABANÓVA: That's right, go on, lay it on thick! I can see now that I'm a hindrance to you.

TÍKHON: You may think what you like, you always have your own way; only I don't know why such a wretched man as me was ever born into the world, for I can't do anything to please you.

MRS KABANÓVA: Doing the poor little boy are you? Baby's going to cry! Come on, what sort of husband are you? Take a look at yourself. Is your wife going to be afraid of you after this?

TÍKHON: Why should she be afraid of me? All I want is for her to love me.

MRS KABANÓVA: Why should she be afraid of him? Why should she be afraid of him? Have you gone crazy, or what? If she isn't afraid of you she certainly won't be afraid of me. What sort of order will there be in the house? You know, you're supposed to be living with her in holy wedlock. Or doesn't holy wedlock mean anything to you? Even if you do have these foolish ideas in your head you might at least not blurt them out in front of her and in front of your sister – a young girl. She'll be getting married too and if she listens to all your blether her husband is going to have something to say presently about the way she's been trained. You see now what sort of sense you have, and yet you still want to live your own life.

TÍKHON: But, Mama I don't want to live my own life. How could I live my own life?

MRS KABANÓVA: So you think you have to be all sweetness to your wife? Why don't you try shouting at her and threatening her sometime?

TÍKHON: But, Mama! I . . . !

MRS KABANÓVA [bitterly]: Go on, let her take a lover! Eh!

Perhaps that's nothing to you either. Eh? Come on and tell me!

TÍKHON: But, Mama, as God's my witness . . .

MRS KABANÓVA [*quite coldly*]: Fool! [*She sighs*] What's the good of talking to a fool! Nothing comes of it but sin!
[*Silence.*]
I'm going home.

TÍKHON: We'll come in a minute too. We're just going to have a couple of turns up and down the promenade.

MRS KABANÓVA: Do as you like then, only you mind I'm not kept waiting for you! You know I don't like that.

TÍKHON: No, Mama. Good Lord no!

MRS KABANÓVA: Well, mind what I say. [*She leaves.*]

TÍKHON: There now, you see the way I keep on catching it from Mama over you. That's the kind of life I have.

CATHERINE: Well, is it my fault?

TÍKHON: I just don't know whose fault it is.

BARBARA: You wouldn't!

TÍKHON: First she kept on at me 'Marry! Marry! If only I could see you married.' And now she's got her knife into me, and never lets up – all on your account.

BARBARA: As if it was her fault! Mother goes for her and so do you. And you still say that you love your wife. I'm sick of the sight of you. [*She turns away.*]

TÍKHON: It's all very well for your to talk, but what am I to do?

BARBARA: That's your business – if you can't think of anything better to say, keep quiet. What are you doing, shifting from one foot to the other? I can see by your eyes what you're thinking about.

TÍKHON: Well, what?

BARBARA: I know what it is. You want to go over to Mr Saul Dikóy and have a drink with him. That's it, isn't it?

TÍKHON: Right you are, girl.

CATHERINE: Come back quickly Tíkhon dear, or Mama will start scolding again.

BARBARA: Yes, you make it a real quick one, or else you know what.

TíKHON: Don't I just!

BARBARA: We're not too keen either on getting scolded for you.

TíKHON: I won't be a moment, wait here. [*He exits.*]

CATHERINE: Then you are sorry for me, Barbara?

BARBARA [*turning her face away*]: Of course I am.

CATHERINE: Then you must like me. [*She gives* BARBARA *a big kiss.*]

BARBARA: Why shouldn't I like you?

CATHERINE: Bless you! You're such a dear, I'm awfully fond of you too.

[*Silence.*]

Do you know what's come into my head?

BARBARA: What?

CATHERINE: Why don't people fly?

BARBARA: I don't understand what you're talking about.

CATHERINE: I say, why don't people fly like birds? You know, sometimes I think I am a bird. When you're up on a hill there's something that makes you want to fly. Look now, suppose I were to run forward, spread out my arms and fly away? Why not try it now? [*Prepares to run.*]

BARBARA: Whatever are you thinking of?

CATHERINE [*sighing*]: I used to be such a lively thing. I've wilted, living with you.

BARBARA: Do you think I don't see it?

CATHERINE: Used I to be like this? I lived without a care in the world, as free as a bird. My Mama adored me, dressed me up like a doll, didn't force me to work; if I wanted to do a thing I used to do it. Do you know how I lived, before I was married? Well now, I'll tell you. I used to get up early; if it was summertime I went over to the spring, I washed, and I brought back a nice drop of water and watered all the flowers in the house, all the flowers. We had lots and lots of flowers. Then, Mama and I went to Church and so did all the pilgrims – our house was full of pilgrims and praying-women. When we got back from Church, we sat down to some kind of work, mostly gold thread on velvet, and the pilgrims would start to tell us stories about where they'd been and what they'd seen, or some of the lives of the saints, or else they'd sing some of the spiritual songs.[5] That was how time passed until dinner. Then the old women went to lie down and go to sleep, and I walked round the garden. After that came Vespers, and in the evening we had stories and singing again. It was so lovely!

BARBARA: It's the same with us, you know.

CATHERINE: Yes, but here it's all like something you've got to do, whether you want to or not. And I did so terribly love going to Church! It used to be like entering Paradise; I didn't see anybody. I didn't remember the time and I didn't hear when the service ended. Mama said that everybody used to look at me to see what was happening! And do you know? On a sunny day, a sort of pillar of light used to come down from the dome, with clouds of smoke floating in the light, and I used to see angels flying and singing in the pillar of light. And another thing, my girl. I used sometimes to get up in the night – we had the same as you, lamps burning before the icons all round the house – and I used to pray all night in front of one of them. Or else I went out into the garden, when the sweet sun was just rising, and dropped on to my knees, praying and weeping, and I didn't know what I was praying about, and weeping about, and that's how they would find me. And I don't know what I used to pray for then, or what I asked for – I wanted for nothing, I had plenty of everything. Such dreams I used to have, Barbara dear, such dreams! Either it was golden churches, or else some kind of wonderful gardens; and all the time there were invisible voices singing, and there was a smell of cypress-wood, and there were hills and trees, only they weren't like ordinary ones, but like the ones painted on the icons. Or else I seemed to be flying and flying through the air. I have dreams sometimes now too, only not often, and not like that.

BARBARA: Like what then?

CATHERINE [*after a silence*]: I'm going to die soon.

BARBARA: Don't! What are you saying?

CATHERINE: Yes, I know I'm going to die. Oh my dear, something bad is happening to me, something uncanny. I've never had it like this before. There's something out of the ordinary inside me. As if I was beginning life over again or . . . oh, I don't know.

BARBARA: Whatever's the matter with you?

CATHERINE [*taking her hand*]: The matter is, Barbara dear, that something wicked is going to happen. I'm in such a fright, such a fright. It's as if I was standing on a precipice and someone was trying to push me over, and I'd got nothing to hold on to. [*She clutches her head with her hand.*]

BARBARA: What's the matter with you? Are you all right?

CATHERINE: Yes, I'm all right . . . it would be better if I were ill. It's horrible to be like this. There's a kind of dream that comes into my head, and there's nothing I can do to get away from it. I begin to think, and I just can't collect my thoughts; I begin to pray, and the prayer just doesn't come. I gabble the words with my tongue but my mind isn't on them at all; it's as if the Evil One were whispering in my ear, and all about horrible things. Then I begin to think it must be me, and I'm the one that ought to be ashamed. What's the matter with me? There's some disaster coming. I can't sleep at night,

Barbara. I keep imagining that I can hear a sort of whispering, somebody talking to me in such a loving way, fussing over me like a cooing pigeon. And Barbara dear, I don't have the dreams I used to have about the trees and hills of Paradise; it's as if somebody was holding me in a hot, hot embrace, and he took me away somewhere and I went with him, I went . . .

BARBARA: Well?

CATHERINE: What am I doing, talking like this to you? You're not married.

BARBARA [*looking round*]: Go on! I'm worse than you.

CATHERINE: Well, what else can I say? I'm ashamed.

BARBARA: Go on! You needn't be.

CATHERINE: I'm beginning to feel so stifled at home, so stifled I could run away. This is the sort of thought that comes to me – if I had my freedom I'd like to be out now in a boat on the Volga, with singing, or else in a smart three-horse carriage, with my arm round . . .

BARBARA: Not round your husband though.

CATHERINE: How do you know that?

BARBARA: As if I didn't know!

CATHERINE: Oh Barbara dear, I've got a sin on my mind! Poor me, the tears I've shed, the state I've been in! I can't get away from it. There's nowhere I can go. It's a horrible thing, you see, it's a dreadful sin, isn't it, dearest Barbara, that I'm in love with another man?

BARBARA: What! Me to judge you! I've got sins of my own.

CATHERINE: What am I to do? I haven't the strength. Where can I go? I'll do something to myself, out of misery.

BARBARA: What are you saying? What's the matter with you? Wait now, Brother is going away tomorrow, we'll think of something; maybe you'll be able to meet.

CATHERINE: No, no! You mustn't! What are you saying? God forbid!

BARBARA: What are you so frightened about?

CATHERINE: If I ever once meet him, I shall run away from home and I shan't come back, not for anything in the world.

BARBARA: Wait now till we see.

CATHERINE: No, no! Don't you speak to me; I don't want to hear it even.

BARBARA: Fancy wanting to wither and shrivel up! Go on, pine away and die – do you think they'll be sorry for you? Come then, let's see what happens. Why have you got to torment yourself?

[*Enter* THE LADY, *with a stick, followed by* TWO FOOT-MEN *in three-cornered hats.*]

THE LADY: Well, my pretty ones? What are you doing here? Looking out for fine young men, looking for your partners? Gay, are you? Gay? Enjoying your beauty? That is where beauty leads. [*She points to the Volga.*] Down there, down there, right down in the deep water! [BARBARA *smiles.*] What are you laughing at? You mustn't enjoy yourselves. [*She thumps her stick.*] You shall all burn in unquenchable fire. You shall all boil in ever-lasting pitch. [*Going away*] Away down there, that's where beauty leads! [*She leaves.*]

CATHERINE: Oh but she gave me a fright! I'm shaking all over, as if she had been prophesying something for me.

BARBARA: On your head be it, you old witch!

CATHERINE: What was it she said? Tell me, what did she say?

BARBARA: Rubbish, all of it. A lot of need there is to listen to what she says. She prophesies like that to every-body. She's been a sinner all her life, beginning when she was young. You ask and see what they'll tell you about her! There you are, she's afraid to die. So she frightens other people with what she's afraid of herself. Even the little boys in town all hide from her; she shakes her stick

at them and she shouts [*imitating her*] 'You shall all burn
in the fire'.

CATHERINE [*wincing*]: Oh, oh, stop it! I feel so awful.

BARBARA: What's there to be afraid of? Silly old fool . . .

CATHERINE: I'm frightened, frightened to death! I keep
on thinking I can see her.

[*Silence.*]

BARBARA [*looking round*]: Why doesn't Brother come?
That looks like a thunderstorm getting up over there.

CATHERINE [*in horror*]: Thunder? Let's run home! Quick.

BARBARA: Have you gone off your head, or what? How
could you turn up at home without Brother?

CATHERINE: No! Go home! Never mind about him!

BARBARA: Why, what are you so scared of? The storm's
still quite a long way off.

CATHERINE: If it is a long way off, then I suppose we can
wait a bit. But it really would be better to go. Let's go;
it's better to!

BARBARA: But you know, if anything's going to happen,
you can't hide from it, even at home.

CATHERINE: Yes, but all the same it would be better.
More peaceful. At home I could go to the icons, and say
my prayers to God.

BARBARA: I never knew you were so frightened of thunder.
I'm not.

CATHERINE: What, girl! Not frightened? Everybody
ought to be frightened. The dreadful thing is not that it
can kill you, but that death can come upon you suddenly,
just as you are, with all your sins, with all your wicked
thoughts. I've no dread of dying, but when I think that
there I'd suddenly be, in the presence of God, just as I
am here with you, after that talk we had – that's what's
dreadful! What have I got on my mind? What a sin!
I'm terrified to mention it.

[*Thunder.*]

Oh!

[TÍKHON *comes in.*]

BARBARA: Here comes Brother. [*To* TÍKHON] Hurry up!
Run!

[*Thunder.*]

CATHERINE: Oh! Hurry, hurry!

ACT TWO

A room in the KABANÓVS' *home.* GLÁSHA *is tying up linen clothes in knotted bundles. Enter* FEKLÚSHA.

FEKLÚSHA: Dearie, you're always working! What are you doing, my dearie?

GLÁSHA: Packing up the Master for the road.

FEKLÚSHA: Is the dear man travelling somewhere?

GLÁSHA: He is.

FEKLÚSHA: Will he be away long, my dearie?

GLÁSHA: No, not for long.

FEKLÚSHA: Well may the road before him be as smooth as a tablecloth! Tell me now, will the young mistress be wailing, or not?

GLÁSHA: I don't know what I'd say to you about that.

FEKLÚSHA: Do you ever hear her wailing?

GLÁSHA: I've never heard it at all.

FEKLÚSHA: I do love to hear it, dearie, when someone puts up a good wail. [*Silence.*] You had all better keep an eye on the beggar woman, girl, or she'll be pinching something.

GLÁSHA: There's no understanding you people; you're always telling tales on one another; can't you live peacefully together? Do you travellers have such a bad time, here with us, that you must be forever squabbling and quarrelling? Have you no fear of sin?

FEKLÚSHA: There's no escaping sin, my dear; we live in the world. I'll tell you what now, dearie, every one of you common people has one devil to lead you astray, but for us, for the travelling people, there are appointed to some six devils, to some twelve. There – all of them to fight against. It's hard, dearie.

341

GLÁSHA: Why then so many for you?

FEKLÚSHA: The Adversary, my dear! He does it out of envy, because we live righteous lives. I'm not quarrelsome, dearie; I don't have that sin. I've got just the one sin, and I know what it is – I'm fond of good food. Well and what of it? The Lord will send to me in accordance with my infirmities.

GLÁSHA: Have you travelled far, Feklúsha dear?

FEKLÚSHA: Not far, dearie, with my infirmities I have not gone far. But I have heard a lot. They say, dearie, that there are countries where there are no true Christian Tsars, but Sultans rule the land. In one land, Sultan Mahound the Turk sits on the throne; and in another, it's Sultan Mahound the Persian; and they sit in judgement, dearie, over all the people, and any judgements that they give are always wrong. And dearie, they can't decide even one case rightly; it's a constraint that has been laid upon them. We have the Law of Righteousness, dearie, and they have the law of Unrighteousness; whatever way anything comes out by our law, dearie, it always comes out the opposite way by theirs. And all the judges they have in their countries, they're all unrighteous too, so when people present a plea to them, dearie, they put in it 'Judge me, thou unrighteous Judge!' And then there's another land where all the people have dogs' heads.

GLÁSHA: But why do they have dogs' heads?

FEKLÚSHA: For their faithlessness. I'm off now, dearie, I'm going round the merchants, to see if there would be anything for the poor. Good-bye for now!

GLÁSHA: Good-bye!

[FEKLÚSHA *goes out*.]

Fancy there being all those other lands! Is there any end to them, any end to the marvels in the world? And we stick here and we know nothing. Well for us that there are good people, so that in spite of it all you can sometimes hear about what happens in the wide world; but for them we'd be fools to our dying day.

[*Enter* CATHERINE *and* BARBARA.]

BARBARA [*to* GLÁSHA]: Take those bundles to the waggon, the horses have come. [*To* CATHERINE] You were married too young, you didn't get a chance to have your fling when you were a girl, so your heart hasn't settled down yet.

[GLÁSHA *leaves.*]

CATHERINE: It never will.

BARBARA: Why not?

CATHERINE: It's the way I was made, fiery hot! What do you think I did when I was six years old, only six? They'd somehow offended me at home, and it was coming on towards evening, dark already. I ran off to the Volga and got into a boat and shoved off from the bank. They found me next morning, seven miles downstream!

BARBARA: Well, and did the boys sometimes look at you?

CATHERINE: Of course they did.

BARBARA: What about you though? Weren't you in love with anybody?

CATHERINE: No, I only laughed.

BARBARA: You know, Kate, you're not in love with Tíkhon.

CATHERINE: Indeed I am! I'm very sorry for him.

BARBARA: Then you're not in love with him. Not if you're sorry for him. And to tell the honest truth, why should you be? It's no good your trying to hide it from me! I saw long ago that you were in love with a certain person.

CATHERINE [*In terror*]: How did you see it?

BARBARA: It's ridiculous to talk like that! Am I a baby, or what? Here's the first sign; when you see him, your expression changes.

[CATHERINE *looks down at the ground.*]

And that's not all . . .

CATHERINE [*eyes on the ground*]: When I see who?

BARBARA: Look here, you know who it is yourself. Why should I say who?

CATHERINE: Yes, do say it! Say his name!

BARBARA: Borís Dikóy.

CATHERINE: Oh yes, that's him, Barbara dear, that's him! Only darling Barbara, for God's sake . . .

BARBARA: Oh go on! Take care that you don't say something to give yourself away.

CATHERINE: I can't be a deceiver; I can't hide things.

BARBARA: Well, but you know you can't get along without deception; remember where you are living. That's what holds the whole of our home together. I usen't to be a deceiver, but I learned how when I had to. I was out yesterday, and I saw him and spoke to him.

CATHERINE [after a prolonged silence]: Well, what then?

BARBARA: He sent his regards to you. He says it's a pity there's nowhere to meet.

CATHERINE [looking even more fixedly at the ground]: How could we meet? And what for . . .

BARBARA: He has a dull sort of life.

CATHERINE: Don't speak to me about him! Please be kind enough not to mention him! I don't want to know him! I will love my husband. Darling Tíkhon, I won't give you up for anybody! I didn't want even to think about him, and you come and upset me.

BARBARA: All right, don't think about him. Who says you must?

CATHERINE: Haven't you any mercy for me! You say 'Don't think' and you remind me about him yourself. It isn't as if I wanted to think about him, but what can I do if he won't go out of my head? Whatever I think about, there he is, standing before my eyes. I want to break myself of it, but I just can't. Do you know, a devil came again to tempt me last night. I tell you, I nearly walked out of the house.

BARBARA: Good heavens, you're a hard one to understand! What I say is, do what you want to do, but mind you keep it dark.

CATHERINE: I won't have that! Besides, what's the good? I'd better stick it as long as I can.

BARBARA: But suppose you can't stick it out, what'll you do then?

CATHERINE: What will I do?

BARBARA: Yes, what'll you do?

CATHERINE: When I want to do something, I'll go straight out and do it.

BARBARA: Try that here, and they'll eat you.

CATHERINE: What's that to me? I'll go away. I'll vanish.

BARBARA: Where to? You're a married woman.

CATHERINE: Ah, Barbara dear, you don't know what I can be like! Please God, of course, it won't come to that, but if I get to really loathe this place, no power on earth will stop me. I'll jump out of the window, I'll chuck myself into the Volga. If I don't want to live here I won't, I don't care what you do to me! [*Silence.*]

BARBARA: Tell you what, Kate. When Tíkhon goes, let's sleep in the garden, in the summerhouse.

CATHERINE: But why, Barbara?

BARBARA: Why not? What difference does it make?

CATHERINE: I'm afraid to spend the night in a strange place.

BARBARA: What's there to be afraid of? Glásha will be with us.

CATHERINE: I still somehow don't like it. All right, perhaps I will.

BARBARA: I wouldn't have asked you, only Mama won't let me go by myself, and I want to do it.

CATHERINE [*looking at her*]: Why do you want to?

BARBARA [*laughing*]: We're going to tell our fortunes in there, you and I.

345

CATHERINE: You're joking, aren't you?

BARBARA: Of course I am. You didn't think I meant it?

CATHERINE: Wherever is Tíkhon?

BARBARA: What do you want him for?

CATHERINE: I just want him. You see he's going soon.

BARBARA: He and Mama are sitting together behind closed doors. She's grinding him down, digging into him like rust into iron.

CATHERINE: What's he done then?

BARBARA: Nothing, she's just telling him how to be a good boy. Two weeks on the road, where she can't see what he's doing! Judge for yourself! She'll be eating her heart out, that he should be free and gallivanting around. There she is now, giving him all his orders, with more and more awful warnings, and presently she'll take him over to the Icon, and make him swear always to do exactly what he's been told.

CATHERINE: He's tied, in a way, even when he's free.

BARBARA: Tied? Him? The minute he gets away he'll start drinking. He's listening to her now, and thinking all the time what can he do to get quickly away from her.

[*Enter* MRS KABANÓVA *and* TÍKHON.]

MRS KABANÓVA: Now you will remember all I've told you? Mind you do! Make sure somehow you don't forget.

TÍKHON: I'll remember, Mama.

MRS KABANÓVA: Well, everything's ready now. The horses have come, you've only got to say good-bye, and then God speed you.

TÍKHON: Yes, dear Mama, it's time.

MRS KABANÓVA: Well!

TÍKHON: Yes, Mother?

MRS KABANÓVA: What are you standing there for; don't you know how to behave? Give your orders to your wife. Tell her what to do while you're away.

[CATHERINE *looks down at the ground.*]

346

TÍKHON: But I think she knows that herself.

MRS KABANÓVA: Are you going to keep on with your back answers? I want to hear you giving her your orders! Then when you come back you'll ask if she's done it all properly.

TÍKHON [*standing in front of* CATHERINE]: Do what Mama tells you, Kate!

MRS KABANÓVA: Tell her not to be rude to her mother-in-law.

TÍKHON: Don't be rude!

MRS KABANÓVA: And to respect her mother-in-law as she would her own Mother!

TÍKHON: Kate, you're to respect Mama, as you would your own Mother!

MRS KABANÓVA: And not to sit with her hands in her lap, like a lady!

TÍKHON: Do some work while I'm away!

MRS KABANÓVA: And not to be mooning and gaping at the windows!

TÍKHON: But Mama, when did she ever . . .

MRS KABANÓVA: Go on, go on!

TÍKHON: Don't look out of the windows!

MRS KABANÓVA: And not to go looking at the young lads while you're away!

TÍKHON: Oh for goodness' sake, Mama, why that!

MRS KABANÓVA: It's no good making a fuss about it! Got to do what Mother says! [*With a smile*] It's all the better if it's an order.

TÍKHON [*embarrassed*]: Don't go looking at young men.

[CATHERINE *raises her eyes and gives him a hard stare.*]

MRS KABANÓVA: Well, now you can talk to one another, if there's anything you want to say. Come on, Barbara.

[MRS KABANÓVA *and* BARBARA *leave.* CATHERINE *stands numbly in front of* TÍKHON.]

TÍKHON: Kate!

[*Kate is silent.*]

Kate, you aren't angry with me?

CATHERINE [*after a short silence, shaking her head*]: No!

TÍKHON: What are you like that for? Come, forgive me.

CATHERINE [*still in the same state, gently shaking her head*]:
Bless you! [*Covering her face with her hand*] She insulted me!

TÍKHON: If you take everything to heart you'll soon go into
a decline. Why listen to her? Don't you see, she has to
say something? Well, let her say it, and let it go in at
one ear and out at the other. Well, good-bye, Kate!

CATHERINE [*flinging herself on her husband's neck*]: Tíkhon,
don't go away! For God's sake, don't go away! Please
darling!

TÍKHON: It's no good Kate. If Mummy sends me off, how
can I help going!

CATHERINE: Take me with you then, take me!

TÍKHON [*extricating himself from her embrace*]: Can't do it!

CATHERINE: Why can't you, Tíkhon mine?

TÍKHON: A lot of fun it would be if I went with you!
You've been riding me to death, all of you here have!
All I want is to get away, and now you start worrying to
be taken along.

CATHERINE: Don't say you don't love me any more?

TÍKHON: No, I haven't stopped loving you, but a man
would run away from the sweetest wife in the world to
escape from this slavery. Just you think; whatever else I
may be, I am still a man, and a man living the way you
see me live would run away even from his wife. I know
now that for a fortnight there's going to be no thunder
hanging over me, and no shackles on my legs, so what do
I want with a wife?

CATHERINE: How can I love you, when you say such
things to me?

TÍKHON: Words, just words! What else do you want me to
say? Can't make you out, what are you frightened of?

348

You're not alone, you know, you're staying with Mama.

CATHERINE: Don't talk about her, don't torment my heart! [*She weeps.*] Oh my grief, my grief! What can I do with myself, poor thing that I am? Who is there that I can hold on to? Oh dear me, I'm done for.

TÍKHON: There now, there, don't go on like that.

CATHERINE [*going up to her husband and squeezing herself against him*]: Tíkhon darling, if you'd stay, or if you'd take me with you, wouldn't I love you, wouldn't I pet you, my sweetie! [*She strokes him.*]

TÍKHON: There's no understanding you, Kate; one minute I can't get a word out of you, let alone love, and the next minute it's you who are all over me.

CATHERINE: Tíkhon, what are you leaving me for? There'll be trouble while you're away. There surely will.

TÍKHON: But don't you see it's no go, so we can't do anything about it.

CATHERINE: Well then look! Will you get me to swear an awful oath . . .

TÍKHON: What sort of an oath?

CATHERINE: Like this – That while you're away on no account whatever will I dare to speak to any stranger, nor to meet them, nor ever dare to think of anyone but you.

TÍKHON: What's all this about?

CATHERINE: Do it for my peace of mind, do this kindness for my sake!

TÍKHON: How can you promise that? All sorts of things can come into one's head.

CATHERINE [*falling on her knees*]: That I won't even see my father or my mother! That I may die impenitent if . . .

TÍKHON [*raising her*]: What are you saying? What are you saying? What a wicked thing! I don't want even to hear it!

MRS KABANÓVA [*off*]: Time Tíkhon!

[MRS KABANÓVA, BARBARA *and* GLÁSHA *enter.*]

349

MRS KABANÓVA: Come on Tíkhon, it's time. Go now and
God speed! [*She sits down.*] Everyone sit down!
[*All sit down. Silence.*]
Now good-bye!
[*She stands, and all stand.*][6]

TÍKHON [*coming up to his Mother*]: Good-bye, Mama!

MRS KABANÓVA [*Pointing to the ground*]: Down you go!
Down you go! [TÍKHON *bows at his Mother's feet and then
kisses her.*] Say good-bye to your wife!

TÍKHON: Good-bye, Kate! [CATHERINE *flings herself on his
neck.*]

MRS KABANÓVA: What are you doing, hanging on to his
neck. Brazen hussy! You're not saying good-bye to your
lover! He's your husband, your Head! Don't you know
how to behave? Down you go, at his feet!
[CATHERINE *bows at his feet.*]

TÍKHON: Good-bye sister! [*He kisses* BARBARA.] Good-bye
Glásha! [*He kisses* GLÁSHA.] Good-bye Mama! [*He bows.*]

MRS KABANÓVA: Good-bye. The longer the leave-taking,
the more the tears.
[*Exit* TÍKHON *followed by* CATHERINE, BARBARA *and*
GLÁSHA.]

MRS KABANÓVA [*alone*]: What is it about the young people?
Just look at them – it's ridiculous! If they weren't my
own I'd have a good laugh at them. They don't know
anything, they've no idea how to behave. Can't even say
good-bye properly. It's all right, as long as there are old
people in the house; they are the ones that keep the home
together. And now, you see, when they want to have their
own way, the sillies, they'll go their own way and they'll
get muddled and disgrace themselves and become a
laughing-stock to decent people, some of whom of course
are sorry for them, though most of them just laugh. But
you can't help laughing; they'll invite guests, and not
know how to seat them at table. Quite likely they may

even forget about one of the relations. Simply ridiculous! But there you are; the old customs are dying out. You wouldn't even want to go inside some people's houses; if you did you'd give one spit, and get quickly away. What will happen when the old people die off, how the world is going to carry on, I don't know. But there's one good thing, and that is that I shan't see any of it.

[CATHERINE *and* BARBARA *enter.*]

MRS KABANÓVA: You were flaunting your great love for your husband; now I can see what that love is like. Any good wife who has seen her husband off, lies down in the porch and wails for an hour and a half; you don't seem to mind.

CATHERINE: What's the point? Besides, I don't know how to do it. Why make people laugh at me?

MRS KABANÓVA: You don't have to be very clever to do it. If you loved him, you'd learn how. If you can't do it properly you might make some attempt at it. That would at least be more decent; as it is, there seems to be nothing but words. Well, I'm going to say my prayers; don't disturb me.

BARBARA: I'm going out.

MRS KABANÓVA [*affectionately*]: What's that to me? Go on, enjoy yourself till your turn comes. Time enough then to be sitting at home!

[MRS KABANÓVA *and* BARBARA *go out.*]

CATHERINE [*alone in thought*]: Now our home will go all silent. Oh, but it's dreary! If only somebody here had children! It's such a shame! I haven't any babies; I could have stayed with them all the time and played with them. I love talking to children – you see they are angels. [*Silence.*] It would have been better if I had died when I was little. I would have looked down from Heaven at the earth, and rejoiced in it all. Or else I would have gone flying invisibly, wherever I wanted. I'd

have flown out over the fields, and gone from one blue
cornflower to another blue cornflower, flying on the wind
like a butterfly. [*She pauses to think.*] I know what I'll do.
I'll make a vow, and start some good work. I'll go down
to the market square, and buy some plain linen, and I'll
make undergarments, and then I'll give them away to the
poor. They'll pray for me. Barbara and I can sit here and
sew, and we won't notice the time passing and then
Tíkhon will come back.

[*Enter* BARBARA.]

BARBARA [*putting a head-scarf on in front of the looking-glass*]:
I'm going out for a walk now. Glásha will be making up
beds for us in the garden; Mama says we can. There's a
wicket-gate in the garden, behind the raspberries;
Mama keeps it locked and hides the key. I've got it, and
I've put another one instead, so she won't notice. Here it
is, maybe it will come in useful. [*She offers* CATHERINE
the key.] If I see him, I'll tell him to come to the wicket-
gate.

CATHERINE [*in terror, thrusting the key away*]: What's it for?
What's it for? I don't want it, I don't want it.

BARBARA: You may not want it, but I'm going to. Take it,
it won't bite you.

CATHERINE: What are you doing, tempting me, you
wicked girl? How could you! What are you thinking of!
You, you . . .!

BARBARA: Let's get on. I don't care for a lot of discussion,
and besides, I can't stay now. It's time for my walk. [*She
goes out.*]

CATHERINE [*alone, holding the key in her hand*]: What is she
doing? Whatever can she be up to? Oh, I'm mad, I
really am, mad! Ruination, that's what it is! Throw it
away, throw it right away, pitch it into the river, where
it'll never be found. It's burning my hands like a hot coal.
[*She stops to think.*] This is the very way we women get

ruined. How could anybody enjoy life, when they're in bondage! All sorts of things come into your head. A chance has turned up that many a woman would be glad of. Jump at it, head first. But how could she do such a thing without any thought or consideration? She won't have long to wait for trouble. And then there'll be the regrets and the agony, to the end of her days. And the bondage more bitter than ever. [*Silence*] And it is bitter, the bondage; oh, how bitter it is! Who wouldn't shed tears over it? Most of all us wives – like I am now. I go on living and struggling, and I can't see even a glimmer of hope, and I don't suppose I ever shall. The longer I live, the worse it gets. And on top of it all I've got this sin on my conscience. [*She pauses and thinks.*] If it hadn't been for my mother-in-law! . . . She's broken me . . . she's made me hate the place; I loathe the very walls. [*She looks thoughtfully at the key.*] Throw it away? It stands to reason; I must throw it away. And how did it get into my hands? To tempt me to my ruin. [*She listens a moment.*] Oh! That's somebody coming. I feel so dreadful. [*She puts the key away in her pocket.*] No . . . it's nobody . . . what a fright I got! I've put the key away; well, I suppose it can stay there now! It looks as if that's where Fate wants it to be. And what's wrong in taking one look at him, from a distance, say? And even supposing I were to have a bit of talk with him, there's still no harm in that. But what did I tell my husband? Well you know, he wouldn't have me promise. A chance like this won't turn up again in all my life, perhaps. And then I'd have myself to blame; there was my chance and I wasn't up to taking it. What am I doing, talking like this and deceiving myself? I don't care if I die, I've got to see him. Who am I making this pretence for? Throw away the key? Not for all the world! It's mine now . . . come what may, I am going to see Borís. Oh, if the night could come quickly!

ACT THREE

Scene One

A street. MRS KABANÓVA *and* FEKLÚSHA *are sitting on a bench in front of the gate of the Kabanóvs' home.*

FEKLÚSHA: It's the end of time, Mrs Kabanóva my dear, the end. By all the signs it is the end. In your town you still have the holy calm of heaven, but my dear in other towns it's just pandemonium. Uproar, tearing around and incessant travelling! And the people darting to and fro, one goes this way, one the other way.

MRS KABANÓVA: There's nowhere for us to hurry away to, my dear; we live without making haste.

FEKLÚSHA: No my dear, you have peace in the town because there's so many people, take for instance yourself, who are adorned with the flowers of good deeds; that is why everything here is done comfortably and decently. All this tearing around, my dear, what does it signify? Why, it's just vanity. Take for instance now Moscow; the people run backwards and forwards without knowing why. That too is vanity. The people are given to vanity, Mrs Kabanóva my dear; that is why they run. Here's a man who imagines he's got something important to run for – poor man, hurrying along, recognizing nobody! He thinks he sees somebody beckoning to him; but no, when he gets to the place it's empty – nothing but a dream. And he goes his way in sorrow. And another thinks he's running to catch up with an acquaintance, but someone else fresh sees at once that there's nobody there. Because it is all

vanity, his thinking that he is catching up. Vanity, you
see, is like a kind of mist. Here now, on a lovely evening
like this, a few people come out to sit at their gates, but
in Moscow it's all entertainments and pleasure-gardens
till the streets are filled with roaring and rattling and
unceasing din. And do you know what, Mrs Kabanóva,
they've started putting harness on to a fiery dragon. And
all it's for, you know, is for the sake of speed.

MRS KABANÓVA: So I've heard; my dear.

FEKLÚSHA: But, Mrs Kabanóva, I've seen it with my own
eyes. The others of course in their vanity see nothing.
They think it is an engine; that's what they call it, an
engine. But I saw it go like this [*spreading out her fingers*]
with its paws. And the roaring of it can be heard even
among decent-living people.

MRS KABANÓVA: They may call it any name they like; I
dare say they do call it an engine. People are stupid
enough to believe anything. But I wouldn't ride in it, not
if you showered me with gold.

FEKLÚSHA: Oh but my dear! Pray God you may never
come to such an extremity of misfortune. And another
thing, Mrs Kabanóva my dear, I had a kind of vision
when I was in Moscow. I was going along early one
morning, when it was hardly yet light, and I looked up at
a great tall house and on the roof I saw Someone with a
black face.[7] I'm sure you'll understand who that was.
And he was moving his hands as if he was scattering something, yet there was nothing coming down. Then it came
to me that he was sowing his tares, and they were invisible,
and the people in their vanity were picking them up in
broad daylight. That, then, is why they keep running
about, why the women are all so thin, and can't get any
flesh on their bones; it's as if they had lost something, or
were searching for something. They've a sad look on their
faces; it's really pitiful.

MRS KABANÓVA: It may well be, my dear! Can't be surprised at anything in times like ours.

FEKLÚSHA: Grievous times, Mrs Kabanóva, my dear, grievous times. And now time itself has begun to dwindle away . . .

MRS KABANÓVA: Dwindle away, my dear? How so?

FEKLÚSHA: We can't tell, of course; how could we in our vanity? But there are clever people who can tell that with us time itself is getting shorter. Summer and winter used to go on and on, and you'd think you'd never come to the end of them, but now they have flown away before you see them. Days and hours seem to be just the same, but time, for our sins, is getting shorter and shorter. That's what clever people say.

MRS KABANÓVA: And there'll be worse than that, my dear.

FEKLÚSHA: If only we don't live to see it.

MRS KABANÓVA: Maybe we shall.

[*Enter* DIKÓY.]

MRS KABANÓVA: What are you doing, Brother Saul, wandering abroad so late?

DIKÓY: Who says I shouldn't?

MRS KABANÓVA: Who says you shouldn't? Who'd want to?

DIKÓY: Say no more about it then. Who's going to come it over me, I'd like to know? And what are you still here for? Why the blue blazes are you still out here?

MRS KABANÓVA: Now then, you needn't open your great mouth so wide. You find someone softer than me! I'm too tough for you! On your way with you, wherever you were going. Come on Feklúsha, let's go home.

DIKÓY: Wait, Sister Martha, wait. Don't be angry. Time enough yet for you to get home; your home isn't over the hills, it's here!

MRS KABANÓVA: If you've come on business, stop yelling and talk sensibly.

DIKÓY: There isn't any business. I'm drunk, that's what.

MRS KABANÓVA: You aren't asking me to praise you for that, are you?

DIKÓY: I don't want praise, I don't want blame. The thing is that I'm drunk, and that's the end of the business. And it's a business that can't be set to rights till I've slept it off.

MRS KABANÓVA: Go on then, go to bed.

DIKÓY: Where am I to go to?

MRS KABANÓVA: Home. Where else?

DIKÓY: And suppose I don't want to go home?

MRS KABANÓVA: Why not, may I ask?

DIKÓY: Because I've got a war on there.

MRS KABANÓVA: Who have you got to fight with? Why, there's only one fighter there, and that's yourself.

DIKÓY: I'm a fighter am I? So what? What of it?

MRS KABANÓVA: Nothing. But it isn't much credit to you, to spend your whole life fighting with a lot of women. So there.

DIKÓY: Why then, they ought to give way to me. Or have I got to start giving way to them?

MRS KABANÓVA: I really am surprised at you. All those people in that house, and you the only one they can't please.

DIKÓY: Oh, go on!

MRS KABANÓVA: Well then, what is it you want of me?

DIKÓY: Look, I want you to talk me round, to make my temper go away. You're the only one in the whole town who can talk me round.

MRS KABANÓVA: Feklúsha, you go and tell them to get a bite of something ready.

[*Exit* FEKLÚSHA.]

Let's go indoors.

DIKÓY: No, I won't go indoors; I feel worse indoors.

MRS KABANÓVA: What have they done to upset you?

DIKÓY: Ever since first thing this morning.

MRS KABANÓVA: I suppose they asked you for money.

DIKÓY: You'd think they had it planned, confound them! First one comes bothering me, then another, the whole day long.

MRS KABANÓVA: If they come bothering you for it, they must want it.

DIKÓY: I understand that; but what would you have me do, when I've got this temper? Of course I know I've got to let them have it, but I can't do it nicely. You're a friend of mine, and suppose I'm owing you for something; if you come and ask me for it, I'll swear at you. I'll give it you, I'll give it you, but I'll swear. Because if anybody so much as opens their mouth to mention money to me it makes me go all hot inside, that's it, all hot inside. And when I'm like that I swear at them for nothing at all.

MRS KABANÓVA: You've got none of the older generation over you. That's why you're such a bully.

DIKÓY: Now you be quiet, Sister Martha, you listen, and I'll tell you the sort of thing that happens to me. It was in Lent one time and I was fasting and preparing to make my Communion, and what did the Devil do but slip a wretched little peasant on to me; he'd been delivering wood for the fire and he came for his money. It was to make me sin that he was brought at a time like that. And sin I did; I cursed him up and down, up and down, you couldn't have asked for any thing better, and I all but hit him. That's what my temper is like! Afterwards I begged him to forgive me, I bowed at his feet, I really did. It's the truth I'm telling you; I bowed at the feet of a peasant. That's what temper leads me into; there was I, outdoors in the mud, bowing before him in front of everybody.

MRS KABANÓVA: But why do you deliberately work your-self up into a temper? That isn't nice, Brother Saul.

DIKÓY: What do you mean, deliberately?

MRS KABANÓVA: I know, I've seen it. What you do, when you see that someone's going to ask you for something, is to go and deliberately set upon one of your family, in order to get yourself angry. Because you know that nobody will come near you when you're in a temper. That's what I mean, Brother Saul!

DIKÓY: Well, and what of it? Does anybody like parting with what is his own?

[*Enter* GLÁSHA.]

GLÁSHA: Supper's ready please, Mrs Kabanóva.

MRS KABANÓVA: Come on now, Brother Saul. Have a bit of what the Lord has sent us.

DIKÓY: All right.

MRS KABANÓVA: Pray be our guest!

[*She lets* DIKÓY *in ahead of herself and follows after him.* GLÁSHA *stands by the gate with her arms folded.*]

GLÁSHA: Isn't that Mr Borís coming? Is it his uncle he wants? Or is he just out for a walk? I expect he's just out for a walk.

[BORÍS *enters.*]

BORÍS: Have you got my uncle here?

GLÁSHA: We have. Might you be wanting him?

BORÍS: They sent me from home to find out where he was. If he's with you he can stay there – who wants him? They're only too glad at home that he's gone.

GLÁSHA: He ought to have married our mistress. She'd have stopped him quick enough. What am I doing, stupid girl, staying out here with you! Good-bye.

[GLÁSHA *goes out.*]

BORÍS: Oh Lord! Just to have one peep at her! I mustn't go into the house; you can't go there uninvited. What a life! We live in the same town, almost next door, and we see each other once a week, either in Church or on the way there and that's all. When a girl here gets married, she might as well have been buried! [*Silence.*] I wish now I'd never set eyes on her; it would have been easier so! As it is, I see her in snatches, and besides, it's in front of

other people, eyes everywhere watching you. It's just
heart-breaking. I can't even control what I'm doing; go
for a walk, and I always end up here, outside their gate.
Why do I keep on coming here? I mayn't ever see her,
and as for talking to her – if such a thing ever happened
I'd probably get her into trouble. What a hole this place
is!

[*Enter* KULÍGIN, *who comes towards* BORÍS.]

KULÍGIN: Well, Mr Borís? Out for a walk, Sir?

BORÍS: Yes, I'm just having a walk; very pleasant weather
today.

KULÍGIN: A very nice time, Sir, to go walking now. Calm,
lovely air, the smell of the flowers blowing in from the
meadows across the Volga, a clear sky. . . .

    'Behold, a bottomless abyss display'd
    'Infinite Space, with countless stars array'd.'[8]

Let's go to the Promenade, Sir, there isn't a soul there.

BORÍS: Let's!

KULÍGIN: You see, Sir, what a wretched sort of a place
we've got here! They've made a Promenade; but they
don't walk there, except only on holidays, and even then
they're only pretending to be taking a walk when they
really come to show off their fine clothes. All you'll meet
is some drunken clerk, staggering home from the tavern.
Poor folk haven't the time to go for walks Sir; they have
work to do, night and day. All the sleep they get is three
hours out of the twenty-four. And what do rich people do?
You'd have thought they'd be out walking and breathing
the fresh air? Not they. They all bolted their gates long
ago, Sir, and turned out the dogs. . . . Do you think they
are doing business, or saying their prayers? No Sir! It
wasn't to keep thieves out that they bolted themselves in,
but to prevent people from seeing the way they bully
their servants and oppress their families. The tears that
are shed, unseen and unheard, behind those bolted

doors! What is there that I can tell you Sir? You can judge from your own home. And Sir, what about the black vice and the drunkenness? All under lock and key, all hidden, all kept dark! Nobody sees anything and nobody knows anything except One – God. 'You may see me in company,' they'll say, 'or in the street, but my family is nothing to do with you. That', they'll tell you, 'is what I have locks for, locks and bolts and savage dogs. The family', they'll say, 'is a secret matter.' We know those secrets! Sir, there's only one person who has any joy of the secrets, and that's the man himself. The rest of them can weep and wail. And what are the secrets? Who doesn't know that? Pillaging orphans and kinsmen and nephews, and thrashing the servants till they wouldn't dare to utter a word about what goes on. That's the whole secret. But never mind about them; do you know, Sir, who do go for walks here? The young boys and girls. They steal a couple of hours or so from the night, and they go walking in couples. Here comes a couple.

[KUDRYÁSH *and* BARBARA *appear. They kiss.*]

BORÍS: They're kissing.

KULÍGIN: We don't mind about that here.

[*Exit* KUDRYÁSH. BARBARA *goes up to her own gate, and beckons to* BORÍS, *who comes over to her.*]

KULÍGIN: I'll go to the Promenade, Sir. Why should I hinder you? I'll wait for you there.

BORÍS: All right, I'll come in a minute.

BARBARA [*with her scarf over her face*]: Do you know the ravine behind the Kabanóvs' garden?

BORÍS: Yes, I do.

BARBARA: You go there presently, a bit later.

BORÍS: What for?

BARBARA: You are a silly! When you get there you'll see what for. Go on then and hurry up; they'll be expecting you.

361

[BORÍS *exits.*]

Why, he never recognized me! That'll be something for him to think about now. I know too that Catherine won't be able to hold back. She'll pop out. [BARBARA *leaves through the gate.*]

Scene Two

Night. A ravine, overgrown with bushes. Above, the KABANÓVS' *garden fence and wicket-gate; a path leading down.* KUDRYÁSH *enters with a guitar.*

KUDRYÁSH: Nobody here. What's she doing, up there? Well, let's sit and wait. [*He sits down on a stone.*] And to pass the time, we'll have a song. [*He sings.*]
A Don Cossack has come with his horse to the watering
A goodly young man is he. By the gate he stands,
And as he stands by the gate he has thought a thought
And the thought he has thought is of doing his wife to death.
Now she, his wife, has come to make prayer to him;
Before his swift-running feet she has bowed herself
'Ah my good lord, my love and my heart's delight!
Don't beat me and do me to death in the evening!
Wait till midnight comes to destroy me and murder me
Give my little ones time to go off to sleep,
All the sweet children, so near to us and so dear to us!'[9]
    [BORÍS *enters.*]
KUDRYÁSH [*stops singing*]: Look at that now! Meek as meek, and him out on the spree too!
BORÍS: Is that you, Kudryásh?
KUDRYÁSH: It's me, Mr Borís.
BORÍS: What are you here for?
KUDRYÁSH: Me? If I'm here, Mr Borís, you can take it that I want to be here. If I hadn't wanted to I wouldn't have come. Where on earth are you going?

BORÍS [*looking round the place*]: Look here Kudryásh, I want to stay here and I suppose it's all the same to you, so you might go on somewhere else.

KUDRYÁSH: No, Mr Borís. I can see you haven't been here before, but this happens to be my particular place, and that path has been trodden out by me. I like you, Sir, and I'm ready to do anything to oblige you but don't you cross my track down here at night if we're not to have something bad happen which we pray God it won't. Fair play is a jewel.

BORÍS: What's the matter with you, Johnny!

KUDRYÁSH: Johnny indeed! I know I'm Johnny. But you go your own road, that's all. Nobody will mind anybody who gets one for himself and walks out with her. But no touching other people's. We don't have anything like that here, or the lads would break their bones for them. If it was my girl, I don't know what I wouldn't do. Scrag him!

BORÍS: There's nothing for you to get hot over; I wasn't even thinking of cutting you out. I wouldn't have come here, only I was told to.

KUDRYÁSH: Who told you?

BORÍS: I couldn't see, it was dark. Some girl stopped me in the street and said I was to come just here, behind the Kabanóvs' garden where the path is.

KUDRYÁSH: But who could it have been?

BORÍS: Listen, Kudryásh. Can I talk heart to heart to you; you won't blab?

KUDRYÁSH: Go on, don't be afraid. Leave it with me, and it's as good as dead and buried.

BORÍS: I don't know anything about this place, I don't know your rules or your ways, but the thing is . . .

KUDRYÁSH: You've fallen in love with somebody, haven't you?

BORÍS: Yes, Kudryásh.

KUDRYÁSH: Well and what of it? That's all right. We're

363

easy about that here. The girls go walking when they want to; Father and Mother don't mind. Only the wives are kept shut up.

BORÍS: That's just my trouble.

KUDRYÁSH: Don't say you're in love with a married woman?

BORÍS: Yes, Kudryásh, she is married.

KUDRYÁSH: Now look here Mr Borís, you've got to drop that!

BORÍS: It's easy to say drop it! Maybe it's all the same to you; you can drop one and find another. I can't do that! If now I'd fallen in love ...

KUDRYÁSH: You know what this means? You're going to ruin her entirely, Mr Borís.

BORÍS: God forbid! God forbid that I should! No, Kudryásh, how could you say such a thing! Me want to harm her! If only I could see her some place; I mustn't do more than that.

KUDRYÁSH: How can you be sure of yourself, Sir? And think of the kind of people there are here! You know them. They'll eat you, they'll bash you down into your coffin.

BORÍS: Oh Kudryásh don't say that! Please don't you try to scare me.

KUDRYÁSH: And does she love you?

BORÍS: I don't know.

KUDRYÁSH: Have you ever met each other, or not?

BORÍS: I've only once been to their house, with my uncle. Besides that I see her in Church, and we pass each other on the Promenade. Oh Kudryásh, if you'd seen her when she's at prayer! She's got such an angelic smile, and it seems as if a light shone out from her face.

KUDRYÁSH: Would it be young Mrs Kabanóva?

BORÍS: It's her, Kudryásh.

KUDRYÁSH: Yes? So that's how it is then! Well, we have the honour to congratulate you.

BORÍS: What on?

KUDRYÁSH: But of course! If you were told to come here, it must mean that things are going right for you.

BORÍS: Don't say it was she that told me to come?

KUDRYÁSH: Who else could it be?

BORÍS: No, you're joking. It can't be that. [*He clutches his head.*]

KUDRYÁSH: What's the matter with you?

BORÍS: I shall go mad with joy.

KUDRYÁSH: Steady on, you've got nothing to go mad about. Just you mind you keep yourself clear of scrapes, and don't you go and get her into trouble. Her husband's a fool, I grant you, but that mother-in-law of hers is a regular terror.

[BARBARA *comes out from the wicket-gate.*]

BARBARA [*singing in the gateway*]:

Far beyond the rushing river, my Johnny goes walking.
There my boy Johnny goes walking.

KUDRYÁSH [*joining in*]:

A' buying his trade-goods [*he whistles.*]¹⁰

[BARBARA *comes down the path and goes up to* BORÍS *with a scarf over her face.*]

BARBARA: You wait a bit, lad. There's something for you to wait for. [*To* KUDRYÁSH] Let's go down to the Volga.

KUDRYÁSH: Why were you so long? Keeping us waiting! You know I don't like it.

[BARBARA *puts one arm round him and they go off.*]

BORÍS: It's all like a dream! The night, the songs, the meetings! Walking with arms round one another! It's all so new to me, so lovely and gay. And there's something for me to wait for! What it is I don't know and I can't even imagine; only my heart is thumping and every vein is throbbing. I can't even think now what to say to her; I catch my breath, I'm weak at the knees! When this foolish heart of mine suddenly boils up, there's nothing that will calm it. Here she comes.

[CATHERINE *comes quietly down the path covered with a big white scarf, eyes on the ground. Silence.*]

BORÍS: Catherine, is that you?

[*Silence.*]

I just don't know how I can thank you.

[*Silence.*]

If you knew, Catherine, how much I love you! [*He goes to take her hand.*]

CATHERINE [*in terror, but without raising her eyes*]: Don't touch me, don't touch me! Oh! Oh!

BORÍS: Don't be angry!

CATHERINE: Get away from me! Get right away, accursed man! Do you know that all my prayers won't take away this sin, won't take it away ever! It will lie on my soul like a stone, like a stone!

BORÍS: Don't make me go away.

CATHERINE: Why have you come? Why have you come to ruin me? You know I'm a married woman, and I've got to live with my husband till death us do part . . .

BORÍS: It was you yourself told me to come . . .

CATHERINE: Understand what I'm saying, you fiend! It's till death us do part!

BORÍS: Better for me never to have seen you!

CATHERINE [*with emotion*]: See what I am laying up for myself. Where am I going to – do you know that?

BORÍS: Calm yourself. [*He takes her hand.*] Sit down.

CATHERINE: Why do you want to destroy me?

BORÍS: How could I want to destroy you, when I love you more than all the world, more than my own self?

CATHERINE: No, No! You've ruined me!

BORÍS: I'm not an evil kind of man, am I?

CATHERINE [*shaking her head*]: Ruined me, ruined me, ruined me!

BORÍS: God help me! Better I should perish myself!

CATHERINE: Indeed you have ruined me, if I've abandoned my home and come to you in the night time.

BORÍS: You did it of your own will.

CATHERINE: I haven't any will. If I had a will of my own I wouldn't have come to you. [*She raises her eyes to look at* BORÍS. *Brief silence.*] Can't you see that you have got your will of me now! [*She flings herself on his neck.*]

BORÍS [*embracing her*]: My life!

CATHERINE: Do you know? I suddenly feel as if I'd like to die now.

BORÍS: Why die, when living is so good?

CATHERINE: No, life is not for me! I know now that I'm not going to live.

BORÍS: Please don't say such things. Don't make me sad . . .

CATHERINE: Yes, it's all right for you; you have your freedom, but I . . .

BORÍS: Nobody even knows about our love. Do you think I won't take care of you!

CATHERINE: Oh, but why take care of me? It's nobody's fault; I got into this myself. Don't take care of me, ruin me! Let them all know, let them all see what I'm doing! [*She embraces* BORÍS.] If for your sake I had no fear of sin, what fear will I have of human judgement? They even say that it's made easier for you, when you have had to suffer a lot for some sin here on earth.

BORÍS: Come, why think about that? We're in luck, we're all right now.

CATHERINE: So? I shall have time enough, and leisure enough, to think all my thoughts and weep all my tears.

BORÍS: I was half afraid you'd send me away.

CATHERINE [*smiling*]: Send you away? The idea! With hearts like ours? If you hadn't come I think I would have gone to you.

BORÍS: I didn't know you loved me.

CATHERINE: I've loved you a long time. Your coming to
our house must have been intended. The minute I saw
you I lost hold of myself. That first time, I think, if you
had crooked your finger at me I'd have gone after you;
you could have gone to the end of the world and I would
have gone along after you, and never looked back.

BORÍS: Is your husband away for long?

CATHERINE: A fortnight.

BORÍS: Oh, then we'll have some good times. It's long
enough.

CATHERINE: Have some good times. And then ... [*She
pauses to think.*] When they turn the key in the lock – death.
But if they don't lock it, I'll find a chance to meet you!

[*Enter* KUDRYÁSH *and* BARBARA.]

BARBARA: Well, are you fixed up?

[CATHERINE *hides her face on* BORÍS's *chest.*]

BORÍS: Yes we're fixed up.

BARBARA: You'd better go and have your walk, and we'll
wait. Johnny will give a call, when it's time.

[*Exeunt* BORÍS *and* CATHERINE. KUDRYÁSH *and*
BARBARA *sit down on a stone.*]

KUDRYÁSH: That was a smart idea of yours, slipping out
by the garden gate. Very handy for us boys.

BARBARA: Just like me.

KUDRYÁSH: Trust you for a thing like that. But won't your
Mother catch on?

BARBARA: Pooh, why should she? Never enter her head.

KUDRYÁSH: But suppose somehow she does?

BARBARA: Her first sleep is heavy. Towards morning –
that's when she wakes up.

KUDRYÁSH: How can you be sure then? Suppose some
devil comes along and gets her out of bed?

BARBARA: What of it? The gate leading out of the yard is
bolted on the garden side; she'll bang and bang on it and
then go away. And in the morning we'll say we were too

fast asleep to hear her. Besides, Glásha's on watch, she'll
give us a call at once if there's anything. Mustn't leave
things to chance! Can't have that! You never know,
trouble can come at any time.

[KUDRYÁSH *strikes a few chords on his guitar.* BARBARA
*leans back against his shoulder; he takes no notice of her but
goes on quietly playing.*]

BARBARA [*yawning*]: I'd like to find out the time.

KUDRYÁSH: Past midnight.

BARBARA: How do you know?

KUDRYÁSH: The watchman struck on his plate.[11]

BARBARA [*yawning*]: Time to go. Give them a call! We'll
come out a bit earlier tomorrow and have more of a walk.

KUDRYÁSH [*whistles and sings out loudly*]:
All come home, all come home!
But I don't want to go home!

BORÍS [*off-stage*]: I hear you.

BARBARA [*getting-up*]: Good-bye then! [*She yawns, and gives*
KUDRYÁSH *a cool kiss, as to an old acquaintance.*] Mind and
come a bit earlier tomorrow. [*Looking to the side where*
BORÍS *and* CATHERINE *went out*] You'd better say good-
bye now, you're not parting for ever – you'll see each
other tomorrow. [*She yawns and stretches.*]

[CATHERINE *runs in, followed by* BORÍS.]

CATHERINE: Come on now, come on now! [*They go up the
path.* CATHERINE *turns round.*] Good-bye.

BORÍS: Till tomorrow?

CATHERINE: Yes, till tomorrow! Tell me what you dream
about! [*She goes up to the wicket-gate.*]

BORÍS: I surely will.

KUDRYÁSH [*singing to the guitar*]:
Come then Maiden, come away
Till the ending of the day!
Hey nonny come away
Till the ending of the day.

BARBARA [*at the wicket-gate*]:
 I, the maiden, come away
 Till the dawning of the day.
 Hey nonny come away
 Till the dawning of the day.
KUDRYÁSH: When the dawn light filled the sky
 In my house then up got I. [*Etc.*]

ACT FOUR

In the foreground is a narrow, vaulted gallery of antique construction, rather dilapidated, with weeds and bushes here and there; beyond the arches is the riverbank and a view of the Volga. Several persons of both sexes are out walking beyond the arches.

FIRST MAN: Those are spots of rain; there'll be a thunderstorm brewing, eh?

SECOND MAN: Any minute now.

FIRST MAN: It's lucky we've somewhere to take shelter.

[*All come in under the vaulting.*]

A WOMAN: What a lot of people walking on the Promenade! It's the holiday; they've all come out for a turn. Merchants' wives too, all dressed up.

FIRST MAN: They'll have to get under cover somewhere.

SECOND MAN: You'll see, they'll all come crowding in here.

FIRST MAN [*looking at the walls*]: Look, my dear man, there must have once been paintings in here. They still show in places, even now.

SECOND MAN: Why yes, of course there were! Anyone can see there were paintings. Now, look you, the whole place has been let go, and it has got ruinous and overgrown. They never repaired it after the fire. You wouldn't remember that fire, it must have been about forty years ago.

FIRST MAN: Tell me now, my dear man, what would this be a picture of here? It's a bit hard to make out.

SECOND MAN: That's the fire of Gehenna.

FIRST MAN: So it is, my dear man!

SECOND MAN: And all sorts and conditions of men going into the fire.

371

FIRST MAN: So they are, so they are! I've got it now.

SECOND MAN: People of every rank too.

FIRST MAN: Black men too?

SECOND MAN: Yes, black men too.

FIRST MAN: What's this then, my dear man?

SECOND MAN: That's the time of the Lithuanian Troubles. A battle! Do you see? When our men fought against the Lithuanians.

FIRST MAN: And what are Lithuanians?[12]

SECOND MAN: Just that – Lithuanians.

FIRST MAN: But they say, my dear man, that they fell upon us out of the sky.

SECOND MAN: I don't know what to tell you about that. Maybe it was out of the sky.

THE WOMAN: What are you talking about! Everybody knows it was out of the sky. And in all the places where there were fights against them, there are barrows built up, for a memorial.[13]

FIRST MAN: There you are my dear man! Isn't that just what I said?

[*Enter* DIKÓY, *followed by* KULÍGIN, *cap in hand. All bow and take up respectful attitudes.*]

DIKÓY: There now, soaking wet. [*To* KULÍGIN] You get away from me! Get away! [*Irate.*] Fool of a man!

KULÍGIN: But you see, Mr Díkóy, Your Worship, this will be a public benefit for everyone in the town.

DIKÓY: Clear out! What benefit? Who wants this benefit?

KULÍGIN: Perhaps even you yourself, Your Worship, Mr Dikóy, Sir. Look, Sir, we could put it in the open space on the Promenade. Expense? Expense would be negligible; a little stone pillar [*illustrates the size of each item by gestures*], a small brass dial – round-like – and the style, an upright style like this [*illustrates with a gesture*] perfectly plain.[14] I'll install the whole thing, and do all the engraving of the figures myself. And then you, Your

Worship, if you were taking a walk, or anyone else who was out for a walk, could come up to it and see at once what time it was. As it is, you've got a lovely place there, with a view and all, but it's somehow bare. And, besides, Your Worship, we get travellers passing through, and they go up there to look at our views. Anyway, it would be an ornament – more pleasing to the eye.

DIKÓY: What are you bothering me for, with all this rubbish? Perhaps I don't want to speak to you. You ought to have found out first whether or not I was in the mood to listen to a fool like you. What am I to you? Your equal, or what? Important business you've got, haven't you? Barging up like that, and talking out of that great ugly mouth of yours!

KULÍGIN: If it had been my own business that I bothered you about, why then I would have been to blame. But this is for the public benefit, Your Worship. Come, what's a matter of ten roubles or so to the Community? It wouldn't take more than that, Sir.

DIKÓY: But perhaps you want to steal it; who knows about you?

KULÍGIN: If I'm willing to put my own labour into it for nothing, what is there that I can steal, Your Worship? Besides everybody knows me here; nobody is going to say anything bad about me.

DIKÓY: All right then, they can know you; I don't want to.

KULÍGIN: Mr Dikóy, Sir, why abuse an honest man?

DIKÓY: Have I to start accounting for myself to you, or what! I won't be accountable to anybody, not even to some folk who are a bit more important than you. If I want to think that about you, I'll think it. You're an honest man to some people, but I think you're a robber, and that's that! Is that what you wanted to hear from me? Listen then! I say that you are a robber! That's the end of it! What are you going to do about it? Go to Law with

373

me, or what? I'll have you know that you're a worm. I'll let you off if I like, and I'll squash you flat if I like.

KULÍGIN: Bless you, Mr Dikóy! I'm a small man, and it's easy enough to abuse me. But I beg leave to say this to you, Your Worship. 'Virtue is honoured, even when she goes in rags.'[15]

DIKÓY: Don't you dare to be impertinent to me! Do you hear?

KULÍGIN: I'm not being impertinent, Sir. I'm speaking to you, because you may be thinking some time of doing something for the town. You have the means to do much good, Your Worship, if only you had the will. Take now this for instance; we have frequent thunderstorms, but we don't put up lightning conductors.

DIKÓY [*arrogantly*]: Perfectly futile.

KULÍGIN: How can they be futile, when experiments have been made?

DIKÓY: What sort of things are they, your lightning conductors?

KULÍGIN: They're made of steel.

DIKÓY [*angry*]: Well and what else?

KULÍGIN: Steel rods.

DIKÓY [*getting more and more furious*]: Rods! I heard that, you poisonous reptile, but what else is there? You keep on about the rods; well and what else?

KULÍGIN: Nothing else.

DIKÓY: And what is thunder, in your opinion? Eh? Come on, tell us?

KULÍGIN: Electricity.

DIKÓY [*stamping his foot*]: What has ellistrixity to do with it? And you mean to tell me you're not a robber? Thunder is sent to punish us, to make us think what we're doing, and you, Lord forgive you, want to protect yourself with a lot of rods and stakes. Are you a heathen, or what? Are you a heathen? Tell me, is that it? A heathen?

KULÍGIN: Mr Dikóy, Your Worship, Derzhávin said
'Dust unto dust moulders my earthly form
'Yet with my mind I rule the thunderstorm.'[16]

DIKÓY: Say things like that! . . . send you to the Prefect!
. . . he'll give it to you! . . . Hey good people! Listen now
to what he's saying.

KULÍGIN: There's nothing for it but to give way. But when
I've got my million, then I'll talk. [*He leaves with a wave
of his hand.*]

DIKÓY: What are you going to do? Steal it from somebody?
Stop him! Dirty little swindler! What can a man do with
people like that! I don't know. [*He turns to the bystanders.*]
Confound the lot of you, you'd make anybody go wrong!
There, and I didn't want to lose my temper today, and
he's deliberately gone and made me do it. Damn him!
[*Angrily*] Has the shower stopped?

FIRST MAN: I think it has.

DIKÓY: You think! Get outside, fool, and have a look!
Think it has!

FIRST MAN [*going out from under the vaulting*]: It has stopped.
[DIKÓY *leaves, followed by all the rest. The stage is empty
for a short while.* BARBARA *enters; she comes quickly in under
the vaulting, hides herself and peeps out.*]

BARBARA: I think that's him! [BORÍS *passes across the back
of the stage.*] Psst!
[BORÍS *looks round.*]
Come over here.
[*Beckons with her hand;* BORÍS *comes inside.*]
What are we going to do about Catherine? Tell me that,
for goodness' sake.

BORÍS: Why?

BARBARA: She's in trouble, real trouble. Her husband's
back, did you know that? They weren't expecting him,
but he's back.

BORÍS: No, I didn't know.

375

BARBARA: She's simply out of her mind.

BORÍS: It seems that all I got was ten little days of life, while he was away. Shan't see her any more now.

BARBARA: Oh you are . . . Now listen here! She shakes all over, as if she had the fever, and she's so pale, and she dashes round the house as if she was trying to find something. There's a crazy look in her eyes! Just now this morning she started crying, and she keeps on sobbing. Oh dear dear me, what am I going to do about her?

BORÍS: But maybe it will pass off.

BARBARA: I don't think it will, though. She daren't look her husband in the face. Mama has begun to notice it, she keeps on darting ugly glances at her, watching her like a snake. And that makes her worse than ever. It's just torture to see her. And I'm afraid . . .

BORÍS: Afraid? What of?

BARBARA: You don't know her. We've got a queer sort of girl there. Anything can happen with her. She'll go and do something . . .

BORÍS: Oh my God! What can we do? You'd better give her a good talking to. Don't say you can't talk her round?

BARBARA: I've tried. She won't listen to anything. It's better to leave her alone.

BORÍS: So what do you think she might do?

BARBARA: Look here; she might flop down at her husband's feet, and tell him all about it. That's what I'm afraid of.

BORÍS [alarmed]: Is that possible?

BARBARA: Anything is possible with her.

BORÍS: Where is she now?

BARBARA: At this moment she's walking with her husband on the Promenade, and Mama is with them. You walk past, if you like. No, better not go, she might get quite distraught.

[Distant sound of thunder.]

376

Isn't that thunder? [*She looks round.*] Yes, and here's the rain. Look at all the people rushing in. You shelter somewhere over there, and I'll stand here where I'm seen, so that people don't think things.

[*Enter* KULÍGIN *and several people of various classes and both sexes.*]

FIRST MAN: That little woman must be very frightened, to be in such a hurry to get under cover.

THE WOMAN: What's the good of hiding? There's nowhere you can get away from what's written in your birth-lines.

[*Enter* CATHERINE.]

CATHERINE [*running in*]: Oh Barbara! [*She seizes her hand and holds tightly to it.*]

BARBARA: Stop that! What's the matter with you!

CATHERINE: It's the death of me!

BARBARA: You take a hold of yourself! Pull yourself together!

CATHERINE: I can't! I can't do anything. My heart aches so much.

[*Enter* MRS KABANÓVA *and* TÍKHON.]

MRS KABANÓVA: There you are, you see. We ought to live our lives so as to be ready for anything; and then there wouldn't be all this fright.

TÍKHON: But Mama what special sins can she have? They're all just the same ones that we've all got, and she's timid by nature.

MRS KABANÓVA: How do you know that? No one can see into anyone else's soul.

TÍKHON [*joking*]: Unless it was something while I was away. I don't think it was anything while I've been here.

MRS KABANÓVA: Maybe it was while you were away.

TÍKHON [*joking*]: If you've got any sins, Katie my girl, you had better confess them. You know you can't hide them from me. No fooling now! I know all about it.

CATHERINE [*looking into* TÍKHON's *eyes*]: My darling!

377

BARBARA: Why do you keep on at her! Can't you see she's upset already, without you starting?

[BORÍS *comes out from the crowd and bows to the* KABANÓVS.]

CATHERINE [*screams*]: Oh!

TÍKHON: What's the fright about? Did you think it was a stranger? This is somebody we know! How's your uncle?

BORÍS: Quite well, praise be.

CATHERINE [*to* BARBARA]: What more does he want of me? Isn't it enough for him, that I am so tormented?

[*She clings to* BARBARA, *sobbing.*]

BARBARA [*in a loud voice, for her Mother to hear*]: We're run off our legs, we don't know what to do with her, and now we've got outsiders on top of us.

[*She signals to* BORÍS, *who goes right over to the exit.*]

KULÍGIN [*coming out into the middle, and facing the crowd*]: Come, what are you afraid of, for goodness' sake! Now every blade of grass and every flower is rejoicing, and we hide ourselves, as if fearful of some disaster hanging over us! Thunder's a sign of wrath; it kills! It is not a sign of wrath, it's God's Grace! Yes, Grace! Everything is a sign of wrath to you. The Northern Lights shine out – you ought to be admiring them, and wondering at the Infinite Wisdom:

'Out of the Midnight Lands doth rise the dawn!'[17]

But you're in dread of them, pondering whether they mean war or a plague. Or a comet comes – you ought not to take your eyes off it! The beauty of it! You have seen plenty of stars and they are all alike but here is something new; come on, gaze at it, admire it! But you shiver and shake, and you're afraid to take even one look at the sky! You have made bogies for yourselves out of everything. Ah, you people you! See, I'm not afraid. . . . Let's go, Sir.

BORÍS: Let's go. There's more to frighten one inside here.

[BORÍS *and* KULÍGIN *go out.*]

MRS KABANÓVA: There's an oration for you! Something to

378

listen to, but nothing to say! See to what times we have
come, when teachers such as these have arisen among us.
If this is what an old man thinks, what can we expect of
the young!

THE WOMAN. Now the whole sky is overcast. Covered all
over, as if it had a cap on it.

FIRST MAN: Look at that, my dear man! That cloud is
rolling itself all up in a ball, as though there were some
live creature twisting and turning inside it. There it is,
creeping and creeping up on us, like as if it were alive.

SECOND MAN: Mark my words; that storm isn't coming this
way for nothing. It's the truth I'm telling you, because
I know. Either someone will be killed, or there'll be a
house burnt down. You'll see! Because, look what an
extraordinary colour!

CATHERINE [*listening*]: What are they saying? They are
saying that somebody is going to be killed.

TÍKHON: Of course it's nonsense; they say anything that
comes into their heads.

MRS KABANÓVA: Don't you criticize your elders! They
know more than you do. Old people know the signs
for everything. An old person doesn't waste his breath
on the wind.

CATHERINE [*to her husband*]: Tíkhon dear, I know who's
going to be killed.

BARBARA [*to* CATHERINE, *quietly*]: Will you keep quiet
now!

TÍKHON: How do you know?

CATHERINE: I'm the one who'll be killed. Pray for me
when it comes.

[THE LADY *with her* TWO FOOTMEN *comes in.* CATH-
ERINE *screams and hides herself.*]

THE LADY: Hiding are you? It's no good hiding! You're
afraid, by the look of it; you don't want to die! You want
to go on living! Of course she does; do you see now what

379

a beauty she is? Ha Ha Ha! Beauty! You pray to God to take away that beauty! Beauty, you know, is the ruination of us! When you have destroyed yourself and seduced others to their ruin, then let you be rejoicing in your beauty! Many and many are the people that you will lead into sin! Giddy young fools will go out and fight duels, stick swords into one another! Jolly! Ancient and honourable old men, forgetting about death, seduced by beauty! And who will be answerable for it? You will have to answer for it all. You had best put that beauty of yours down into the deep water! And quickly, quickly!

[CATHERINE *hides.*]

Where are you hiding, you silly creature? You can't get away from God!

[*Clap of thunder.*]

You shall all burn in unquenchable fire! [*Exit.*]

CATHERINE: Oh, I'm dying!

BARBARA: Now, really, what are you tormenting yourself for! Kneel over there, and say a prayer and you'll feel better.

[CATHERINE *goes over to the wall and kneels down, then quickly jumps up.*]

CATHERINE: Oh! It's Hell, it's Hell, it's the fires of Gehenna!

[MRS KABANÓVA, TÍKHON *and* BARBARA *come round her.*]

My heart's all ripped and torn. I can't bear it any longer! Mother! Tíkhon! I have sinned before God and before you! Wasn't it I that swore to you that I wouldn't look at anybody while you were away? Remember? Remember? And do you know what I did? What I, the wanton, did while you were away? On the very first night I went out of the house.

TÍKHON [*distraught, in tears, plucking at her sleeve*]: Don't! Don't say it! What are you doing? Mother is here!

MRS KABANÓVA [*sternly*]: Go on, go on and say it, now you've started.

CATHERINE: And all those ten nights I was out. [*She sobs.* TÍKHON *is about to put his arm round her.*]

MRS KABANÓVA: Let go of her! Who with?

BARBARA: She's talking nonsense, she doesn't know what she's saying.

MRS KABANÓVA: Quiet you! So that's it! Come on now, who with?

CATHERINE: With Borís Dikóy!

[*Thunderclap.*]

Oh! [*She falls fainting into her husband's arms.*]

MRS KABANÓVA: Now, my little son! See where freedom takes you! I told you, and you wouldn't listen. Now you've got what was coming to you!

ACT FIVE

Scene as in Act One. Twilight. KULÍGIN *is sitting on the bench,* *and* TÍKHON *walking along the Promenade.*

KULÍGIN [*sings*]: ' 'Twas at the dark of midnight
                'When murky was the sky
                'And people with their eyes shut
                'Upon their beds did lie . . .' (*etc.*)[18]

[*Sees* TÍKHON.]

Good evening, Sir. Might you be going far?

TÍKHON: I'm going home. Have you heard, man, how things are with us? It's the whole family, man; we've got ourselves into a terrible state.

KULÍGIN: I did hear, Sir, I did hear.

TÍKHON: I had been to Moscow – you knew that? Mama lectured me and lectured me about going, and directly I was off I went on the spree. I was so glad that I had broken loose. I kept on drinking all the way and all the time I was in Moscow; I had a rare old frolic – enough fun to last me a twelvemonth. Never once thought about home. And even if I had, I'd never have imagined what was going on there. Have you heard?

KULÍGIN: Yes, Sir, I've heard.

TÍKHON: My dear man, there's no luck now for me. Blighted, and for no reason at all. Not a ha'p'orth of reason.

KULÍGIN: That Mama of yours, she's terrible hard.

TÍKHON: Yes indeed. And she's the one that caused it all. Why am I blighted, will you tell me that, for goodness' sake! Look, I've been in to see Mr Dikóy; well, and we had a few drinks together. I thought it would make me feel better but it didn't, Kulígin, I feel worse! Do you know what my wife did to me? Nothing could have been worse . . .

KULÍGIN: It's a hard case, Sir. It's hard to judge between you.

TÍKHON: Steady on now! There isn't anything worse than that. Killing her for it is too good for her. Mama says she ought to be buried alive in the earth, so as to make her suffer. But I love her, and it hurts me to lay a finger on her. I have beaten her a bit, but that was only because Mama told me to. It hurts me to look at her, do you understand that, Kulígin? Mama keeps on and on at her and she never answers back, but goes round like a sort of a shadow. Just crying, and melting away like wax. It's killing me to look at her.

KULÍGIN: There ought to be some way of setting things to rights, Sir. Suppose now you were to forgive her, and not mention it ever again. Have you done nothing wrong yourself? I expect you have.

TÍKHON: You don't need to tell me that!

KULÍGIN: So you can't say much, especially when you're drunk. She would be a good wife to you, Sir; better than any, I dare say.

TÍKHON: But understand this, Kulígin! I'd be all right, if it wasn't for Mama. You try and get round her.

KULÍGIN: It's time, Sir, that you had a mind of your own and went by it.

TÍKHON: Do you want me to tear myself in two? They tell me I haven't got a mind of my own, so I've got to go by someone else's all my life. They say, I'd go and spend my last penny on drink; that's why Mama has to dry-nurse me like an idiot.

KULÍGIN: Dear, dear, Sir, that won't do! Tell me now, Sir, what about Mr Borís?

TÍKHON: The wretched man has got to go to Kyákhta,[19]

where the Chinamen are. His uncle is sending him to
some merchant he knows there, to work in his office.
He'll be there for three years.

KULÍGIN: And how is he, Sir?

TÍKHON: He dashes about too, and weeps. His uncle and
I had a go at him just now; we called him all sorts of
names, and he didn't say anything. He's become a sort of
wild creature. 'Do what you like to me,' he says, 'only
don't hurt her!' So he feels sorry for her too.

KULÍGIN: He's a good man, Sir.

TÍKHON: He's all packed up, and the horses are ready. He's
so miserable, it's dreadful! I can see now that he wants to
say good-bye to her. Is that all he wants? So much for
him. He's my enemy, Kulígin. I ought to hack him to
pieces; that'd teach him.

KULÍGIN: Sir, we must forgive our enemies.

TÍKHON: Go and tell that to Mama and see what she'll say
to you! Kulígin, man, our whole family has been knocked
to bits. We're not like relations, more like foes to one
another. Mama nagged and nagged at Barbara till she
couldn't stick it, so she vanished – she just took and went.

KULÍGIN: Where has she gone to?

TÍKHON: Nobody knows. They say she's eloped with
Kudryásh, with Johnny Kudryásh; he can't be found
anywhere either. This time, Kulígin, I must say straight
out that it's Mama's fault, because she started bullying
her and locking her in. 'Don't you lock me up,' she said
'or it will be the worse for you.' And so it turned out.
What am I to do, will you tell me that? Will you teach
me how to live now! I've come to loathe my home, I'm
ashamed to meet people, I start to do a thing and my
hands drop down. Here I am now on my way home, and
do you think it'll be any pleasure to get there?

[*Enter* GLÁSHA.]

GLÁSHA: Mr Tíkhon, my dear!

TÍKHON: What is it now?

GLÁSHA: We've got trouble at home, my dear!

TÍKHON: Good Lord! First one thing and then another! Tell me what's happened there?

GLÁSHA: It's the little mistress . . .

TÍKHON: Go on, what about her? Is she dead, or what?

GLÁSHA: No, Mr Tíkhon my dear, she's gone away somewhere and we can't find her anywhere. We're run off our legs, looking for her.

TÍKHON: Kulígin! We must run, man, and look for her. Do you know what I'm afraid of? That in her misery she might do something to herself. She's so miserable, oh she is miserable! It's enough to break your heart to look at her. What do you suppose? Is she long gone?

GLÁSHA: Not so very long, Mr Tíkhon my dear. It's our fault, we didn't watch her properly. But when all's said and done, one can't be on guard every moment of the day.

TÍKHON: Come on, what are you standing here for? Run!

[*Exit* GLÁSHA.]

And we'll go too, Kulígin.

[*Exeunt* TÍKHON *and* KULÍGIN. *The stage remains empty for a short time.* CATHERINE *comes on from the opposite side and walks quietly over the stage. All through the two soliloquies and the scene with* BORÍS *she draws out her words and repeats them, speaking pensively, as if not conscious.*]

CATHERINE [*alone*]: No, he isn't anywhere! Poor man, what is he doing now? All I want is to say good-bye to him and then . . . and then just die. What did I get him into trouble for? You see, it hasn't made it any easier for me. I ought to have gone down alone. And now I've destroyed myself, and I've destroyed him; for me dishonour – for him an everlasting reproach. Yes, for me dishonour – for him an everlasting reproach. [*Silence.*] Can I remember what he said? How sorry he was for me?

What were the words that he spoke? [*Holds her head.*] I can't remember. I've forgotten everything. The nights, the nights are heavy on me! They all go to bed, and I go too; it's all right for them, but for me it's like going to the grave. I'm so frightened in the dark. A sort of noise starts up and there's singing as if it were someone's funeral, only it's so soft I can hardly hear it; it's far away from me, far away. Daylight, and you're so glad to see it. But you don't want to get up; the same people again, the same conversations, the same torments. Why do they look at me like that? Why aren't you killed for it today? Why have they done it like this? They say you used to be killed. They could take and throw me into the Volga, and I'd be glad. 'If we were to put you to death,' they say 'that would take away the sin from you, but you're to go on living, and be tormented by your sin.' I have been tormented! How much longer is it to go on? What have I got to live for? Come – what have I? I don't want anything, I don't care about anything, I don't even care about God's world! And death doesn't come. You call it, and it doesn't come. Whatever I see, whatever I hear, is nothing but pain [*pointing to her heart*] here. Yet even now if I could live with him I might see some kind of happiness ... Well, it makes no difference now; you see, I've damned my soul already. I'm so lonely for him! Oh, I am so lonely for him! If I may not see you, then let me hear your voice in the distance. Oh you rough winds, carry to him my sorrowful yearning! Oh goodness me, I'm lonely, lonely! [*Goes to the riverbank and calls at the top of her voice*] Joy of mine, life of mine, soul of mine; I love you! Call back to me! [*She weeps; enter* BORÍS.]

BORÍS [*not seeing* CATHERINE]: My God! Why, that's her voice! Wherever is she? [*Looks around.*]

CATHERINE [*runs up to him and falls on his neck*]: I did see you after all! [*Weeps on his chest. Silence.*]

BORÍS: There now, we've had a cry together. God has granted us that.

CATHERINE: You hadn't forgotten me?

BORÍS: How could I! What are you saying?

CATHERINE: Oh no, I didn't mean that, I didn't mean that! You're not angry?

BORÍS: What is there to be angry about?

CATHERINE: Come then, forgive me! I didn't mean to do you a wrong, but I couldn't help myself. I wasn't conscious of what I was saying or doing.

BORÍS: Stop! What are you saying? What are you saying?

CATHERINE: Well, and what about you? How are you now?

BORÍS: I'm going away.

CATHERINE: Where are you going to?

BORÍS: A long way, Kate. To Siberia.

CATHERINE: Take me with you, away from here.

BORÍS: I can't do it, Kate. I'm not going of my own accord; my uncle is sending me, the horses are ready now. I've just begged a little minute from my uncle, so as at least to say good-bye to the place where you and I met.

CATHERINE: Go and God be with you! Don't grieve for me. I dare say you'll be a bit lonely at first, poor you, and then you'll begin to forget.

BORÍS: Why mind about me! I'm as free as a bird. What about you though? What about your mother-in-law?

CATHERINE: She torments me, locks me in. She says to everybody, my husband included, 'Don't believe her, she's a sly one.' They all follow me about all day, and laugh right in my face. And with every word they keep on throwing you up at me.

BORÍS: What about your husband?

CATHERINE: Sometimes he's affectionate, sometimes he gets angry, and he drinks all the time. And I've got to loathe him, loathe him. That love of his is worse than the beatings.

BORÍS: It's hard for you, Kate, isn't it?

CATHERINE: It's so hard now, so hard, that to die would be easier.

BORÍS: Who could have known that you and I would have had to suffer so for our love? It would have been better if I had run away that time!

CATHERINE: It was bad luck my setting eyes on you. I had seen little enough joy, but sorrow, and what sorrow! And how much more of it is there ahead of me? But why think about what's to come? There, I have seen you now; that's something they can't take from me, and I don't need anything more. Only you know I did so want to see you. There, it's much easier for me now, as if a load of sorrow had slipped off my shoulders. And all the time I thought you were angry with me, and cursing me.

BORÍS: What are you saying? What are you saying?

CATHERINE: No, I keep on saying the wrong thing; that wasn't what I meant to say. I was lonely without you, that's what it was. Well, and so now I have seen you . . .

BORÍS: They had better not find us here.

CATHERINE: Stay, stay! There was something I was going to say to you. And now I've forgotten. Something I wanted to say! My head's all in a muddle; I can't remember anything.

BORÍS: My time's up, Kate.

CATHERINE: Wait, wait!

BORÍS: Well, what was it you were going to say?

CATHERINE: I'll tell you in a minute. [*Pauses to think.*] Yes! As you go along the road, you're not to miss a single beggar. Give something to each one of them, and tell them to pray for my sinful soul.

BORÍS: Oh, if those people knew what it was like for me, saying good-bye to you. My God! God grant that some day it may be as sweet for them as it is now for me.

Good-bye, Kate! [*He embraces her and is about to go.*] You wicked, cruel monsters! Oh, if I had the strength!

CATHERINE: Stay, stay! Let me have a last look at you! [*She gazes into his eyes.*] There! That's enough from me! Now go your way, and God be with you. Off with you now, quickly, off with you!

BORÍS [*walks away a few steps and then stops*]: Kate, there's something I don't like! You weren't thinking of doing anything? I shall be destroyed with anxiety on the road, thinking about you.

CATHERINE: It's all right, it's all right. Go and God speed! [BORÍS *is about to come towards her.*] You mustn't, you mustn't. Stop it!

BORÍS [*sobbing*]: Well, may God be with you! There's only one thing I must ask God for now, and that is for her to die quickly, so as not to suffer too long! Good-bye! [*Bows.*]

CATHERINE: Good-bye! [*Exit* BORÍS. CATHERINE *follows him with her eyes and stands awhile in thought.*]

CATHERINE [*alone*]: Where to now? Home? No, whether I go home, or to my grave, it's all the same to me. Yes, home or to my grave . . . to my grave! Better in the grave . . . under a little tree, a little grave . . . how lovely . . . and it's kept warm by the sweet sun, and kept moist by the gentle rain . . . in the springtime the grass will grow on it, so soft . . . and the birds will come flying to the tree, they'll sing, they'll bring out their babies, and the flowers will bloom, flowers yellow, flowers red, flowers blue . . . all the flowers. [*She stops and thinks.*] All the flowers . . . So quiet, so lovely! I seem to feel easier! But I don't even want to think about life. Live again? No, no! Mustn't do it . . . not nice! The people are horrible to me, the house is horrible to me, the walls are horrible. I won't go there! No, I won't, I won't. Go to them, and they walk about and they talk, and what's that to do with me?

Oh, it has got dark! And there's the singing again, somewhere! Singing what? Can't make it out . . . I'd like to die now. . . . What are they singing? It doesn't matter, whether death comes to me, or I go to it . . . but I can not go on living! It's sinful! Won't there be any prayers? If anyone loves me they will say prayers. They put your hands cross-wise . . . in the coffin! Yes, that's it . . . I've just remembered. But if they catch me here, they'll drag me back home by force . . . Oh, quick now, quick! [*She goes to the riverbank. In a loud voice.*] Dearest mine, joy of mine! Good-bye! [*She goes out. Enter* MRS KABA-NÓVA, TÍKHON, KULÍGIN *and a* WORKMAN *with a lantern.*]

KULÍGIN: They say they saw her here.

TÍKHON: But is that true?

KULÍGIN: They had a clear view of her, they say.

TÍKHON: Well, thank God. At least she's been seen alive.

MRS KABANÓVA: And you got into such a fright, crying your eyes out! A lot you've got to cry about. Never fear, we're going to have her to worry over for a long while yet.

TÍKHON: But who'd have thought of her coming here! The place is so public. Who would take it into their head to come here to hide?

MRS KABANÓVA: You see what she's doing? There's a minx for you! She's going to run true to character.

[*People gather from all sides, with lanterns.*]

ONE OF THE PEOPLE: What? Found her?

MRS KABANÓVA: Oh no, no. It looks as if she's vanished somewhere.

SEVERAL VOICES: That's funny! Here's a queer business! Where could she have got to?

ONE OF THE PEOPLE: She'll be found!

ANOTHER: Bound to be!

A THIRD: Any minute now, she'll come walking in on her own.

VOICE OFF STAGE: Boat ahoy!

KULÍGIN [*from the bank*]: Who's calling? What's that there?

THE VOICE: A woman's chucked herself in the water.

[KULÍGIN *runs off, followed by several others.*]

TÍKHON: Gracious, that must be her. [*He is about to run off. MRS KABANÓVA holds him by the arm.*] Let me go Mama, or it will be the death of me! I'll get her out or I'll ... What is there for me with her gone!

MRS KABANÓVA: I won't let you go, you're not to think of it! Destroy yourself on her account, is she worth it? Hadn't she put enough shame on us? What has she gone and done now?

TÍKHON: Let me go!

MRS KABANÓVA: There's plenty of them without you. I'll curse you if you go.

TÍKHON [*falling on his knees*]: Only to have one look at her!

MRS KABANÓVA: You can have a look at her when they get her out.

TÍKHON [*stands up and calls to the men*]: Tell me, friends, is there nothing you can see?

FIRST MAN: It's dark down there, you can't see a thing.

[*A noise off stage.*]

SECOND MAN: It sounds as if they are shouting something, but you can't make it out.

FIRST MAN: And that's Kulígin's voice.

SECOND MAN: It's him there, walking about on the bank, with a lantern.

FIRST MAN: They're coming this way. There they are, and they're carrying her.

[*Several of the men coming back.*]

ONE OF THE RETURNING MEN: Good man, Kulígin! It was quite close to here, in a bit of deep water, by the bank. You can see a long way down into the water with a light; he saw her dress and he got her out.

TÍKHON: Is she alive?

ANOTHER MAN: Alive? How could she be! She threw herself off from a height; it's steep there, and she must have fallen on to an anchor. Knocked herself, poor thing! But boys, she looks just as if she was alive. Only a small wound on the temple, and only one little drop of blood. Just the one drop.

[TÍKHON *dashes forward; he is met by* KULÍGIN *and men carrying* CATHERINE.]

KULÍGIN: There's your Catherine for you. You can do what you like with her. Her body is here, take it, but her soul is not yours now; it is now before the Judge, Who is more merciful than ye. [*Lays her down on the ground and runs off.*]

TÍKHON [*flinging himself towards* CATHERINE]: Kate! Kate!

MRS KABANÓVA: Stop that! It's wicked to weep for her.

TÍKHON: You killed her Mama. You, you, you!

MRS KABANÓVA: What are you saying? Have you forgotten yourself. Don't you remember who you are speaking to?

TÍKHON: You killed her, you, you!

MRS KABANÓVA [*to her son*]: All right, I'll talk to you when we get home. [*Deeply bowing to the men.*] Thank you, good people, for the service you have done us.

[*All bow.*]

TÍKHON: It's well for you Kate! But why am I left in the world to live and to suffer! [*He falls on his wife's body.*]

Notes to *Thunder*

1. p. 320. See Introduction, Section 2.
2. p. 321. A very well-known popular song, words by A. F. Merzlyakóv, Professor of Poetry and Russian Composition at the University of Moscow; one of his pupils was Griboyédov.
3. p. 327. Kulígin is well up in eighteenth-century Russian literature, but never mentions Púshkin, or any other nineteeth-century author. Lomonósov (1711–1765) – poet, 'Father of Russian Literature', scientist and much else besides was the son of a White Sea fisherman. Derzhávin (1743–1816) was the chief poet of the age of Catherine II.
4. p. 328. The organization that administered benevolent funds etc., belonging to the 'townsmen'. (See Introduction, Section 2.)
5. p. 335. 'Spiritual songs' were anonymous narrative poems on religious themes, chanted in popular 'accentual' verse (see note 9 below).
6. p. 350. All sit together for a minute in silence, then rise and cross themselves; part of the traditional leave-taking ceremonial.
7. p. 355. What she saw on the roof was an old-fashioned chimney-sweep!
8. p. 360. From Lomonósov's 'Evening Meditation upon the Divine Majesty, on the occasion of the Great Northern Lights.'
9. p. 362. A cossack song; one of the cycle of so-called 'women's songs'. The verse-translation is in imitation of the popular 'accentual' verse, the rules of which are simple and few. Every line here contains four heavily accented syllables, or 'main accents': any number of un-accented syllables (or none at all) may precede each of these 'main accents', the last of which is followed by (usually) two unaccented syllables, to form a kind of cadence. This song makes its first appear-ance in print in this play, and it may well be that Ostróvsky collected it himself.
10. p. 365. Folk song again, as are the two other snatches sung in this scene – 'All come home' and 'Come then Maiden, come away'. (The latter is a strongly rhythmic dance song).
11. p. 369. In small towns there was a watchman, who used to bang on a brass plate to show that he was awake, and to mark the hours.
12. p. 372. The Grand Duchy of Lithuania, the western neighbour of Muscovy in the latter Middle Ages, included not only Lithuania proper, but also a great part of what are today the Byelorussian and Ukranian republics of the USSR; eventually this Grand Duchy was

united into a single state with the Kingdom of Poland. Consequently, when Russians talk about 'Lithuanians' they sometimes mean Poles, as here, where the 'Lithuanian Troubles' is a name for the seven years' anarchy that began with the invasion of Russia from Poland in 1606.

13. p. 372. These 'barrows' are prehistoric, and nothing to do with 'Lithuanians'!

14. p. 372. Kulígin is a clockmaker, but what he is proposing here seems to be simply a sundial.

15. p. 374. Misquotation from Derzhávin – 'Even in rags, a hero is honoured'.

16. p. 375. From the 'Ode to God', a famous poem by Derzhávin.

17. p. 378. Lomonósov's 'Evening Meditation' again.

18. p. 382. From Lomonósov's translation of the Anacreontic poem about the man who let Cupid into his house.

19. p. 383. Kyákhta, now in the Buriat republic of the USSR, was the Siberian end of the great caravan-route from China across the Gobi desert; it was a very important centre of Far Eastern trade until the building of Vladivostók and the Trans-Siberian Railway.

FOR THE BEST IN PAPERBACKS, LOOK FOR THE 🐧

In every corner of the world, on every subject under the sun, Penguin represents quality and variety – the very best in publishing today.

For complete information about books available from Penguin – including Puffins, Penguin Classics and Arkana – and how to order them, write to us at the appropriate address below. Please note that for copyright reasons the selection of books varies from country to country.

In the United Kingdom: Please write to *Dept E.P., Penguin Books Ltd, Harmondsworth, Middlesex, UB7 0DA.*

If you have any difficulty in obtaining a title, please send your order with the correct money, plus ten per cent for postage and packaging, to *PO Box No 11, West Drayton, Middlesex*

In the United States: Please write to *Dept BA, Penguin, 299 Murray Hill Parkway, East Rutherford, New Jersey 07073*

In Canada: Please write to *Penguin Books Canada Ltd, 2801 John Street, Markham, Ontario L3R 1B4*

In Australia: Please write to the *Marketing Department, Penguin Books Australia Ltd, P.O. Box 257, Ringwood, Victoria 3134*

In New Zealand: Please write to the *Marketing Department, Penguin Books (NZ) Ltd, Private Bag, Takapuna, Auckland 9*

In India: Please write to *Penguin Overseas Ltd, 706 Eros Apartments, 56 Nehru Place, New Delhi, 110019*

In the Netherlands: Please write to *Penguin Books Netherlands B.V., Postbus 195, NL–1380AD Weesp*

In West Germany: Please write to *Penguin Books Ltd, Friedrichstrasse 10–12, D–6000 Frankfurt Main 1*

In Spain: Please write to *Longman Penguin España, Calle San Nicolas 15, E–28013 Madrid*

In Italy: Please write to *Penguin Italia s.r.l., Via Como 4, I-20096 Pioltello (Milano)*

In France: Please write to *Penguin Books Ltd, 39 Rue de Montmorency, F-75003 Paris*

In Japan: Please write to *Longman Penguin Japan Co Ltd, Yamaguchi Building, 2-12-9 Kanda Jimbocho, Chiyoda-Ku, Tokyo 101*

PENGUIN CLASSICS

Carl von Clausewitz	**On War**
Friedrich Engels	**The Origins of the Family, Private Property and the State**
Wolfram von Eschenbach	**Parzival**
	Willehalm
Goethe	**Elective Affinities**
	Faust
	Italian Journey 1786–88
	The Sorrows of Young Werther
Jacob and Wilhelm Grimm	**Selected Tales**
E. T. A. Hoffmann	**Tales of Hoffmann**
Henrik Ibsen	**The Doll's House/The League of Youth/The Lady from the Sea**
	Ghosts/A Public Enemy/When We Dead Wake
	Hedda Gabler/The Pillars of the Community/The Wild Duck
	The Master Builder/Rosmersholm/Little Eyolf/John Gabriel Borkman
	Peer Gynt
Søren Kierkegaard	**Fear and Trembling**
	The Sickness Unto Death
Friedrich Nietzsche	**Beyond Good and Evil**
	Ecce Homo
	A Nietzsche Reader
	Thus Spoke Zarathustra
	Twilight of the Idols and **The Anti-Christ**
Friedrich Schiller	**The Robbers** and **Wallenstein**
Arthur Schopenhauer	**Essays and Aphorisms**
Gottfried von Strassburg	**Tristan**
August Strindberg	**Inferno** and **From an Occult Diary**

FOR THE BEST IN PAPERBACKS, LOOK FOR THE

PENGUIN CLASSICS

Molière	The Misanthrope/The Sicilian/Tartuffe/A Doctor in Spite of Himself/The Imaginary Invalid The Miser/The Would-be Gentleman/That Scoundrel Scapin/Love's the Best Doctor/ Don Juan
Michel de Montaigne	Essays
Marguerite de Navarre	The Heptameron
Blaise Pascal	Pensées
Marcel Proust	Against Saint-Beuve
Rabelais	The Histories of Gargantua and Pantagruel
Racine	Andromache/Britannicus/Berenice Iphigenia/Phaedra/Athaliah
Arthur Rimbaud	Collected Poems
Jean-Jacques Rousseau	The Confessions A Discourse on Equality The Social Contract
Jacques Saint-Pierre	Paul and Virginia
Madame de Sevigné	Selected Letters
Voltaire	Candide Philosophical Dictionary
Émile Zola	La Bête Humaine Germinal Nana Thérèse Raquin

FOR THE BEST IN PAPERBACKS, LOOK FOR THE 🐧

PENGUIN CLASSICS

Anton Chekhov	The Duel and Other Stories
	The Kiss and Other Stories
	Lady with Lapdog and Other Stories
	Plays (The Cherry Orchard/Ivanov/The Seagull/
	Uncle Vanya/The Bear/The Proposal/A
	Jubilee/Three Sisters)
	The Party and Other Stories
Fyodor Dostoyevsky	The Brothers Karamazov
	Crime and Punishment
	The Devils
	The Gambler/Bobok/A Nasty Story
	The House of the Dead
	The Idiot
	Notes From Underground and The Double
Nikolai Gogol	Dead Souls
	Diary of a Madman and Other Stories
Maxim Gorky	My Apprenticeship
	My Childhood
	My Universities
Mikhail Lermontov	A Hero of Our Time
Alexander Pushkin	Eugene Onegin
Leo Tolstoy	Anna Karenin
	Childhood/Boyhood/Youth
	The Cossacks/The Death of Ivan Ilyich/Happy
	Ever After
	The Kreutzer Sonata and Other Stories
	Master and Man and Other Stories
	Resurrection
	The Sebastopol Sketches
	War and Peace
Ivan Turgenev	Fathers and Sons
	First Love
	A Month in the Country
	On the Eve
	Rudin